sebastijan pregelj

IN ELVIS'S ROOM

T0340921

COPYRIGHT © 2023 Sebastijan Pregelj
TRANSLATION COPYRIGHT © 2023 Rawley Grau
COVER DESIGN BY Nikša Eršek
DESIGN & LAYOUT Sandorf Passage
PUBLISHED BY Sandorf Passage
South Portland, Maine, United States
IMPRINT OF Sandorf
Severinska 30, Zagreb, Croatia
sandorfpassage.org
PRINTED BY Znanje, Zagreb

Sandorf Passage books are available to the
trade through Independent Publishers Group:
ipgbook.com | (800) 888–4741.

Library of Congress Control Number:
2023941709

ISBN: 978-9-53351-474-1

Also available as an ebook;
ISBN: 978-9-53351-475-8

Funded by the European Union. Views and opinions
expressed are however those of the author(s) only and
do not necessarily reflect those of the European Union
or the European Education and Culture Executive Agency
(EACEA). Neither the European Union nor EACEA can be
held responsible for them.

This book is published with financial support by the
Slovenian Book Agency.

This book is published with financial support by the
Republic of Croatia's Ministry of Culture and Media.

Co-funded by
the European Union

SLOVENIAN
BOOK
AGENCY

Republika
Hrvatska
Ministarstvo
kulture
i medija
Republic
of Croatia
Ministry
of Culture
and Media

sebastijan pregelj
IN ELVIS'S ROOM

Translated from the Slovenian by
RAWLEY GRAU

**SAN-
DORF
PAS-
SAGE**

SOUTH PORTLAND | MAINE

1

I SLOWLY OPEN my eyes. I am lying on my back; there is a pleasant smell in my nostrils. I turn my head and see my mother. She is lying on her side, completely still. Her breathing is so soft it's impossible to tell when she inhales or exhales. I turn my head to the other side. My father is there. He is sleeping on his back; his mouth is open and he is snoring. I copy him. I want to wake up my parents as quickly as I can. Today is my birthday. But they are still asleep, so I start jumping up and down on the bed. It's my birthday! My birthday! My birthday!

Mom and Dad wake up at once. Dad grabs me and hugs and kisses me; then Mom hugs me. Happy Birthday, Bean! I don't feel like being cuddled so I jump off the bed and run into the hallway. My parents are right behind me. My present! Breakfast first, Mom says, then your present. But Mommy! I stand there with my arms spread out. Breakfast first. She is not giving in.

All through breakfast I glance impatiently at the door to the front hall. I know I'm getting a bicycle but I don't know where they've hidden it. I want to be sitting on it right now, I want to be riding it. Just a little, just in the hallway. My parents see what I'm feeling but they pretend not to notice. They think it's funny. After a while Mom looks at the clock and says, Martin will be here soon. Oh boy, I exclaim.

Martin is my cousin. He is two years and two months older than me. I've learned basically everything from him, the kind of things younger boys learn from older boys. From Martin I learned how to pee standing up (and I peed on my pants when I did). Martin showed me how to jump down the stairs two at a time, and then three or four at a time. From Martin I learned how to spit and how to make iceballs in the winter that fly farther and hit their mark better. Martin told me about Superman after he went to see the movie. Then my parents had to buy me the action figure. Martin has a racetrack with electric cars, so I had to have one too. Mom often worries about what Martin and I get up to when we're by ourselves, but Dad always tells her that if I didn't learn things from Martin, I would learn them from somebody else.

After breakfast, it's time for my present. We go out in front of our building. The bicycle is hidden under the steps. It's blue like I wanted and there's a big bow on the right grip of the handlebars. Yay! I run to the bike and push it to my parents. Mom takes off the bow and Dad holds the seat and waits for me to sit on it and put my feet on the pedals. Mom makes sure I won't fall off, Dad gives me a light push, and the bike moves forward. Pedal, he yells. I'm trying but I'm not very good at it and every so often I stop pedaling or start pedaling backward. Dad is walking behind me to help keep the bike going. Pedal! Not backward! Forward!

Pedal, pedal! I'm trying but it's hard; it's like it's all clear in my head but not in my feet. Then I finally start pedaling correctly and Dad starts hanging back. You see, he shouts from behind. You're doing great! Every so often the bike leans onto a training wheel, which starts clacking as if it's not turning at all.

There's not a cloud in the sky and it feels like it's going to be a warm day. Mom is happy because the past few days they've been forecasting rain, but now everything points to good weather. Dad basically doesn't care. He usually says that weather is what it is. You can't choose it.

Look at you, Dad shouts. Before long you won't need the training wheels. I can hear him but I don't look back; I keeping pedaling forward. I'm trying to go as fast as I can, but the bike is heavy and awkward; it's like riding a mammoth. Plus, at the end of the courtyard I have to turn around. There's a big curb at the end, and before I reach the curb I have to grab the mammoth tightly by the fur and, like some prehistoric rider, pull it in the direction I want to go.

I ride the bike up and down the front courtyard, which is separated from the street by a hedge. I'm doing well. Mom and Dad are standing near the entrance to our building. Now and then one of them comes to help me turn the bike or gives it a little push so I can keep riding, but I feel like I already know what I'm doing and that I'm doing really well.

At a few minutes past ten, Martin, Uncle Gorazd, and Aunt Taja arrive. Aunt Taja doesn't want me to call her *Aunt*, just Taja. *Aunt* makes me sound old, she says whenever I forget.

I am trying as fast as I can to ride to them, but Martin is faster. In a moment he's next to me shouting, You got a bike! He walks alongside me awhile; then he starts pushing me. Faster, I cry. Faster! Not too fast, Mom shouts. You boys be careful. Martin, don't push too hard! Okay, okay, the red-headed boy nods and starts pushing me more slowly because the curb is in front of us now and I have to turn around. When I manage to turn around and we're going in a different direction, he starts pushing me faster. A minute later and he's running as fast as he can. I'm scared but I wouldn't admit it for the world. I hold on tight to the rubber grips on the handlebars and make sure that I start turning the bike at the right moment.

When we come to a stop, Dad says, Why don't you let Martin ride for a while? Okay. I climb off and watch as my cousin gets on the bike and starts pedaling. Martin is riding my new bicycle incredibly fast. He does two circles, then stops next to my father. In a serious voice he says, You know what? I don't need training wheels. I know, Dad says with a smile. So maybe you'll help me teach Jan how to ride without them? Sure. You know I will, Martin replies and rides the bike over to me.

At a little before eleven Mom says she should go up if we want to have lunch. You coming with me? She looks at my aunt. Of course. You boys stay down here for a while, she tells my father.

After lunch, we all go into town. Dad suggests we go to the Skyscraper Building and all the grown-ups agree. It's less than an hour's walk along the main road. The sidewalk is wide, and no one worries about me taking the bicycle. Mom and Aunt Taja walk in front, Martin and I are in the middle, and Dad and Uncle Gorazd bring up the rear.

When we reach the Skyscraper Building, Dad tells us that at the time it was built it was the tallest building in the country.

It was built and paid for by the Pension Fund and was designed by the architect Vladimir Šubic. When your grandfather was a young man, not long after he arrived in Ljubljana, he helped build it, Dad tells Martin and me. He said there used to be a medieval monastery here. And when the workers started digging, they found an old fountain. The ones who dug it out became convinced later on that it was a fountain of wishes. They all had their wishes come true—whatever they were wishing for when their shovels hit the top stones. They didn't realize it at first, Dad says, shaking his head. But eventually it became obvious. And your grandfather was one of them.

Dad pauses a few seconds, then continues. He told me about a man named Janez, who was already well over forty. He was an honest fellow with a good soul; there weren't many like him. He wanted to have a family, but he didn't have a wife. No woman would take him because one of his legs was shorter than the other and he had walked with a limp since he was a child. But otherwise, he was as healthy and strong as an ox. Whenever they came to some particularly big rock when they were digging, they always called Janez. For him it was a piece of cake. He'd tell the men to give him some room; then he'd dig up the rock all by himself and sometimes even roll it to the side, where the men would break it into pieces with big sledgehammers and cart the pieces off the construction site. Anyway, less than a year later, Janez married the beautiful Anica. For years and years, all the unmarried men had been wooing this girl, Anica Turk, and the married men, too, couldn't get her out of their minds, but Anica never seemed to have eyes for any man. So people started saying she preferred women; they started saying she was a lesbian, a feminist, a vegetarian. That is, until Janez came along. Nobody could understand what she saw in this man with a limp, who would rather keep his thoughts to himself than talk, who would rather work than eat or drink. Malicious tongues said she did it to spite her parents, because she wanted to hurt them. They said that's the way those women are who think for themselves. This well-educated, beautiful young woman, who could have married a lawyer or a doctor, instead chose a common laborer, who on top of everything else walked with a limp and was as silent as if he couldn't talk. Whatever the reason, in the years that followed she bore him four beautiful children. The family survived the war, and Janez and Anica stayed together happily ever after. Like in a fairy tale, Dad says.

While we're waiting for the elevator, he goes on. He also told me about Bratko, a greedy mountain hick who believed that money was everything. But he himself never had any, even though the men who worked on the Skyscraper construction site were well paid. He squandered most of his earnings on booze, gambling, and lottery tickets. He always talked about how one day he'd strike it rich and never have to work again; he'd live a life of leisure. Well, not long after the construction work was completed, he won the jackpot in the lottery, which all of Yugoslavia, from Jesenice to Strumica, had been talking about for weeks on end. The State Lottery paid him millions. Well, Dad smiles, the money came in but it also went out. When Bratko died in unexplained circumstances a few years later, all he had left in the bank was small change. Your grandfather, however, was convinced that Bratko hadn't spent all that money—even for him it would have been impossible to spend so much. He was convinced that, while Bratko may have put some of it in the bank, most of the money he must have buried somewhere, since, among other things, he didn't trust banks. Of course, nobody knows this for sure. The secret went with him to the grave. Once he got the money, Bratko moved into Hotel Evropa. He took the royal suite, where he had a closet the size of a small room, which was filled with custom-made suits and hand-crafted shoes. Bratko liked to walk to the train station; there he would board a train and sit with the first-class passengers, and, depending on where they were headed, he'd say, I'm going to Zagreb for a slice of vanilla cream cake, or I'm going to Belgrade for a Karadjordjević schnitzel, or I'm going to Sarajevo for a Turkish coffee. People would laugh and not believe him. But they had no objections when throughout the trip he'd be ordering sparkling wine, toast, butter, and caviar for everyone in the compartment. On one such trip, Bratko fell off the train. Since it happened at night, he wasn't found until the morning. A farmer named Juraj discovered him when he was plowing the fields. He drove him to a doctor right away, but Bratko was already past saving. His body was broken and battered and he didn't have a dinar on him, which is why many people thought he didn't just happen to fall off the train but had instead been beaten and robbed while he was still on it and then pushed off. But that's not important. In the end, there was no more Bratko and no more money.

For goodness' sake! Mom is tugging at Dad's arm. Couldn't you find a more cheerful story to tell us? A more cheerful story? Dad is surprised. Well, yes, more cheerful, she repeats. Or at least tell us what wish came true for your father! After all, you said he was one of them. The thing is . . . Dad scratches his head. I don't actually know. Of course you don't know, because not a word of that is true! Mom claps her hands in triumph. And what about you? She turns to Uncle Gorazd. Do you know anything about this? No. My uncle shakes his head. Our father didn't tell me any stories. With me he did calculations; he would explain physics and mathematics to me. He may have been a bricklayer, but in fact he was in love with numbers. He kept the fairy tales for his younger son. Uncle Gorazd punches Dad's shoulder and lets out a big laugh.

Remember, boys, the Skyscraper is a very important and special building, Dad begins again, but quickly concludes, Today almost every big tower that gets built is taller. But not more beautiful. It seems that's not so important these days. It's called progress, he says as he opens the door when the light comes on and the elevator is on the ground floor.

Inside the elevator, which we can barely squeeze into, Martin starts making faces. Are you feeling sick, my aunt asks. My cousin shakes his head and says, I'm not sick. So behave. My aunt places her hand on his head. Let go of me! Martin jerks his head away. Okay, I have already. When the elevator stops, Martin and I dash out. Slowly! Dad leaps out and grabs us. We're not the only ones here, you know. See? You could have run into a waiter. Waiters carry big, heavy trays. They can't always be watching their feet, so you boys need to watch out. Understand? We nod. Okay, we'll watch their feet for them, Martin adds. That's not what I mean, Dad says. Just be careful you don't run into anyone. That's all. Okay? We nod again. Dad puts the bicycle under the wooden spiral staircase. Mom and my aunt and uncle are already outside on the rooftop terrace. They choose a corner table. Before we join them, Dad, Martin, and I walk around the terrace. Dad stops at each corner and looks down. Martin and I look down too. Dad tells us what we're looking at. Mostly it's nothing very interesting. By the time we reach our table, the waiter is already there. The grown-ups order wine for themselves and juice and cake for Martin and me. That's the only way they'll sit still for five minutes, Aunt Taja says with a smile. I wouldn't be so sure about that, Mom quips.

Before the waiter brings the cake and juice, I notice a man opposite me at another table. He is wearing a black hat, which makes him seem special to me. I watch him awhile, and then, in a whisper, tell Martin to turn around and look. I ask, Do you think he's a magician? I don't think so, Martin says. Magicians wear top hats, but that man has an ordinary hat. You can't keep flowers or a rabbit or a dove in an ordinary hat. I guess you're right, I say. Martin has been to the circus a few times and seen a few magic shows. I've only been to one, and we sat so far back I couldn't see exactly what the magician was doing. If the man in the hat isn't a magician, then what could he be? I have no idea.

When everything is on the table, Uncle Gorazd picks up his camera, stands up, and takes two steps back. Aunt Taja tells Martin not to make faces. But I'm not, Martin says, offended. I didn't say you *were* making faces. I was just reminding you *not* to. So behave. We have to look nice for the camera, don't we? Uncle Gorazd takes the picture, winds the film, takes a second one, and sits down again.

As I eat, I keep glancing at the man in the hat. Mom always tells me not to stare at people, that it's not polite, but I can't help myself. It's like I'm under a spell. I look at the cake I'm eating and start counting. I almost never get to ten before I have to look at the man again. One time when I look at him, the man is looking back at me. At once I feel hot all over. We look at each other for a few moments. For a few long moments, with my mouth full of chocolate cake, I feel like I can't turn my eyes away, even though I want to, just like I want to swallow the cake but there only seems to be more and more of it in my mouth. I'm scared. I wonder if now that he's caught me staring at him, the man is going to come over to our table. Maybe he really is a magician, although Martin says he isn't. If he is a magician, he could put a spell on us. He could come over to our table and blow us all away, across the tops of the buildings and ever farther, over the castle and the mountains, all the way to the enchanted forest, from which there is no escape. Magicians have that kind of power. Or he could cast his spell only on me, since I was the one looking at him. He could turn me into a rabbit, put me in his hat, and carry me away with him. Or he could turn me into a pig and put me on the ground. When I start running around the tables, people will be surprised at first and scream and shout, but then they'll start laughing and making pig faces and pig noises. Maybe, among all the shoving and overturning of tables, somebody will try to catch me, but they won't be able to. In the end, I'll run to my mother and jump into her arms. My darling, what have they done to you, she'll sigh and try to break the spell by kissing me, but who knows if she'll succeed.

None of this happens. The man smiles at me, lights a cigarette, and looks away. Suddenly I can move again, I can look where I want again, and I can chew the cake that's in my mouth

SEBASTIJAN PREGELJ

and finally even swallow it. I find the courage to inhale and exhale; I'm not scared anymore and I'm not hot all over. Everything is fine. I gulp down the last bit of my cake and a moment later jump off the chair and run after Martin, who is gesturing for me to hurry up. Slowly, Mom says. No running!

On the other side of the terrace we stop for a moment. Look! Martin points in the direction of the Ljubljana Marsh. People lived there in prehistoric times, he says, mimicking my father. We call them pile-dwellers, he says, repeating what Dad had told us earlier. But then the dinosaurs came and ate them up. Then Superman came and threw the dinosaurs into a black hole. That's why they're not here anymore. Come on! He starts running and I run after him. We stop by a pair of binoculars on a thick metal pole that is fastened to the ground. If you want it to move and rotate you have to put a coin in the slot, but anyway, Martin's eyes don't reach the eyepieces even when he stands on tiptoe. Still, he grips the binoculars with both hands for a minute or so; then he looks at me and says, This is stupid. Let's keep going!

We do a lap and then start running back to our parents. When we're almost at our table, I feel somebody's hand on me, stopping me. I turn my head to see who it is and what they want. It's the man in the hat! I freeze in horror. I probably would have wet my pants if the man hadn't smiled, circled my head with his free hand, and held a silver coin in front of my nose. Here, he says, it's your lucky number and our secret. Shh! He places a finger over his mouth and releases me. Swallowing hard, I take the coin and return to our table. I am utterly beside myself, but I don't want to say anything; I don't want to tell anyone because I know what would happen. Mom would say I must never accept anything from a stranger, certainly not money. She would tell me to go straight back to the gentleman and return the coin. If I refused, she would take me by the arm and go with me. So I drop the coin into my pants pocket and sit down. I don't tell anyone, not even Martin, even though I would like to tell him that he's wrong. The man is a magician. He just showed me a trick. But now isn't the right time.

Uncle Gorazd asks if anyone wants anything else. If not, then let's go, all right? He turns in the direction the waiters have been coming from, raises his right hand, and waves a few times. While he's paying, the rest of us head to the glass doors. The terrace is almost empty. As we walk toward the spiral staircase and the elevator, I look back at the man in the hat. The man is looking away. He doesn't see me. A moment later we step into the small elevator.

As we're going down, Dad and Uncle Gorazd talk about Tito and illness. I know who Tito is, but I'm not interested in his illness. I prefer the heroic stories about the battles between the Partisans and the Germans or about Tito's travels to distant lands on the good ship *Seagull*. Do you really think there will be a war when the old man's gone is the last thing I hear my uncle say. Then I look at my cousin, who has been tugging my arm. Martin is making faces as if he feels sick to his stomach and is about to throw up. I think it's funny and laugh. Mom and Aunt Taja are chatting. They're talking about some guys named Robert Redford and Oskar. That's lucky for us. If my aunt had seen what Martin was doing, she would have yelled at him again and our fun would be over in a second, but now it ends only when the elevator stops with a jolt on the ground floor.

We stand for a moment in front of the entrance to the building. While Mom and my aunt go on talking about Robert and Oskar, and Dad and my uncle about Tito and illness, Martin and I stand beneath a wooden frame in which there are photographs of naked women. Naked ladies, Martin says, as he looks at each of them in turn. She's got a hairy one, he points, and this one's smooth. When Aunt Taja sees what we're doing, she shepherds us away. Kids, that's for grown-ups! I don't understand why it should be just for grown-ups. When we're at the beach everyone is naked. I've seen Mom and Dad naked, I've seen my aunt and uncle naked, and everyone else too. Out of the corner of my eye I watch as my aunt tells Mom what we were doing and I see them both chuckle about it. Then I look at Dad, who eventually says, Well, let's go.

We've only taken a few steps when we hear a whistling sound behind us and a dull thud. We all turn around.

My mother shrieks, my aunt screams. Martin shouts, Superman! I look to see what's happened, but Dad quickly turns my head away so I can't see what's behind me. But I do see what's above me: a black hat is falling toward us. Hurry, hurry! My aunt grabs Martin and tugs him behind her. Don't look back, Mom says hoarsely. We're leaving! I don't understand why there's such a panic all of a sudden. Dad grabs me firmly by the arm and pulls me after him; Uncle Gorazd is walking at a brisk pace next to my father and saying over and over that it's better not to see anything. If you don't see anything, you don't know anything. If you don't know anything, they can't ask you anything. And I don't want to be asked anything ever again, dammit.

We cross the street quickly, passing a guard box where moments before a policeman was standing, but now he is running toward the Skyscraper Building. My uncle looks back. He sees a crowd of curious onlookers gathering. A bus has to merge into the left lane to avoid them, and even then it can barely get past. The policeman is trying to disperse the crowd and direct the traffic, but without much success. More and more people are gathering and cars are stopping right in the middle of the road. If the streets and sidewalks had seemed empty not so long ago, now there are suddenly people and cars everywhere. There are plenty of other people here, my uncle says. Let the police ask *them* what happened, let them take down *their* names and addresses. He hurries after us. Martin won't stop asking what happened. Mommy, what happened? Daddy, tell me what happened. Mommy? Daddy? Stop it, my uncle says firmly. Nothing happened, he hisses. Nothing you need to know about.

At home they send us to my room. Martin starts building a tower; I crouch beside him, handing him blocks from the pile. When the blocks of one color run out, he continues with a different color. When there are no more blocks left, Martin takes the Superman action figure and stands it on top of the tower. That's him, he says and then he flicks it with his finger so the plastic figure wobbles a bit, then falls. I don't understand. He should have grabbed Superman and lifted him into the air. Superman flies! That's how you play with him. Martin told me this himself after he saw the movie. He told me everything about the superhero: how he takes off from the ground, how he flies, how he has superhuman strength. Superman can use his body to replace the missing part of the train tracks so the train can run across him, he can stop the earth and spin it in the opposite direction so time goes backward; and he can do lots of other things too. He told me endless stories about him. But no. Martin has just now flicked Superman with his finger and let him fall down, as if he wasn't a superhero, as if he didn't have superpowers. He threw himself off the Skyscraper, Martin says in a serious voice. He killed himself. Do you understand? Who killed himself? Superman? No, Martin says, waving his hand. The man in the hat. He threw himself off the building. I told you he wasn't a magician. If he was a magician, he would have been able to fly. I still don't understand. In my head, the image I have of the man and what Martin is saying about how he threw himself off the building are all mixed up. I'm about to ask Martin how he knows this when the door opens and my mother sticks her head into the room. Come on, boys. The cake is ready. Cake, we both exclaim and dart out of the room. In an instant we forget all about Superman and the man in the black hat.

2

IT'S THE MORNING of the first day of school, and the school courtyard is swarming with children. With us are our parents, who are going in to work late today or not going in at all because they've taken the day off. While our mothers are making sure we look nice, our fathers are taking a few steps back or a few steps forward, trying to frame the best possible shot in the camera lens. Mom is constantly fiddling with my hair and clothes, while Dad has shot nearly an entire roll of film in just a few minutes. When he's finished taking pictures, we step into the imposing building. I look at the high ceiling, the big doors, and the innumerable mass of people. It all feels special, but I can't make up my mind whether I like it or not. When we come to my homeroom, Mom softly knocks on the door, opens it, and looks inside; then we enter. Inside it's already full of children and their parents. Mom, in a half whisper, reads me the words of welcome on the chalkboard. Meanwhile, I'm looking at the desks to see if I know anyone. Of all the children there I see only a few I remember from nursery school or kindergarten. But none of my friends. Look, Mom says, stroking my head, isn't that Janez? You remember him from nursery school, don't you? And there, just behind him, isn't that Alenka? And isn't that Peter sitting up there in the first row? Would you like to share the desk with Peter? I shrug. Actually, I don't know what I would like. Mainly I'd like to go home. Or if I can't go home, then I'd rather be back in kindergarten. Kindergarten was good. I had friends and we played together. But not a single one of them is here. Well, come on. Mom takes my hand and says, Let's go there. You can sit with Peter. Dad follows us.

There are no lessons that first day. We are there to meet each other. I meet my teacher; I meet my classmates. When our parents leave, the teacher takes us to the auditorium, where we watch *The Red Balloon*. I don't like the movie. I think it's stupid because the children in it never talk; all they do is shout and shove and run through the narrow streets, chasing that balloon, and one of the brats even shoots at it with his slingshot, but luckily he misses. I don't like the movie, but I do like sitting in the auditorium with the others, watching what happens on the screen, where every so often a black silhouette appears when a person stands up and leaves and again when they come back. I've only been in a movie theater once. At the beginning of summer Mom took me to a children's theater to see a movie about animals. It took place somewhere in Africa. The animals were eating fruit and then got drunk and did silly things. The giraffes were stumbling around on their long legs, the zebras were laughing and braying, and the monkeys were doing somersaults backward and forward, rolling around and picking themselves up. I think going to the movies is great, so there's nothing wrong with watching a film in the school auditorium either. It's almost like a movie theater. Not even a movie I don't like can ruin this feeling. I'll be able to tell Martin we watched a movie.

When the movie is over we have a snack. They pass out hot dogs and bread. Then the first day of school is over.

I am happy to see my mother, who is waiting for me in the hallway. Mom keeps asking me how it was. I tell her a few times that it was good. The teacher is nice. My classmates are okay. Mom asks me if I want to go somewhere for cake or ice cream. I'm quiet a few moments; then I shake my head. No, thanks, I say. I would rather go home because I know Martin is coming over this afternoon. On Saturday, when we were all at the beach, my aunt and uncle said they would come by. The boys should be together on such an important day. So I don't feel like having cake or ice cream. I want the afternoon to be here as soon as possible. Maybe I could have an ice cream cone, but I know Mom wouldn't buy it for me. We don't eat on the street, she'd say. And you'll get some on your clothes. You always do.

At home I go straight to my room. I take Superman off the shelf and tell him that I don't like school. If Martin was in my class, it would be okay. But that's impossible. Martin is in third grade and I'm only in first, and we don't even go to the same school. Well, you understand, I say, setting the plastic figure on my desk; then I run into the kitchen and ask when lunch is. You hungry? Mom strokes my head. No, I say. But I want Martin to get here as soon as possible. Mom smiles. They'll be here soon. You'll see.

At a little after two, Dad comes home from work. The first thing he asks is how school was. Did you like it? I wait for a moment before I nod, but I don't say anything. If I just nodded, that still wouldn't mean definitely yes. It depends on how many times I nod. It depends on whether I first wait and nod or nod right away. Or something like that. The three of us sit down at the table. Dad talks for a while about what his first day of school was like, and Mom and I listen, although we know the entire story because ever since the beginning of summer, when they bought me a red bookbag, he's been talking about his first day at school every chance he gets.

After lunch, Dad goes into the living room. He opens the newspaper on the glass coffee table and reads. Mom does the dishes and puts them away; then she goes to the balcony to water the plants. I find two of my toy cars in the living room and play with them.

Martin, I cry when the doorbell finally rings. I run to the door and turn the key. Well, where's our schoolboy? Uncle Gorazd grabs me. So how was it? Any cute girls in your class? I manage to wriggle out of his arms and shake my head; then I turn to Martin and gesture for him to follow me. We head to the living room while the grown-ups stay another few minutes by the door.

Martin and I are pushing cars around the carpet; the road, which is made by the carpet's Persian design, runs past the door to the balcony, where Dad and my uncle are talking. My uncle lights a cigarette and wrinkles his forehead, as if to say it's all very strange. It's happened before. We've had them at the company before—guys from State Security who are there mainly to hear what we say. But they simply don't understand what we do. On the one hand, I get it. We do a lot of work for the military, and this involves classified information and military secrets. But recently it's been fucking crazy. Novak and Knežević are like foxes—they're always watching us. A few days ago some people showed up from General Staff. Then two guys in production were hauled off to be interviewed. As far as I know, they hadn't done anything that serious, certainly not passing secrets. Mainly they're trying to scare us. That's the point. Novak told me face-to-face that we engineers are brainy types who think we're better than everyone else, but I should watch my head. Comrade, brainy heads roll just the same as stupid ones. That's what he told me. Uncle Gorazd stubs out his cigarette. Then they come back inside.

Here, Dad says, as he takes a package off the top of the television set and walks over to Martin. This is for you. Martin turns around, looks up, and holds out his hand. Well, what do you say, Uncle Gorazd says. Thank you, Uncle Samo, the boy says and the next moment rips off the wrapping paper. He holds the big book in front of him and reads the title in a monotone: *The Illustrated Encyclopedia of Technology.* Dad smiles. I think you will like it. Inside you'll find big construction equipment, transoceanic ships, airplanes, satellites, and rockets. You'll learn all about what they do and how they work. Thanks, Martin says again. He puts down the book, grabs the red car, and rolls it over to my green one.

Oh, Maja, there was no need, I hear my aunt say a few moments later when she and Mom enter from the kitchen. Sure, sure, Mom says softly as she sets a cake on the table along with

SEBASTIJAN PREGELJ

the dessert plates and little forks. Boys, look, Aunt Taja calls to us. Cake, Martin shouts, but I, like an expert, say that it's reh-rücken. Do you like rehrücken cake, I ask my cousin. You bet, Martin says as he climbs on a chair.

I used a new recipe, Mom says as she cuts the cake. I got it from the cook at work. Her husband is Hungarian. His mother, or maybe it was his aunt, I'm not sure, had been the cook at a castle before the war. For a count or something. She told me she has a lot of her recipes at home. And they're all splendid, she said. But here, you know, you can't work directly from those recipes because you can't get the ingredients. It's hard to find chocolate, it's hard to find lemons and bananas, and don't even dream about ginger. So you have to adapt them a little, be a little creative.

Mom goes on talking about the cook at work, her husband, his mother or aunt, and the count or something. Dad brings a bottle of wine from the refrigerator. Before he opens it, he arranges the wineglasses on the table. Even Martin and I get crystal wineglasses, into which Dad pours us apple juice. Then we all toast each other's health.

As we're eating, Uncle Gorazd tells us a story about a violin. My family was determined that I learn a musical instrument. And not just any musical instrument, he says, lifting his left index finger. Dad insisted on the violin. Flutes are for shepherd boys, he said, and the piano is for young ladies. But the violin, o-ho-ho! The violin is for gentlemen! Dad said that any true gentleman plays the violin. I have no idea where he heard that. But that's beside the point. My uncle waves his hand. But it didn't last long. Lojze, the neighbors' boy, started teasing me, said violins were for girls. And he wouldn't stop. Not until I opened my violin case, took out the violin, and bashed him over the head with it! My uncle laughs so hard he can barely breathe. Oh please, the things you say, Aunt Taja snaps at him. I'm just saying what happened! Uncle Gorazd can't stop laughing. More than two weeks I carried that case back and forth with the smashed violin in it. Then Dad found out I wasn't going to my music lessons. He asked me where I was going if not to the music school. Where are you taking that violin? I can still hear his voice today, my uncle says, raising his eyebrows. He got the black violin case out of the cabinet and told me, If you think you know everything already, then play me something. Of course, there was no need for me to play anything. Dad grabbed the violin by its neck and slowly picked it up. He stared at the broken instrument; then, without uttering a word, he turned around, grabbed me, placed me across his knee, and gave me a good spanking. I couldn't walk for two days! Again my uncle bursts out laughing. But Lojze left me alone after that and I never went near the violin again.

As soon as our plates are empty, Martin and I go back to the carpet. The grown-ups remain at the table.

Help, Martin cries. Help me! My mother and aunt are alarmed at first, but then they see it's only a game. Here comes Superman! I put down my car, pick up the plastic action figure, and fly it through the air to the car on the edge of the sofa. The car is about to go off the cliff, I say. If I don't help you, you'll fall. Help me, Martin cries again. With my left hand, I set the car on its wheels and push it to the back of the sofa. There you go. I saved you. Thank you, Superman, Martin says. Thank you!

At a little before six Uncle Gorazd looks at his watch and says they'll be going. We've got school and work tomorrow.

The sky is bright outside and you can still feel the heat through the windows. Summer is not over yet.

3

IT RAINED YESTERDAY and all through the night. The rain stopped before morning, but there are still big puddles on the sidewalks and in the streets.

Peter, Elvis, and I are almost home when we see the Hornets by the garages. We could turn around and try to run, but we know the Hornets would catch us; they're older, bigger, and stronger than we are. The Hornets are in the fourth grade.

At the sight of these boys, we stop in our tracks. It looks like we have no choice. When we reach the garages, Robi steps out in front of us; he's the biggest and scariest of them. His friends call him by his last name—Sršen, which actually means "hornet." So what's going on? He grins. We stand there. Nothing, I say with a shrug, and adjust the strap on my bookbag, which has slipped a little. Sršen nods. You say nothing's going on. Good. If nothing, then nothing. So *you* can go on your way. He gestures to me with his head. You're a funny one, kid, he says, and flicks my ear as I go past. I duck a little but don't stop.

You! Nerd! Sršen points to Peter. Come here. When Peter is directly in front of him, Sršen stretches out his arm and takes a swing as if he intends to slap Peter, but just before his hand reaches Peter's cheek, it stops. Peter lets out a shriek all the same, and Sršen and the other boys burst into laughter. Forget the nerd, one of them cries. He's shit his pants already. Let's get gypsy boy instead. Gypsy boy! Gypsy boy! Elvis mumbles that he's not a gypsy and takes a step back, but Sršen grabs him by his bookbag and drags him over to the other boys. So now you're all by yourself, he says, wrinkling his forehead. When there are more of you, you're braver. When there are more of you, you make trouble. So tell me. Who sliced the tires on my old man's car? Huh? It wasn't me, Elvis says. Oh, it wasn't you. Sršen smiles and a moment later shoves him. Elvis staggers back and falls over a boy who is kneeling behind him. Come on, Hornets! Sršen waves his arms. Sting him! Sting him, he cries and lunges at Elvis, who is on the ground trying to cover his head while the Hornets kick him from every side.

Leave him alone, I shout, even though I'm scared. I hurl myself at them. One of the Hornets turns around and punches me in the stomach. I double over. I expected them to hit me, but I didn't realize how much it would hurt. My bag slides over my head and falls on the ground. Then I fall too. Two or three of the boys give me a kick and then go after Peter. They knock him down and kick him a few times. The Hornets would have certainly kept beating up on Elvis and Peter if an old woman in the building next door hadn't shouted from her window. You down there, stop that right now! I'm calling the police! When Sršen hears her, he stands up straight and turns toward the window.

What's your problem, old lady? You trying to stick your nose into our business? Is that what you're doing? He leans over, picks up a rock, and throws it at the window but doesn't hit it. You want me to break your window? Get the fuck back inside, and don't let me hear another peep out of you. Fuck you! And go ahead, call the police. You'll get to meet my old man. He'll clobber your ugly mug! Sršen hikes up his pants with both hands and yells to the others, That's enough. Let's go.

Peter and Elvis and I are sitting on the wet ground. Elvis has a bloody lip and a black eye, and Peter's glasses are broken. They're both wiping away tears. I'm sitting there, staring into the distance and clenching my teeth. After a while we stand up and put on our bookbags. We walk a few steps together and then, without a word, we split up. I am in a rage, mostly because I have no idea what to do. If I told my parents it wouldn't solve anything. If I told Martin, he wouldn't be able to help me because the Hornets are bigger and stronger than him too.

At home I go straight to the bathroom, quickly change my clothes, wash up, and shove my wet things to the bottom of the hamper; then I go into the living room. Mom smiles and kisses me on the forehead. How are you doing? Fine. I pick up one of my cars from the floor. She asks, Are you hungry? No. How was school? I don't know. How do you not know? Mom smiles. Either you know it was good or you know it was bad. Which was it? Did you get a bad grade? A teacher's note? I shake my head. Well, then, I guess everything's all right, Mom says.

Everything's all right. I go into my room, throw myself on the bed, and open a book. I read about prehistoric humans. I read about how they hunted mammoths. They would dig big pits into which they stuck poles sharpened at both ends; then they covered the pits with branches and grass. After that, they waited for the animals to come and chased them into the pits. We should make something like that for Sršen and the Hornets. The thought makes me smile, and at the same time I feel the pain in my gut. It's still hurting but I don't care. When that creep falls into the pit we'll clobber him with rocks, I think. Then they'll leave us alone. But that won't work. So I take Superman off the shelf and ask, You got any ideas?

That evening I go straight to bed. I want to be alone. I want to think. I'm scared the Hornets will be waiting for us tomorrow. I wonder if that's what every day is going to be like from now on. Will we have to hide after school and always be on the lookout when we walk home? Will we have to take different routes to avoid them, even going where our parents have told us not to go because it's dangerous? Will we be constantly afraid, worrying about when Sršen's going to show up? I guess so, I sigh and wipe away a tear trickling down my temple.

The next day everything goes wrong. First, as I expected, on our way home from school the Hornets start chasing us, but not for long. They stop and laugh because we keep running and our big, heavy bookbags are bouncing up and down and hitting us in the head. Elvis finally throws his bag off and, like a weasel, slips between the parked cars, runs past the garages, past the stores, and darts across the main road, even though the crossing light is red. Brakes squeal and drivers honk like mad. Elvis runs on toward the old, peeling building where he lives. I run in a different direction, and Peter is lagging behind me, but it actually makes no difference.

I dash up the stairs of my building. I stop for a moment in front of our door. I don't hear footsteps below, but I'm not going to wait. The Hornets could be coming up on tiptoe. They're sneaky like that. It's best if I go inside right away. When I unlock the door and step into the apartment, my parents are already in the front hall. What's going on, Dad asks. Nothing, I say, totally out of breath and sweating all over. And yesterday? He gives me a serious look. Did anything in particular happen yesterday? I don't know, I say as I put down my bag. I see. So you don't want to say? Well, you don't have to, your mom and I know everything anyway. Somebody beat you boys up at the garages. Tell me, Mom says, crouching down, has this happened to you before? Do they often wait for you there? Do they often hit you? Not me, I say. What about the others? Dad wrinkles his forehead.

I nod. Sometimes. Dad, scratching his chin, says, That's what I thought. Peter's mom called me and said they've been chasing you after school. She said they chase you on the way home. A few days ago they dragged Peter into the gym and locked him inside a vaulting box. He was there for two hours. Yesterday they broke his glasses. They leave me alone, I say. Yesterday, Robi Sršen flicked my ear. That's all. He let me go, but Peter and Elvis had to stay. Mainly they go after Elvis, Peter too sometimes. I wanted to help them. I see, Dad says. What do they have against Elvis? At first I say nothing, but then I tell him, Sršen said Elvis sliced the tires on his father's car. His father's car, Dad repeats. His father is a policeman. But that doesn't mean his kid can do whatever he wants. And what about Peter? They call Peter a nerd, I say. They say nerds need a good beating. I look down at the floor. Rotten kids, Dad hisses through his teeth.

I go to my room. I can hear my parents talking so I leave the door slightly open and stand behind it, listening. I hear Mom say she had been talking to Sonja, Neža's mother. Sonja knows the principal and, besides, she works in local government. I think things will calm down now. You know, no principal can afford to let the older students attack the younger ones at their school, especially if they're attacking students from the other republics. You know what I'm saying?

I feel hot all over, worse than I felt when I was punched in the gut. I don't understand everything Mom is saying, but I understand enough to know that I don't like what I'm hearing.

And I wasn't wrong. The next day our teacher comes into the classroom with the principal, who gets right to the point. As soon as we're all sitting down, she stands between the desks in the first row. I am here because I will not tolerate older students picking on the younger ones, I will not tolerate stronger students attacking weaker ones, and I will not tolerate Slovenian students attacking students from other republics. Is that clear? If anything like this happens to you, tell your teacher. If you see anything like this happening, it is your duty to tell her. If you say nothing, then the same thing could happen to you. If you say nothing, then no one will be able to help you when it does.

I swallow hard. My heart is racing; I have a knot in my stomach that's getting bigger and more painful every second. I'm sure the principal is here because my parents squealed. I don't understand why they had to tell anyone. Why couldn't they keep their mouths shut like other parents? Now it will only get worse. I can't even look at the principal. Right up to her very last words, following which our teacher walks her to the door,

I am terrified she's going to mention me; I am terrified she's going to mention my parents, and Peter and Elvis too; and I am terrified she's going to tell everybody what happened a couple of days ago. I am sure the principal knows everything. Just like Tito sees everything. Once Peter and I changed our seats a few times in the dining hall and looked at the framed photograph of the president from different angles, and each time we discovered that Tito was always looking back at us no matter where we sat. It's the same with the principal: no matter where or when something happens, she knows everything. When the classroom door closes behind this tall, skinny woman, I feel a little relieved. The knot in my stomach slowly unwinds and my heart stops racing. But my legs continue to shake all through the lesson.

On our way home, we are constantly looking around us. We are convinced the Hornets are waiting for us somewhere and will sooner or later get us, but they're not lurking behind the school or by the garages. When we split up, I run to the door of our building. My heart is pounding as if I'm being chased. When I'm inside, I stop for a second; then I run up the stairs.

Just as she did the day before, Mom asks me how school was. I say it was okay. Did anything in particular happen, she asks. I shake my head and go into the bathroom, where I wash my hands; then I go to my room. Mom is right behind me. What about those boys, she asks, standing in the doorway. Are they leaving you alone now? Yes, I say. Good, she says and goes into the kitchen.

When Dad comes home from work we have lunch. At the table, no one says anything for a while; then he looks at me.

SEBASTIJAN PREGELJ

We've been invited to lunch on Saturday. Okay, I mumble with my mouth full. Don't you want to know where, he asks. Where? I look up. To Elvis's, Dad says. Elvis's father came to see me at work today. He said he wanted to invite us to lunch on Saturday. He said he would be happy if we could come. He wants to meet you. He wants to thank you. I stare at my father and don't understand. Why would Elvis's father want to meet me and what does he want to thank me for? Isn't that wonderful, Mom says. You can play with your classmate. I shrug. Sure, Elvis and I walk home together, but that's mainly because we live close to each other. At school we mostly don't hang out together. But I don't say this. It's better if we go to Elvis's for lunch than to some co-worker of my father or mother. I nod and take another helping of mashed potatoes.

4

ELVIS'S FATHER IS a short, fat man. I know him by sight. Fikret—that's his name—often sits in front of the building where he and his family live, and even more often he walks around his shiny car with a soft cloth and wipes off any spots. There are always taxis parked in the lot in front of their building, mostly big cars, Mercedes and Audis. And out of all of them, it's Fikret's red Mercedes that stands out. It's the biggest and shiniest car and people are always admiring it. The only time we ever see this kind of car is when there's an official delegation passing through town.

On Saturday morning, Mom goes to the florist to buy flowers for Elvis's mother, while Dad brings home from the store a bag full of candy for the children and a big box of chocolates with lilies on it. I expect they're Muslim, he says. You can't bring wine or pear brandy to a Muslim. But everyone likes a box of chocolates. Mom agrees. While I play with my cars, Mom lays some freshly ironed clothes on the sofa for me. So you'll look nice, she says. I put up a fight but Mom doesn't give in and in the end I change clothes. Dad, meanwhile, is standing by the door glancing impatiently at his watch. Come on, hurry up, he urges, as if we are going somewhere far away and every minute is precious. When we get to their building, Elvis's father is not out front. We see him standing on the long balcony; he waves to us and calls out that we should come on up. Take the stairs on the right. We're on the second floor.

When we're at the top of the stairs he comes over to my father and squeezes his hand; then he shakes hands with my mother. Finally, he crouches down in front of me and looks into my eyes. You're a brave boy, son, he tells me. And a good friend. If we were all like you, the world would be a better place. He smiles, then he stands up and steps toward the door. Come on in. He opens the door and goes in and we follow him. Inside, lined up in the large front hall, are the mother, Farhana, the two sons, Elvis and Ali, and the daughter, Defne. We brought you a little something, Dad says, and hands Elvis's father the box of chocolates and gives the bag of candy to the children. Mom gives the flowers to Elvis's mother. There really was no need, Fikret says, shifting his weight; then he points his arm at the open door to the living room. Please, do come in, straight ahead.

Our parents start talking, and we children go into a smaller room. Elvis takes a few toys off the top of a low chest, including an action figure that looks sort of like my Superman. This is Sandokan, he says, holding him in front of me. Ali brags, I've seen all his movies. Have you heard of him? I shake my head. I've never heard of him. Okay, then, listen. Ali stretches out on the floor and starts telling me the story of the pirate Sandokan, who people call the Malaysian Tiger. Elvis sits down next to him, and their sister is somewhere behind me, resting on the bed, watching us.

When Ali finishes the story, he says that one day he's going to be a pirate too. I'm going to get on a boat in Trieste and sail to the South China Sea. There I'll join Sandokan and his tigers. Just so you know. He stands up, runs to his own room, and comes back with a sticker album. Do you collect World Cup stickers? No, I say. That's too bad. He places the album in front of me. I already filled it. But I have lots of stickers left over. If you were collecting them, I could give them to you. Here, he says, pushing the album in my direction. Take a look.

Although I'm not really into football and footballers, I pull the album toward me anyway and start looking through it. I know footballers mean a lot to Elvis and Ali. They're always talking about them at school. One day Mario Kempes is the best; the next day it's Rob Rensenbrink.

Before I get to the end of the album, Elvis's father enters the room. Great, great, I see you're getting along, he says happily. Then he tells us that lunch is ready. Come and sit down. But first wash your hands.

When everyone is at the table, Elvis's father says a few words about friendship and loyalty and then wishes us all bon appétit. Elvis's mother serves us soup that has a peculiar smell, and, in fact, everything floating in my bowl looks very peculiar. It's lamb soup, Elvis's father says. Where Farhana and I come from, this is the soup people make when friends come to dinner. I should have given you the biggest piece of fat. The biggest piece of fat is found under the sheep's tail. But you city folks, the mustached man smiles, you don't like fat. If you want, I'll let you try it later. He glances at my father, who is holding his spoon in his hand as if he is summoning the courage to start eating and now Fikret's words have offered him an excellent reason to delay dipping the spoon into the soup. Maybe later, my father says. My mother, meanwhile, takes her first spoonful and lifts it into her mouth. It's wonderful, she says when her mouth is empty. Well, aren't you going to try it? She looks at me. The soup is very good. You haven't had this kind of soup before. It's quite special.

I know I won't like it. I suspect Mom doesn't like it either. Whenever she says something is special it usually means it's strange. And strange means it isn't good or she doesn't like it. But people don't say things like that. It's not polite. Especially not when you're a guest in somebody's home.

Eventually, with a little effort, my bowl is empty. Dad's bowl is empty too. Mom accepts another ladleful, but Dad says thanks but he'll pass. They don't try to force it on me. Elvis, Ali, and Defne all ask for seconds and their mother fills their bowls to the rim.

While Elvis's mother is clearing the empty bowls, his father tells us that they are both from Macedonia. But we're not Macedonians, he says, raising his index finger. We are Turks. Yes, yes, that sounds rather wild and exotic, but if you remember that the Ottomans ruled our region for six hundred years, there's nothing so unusual about it. You know, he goes on, shifting in his chair, the area around Gostivar is full of Turkish villages, and there are others all over Macedonia. Years ago, large numbers of our people started migrating to Turkey. The authorities gave us passports and opened the door so we could go. I don't know what we did to upset them, but the message was clear. Entire villages emptied out. Albanians moved into some of them, but others were eventually abandoned. Farhana and I decided to move to Slovenia. It's true that our ancestors were Turks, but really...

In Slovenia, people used to be afraid of Turks, Dad says with a smile. When I was little, my grandmother would scare us with them. She'd say, If you don't behave, the Turks will come and get you. What nonsense! I am happy that you are here. Dad reaches his hand across the table. He and Elvis's father shake hands, as they will several more times this day. I have never seen my father shake hands with someone so many times in a single day, but it's probably a good thing and I like it.

Just before Elvis's mother places a large baking dish with pieces of meat on the table, she warns us, Careful, it's hot. Everyone sits up a little. It's goat meat, Elvis's father says, pointing at the dark, steaming pieces. I have my own butcher. He always saves the best pieces for me. My father smiles and says it looks good. And so it is. Fikret pats down his mustache. You'll see. It simply melts in your mouth.

While we're eating the thready meat, our parents talk among themselves. At one point I catch that the boys were named after men Fikret wanted them to be like when they grew up. A good heart, a velvet voice, and an iron fist. The older boy was named after the world's greatest boxer; the younger, after the world's greatest singer. The girl was named after her grandmother. I don't listen to the rest. I'm trying to eat as fast as I can so I can leave the table as soon as possible. I'm certain Elvis and Ali have more things to show me. And besides, I want to hear more about Sandokan. Ali has to know a lot more than he's told me so far. I'm glad that I met someone who's going to be a pirate.

A few hours later, when we are getting ready to go home, it's already growing dark outside. Elvis's father asks us more than once if he can give us a lift. My parents say there's no need. After all, we're practically neighbors. At last, we all shake hands, each in turn, and say goodbye.

As we're walking home, Mom keeps saying what nice people they are. I would never have guessed they're Turkish. I didn't even know there was a Turkish minority in Yugoslavia. Dad is mostly quiet, but then he says that we're too superficial. For us Slovenians they're all one and the same; it doesn't matter if they're Croatians, Serbians, Muslims, Montenegrins, Macedonians, Albanians, or Turks. We call all of them Bosnians and have no idea what makes them different from each other.

When we're home, I run to my room. I pick up Superman and tell him I have news. I just met Sandokan!

Then I tell him that from now on I'm going to be friends with Elvis's brother, Ali, too. If Superman could talk, he would tell me this association will in a very short time cost me some bruises. He would tell me our friendship will not last forever, although right now that seems impossible. He would say a lot of things are going to change, but mainly, in the time that is coming, the two of us—me and Ali—will change. He would tell me that a time will come when we will be completely estranged from each other, to the point where we don't know each other anymore. And sometimes when I think of him, I will be filled with anger and sorrow at the same time, both equally strong. And that many years later, when I ask myself what really happened between us,

I will feel a kind of sadness. I will wish we were children again, sitting on the floor in Elvis's room: one boy saying he's going to join the pirates, the other boy listening and believing every word. He admires him and wants to be like him. If Superman could talk, he would tell me that things in life often turn out differently from what we wish, that wishes and hopes mostly remain unfulfilled, but that some wishes, of course, are fulfilled, and they inspire us with hope for all our later wishes, both big and small. They are why we get excited and look forward to things; they are why we don't despair. If Superman could talk, he would tell me, Be friends with this boy who will soon leave to join the pirates, and never let fear get the better of you. But when it's time for you to part, go your own way and do not look back.

5

ON SATURDAY WE go on a picnic with Martin and my aunt and uncle. Finally!

After breakfast, Dad goes to the store and Mom straightens the apartment; I spend my time making pictures. When Dad returns, Mom takes the dish with the dessert from the refrigerator and carefully puts it in a plastic bag; then we leave. As we're going down the stairs, they call out to me a couple of times not to go so fast and not to jump, but it's useless. I'm holding Superman in my left hand and gripping the railing with my right. I take the stairs two at a time; then I jump the last three all at once and fly into the front door. I grab the handle, push it as hard as I can, and run outside.

The morning sun blinds me for moment; then, squinting my eyes, I start running to our car. But I soon stop. My heart is pounding. Over by the cars I see Sršen, who is crouching down by the front bumper of a white Audi. A soft voice whispers to me to stay where I am, but an unknown force pulls me forward, toward the parked cars and Sršen. I don't know what he's doing there but I'm sure he hasn't noticed me. I creep forward as slowly as I can, but then Sršen turns his head in my direction. When our eyes meet, I freeze.

Time stops. Sršen is crouching by the car and I am watching him. I feel like this has been going on forever: Sršen has been crouching forever by the front bumper of the car and I have been watching him forever from a not-so-safe distance. Sršen could lunge at me at any moment, but that doesn't happen because the scene will never end. Sršen will be crouching until the end of time by the white Audi and I will be watching him in fear until the end of time from a not-so-safe distance.

Come here, kid, he says a second later, gesturing to me with his big brush-cut head. I cautiously step forward and look at what he's doing. Sršen has a screwdriver in his right hand and the nameplate from the car in his left. I collect them, he says. The Kraut cars are the most valuable. The only car better than an Audi is a Beemer, and the only car better than a Beemer is a Mercedes. This will stay between you and me. He peers at me from under his eyebrows. If my old man ever found out what I'm doing, he'd kill me. Understand? So this stays between you and me and nobody else. Just you and me, I say. That's right, Sršen says as he stands up, comes over to me, and pats me on the shoulder; then he runs off between the cars in the direction of the main road.

A second later, my parents are in front of our building. When they reach me, Mom says that next time she'll tweak my ears. But why? I look at her in surprise. I told you very clearly: do not jump down the stairs. She tilts her head a little to the side. I told you very clearly not to do this because it bothers the neighbors and you could fall down the steps. If you fell down the steps, you could hurt yourself. You could break your arm; you could crack your skull. Do you understand what I'm saying? I nod and climb into the back seat. Mom puts the bag with the dessert next to me. Just be careful, she says, looking at me. Dad starts the car.

6

ON OUR WAY home from school, the Hornets surround us by the garages. They haven't bothered us in a long time. We thought they'd lost interest, so we got careless. We stopped looking over our shoulders; we weren't checking all around to see if they were anywhere nearby so we could avoid them. We were certain they weren't and that even if we did run into them they would leave us alone.

And now here they are in front of us, as if time had wound backward, except that in the meantime they have grown. Now they are at least two heads taller than us. They are bristling with hornet anger, as if we had done something to them.

You can go on, Sršen tells me. But as for you two, we need to have a talk. He looks first at Elvis, then at Peter. Well, what? Sršen gives me an idiotic look because I'm still standing there, watching them, and not going on like he told me. If you want, you can stay too. But then we'll treat you the same as gypsy boy and nerdy. Understand? I nod and swallow hard. I think, Now we're in for it, but Sršen has to remember that Elvis has a big brother who isn't going to keep watching this happen forever. Ali is stronger than Sršen. Ali is stronger than all four of them. And besides, I know Sršen's secret. He told me himself that his father would kill him if he ever found out. That has to be worth something, I think.

As I am considering all this, Sršen shifts from one foot to the other and squeezes out a wad of spit from between his teeth, steps on it, and smears it on the concrete so it makes a dark stain. All right, you can all go past the garages. And we'll leave you alone. But not for free. He shakes his head. Understand? Peter is looking at him terrified, Elvis is looking at the ground, but I am watching everything as if it's on television and I'm not really there at all, so I know that nothing can happen to me.

Every Monday each of you is going to bring me five dinars, Sršen continues. If you pay, you pass; if not, you don't. Simple, right? The three of us stare at him, so he says it again. Simple, isn't it? I don't know, I say, lifting my shoulders. I have no idea where I can get money. You don't? Sršen grins and steps toward me. Well, you probably get some money for your birthday and New Year's Eve. Probably for a good report card too. At least that's what I think. I don't get any money, Elvis whispers. Sršen turns to him. But you're a gypsy! You know how to steal. It'll be easiest for you. Then he looks at Peter. How about you? Peter shrugs. Well, it doesn't matter what you think right now, Sršen says, scratching at his neck. Each of you brings me a fiver on Monday and you can go past for the entire week. That's right, says one of the other Hornets, a skinny, grinning boy; he's leaning against a wooden garage door, where shoes and balls have left pale-colored marks. And if you pay extra, we'll carry your bags for you too. All four of them break into laughter.

Today I'm in a good mood. Sršen again shifts his weight. Today I'm letting you pass for free, aren't I? He looks at his buddies. Sure, they nod. Today you can pass for free.

We continue on at a brisk pace toward the apartment blocks. When the garages are far enough behind us, we stop. I have no idea where I'm going to find the money, Elvis says. I'll give it to you, Peter tells him. I've got some money. Maybe we can pay them for one week, I say, while we figure out something. Okay, we pay them for a week, Peter agrees, then we'll see.

Peter turns to go to his building and Elvis and I walk on together a bit. Sršen's a real asshole, I say. Somebody should punch that fat mouth of his; then he'd leave us alone. Maybe Ali could help us. What do you think? I look at Elvis. I don't know, he says with a shrug. Ali would help us of course, but Dad would have his hide if he found out Ali was fighting. He signed him up for football and the engineering club. He's always saying that boys need to keep occupied. If boys aren't occupied they do stupid things. Ali has football practice three times a week and when he's at home he's always making something for the engineering club. Right now he's making a rocket model. Dad bought him a rocket engine at the Young Engineer store. But you're his brother, I exclaim. Dad says you can always find a better solution than your fists. Fists are the last resort. If we always tried to fix things with our fists, we'd still be apes, we'd still be hopping from tree to tree—that's what he tells us. I laugh. But Sršen is an ape! Can't you see that? Sršen's an ape, Elvis repeats after me. If we tell our parents, it'll only be worse, I say before we part. I know, Elvis says, but I don't want Ali to get in trouble because of me. You understand?

I turn around and head toward our building. I'm thinking I should sign up for karate and boxing. Since the start of the year there have been posters at school for karate and judo. I didn't want to sign up for anything before because I thought it was pointless and stupid. Whenever my parents asked me if I wanted to take gym or soccer, I always flatly refused. Dad said it was good for a boy to do sports. Mom said I needed to take English and learn a musical instrument. Would you like to play piano? Or the flute, she asked. Maybe guitar, I told her, but Mom said no, I was too little for guitar. People usually start with piano or recorder. Piano's out, Dad said. We don't have space for a piano. Play the flute. I'm not a shepherd boy, I objected. Well, then you'll do football. Dad wasn't giving up. Or swimming. But I don't want to. I frowned and ran into my room. But I left the door open a little so I could hear what they were saying. We shouldn't force him, Mom said. Well, we have to sign him up for something, Dad insisted. The sign-up time is now. If we miss the start of the school year, we miss the entire year. We'll talk about it, Mom said, ending the discussion.

Now I'm sorry I didn't say I wanted to take karate. Or judo. Or boxing. Mom would think it was dangerous and wouldn't like it; she'd be afraid I'd get hurt or injure myself, but Dad would have backed me. He would have said what he always says, Let him try if he wants. He's a boy, after all. Nothing will go wrong, believe me. It's a sport; it's not fighting. Besides, it won't hurt him if he has to stand up for himself now and then; it won't hurt him if he knows how to use his fists. Mom would say, See?

That's where I don't agree. After that, they would stop talking. If I had signed up then, I'd already know something by now. I could have stood up to Sršen. I could have told him to shut that fat mouth of his or he'd get a bloody lip.

I imagine what it would be like then if the Hornets surrounded us at the garages. First, I would warn them to leave us alone. I would tell them I'm taking boxing and karate and it would be best for everybody if we just went our separate ways, peacefully. But, of course, Sršen and his buddies wouldn't stop. They would laugh in my face and make fun of us. Even when I took a step forward in defiance, they'd be laughing. But they'd probably stop laughing when I punched Sršen's face. Then it would get serious. I can easily imagine Sršen picking himself off the ground and me hitting him one more time, so he falls down again and stays down; then I take care of the other three goons, who are just standing there, watching in shock. With them it's easier because they're cowards. I knock one goon down and the others start running. That's exactly how it would be. But, I tell myself, shaking my head, I didn't sign up for either karate or boxing, so that's not how it is. But it's not too late, I think. I can still sign up. And if I practice every day, it won't take me long to catch up.

By the swings I see Ana and Alenka, two girls in my class. Alenka lives across the road, same as Elvis and Ali, and Ana lives in the building next door to us. Her family moved here last summer, when we were at the seaside. They used to live on the coast, in Koper, but her father got a new job and they moved to Ljubljana. All the boys in our class like Ana. When a few of us are together, we tease her, but when I happen to be alone with her,

I don't tease her. I like being with her. Most of the time I don't know what to say, but I don't feel awkward or embarrassed. Ana is good at starting a conversation.

Ana is in movies. She's quite small for her age, so she usually plays preschoolers. She's been in three movies so far, she told me, and she wants to be an actress when she grows up. In fact, she already is an actress, but it doesn't sound serious when a kid says it. So I always say I'm going to be an actress when I grow up, she said when she was telling me what it was like to be in a movie. I haven't seen any of her movies, but I do watch her every night on television in a chocolate commercial. The commercial is nothing special, but I like it because of Ana. I always ask Mom to buy me Ana's chocolate. That what we call it in our family: Ana's chocolate. It's not really Ana's, of course, it's Gorenjka chocolate, since Ana and her family don't have a factory that makes chocolate they could name after her, but for me it's still Ana's chocolate. Period.

Ana is on one swing, Alenka on another. The girls are swinging and talking. I run over to the swing set, lean against one of the metal poles, and say hi.

Do you want to swing too, Ana asks. No, I say, I don't think so. So then leave us alone, Alenka snaps at me. We're having a conversation. Can't you see that? Sure, I say with a shrug. Then I say goodbye and head home.

Basically, I don't understand the kinds of conversations girls have. But Dad, too, often says that he doesn't understand Mom. Apparently, there are things everybody understands and other things only girls and women understand. But what do I know? I open the door to our building and run up the stairs.

At home, I go straight to my room. When I see Superman, I think of Sršen. In my chest I feel the same anger I felt when he attacked us before. I think about karate and judo and boxing. I decide to talk to Dad about this today. I am sure he'll support me but I won't tell him the real reason. If I told him I was doing it because of Sršen and his goons, he'd want to talk it over with me first and I don't want to talk. Not about this. Not today. So I'll just say I want to take karate or judo or boxing. Dad will say sports are good for boys and that's enough for him. He'll win Mom over too. In the end she'll say, If that's what you think is best.

7

ON MONDAY WE paid Sršen fifteen dinars and on Tuesday I had my first karate practice. Practice takes place in the school's small gymnasium. I felt uncomfortable because I didn't know anybody. There were nine of us—seven boys and two girls. They were all from other homerooms and one boy was even from a different school. Coach Miha introduced me at the beginning of practice and then quickly went through the basic rules with me. He mostly repeated everything he had told my father on the phone, when, after we talked, Dad called him to ask if it was still possible for me to sign up. Then Dad told me everything he learned from the coach during the phone call, some things two or three times. I heard it all again on Tuesday. As I sat there on the blue mat, I thought about how I really don't like karate but I had better start liking it soon if I want to get Sršen off my back. It would be easier if Peter and Elvis were taking it too, or at least one of them. If I could choose, I'd choose Elvis, but I'd be happy with Peter too, but their parents won't let them.

Peter and Elvis are still friends I spend time with mainly on my way home from school and sometimes on my way to school, but when I'm at school, I mainly hang out with Rok. Rok is new in our class. He lives in a different part of the city. His father drives him to school every morning and his mother picks him up in the afternoon.

Rok has a digital watch and *Superman* is his favorite movie. As soon as I met him I knew we would be best friends. At first he was sharing a desk with Matic, but when we had the chance to change seats, we took it and he shared the desk with me. All excited, I told Dad I was sitting with Rok now. What about Peter, he asked. Aren't you friends anymore? Sure, I replied, of course we are. But I'd rather sit with Rok. You know, I had the same experience, Dad said. At first Janez and I didn't sit together in class, but we did later. Eventually, we became best friends. And still are. Uncle Janez, as I call him, is much taller than Dad, has just a few teeth in his mouth, and has a blond mustache. Mom calls him the Walrus. Whenever he and Dad go out, Mom says Dad went out for a beer with the Walrus. Then she laughs. Isn't that funny? He went out with the Walrus!

Rok and I spend all our time together. Our teacher once said we were thick as thieves. But I don't get that. We're not stupid and we don't steal things, so what she said doesn't make any sense.

The best time I have with Rok is in the afternoon, when after lunch the assistant teacher takes us to the exercise field, which is big enough for us to disappear in, although she always tells us to play where she can see us. I don't want anyone going anywhere I can't see you because something might happen. I'm responsible for you. If you don't do what I say, then tomorrow we won't go outside at all, she threatens us day after day. But, of course, her threats don't stick.

How do I know how far she can see, Rok said with a laugh his very first day. She wears those thick glasses and is blind as a bat. She's like a bat, I repeated. That's how the assistant teacher got the nickname Batty. At first, we were the only ones who called her that, but before long everyone else was doing it too.

Rok and I like to go to the concrete platform near the fence where there are train tracks on the other side. Rok knows the train schedule by heart; it's like he worked for the railroad. Not only does he know exactly when a train is coming, he knows if it's express, local, or freight.

Yesterday, we noticed that there was a hole in the fence. We climbed through it and Rok put a coin on one of the rails. We stepped back and waited for the train to come. When the train disappeared in the distance, we went back for the coin. It was completely flat. Look at that! Rok was thrilled. Later, in our classroom, we showed the coin to the other boys. They all wanted to know how we did it. We told them, but they didn't believe we had the courage to go onto the tracks. So we made a plan for all of us to go there today.

As soon as we arrive at the exercise field, all of us boys start running to the concrete platform. Behind us we can hear Batty shouting not to go too far but we keep running as if we're deaf. When we're on the platform, Rok checks his watch and says, An express train will be here in eleven minutes. That gives us enough time. He jumps into the grass and I follow him, and everyone else follows me; they stand by the fence and watch as Rok and I crawl through the hole to the other side.

Rok pulls a coin out of his pocket and shows it to them. See? Take a good look so you don't tell me later that it was already smashed. The boys nod; then Rok crawls over to the tracks and carefully places the coin on the slightly rounded surface of one of the rails. While he is getting it into position, I look right and left to make sure there's no train coming. My heart is pounding, but Rok is completely calm as he pushes the coin to the middle of the rail with his finger. When he decides that it's where it should be, we go back behind the fence. Rok checks his watch and says authoritatively, Seven more minutes.

While we're waiting for the train, we hear Andrej, who's been keeping watch, shout, Batty! Batty's coming! Shit, Rok mutters through his nose and says we have to leave. If she comes and sees that there's a hole in the fence, then the fun's over. The janitor will be here today to patch the hole. Let's go! He runs toward the jungle gym and the other playground equipment, and we're all right behind him. We're shouting as if we're playing cowboys and Indians and Partisans and Germans all mixed up together, but who ever saw Indians chasing Germans or Partisans fighting cowboys?

Midway to the platform, Batty stops. Maybe she had counted us from a distance and saw that we were all there, or maybe she was tired and didn't feel like going farther. She turns around and pulls a pack of cigarettes from her jacket pocket, then walks to the jungle gym, where the other assistant teachers are; they're all standing in a semicircle smoking, and every once in a while they send a glance our way.

Rok checks his watch. We've got three minutes. We can go back, but we need to go a different way. If we go straight back, she'll see us and come after us again. We agree; we'll go a different way. We run to the far end of the field and from there proceed cautiously to the fence. There are a few trees in front of the fence that give us cover. We are still far away when we hear the train coming. Rok starts running as fast as he can. I can barely keep up with him. Everyone else, too, is running as fast as they can, and one boy, Aleš, even passes Rok. When we get to the platform, we stop to catch our breath; then we go to the fence, hold on to it, and wait.

The roar is getting louder and louder until we finally see the engine, which is coming at us like a ferocious beast. When it shoots past us, we feel the wind, and in the wind can smell that distinctive odor trains give off. We watch wide-eyed as the cars go by so fast we can't see the separate windows; instead, the train seems to have just one long window stretching from the first car to the last.

When the train has gone past, Rok creeps through the hole in the fence to the tracks. He searches for the coin among the gray stones. Here it is, he shouts when he finds it, but right at that moment we all freeze in terror. On the other side of the tracks there is a man running toward our friend. Rok is still crouching on the tracks looking at the coin and doesn't see him. Rok, I shout. Rok raises his head and looks at me; then he looks behind him and starts running with all his strength toward the fence. He slips once or twice, sending the dark-gray stones loudly scattering, but the man behind him isn't very fast either. He swipes at Rok with his arm a few times, but he doesn't catch him. Rok dives through the hole in the fence. We are waiting for him on the other side; then we all run together to the middle of the field. The man remains on the other side of the fence. I look back a couple of times to see if he's still there. He is still there. But when we get to the playground area, the man is nowhere to be seen. Fuck, Matic says, leaning over with his hands on his knees. Who was that guy? What did he want?

While we all catch our breath, Rok turns to me. Did I get a scratch? When I look at him I almost shriek. Rok's right cheek is cut and he's bleeding. Hold on, Peter says; he straightens his glasses and pulls out a handkerchief. It's clean. Hold it on the cut. Right, hold it on the cut, I repeat. I'm scared. It's clear to me that Rok won't be able to hide the injury. We'll have to tell Batty and then she'll start asking us what we were doing and where exactly this happened. We need to think a minute, Rok says, pressing the handkerchief to his cheek; the cloth is already red with blood. We can't tell her where we were or what we were doing. But we can say that I was climbing a tree and scratched myself on the branches. She'll maybe believe that. We all agree. We'll say we were climbing a tree and you scratched yourself on a branch.

But what about that guy, Matic says. Who was he? What did he want?

He's probably a homo, Aleš says. I've heard that word a few times, but I don't know what it means and I don't want to ask. Everybody else seems to know it. Everybody is repeating that he's a homo, so I say it too. Yeah, he's a homo.

On Monday, during our breaks, we will all probably be talking about the man on the tracks and the cut on Rok's cheek, for which he had to go to the health center that Friday afternoon. After he told his mother the part of the story he thought he could confide to his parents, she quickly decided not to go home but rather straight to the doctor. Rok was given a tetanus shot and three stitches.

As often happens, events overtook us. The event that on Friday at one o'clock seemed so big to us was overshadowed, on Sunday at four minutes past three, by much bigger and far more momentous news. While the event on Friday may have been important to some boys who had been playing by a chain-link fence, the news on Sunday was important for, essentially, every Yugoslav citizen. What happened to us on Friday was nothing in comparison to what happened on Sunday. And we all understood this, even at our young age.

8

OUR TITO HAS DIED, it says on the chalkboard when I enter the classroom on Monday. But I already know everything. Mom and Dad told me. They told me in a way I would understand. Then I had to repeat a few things after them. So you'll remember, Dad said, and won't blurt out any nonsense.

On Sunday, Uncle Gorazd, Aunt Taja, and Martin had come by in the late afternoon. Martin and I spent most of the time in my room. Whenever we came out, the grown-ups stopped talking.

They look at us like we did something wrong, Martin said. Maybe it's because Tito died. I don't know. But it's not our fault. No, it isn't, I agreed and ran across the room holding Superman in my right hand while Martin moved his plastic robot across the parquet floor. He got it in Italy. This is Droid, he told me. From *Star Wars*. Have you seen *Star Wars*? No, I said. That's too bad. You've got to see it. Mom and Dad wouldn't let me at first, but then Dad took me anyway. What a movie! Martin then told me everything that happens in the movie.

As I was standing by the door, long after I stopped listening to Martin, who was now talking about something else entirely, I heard my father say he was worried. I was worried even before, he said. It's no secret that for some time now the old man hasn't been running the country. The generals and Jovanka have been running it for him. But now that he's gone, well, it's not going to be easy. The old man kept order. Nobody dared make a peep. It's possible the Russians could invade, Uncle Gorazd said. Stop trying to scare me, Dad said. The Russians! There won't be any Russians. What about Hungary and Czechoslovakia, my uncle asked. There they came with tanks. The Americans would never allow them to cross the Yugoslav border, Dad objected. If that happened, they would suddenly be on *their* border. You see? My uncle sighed. The old man knew how to steer the ship between the two sides. Now everything's changed. He's gone, and that's that. I just hope there won't be a war.

Do you think there'll be a war, I asked my father later, when my uncle, my aunt, and Martin left after the evening news. Don't worry. Dad stroked my head. There won't be any war. Were you boys listening to us talk? No, I said, shaking my head. But I heard a little. Oh, you heard a little, did you? Dad smiled. Listen, he said, sitting me down. There are a few things you need to remember: Tito was the country's president. And the Marshal . . .

Now I am standing in my classroom, looking at the white words on the green chalkboard: *Our Tito has died.* I sit down next to Rok, who has a big bandage on his cheek. He tells me about the tetanus shot and the stitches. I ask if it hurt. Of course it hurt, he says. But not a lot. I gritted my teeth. They're taking the stitches out in a week. The doctor said there could be a small scar. Cool! If you want to join the pirates, that'll make them take you more seriously. Only don't say you cut yourself on a fence. You have to say it's a battle scar. That's exactly what I'll tell them, Rok agrees. Then we stop talking because the teacher enters the room.

In her right hand she has a handkerchief, with which she dabs at her tearful eyes, and in her left she carries a thick book with a red cover and a title in gold. Miss Nada is crying. Some of the girls are crying too, including Ana. I look at her and don't understand. Tito was our president, sure, but he wasn't our grandfather or grandmother; he wasn't our uncle or aunt. So why are they crying?

The teacher takes a few deep breaths and then says in a trembling voice that today is a very sad day. We will be talking about Comrade Tito, about his life and work. You probably already know a great deal. She looks at us. Well, she continues, opening the book, you probably don't know everything. If you hear something you already know, that's good too, because you'll remember it better. It's important that you remember. It's important that you know. It's important for both today and tomorrow. We'll start by reading about the boy from the Sutla River.

During the break we remain in our chairs, and Miss Nada stays in the classroom too. We don't leave until it's time for lunch. We stand by the classroom wall in a line that stretches from the door to the last row of desks. We wait for the teacher to stand up, go to the door, and let us out. Unlike ordinary days, we don't shove or run or try to push to the front of the line; we walk single file, one after the other.

When Rok and I are seated at a table, he nudges me with his elbow and gestures at the picture of Tito hanging high on the wall. I need to tell you something, he says. But it's a secret. Oh, yeah? I look at him curiously. So listen, Rok says, leaning over to me. Tito is always looking at me. It doesn't matter where I sit, he's always staring at me. I can be at one end of the dining hall or at the totally opposite end. Only now that he's dead, I don't know if he can still see me. Slowly I raise my eyes and stare at Tito's portrait. There is a picture of him in every classroom. In our homeroom, it's just his face in the picture. In the music room, Tito is sitting at a piano. In shop class, he's standing next to some machinery. In the hallway by the history office, there are photographs from the war. The photo I remember most is Tito with a dog. The dog's name was Luks and he saved Tito's life. I don't respond right away, but then I tell Rok that I already know this. Peter and I realized that Tito is always looking at us a long time ago. I lean a little to the right, and then a little to the left, to see if it's still true. Tito is watching me. His face doesn't change, but his eyes stare straight at me. Rok picks up his spoon and starts eating his soup. A minute or so later he looks at me. Eat up, he says. We'll check the other classrooms too. We'll find all the pictures and see if he's watching us from them too.

We take our trays to the counter. Our plates are nearly full. On any other day, Miss Nada would have been waiting for us at the counter. She would have asked us why we had hardly eaten anything and would have told us that all over the world many people are starving and that because of them we should show greater respect for our food. But today is a special day. None of the teachers are standing at the counter, so we can leave our trays without any problem and run down the hallway to the classrooms.

Rok cautiously opens the doors to the first- and second-grade classrooms. Most of them are empty because the students are still at lunch. If by chance there are any students in a classroom, he quickly shuts the door, but when a classroom is empty we walk in as if it was ours. At first we're a little nervous, but before long we do it with no fear at all.

Once we're in a classroom, the first thing we do is see which picture is hanging over the chalkboard. If it's different from previous ones, we stand directly beneath it. Then we move to the left and to the right, to the windows, and to the wall and the cupboards. Tito is always still looking at us. Even if we crouch behind the desks and chairs, he knows where we are. As soon as we come out from hiding, he's looking at us.

When we are back in our classroom, we do everything the same as in the other ones. Then it hits me: each of us should stand on a different side of the room. I wonder who he'll be looking at if we do that! You're right, Rok says enthusiastically. We both stand in the middle of the classroom; then Rok starts moving toward the windows, and I move toward the door. He's still looking at me, Rok says in a loud voice. Me too!

When I am next to the door, it suddenly opens. It's Miss Nada. What are you doing here? Nothing, I say, startled, and go to my chair. Come here, both of you, she says when she's at her desk. My whole body is shaking. I have the sense that what we did was wrong and that the teacher knows everything. I'm afraid she's going to write a note to my parents or, even worse, say that my father or mother or, even better, both of them should

SEBASTIJAN PREGELJ

make an appointment to see her. I walk slowly to her desk, but Rok does just the opposite; he's right away at the chalkboard, as if he's waiting for her to praise him.

Well now, what thoughts do you boys have about Comrade Tito, Miss Nada asks us. He's always watching us, I blurt out. What? She is surprised. Whatever we do, he's always watching us, and he sees everything, I tell her. How do you mean? The woman wrinkles her forehead. Come over here. I take two steps back and look up at Tito's portrait. Now he's looking at me. And if I go over to the windows, he's still looking at me, and if I run to the other side of the room, he's still looking at me! You see, Miss Nada says with a smile, that's why it matters what you do. That's why it matters how you behave. You must be a good Pioneer, always an example, always a good comrade! Because Tito is watching you. He is watching all of us. He sees everything.

That afternoon I sit with my parents in front of the television. We are looking at the Blue Train, which is carrying the dead president from Ljubljana to Belgrade, where he will be buried. Thousands of people are standing alongside the train tracks. From time to time the camera rests on the face of a soldier, a policeman, a female worker, a male worker, who today are not working but are instead standing by the train tracks waiting for the train to roll past so they can say their final goodbyes to the Marshal, who united the peoples of Yugoslavia and led them on the path of liberation from the Nazi and Fascist occupation, and who brought us to the bright future that we enjoyed right up to that terrible moment at four minutes past three on Sunday, when his great heart stopped beating. The women on the television screen are wiping away tears; the men have somber expressions, many with tears trickling down their cheeks.

Tito is watching all of us, I say. What? Dad looks at me in surprise. Tito is always watching us, I repeat. Where did you read that, he asks. I tell him about Rok and me going from classroom to classroom, and also how Miss Nada had told us we were right. Tito is watching us.

9

PEOPLE IN THE movies don't really kiss, Ana says. It only looks like they do. But actually they don't. So how do they do it then? I want to know. Come here, she tells me, but then she comes and stands in front of me herself, gets on her tiptoes, leans her head forward, and rests it against my head. Her lips are right next to mine; I can feel her breath on my neck. My whole body is pulsating with a feeling I don't recognize. It's different from when my mother, aunt, or grandmother kisses me. It's a little horrible, but in a way it's not horrible. In a way I like it. And then, when Ana steps back, I feel excitement and can only look at her, until she says, Well, did you see? Did our lips touch? Did we kiss? We did not. She shakes her head in a way that makes her dark hair sway left and right. Then she smiles and says we can go on the swings now. She hops on a swing and starts pumping her legs. I stand on the side a few moments, but then I, too, start swinging. In my chest I feel immense strength; I am sure this is exactly what Superman feels. Nothing is impossible. I make the swing go as high as I can.

When we get tired of swinging, we cross the grass to the hill where we go sledding in the winter. As we walk, she tells me people also make movies where actors and actresses really do kiss. They're called erotic films. The men and women in them are naked. I've never seen one, but I know that our janitor watches them. He has a film projector in his basement apartment, like in a movie theater. Mostly he watches them by himself, but sometimes other men come over and they all watch together. When they watch them together, they howl like wild animals, but when he watches them by himself, he's mostly quiet or whimpers and moans. Sometimes I watch him through the gap in his curtains and the partly open window. He's a real bastard, let me tell you. He's a homo, I say emphatically. Well, I don't know if he's a homo, Ana says. What do you mean, you don't know? Well, it's true that men do get together in his apartment sometimes, Ana says, but as far as I can tell, he's interested in women. Homos are interested in men. What do you mean *interested*? Now I'm even more confused. Oh, come on! Ana stops and looks at me in amazement. Do you really not know what a homo is? Of course I do, I insist, but a moment later I mumble that actually I don't. That's what I thought. Ana wrinkles her forehead. Homos are men who are interested in men. Do you understand? Usually men are with women. Like my father and mother, or like your father and mother. A homo is a man who's with a man. You mean they kiss each other too, I ask. Yes, that too, Ana says. She seems to know what she's talking about. But they don't do it in public. Because how would it look if two men were holding hands and getting all lovey-dovey in public? I nod as if now everything is clear to me.

We stop at the top of the hill. I feel like Ana knows everything, and I want to learn everything. I'm sure she would tell me if I asked, but I don't even know what to ask her.

10

ON SATURDAY WE celebrate my grandmother's sixtieth birthday. Grandma, my mother's mother, had her birthday a few weeks ago, but in my mother's family birthdays aren't as important as name days. On her birthday Mom usually just telephones Grandma, but on her name day we always visit her. This year, because it's a round number, we're holding the family celebration in a restaurant.

My parents let me sleep a little later this morning because it's going to be a long day. Mom leaves the apartment just before eight. First she goes to the hairdresser and then to the florist, where she picks up the bouquet she ordered for Grandma.

Dad reads the newspaper and drinks coffee. When I wake up, he makes me breakfast. While I eat, he says that we're going to have a wonderful time today. It's been a while since you last saw your cousins, he says. But I don't think I'm going to have a wonderful time. The grown-ups will badger me with questions—my aunts will smack their lips and say how much I've grown; my uncles will ask me how school is going and what my favorite subject is. My cousins, who I'll be sitting with at the children's table, will be nice to me of course, but I shouldn't expect much more than that. They're all older than me and think of me as *our little cousin*; only Marko and Marija are younger, but they're only three and four. My boy cousins have no idea who Superman is or what happens in *Star Wars*. They're into motorcycles and cars. Some of them already have their own mopeds and a few drive their fathers' cars. But except for Janez, none of them has their driver's license yet. Still, what they mostly talk about is what car is worth buying and why. If I remember right, it's the Opel Kadett. My girl cousins mainly huddle together and whisper to each other, as if what they're saying is not for the ears of boys. When I was little, they liked to hold me, often right on their laps, and I could listen to them. Now I'm too big for such things, and ever since I've been too big for such things, I've sat with the boys.

When we get into the car at a few minutes after ten, Mom says it'd be best if I slept a little. So you won't get carsick, or at least not so much. But how can I fall asleep when I haven't been up very long? I sit in the middle of the back seat so I can look at the road, and as soon as the road starts curving this way and that, the saliva in my mouth gets thicker and a kind of ball forms in my stomach and starts moving up and down. I try to keep it down. I try to think about other things: about karate practice, which I don't like very much but have somehow learned to live with; about Ana, who is going to be a real actress one day and we'll all watch her on television and in the movies; about the stitches on Rok's face; and, finally, about Superman, who doesn't have the kind of problems we have.

When not even that helps, I start asking how long before we get there and what restaurant are we even going to. Dad replies that we'll be driving for another half an hour or so and that it's the restaurant with the stuffed animals. There's a bear as well as a few other animals; he thinks maybe an eagle, a weasel, and a fox. We've been there before. Don't you remember? Then Mom corrects him. She says it's not an eagle, it's a falcon, and it's a marten, not a weasel. They're all one and the same to you city folk, she chuckles. As far as I'm concerned, it makes no difference. Falcon or eagle, weasel or marten, I still feel sick to my stomach.

When Dad parks in the dusty lot in front of the restaurant, my stomach settles down. I get out and breathe the fresh air; Mom and Dad, meanwhile, are already hugging relatives who, like us, have just arrived. Dad opens the trunk so Mom can take out the big, colorful bouquet, which is wrapped in cellophane, and Grandma's beautifully wrapped present. Then we walk to the entrance of the restaurant. Mom tells me it would be nice if I went first when we wished Grandma a happy birthday. But I don't know how, I protest. What do you mean you don't know how? Mom smiles. You look into Grandma's eyes and say, Dear Grandma, I wish you all the very best on your birthday. Then you shake her hand and kiss her on the cheek. That's all. So how about it? I don't know, I say with a shrug. Come on, you can do it, she encourages me. You're a big boy. Fine, I agree and start repeating to myself what she just said.

Grandpa and Grandma are sitting in the middle of a long table covered with a white tablecloth. When they see us, Grandma smiles and says, And here I was starting to think the Ljubljana folks wouldn't make it. Oh, for goodness' sake! The things you say! Mom quickens her step as we walk next to the wood-paneled wall and at the same time nudges me ahead, which makes me lose my balance; I can barely catch myself and land straight in my grandmother's arms. I look into her eyes and recite the words I had been repeating ever since Mom said them. Grandma gives me a noisy kiss on both cheeks, and then releases me so I can go to Grandpa, who gives me a big hug and tells me I'm already a real man. I smile and look into his eyes, which shine in a very special way. More than anyone else I know, Grandpa has especially shiny eyes. Dad says that Mom has her father's eyes, but I don't agree. Only Grandpa has such eyes. I imagine that at night they shine so bright he doesn't need a flashlight even in the darkest forest, because he can see as clearly as the night animals do, maybe more so.

I hear Grandma saying to my parents that there was no need to bring her anything and they should save their money, and Mom replies that she shouldn't talk that way and should look at what she's being given. The flowers are beautiful, Grandma says. Here's something else for you, I hear Dad say. Then there is the rustle of wrapping paper. I know that Grandma doesn't rip it but instead carefully feels for the tape with her fingers and then peels it off slowly so the wrapping paper remains in one piece. Then I hear Grandma sigh. Do you like it, Mom asks. It's a gorgeous blouse, Grandma says. But I'm not getting married, you know. Where can I wear it? Well, if nothing else, you have it for going to mass. But actually you can wear it anytime. Oh, it's too beautiful for just anytime, Grandma says. But you can bury me in it. Oh, Mama, for goodness' sake! The things you say!

Not long afterward we take our seats. Just as I expected, I am sitting at the shorter table with my cousins, right between the boys' part and the girls' part. Bertica sits across from me. Bertica is in the eighth grade; she tells everyone she's going to be a schoolteacher, but whenever the subject comes up, Aunt Meta, her mother, wags her head and says she's afraid the pedagogical secondary school might not take her because her grades aren't good enough. If she wants to be a teacher, she needs to have all As. Mom usually tells her that they're not so strict. They'll take you even if you get Bs. But Bertica also has Cs! Cs and even a D, Aunt Meta insists. Maybe Bertica and I will play together later. If we do, we'll play school. Bertica doesn't know how to play anything else. When she plays by herself in her room, she arranges all her toys in rows, as if the teddy bears and dolls were sitting at desks; then she stands in front of them and writes letters and numbers in chalk on a small blackboard. The last time when I was staying at my grandparents' during vacation, I had to sit with her stuffed bears and answer questions. Whenever I knew the answer, she praised me, but if didn't say anything because I didn't know the answer, she scolded me. Sometimes she would write a note to my parents on a slip of paper and tell me to bring it to school the next day with my mother's or father's signature. Even then I thought the whole thing was stupid, but it was less embarrassing than when we played family. When we played family, Bertica was the mother and I was the father. She put a plastic baby doll in a stroller and carefully covered it with an old diaper; then she pushed the stroller along the edge of the road past all of the neighbors' houses, all the way to the little chapel at the end of the village. Bertica would stop now

SEBASTIJAN PREGELJ

and then and check on the baby, and sometimes she would take the doll out of the stroller and cradle it in her arms. The worst part was when she said it was my turn to take Baby out of the stroller because her hands were full. I felt like sinking into the ground. But in the end I didn't have a choice because I wanted Bertica to play with me again the next day. When I was holding that plastic doll in my arms, I was scared the entire way that we'd run into other boys. In such a small village it was almost impossible not to. And whenever we did, the boys would poke fun at me until Bertica scared them away by threatening to tell their parents.

Sitting next to Bertica is Petra. Petra gets all A's. She's sixteen. She paints her nails. My aunt lets her do this. The other aunts say the girl will go bad. Painted nails are like a push-up bra—they're both magnets for boys. We all know the story. It would be a shame if a girl with good grades who has her whole life ahead of her got pregnant. Goodbye school if she does. Then she'll be working on an assembly line. Goodbye comfortable life!

On my right is Matija, Petra's brother. Matija plays the accordion. At our family celebrations, his accordion is never far away. It was either brought into the restaurant as soon as the family arrives or it's in the trunk of my uncle's car. We usually don't have to wait long before one of my uncles says, Why don't we ask Matija to play us something? What a good idea, everyone responds enthusiastically and loudly. Come on, Matija, play us something! Matija keeps a silk kerchief in the instrument case, which he uses to wipe down the keys. Then he straps the accordion over his shoulders and starts to play. When he plays, his mouth is open and his eyes are shut. My uncle almost always says that the boy has a gift. People with talent don't need sheet music; they play with their eyes closed. When Matija plays, my uncle beams with pride. He says he plays Lojze Slak songs better than Slak himself. May lightning strike me down if that's not true! Since he hasn't been struck down yet, I guess it's true.

Janez is at the head of the children's table. He is seventeen and a half. He completed vocational school and now works as a metal turner and toolmaker. In the spring he will have to do his military service, but after that he's going to buy an Opel Kadett. He says this German sedan is not only a reliable car, but you can also always sell it for a good price, no matter how old it is or how many kilometers you have on it. Janez's words carry weight. When he talks, the other boys at the table are quiet. Everyone listens to him, and my cousins hope to learn something new. Although I'm not interested in what he's saying, I have no choice but to listen with the others. Then all my boy cousins start praising the Kadett. None of them wants to lag behind in their praise. They repeat the things they've heard from their fathers, their uncles, and other boys like Janez, and even from Janez himself. This makes Janez feel good.

Janez's words about the Opel Kadett end only when the waiters start bringing the big tureens to the tables, some with beef broth, others with mushroom soup. Before we start to eat, we pray.

Grandma prays aloud and we respond. Since this is a special occasion, it's a long prayer that doesn't want to end. For a while I look at the table right in front of me, at the white plate and the silverware on the white cloth placemat, at the steaming tureen; then I start looking around me. First I look at Bertica, then at Petra. Then I look at the grown-ups' table. I see my parents' backs and Uncle Tone's face, and, beside him, Aunt Marija. Sitting next to Aunt Marija is Aunt Katja, and next to her, Grandma. But I don't look at Grandma. If our eyes happened to meet she would know that I'm looking around. And if you're looking around, you aren't praying, Grandma likes to say when we walk back from mass in the summer and Grandpa asks her if she saw one thing or another. I like going to mass with Grandma and Grandpa. Grandma stays below and goes to a pew on the left side of the church, where the women sit, while Grandpa and I go up to the choir loft, where there are mostly men, who sing, and the organ, which thunders. I don't know why the women sit on the left in church and the men on the right, but I also never ask because I'm sure this is something I'm supposed to know and if I asked and let on that I don't know I'd get a look of reproach. So instead, I wait patiently to find out about this on my own one day (as I do with a lot of other things too) and then everything will be clear to me and I'll know what to say if someone asks, although I can't imagine who would ask me why the women sit on the left in church and the men on the right. If I sat down below with Grandma, she would always be reminding me to pay attention, but Grandpa leaves me alone. Except when it's time for us to stand up or make the sign of the cross—then he'll give me a nudge. Up in the choir loft, I look at the pictures on the ceiling and the walls. If I look at them long enough, they start coming to life before my eyes; it's like I'm watching a cartoon. And although I know all of the pictures, as if they were in one of my picture books at home, I always discover something new on that vaulted ceiling. Sometimes it's an animal, sometimes a plant, some-times a mountain; sometimes it's a few words that an angel is holding, or a ribbon floating in the air. Whenever I discover something new, it surprises me. All those Sundays I've been looking at the pictures on the ceiling, but I never noticed this before. I love to look at the lilies and the lions and the deer, and the people are interesting, too, from the wicked Romans with their helmets and short swords to the saints with the golden halos over their heads. The only one who scares me is Jesus, who is depicted three times. The body of Jesus is full of wounds. Grandma says he is suffering for the sins of the world, including my sins. I can't imagine what I did that was so awful they have to kick and whip him and finally nail him to the cross up there on the ceiling. Is it such a big sin if you cheat at Black Peter or Uno? Is it such a big sin if you move an extra square in Chutes and Ladders? Is it such a big sin if you say you're hungry even if you aren't just so you can stay up longer? I try not to look at Jesus. I'm afraid he might come to life; I'm afraid he might reach out his arm and pull me into the picture with him. And I don't want to go there.

When the prayer is over, we pick up our spoons and start eating. The beef broth, which Bertica ladles into my bowl, is salty, just the way I like it. Mom doesn't use much salt in her cooking. She says it's not good for you. Maybe it isn't, but the restaurant's salty soup tastes better to me than Mom's. But of course I won't tell her that because she'd be hurt.

Janez is talking again about the Opel Kadett. My girl cousins are whispering about some boy. His name is Zlatko and his fa-ther is an army officer from Montenegro. Speaking in low voices so their parents and the boys don't hear, they say Zlatko has a good body and is very romantic. Petra says he's the only boy she would ever let kiss her. She's sure he's a good kisser. I'm sure he knows just what to do, she whispers. The other girls giggle.

Later, after the waiters have brought platters to the tables with three kinds of meat—breaded turkey cutlets, pork roast, and boiled beef—I hear Uncle Tone ask my father what's going to happen now that Tito is gone. Is this the end of socialism? Is Yugoslavia going to fall apart? Will there be a war? Dad replies that it's hard to say but certainly nothing will happen overnight. Changes take time. For a while everything will be the same. For a while we'll go on living as if nothing has happened. After that, well, we'll see.

If Yugoslavia falls apart, there will be bloodshed again, Grandpa says from across the table. I don't believe that, my father disagrees. Believe it, Grandpa insists. You know the caves are full of bones. And it can happen again very quickly. I saw it all before. Brother against brother. I pray to God I don't see it again. You just hush now, Grandma spits out, trying to stop him. We don't talk about those things. Certainly not in a nice restaurant and not on a day like this! I'm just saying, Grandpa retreats, but it's already too late. Uncle Boštjan speaks up. Not long ago some folks from Ljubljana were here asking about hidden burial sites. They asked me if I knew where they were. I didn't tell them anything. He shakes his head. They may have been relatives of the dead like they said, but even more likely they were provocateurs or State Security agents. You were right not to tell them, Uncle Tone says. It's not the time. We need to wait. Why put yourself at risk? Who for?

Before the meat platters are empty, Uncle Tone says, Matija, do you have your accordion with you? I sure do, my cousin says. So why don't you play us something? Yes, Matija, play something, others chime in. Uncle Mirko is already dashing out to retrieve the instrument from the trunk of his car. And before long Matija is standing in the middle of the room playing his gleaming accordion. At first my aunts and uncles just listen, but then they start clapping along to the beat, until finally they are singing the best they know how. My uncles are trying to sing as loud as possible, while my aunts are trying to sing as high as possible.

When the accordion stops and the singing dies down, two waitresses serve coffee, and then the desserts: first the cookies and roulades my aunts baked, then the cake. As the grownups sip their coffee, Uncle Mirko says he's going to buy his son a Hohner. A red Hohner! That's the best accordion in the world. Real German quality. All the best accordion players have Hohners. You want to know something interesting? My uncle scratches at his red cheeks. Matthias Hohner started out as a clockmaker. He made his first accordion when he was twenty-four. Soon he became famous for his accordions and had the biggest accordion factory in the world. Like I said—real German quality. When my Matija has his Hohner, you'll hear the difference. Now the boy has to put up with a Melodija, but soon I'm going to buy him a red Hohner!

Petra and Janez are the only ones at our table who order coffee. Janez drinks it black, which he's used to from work, but Petra takes hers with milk. She says it's terribly bitter without milk but with milk and sugar it's not too bad. At the first sip she makes a face; then she says you have to get used to it. Just like cigarettes. Just like men.

At the grown-ups' table I hear Aunt Marija bragging about their new washing machine. It's a Bosch automatic. She says that Majda, who lives in Stuttgart, drove one here by car for her mother. Everybody went to look at it. The machine has different programs, depending on what you're washing, and it has a centrifuge too, so by the end of the wash the clothes are almost dry. Uncle Tone, who's an electrician, adds a few things about the kind of electric motors that power washing machines, but then he waves his arm and says it'll be a while before any automatic washing machines are available in our country. If anybody wants one, they'll have to drive it here from Austria or Italy or Germany. That's what we did, Aunt Marija explains again.

11

EARLY IN THE week Elvis's father calls Dad and they arrange for me to go to Elvis's after school on Friday. Elvis has been absent the entire week. After school I'll bring him my notebooks, so he can copy out what he missed. I'll show him what we did in math and what we did in Slovenian.

As soon as he sees me, Elvis's father waves to me from the balcony; then he disappears into the apartment. Even before the door in the entrance hall shuts behind me I hear him on the floor above. Come on up! You know where we live, he says in a loud voice. When I'm on the second floor, I first see Elvis's father, then Elvis, who is smiling to me from the door.

Please, come in, Elvis's father says, putting an arm around my shoulders and gently ushering me into the apartment. I remove my shoes in the front hall and follow Elvis and his father into the kitchen. Let's eat something first, his father says. Then you boys can go over your notebooks. Elvis's mother pats my head and, smiling, says she didn't make lamb soup today. It's something completely ordinary—chicken soup. So you'll eat. I nod and sit down next to Elvis. At first I don't say anything, but then I ask, Have you been sick? No, Elvis shakes his head. I look at him in surprise, but before I can ask anything else, Elvis's father speaks up. The last time you were here, I told you we were from Macedonia. We're Turks and by our religion we're Muslims. According to the Abrahamic Covenant, it is our duty, or I could say, our custom, to circumcise a boy before he grows up. We cut the foreskin off his penis. Really, Fikret! We're at the table! Elvis's mother looks at his father. We're about to eat. Table or no table, I'm telling the boy so he knows. And he should know because they're friends. Friends need to know things about each other; they need to know what's going on with each other. I didn't even say anything so bad. Also, he turns to me, it sounds a lot worse than it really is. It stings a little, that's all. Well, that's how it is with us. He smiles and strokes his mustache.

Ali! Defne, Elvis's mother calls as she's placing the bowl of soup on the table. Lunch is on. Hurry up!

Well, look who's here! Ali lightly punches my shoulder when he comes out from his room. How are you doing? Good, I hope, he continues before I can say anything. And karate? How's that going? Bruce Lee! You know who Bruce Lee is? Yes, I know who he is, I say, glad that I finally know something Ali is talking about.

Hey there, Defne greets me as she sits down next to her mother. There's going to be a dessert after lunch, she says. I made it. That's good, dear, her mother stops her and strokes her head. But lunch first.

While we're eating, we don't say anything. The soup is followed by roast chicken, potatoes, and carrots. Elvis's mother asks a few times if I like it. I nod with my mouth full. I'm trying to eat as fast as Elvis and Ali, who received as much food as I did but their plates are nearly empty.

When we finish the main course, Elvis's father leans back and looks at Elvis's mother. It was delicious, dear Farhana. Thank you. Thank you, the children say in unison and then, with a slight delay, so do I. That's okay, Elvis's mother smiles at me. I'm glad you liked it. Defne, she says, turning to her daughter, would you like to bring in dessert now?

Defne hops off her chair and runs to the refrigerator. She returns with a plate full of pastries that look more like sandwiches, only a little smaller. They're éclairs, she tells me. Do you know what éclairs are? Have you had them before? No, I say, staring at the dessert. I can hardly wait to taste one, although I'm also worried because they're so big. What if I don't like it? But I have no reason to worry. With the first bite still in my mouth, I smile and say, It's good. It's my favorite, Defne says. But they take a while to make. Mom told me you were coming so I made an effort. They're very good, Defne, her mother breaks in. You know—her father now puts in a word—some people say éclairs are French, others say they're British, but if you ask me, well, they're obviously Turkish. He pats down his mustache, where there's still a little vanilla cream. Have another one. He pushes the plate toward me.

When Elvis and I are at last in his room, I open my bookbag and place my notebooks and workbooks on the floor. You didn't miss a lot, I tell him as I page through my math notebook. I stop and run my finger along the top line. That's what we did today. It's not too hard.

As Elvis looks quickly through the notebooks, I'm thinking about his penis and foreskin. I don't understand why it had to be cut off. When Elvis's father was talking, it sounded completely understandable, but now that I'm thinking about it, it no longer makes sense. As soon as Elvis closes the last notebook, I look at him. Did it hurt a lot? Hurt? Elvis is surprised for a second, but then he figures out what I'm asking. No, he says. Not a lot. But it was gross. It swelled up. For a few days, it was thick and black like a sausage. That first night it hurt, and it stung when I went to the bathroom, but now it doesn't anymore and the sausage is gone too. Bye-bye sausage! I laugh.

But I did get lots of presents. Elvis stands up and goes over to his bed. Uncle Idriz came here from Italy, and Uncle Nadir from Bosnia. And all my cousins too. We had a full house, and everyone had presents for me. Look! He pulls out two big boxes from beneath the bed. Which one do you like best?

I go over to the bed and gaze in wonder at all the toys. They don't have that many toys in the store, I say and quickly look them over. I like the soldiers, I say, and the tanks. But no Superman? No robot? My cousin Martin has Droid from *Star Wars*. Do you know about *Star Wars*? Elvis nods and says, Sure, I know about it. Have you seen it, I ask. No, he says. Neither have I, I say. Then I start telling him about it, as much as I remember from what Martin told me. Every so often Elvis adds something or corrects me. He tells me what he heard from Ali and Ali's friend Andrej. Although neither of us has seen the movie, we piece together the story. Since we don't have any *Star Wars* action figures, we position the plastic soldiers around the room. Green soldiers on one side, brown on the other. Then we divide up the tanks. The brown soldiers are the Empire's troops; the green ones are the rebels. They could just as easily be Partisans, and the brown ones Germans. We don't play against each other; we're both greens. We attack the browns and slowly squeeze them into a corner.

After a while Elvis's father opens the door and asks, Have you boys gone through the notebooks? Yes, we both say. Good, he says; then, shifting his weight, he leaves.

When it starts getting dark outside, Defne comes into the room. Can I play with you? No, you can't, Elvis says. The rebels will defeat the Empire, he cries and moves a few of the green figures and, at the same time, knocks down some of the brown ones, as if they're falling under gunfire. I can be the princess, Defne says. *Star Wars* doesn't have any princesses or Barbie dolls in it, Elvis responds. There is too a princess, Defne insists. Ali said there was a princess in *Star Wars*. Wait. She runs to another room and brings back Ali, who says there is indeed a princess in *Star Wars*. Her name is Leia, he says. Fine, Elvis says, you can be Princess Leia. But this is a battle and the princess doesn't fight. Get on the bed. You'll be safe there. Defne isn't especially happy about this, but she still obeys her brother. She gets on the bed and starts watching us as Ali leaves.

Elvis and I are still playing and Defne is still watching us from the bed when the doorbell rings. Aw no, I say, and angrily flick my arm. They're here to pick me up. Maybe they'll stay for coffee, Elvis says. Maybe, I pout and move a green soldier. Down with the Empire, Elvis cries.

I hear my father's voice in the front hall. Then my mother's. If they're both here, then we're probably not going to leave right away, I think, and keep moving figures around as if nothing has changed; Elvis does the same. A moment later the door opens again. I see Dad, Mom, and Elvis's father, who says, Look how nicely they're playing. Are you boys having fun, Dad asks, but when he sees Defne in the room, he corrects himself. Are you all having fun? Sure, I say and keep moving the soldiers. We're playing *Star Wars*, Elvis says. Defne's the princess and we're the rebels. Oh, I see, Dad says. Five more minutes, he tells me, and then we're leaving. We're going to have a quick coffee first. He closes the door. See, I told you, Elvis says, looking at me.

Before we leave, everyone gathers in the kitchen. Elvis's father is holding a camera. We'll take a picture to remember this, he says. First he takes a picture of just Elvis and me. Then he decides he'll take another one of all of us together. For a long time he is flapping his arms as the rest of us take a step to the left and then a half step back to the right by the television set, as he indicates. Then another step to the right, and a half step back to the left. At last, he pushes the button. He looks at us for a few seconds; then he sets the camera on the table, adjusts its position a couple of times, and runs over to us. He places himself next to my father just in time. Then there's a flash and a click. Great, he says with a clap of his hands. We'll have some pictures to remember the day by.

While we're putting on our shoes, Elvis's father says he'll bring my bookbag and notebooks back to me on Sunday. Oh, and one more thing. He lays his right hand on my shoulder. From now on call me Uncle Fikret. Think of us as your Uncle Fikret and Aunt Farhana. Okay? I nod and say goodbye to Elvis, Ali, and Defne, and then to my new uncle and aunt.

On the way home, Mom asks me several times if we had fun. Yes, is all I say. So I guess you and Elvis could get together to play another time too, she says. Sure, I say. Maybe at our place next time. I nod. You'll have to straighten your room first. Did you see how neat and tidy everything was at Elvis's? Whenever we're there, everything is always as neat as a pin. Okay, I say, I will.

At home, I go straight to the bathroom. After I wash up and put on my pajamas, I climb into the armchair in front of the TV. Mom and Dad are watching a movie. Mom hands me a blanket. Cover up so you won't be cold. I pull the blanket over my legs and think for a few moments; then I blurt out, When am I going to get circumcised? What did you say? Dad looks at me in surprise. When are you going to have me circumcised, I repeat. You know, the foreskin on my penis. Whatever gave you such an idea? Mom is bewildered. I want to be circumcised, I say. So I can get a bunch of toys. Oh, I see, Dad says with a chuckle. This is all about the toys. I thought so. Elvis got some toys, didn't he? You wouldn't believe how many, I exclaim. He got circumcised, and then all his aunts and uncles and cousins came. And they all brought presents. But Elvis didn't get circumcised so he could get presents, my mother says. I know that, I say. Did Elvis tell you what happens? His dad did, I say, then add, I mean Uncle Fikret. Elvis told me a little too, but he didn't want to talk about it. Do you know why he didn't want to talk about it? Dad shifts in his seat. Because it's not very pleasant. It hurts and burns. How do you know that, I say. Did you get circumcised? No, but I have friends who did. They told me about it. It burns and hurts for about a week; it's like if you cut yourself. That's why Elvis wasn't in school.

Now I'm not so interested in the toys. If it didn't hurt and burn, then maybe I'd try to convince Mom and Dad to let me be circumcised, but after everything I've heard, I decide against it. I'd rather wait for New Year's Eve and my birthday to get some presents.

In my room I take Superman from the shelf. Did you get circumcised? Did you put up with it so you could get some toys? Or were you never even a kid?

I take the plastic action figure to bed with me and fall asleep.

12

ROK'S NOT IN school on Monday. I sit at our desk by myself. But Elvis is back. Before our first lesson, he handed the teacher a note from his parents. During recess, the two of us go into the hallway. Peter follows. He asks Elvis why he wasn't in school last week. No special reason. Elvis waves his arm and shakes his head. It wasn't important. Let's take a walk, he says and starts off down the wide hallway. Peter and I hurry after him.

We go up the stairs and do half a circle on the second floor, where the seventh- and eighth-grade classrooms are. Ali's classroom is down the hall, Elvis says. Let's take a look. Before Peter and I can say anything, we're surprised by a voice. So where are you boys going? We freeze as if struck by lightning. We don't need to look to know who it is. I turn around slowly and see Sršen. He has a sandwich in his right hand and his left is shoved deep into the pocket of his pants. This isn't what we agreed, is it? I don't think so, he says. Who gave you permission to walk around the school? Why should anyone have to give us permission, Elvis says, stepping forward. Why? Sršen stuffs the last chunk of his sandwich in his mouth, chews, and swallows it; then he wipes his mouth with the back of his hand. I'll tell you why. He steps toward us, but Elvis stands his ground. Because I said so—understand? It takes me a few moments to gather my courage, but then I say, Just leave us alone, why don't you? I would leave you alone, Sršen says with a smile, but you came up here to us. I didn't go down to you. Get it, kid? No, I don't get it. But now you will. He swings his arm to hit me, but I duck just in time. Think you're smart, do you? He lunges at me, swings again, and again misses, only now he loses his footing and starts waving his arms. I take my chance and punch him in the stomach as hard as I can. Then I kick his leg and jump back.

Sršen grimaces, but a second later he comes at me like a bull and knocks me over. So what now, kid? What are ya gonna do now? He sits on my chest and starts slapping my face with both hands as I try to wriggle out from under him. But he's too big and heavy. He's so fat he doesn't even feel me pinching and scratching at him. Let him go, Elvis shouts. Let him go, Peter shouts and charges. Sršen pushes him away with a swipe of his left arm, and Peter stumbles back all the way to the radiator. Now Sršen leans his face over me with drool oozing from his mouth. There are crumbs on his lips and the thick saliva is slowly falling toward me. I shut my eyes and wait for the worst.

Then I hear Ali. Get off him, shithead! What, are you deaf? A moment later, Ali grabs Sršen and yanks him off me. I'm free again. I roll over and get to my feet in a hurry; Sršen, meanwhile, is on the floor. Ali kicks him twice and shouts, You touch them one more time, just one more time! You hear me, shithead?

Sršen smirks up at Ali. Oh yeah? What ya gonna do? Touch them just one more time and I'll break both your arms, Ali shouts.

At that moment Tornado appears in the hallway. My blood freezes, as does the blood of everyone who sees her. Tornado teaches geography. I haven't had geography yet, but I know who she is. Tornado is also the deputy principal and the strictest teacher in the school. All the students are afraid of her, even the ones who haven't had her yet. We all know she's ruthless. First, she grabs Ali by the ear; then she orders Sršen to get up. I gaze at her in terror as she stands in front of us and shouts, The three of you, to the principal's office. Now!

But that's not fair, Peter says. We didn't start it. Tornado turns to him and says, Who asked you anything? And what grade are you in, anyway? Second? Third? What are you doing up here? You should be down in your classroom. Who is your teacher? Miss Nada, Peter stammers. Go downstairs this minute, Tornado shouts. Or would you rather visit the principal too? Peter and Elvis run down the hallway to the stairs, while Sršen, Ali, and I go with the teacher to the principal's office.

I try not to think about what's going to happen in the principal's office. And I try not to think about what's going to happen at home. Sršen glances at me a few times. Before we go in, he whispers, Watch what you do, kid. Or we'll all be screwed.

The principal is a tall, skinny woman. I remember her from our school ceremonies, where she gives long speeches full of complicated words I don't understand. But the teachers always applaud her enthusiastically so the students do too.

My heart is pounding. I don't know if it's ever pounded like this before, not even when the Hornets surrounded us at the garages. But then I knew everything would be over in a few minutes. Even if they beat us up it would be over. It's not like that with the principal and being punished. That will keep repeating itself over and over and never end. First it will be in her office, then in the classroom, and again at home. Nobody will ever forget that I was sent to the principal's office. Even much later, for every little thing I do, I'll hear, Do you want to be sent to the principal again? Wasn't once enough for you?

There's a burning knot in my stomach and my hands are cold and clammy.

The principal looks at us in silence for a few moments; then she turns to the teacher who brought us here. What happened? The boys were fighting, Tornado tells her in a dry voice. I didn't start it, Sršen stammers. Keep quiet, Tornado snaps at him. The principal is talking. You'll speak when you're spoken to. Is that clear?

All right, the principal says softly, we'll all have a chance to speak. But first I'd like you to introduce yourselves. Tell me your first and last names and what class you're in, so I will know with whom I am talking. We all introduce ourselves. First Sršen, then Ali, then me. The teacher asks each of us to tell her what happened. Each of us tells our story. Sršen mostly makes everything up, but neither Ali nor I dare to object.

For a few moments the principal looks at us sternly; then she decides. Today, this is how it will be. I am giving each of you a verbal warning. I am certain this will not happen again. But if it does—she raises the index finger on her left hand—there will be consequences. Do you understand me? Yes, ma'am, we all say in unison, we understand. Good. Now, quickly, back to your classes.

Tornado escorts us to the hallway. Outside the office, she stands in front of us. If it were up to me, you would not have gotten off so easily. If it were up to me, you would all have been severely punished. But the principal has the last word, so we're doing things her way. I will see you two in class, she says, looking at Ali and Sršen. Then she turns to me. You I will see next year. In the meantime, improve yourself. That's my advice.

As I run down the stairs I feel like I've grown wings. Like I can fly! Like I can lift off the ground and make a few circles down the hall and in the lobby. It all turned out all right in the principal's office. Nothing happened—we weren't punished! Although now I don't remember exactly what I expected to happen, but just five minutes earlier I was sure I'd be in for some terrible punishment. And now this—a verbal warning! The principal is a very fair person.

For a few moments I still think about what I would have said to my parents if the punishment had been worse. They would probably have had to come to the school. They would probably have been disappointed in me. That's what they would say. But now it's over. Nothing happened!

I stand for a moment in front of the classroom door. I knock softly and go in. The teacher looks at me and nods for me to go to my desk. I think how lucky I am. Miss Nada doesn't even ask me where I've been or why I'm late. I open the book and try to follow what she's saying, but my thoughts keep drifting off. All at once I'm back in the principal's office and everything that happened is repeating, only much faster. Also, I'm watching it from somewhere overhead and farther away. I can see myself too. It's like I'm watching a movie.

I glance at the chalkboard. The teacher writes: *Mollusks may be divided into eight groups, including shellfish such as mussels and oysters, snails such as slugs and arions, and cephalopods such as cuttlefish and octopuses.* I open my notebook and start copying from the board. I do my best to stay focused, but my thoughts are all over the place. Suddenly, Sršen is standing in front of me. He swings his arm at my head, but I nimbly dodge him. I kick his leg and punch him in the stomach. Then a second punch in the stomach, and a third. Sršen tries to get away but I won't let him. Now you're mine, I say and knock him to the ground. Sršen lies there looking up at me. Kid, please, he stammers. What, I ask, standing over him. What, Sršen? I'll never bother you again, kid, he promises. And what about Elvis and Peter? I clench my teeth. Them too, he says. And Ali? Not him either. Sršen shakes his big brush-cut head. Good, I say, satisfied. If that's the truth, I'll release you. If that's the truth, I'll let you go. I step back. But remember, I tell him as he picks himself up off the ground. I'm watching you, so you had better keep your promise. I will, Sršen says. Then he turns around and runs to his classroom. Ali, Elvis, and Peter come up to me. You really gave it to him, Ali says, patting me on the shoulder. Just like Bruce Lee! At that moment, the bell rings. I come out of my daze. The teacher has put down the chalk and is looking at me; a moment later she calls me to her desk.

Where were you earlier, she asks in a stern voice. I tell her I was in the principal's office. Miss Nada nods. Well, I already know that. She gives me a stern look. Elvis and Peter told me. But now I want you to tell me yourself. I tell her what happened. When I finish, the teacher gives me a good look and then says,

You Pioneers are examples. Every one of you! I nod but don't say anything. I know you're a good boy, she says. Don't change because of the others. Now go to your desk and write something in your diary.

At first, I'm all by myself, but then Ana comes over. Don't feel bad, she says. You did the right thing. How do you know? Peter and Elvis told us. They said you were in a fight with Sršen. Everyone's afraid of him, but you stood up to him. You're really brave. If Ali hadn't shown up, it would have ended badly, I say. But that's what friends are for, Ana exclaims. While we're talking, a few more of my classmates gather at my desk. Mostly they don't say anything. But when the bell rings for the end of the break, Matic says, Good job! Somebody had to punch his fat mouth.

Somebody had to punch his fat mouth—this keeps echoing in my head for a while.

After school, Elvis, Peter, and I head home. We look over our shoulders a few times to see if Sršen is following us. When we reach the garages, we stop. Sršen could be anywhere. He could be hiding behind the garages; he could be on the upper level ready to jump down right in front of us from the top of the metal steps, or he could be calmly waiting behind a corner at the end of garages.

I don't think he's here, I say. Besides, he wouldn't dare do anything now. We'll have some peace from him for a while. But when things settle down and everything's forgotten, he'll probably take revenge. Sršen doesn't forget. My friends agree. Sršen doesn't forget. His father's a cop, Elvis says. So what, I say, looking at him. Dad says it's best not to have anything to do with them. Not in any way. What do you mean, *not in any way*, I ask. Like I said, Elvis says sharply, it's best not to have anything to do with them. I just shrug and keep walking.

When the garages are behind us, we breathe a sigh of relief. Now we're talking more, and louder. Soon we split up. I start running to my building, but then I see Ana on the swings, so I make a detour. When I run up to her, I ask if she's by herself. Do you see anyone else here, she says with a smile. So then I'll stay for a bit, I say. I put my backpack down and sit on an empty swing.

I don't say anything for minute or so, but then I ask if she's making any movies now. Not yet, but we're getting ready to. We'll start right after school ends. What's it about, I ask. I'm not really sure. It won't be a children's movie, though. I'm going to play the daughter of the main character. Who's the main character? His name's Bert, Ana says. Bert's a man with a lot of problems, a lot of obstacles in his life, but he overcomes them through his unbreakable will. He's a fighter. Just like you were today. She glances at me. Oh, I say, and because I'm curious I ask if Bert is maybe a policeman or superhero. No, Bert's a completely ordinary man, Ana explains. It'll be a movie about an ordinary man. I nod and think to myself that it won't be very interesting if Bert is just an ordinary man, but I don't say that. I'd like to see the movie anyway. Because of Ana.

It's too bad that Bert's not a superhero, I say a little later. If I was making the movie, he would have superpowers. And not just one, but several. He'd help people like Superman does. Ana laughs and says, So tell me the story of superhero Bert. I shrug. Well, I don't know. On the one hand, I'm embarrassed because

I'm not sure I know how to make up the kind of story Ana would be interested in, and on the other hand, I like that she wants to hear it. She could have said that Superman is a silly hero because he's not real. But Ana didn't say that; she told me to make up a story. Okay, I say and start making one up.

I give superhero Bert some of Superman's qualities and some of Sandokan's qualities, and add a couple of details from *Star Wars*. Then I come to his enemy. Bert's archenemy is Sršen, I say with a laugh. Sršen used to be a good man, a cop. But then something bad happened to him. He's not a cop anymore but a villain. He has a big shaved head and lips that are always wet. He doesn't appear to be very nimble, but because of his past he has the skills and knowledge of a policeman and detective. He's mastered quite a few of the martial arts, especially karate and judo. Also, he has a lightsaber. Sršen is a very dangerous adversary, I say. But eventually Bert defeats him, Ana exclaims. Yes, I say. At the end, Bert defeats him.

13

EARLY ON SATURDAY, we leave for Austria. For about two weeks, my parents have been saying that we're going across the border to buy a few things we can't get at home, just like other people do. They have been talking about marks and schillings, the kind of money people use in Germany and Austria, and here too. We use dinars in our country, but I already know that it's better to have marks. Or if not marks, then schillings or francs or dollars. I don't understand why dinars aren't any good. Everybody always gives me dinars—for my birthday, or for a good report card, or sometimes for no special reason at all.

At first, I didn't want to go to Austria, but then my parents told me about the big toy stores they have there and I gave in. They may even have some *Star Wars* action figures, Dad told me with a wink. If they do, and if they aren't too expensive, then you can have one. In any case, I have my wallet with me; it has all my money in it. If I hadn't been paying Sršen all this time,

I'd have even more. I'm thinking about how I will finally have something like what Martin and Elvis have.

Martin and Elvis are lucky. Uncle Gorazd goes fairly often to Trieste and he always brings back something for Martin. Elvis has relatives in other countries. When he was circumcised, they brought him two whole boxes of toys. But even before, he and Ali had more toys than anybody else. But now that's going to change. Now I will have some new toys too. Superman, who stands on my desk, is finally going to have some company.

Soon the road starts to rise. There are more and more curves and I'm feeling more and more nauseous. Mom asks me a few times if we should stop, but I don't want to. I want to be in Austria as soon as possible; I want to be in stores full of toys as soon as possible. I gulp down the thick saliva and try looking straight ahead at the road. My breath is short and shallow. Just when I think I'm not going to make it, the car stops. There's a long line of vehicles in front of us and they're not moving. Mom looks at Dad and asks him if it's always like this at the border. It depends, he replies. Sometimes you can be stuck for an hour or two. Look at that, Mom says, turning to me and pointing outside. Do you see the chamois? They've come right down to the road! They're obviously used to people.

Let's get out, I exclaim. Mom nods. All right, she says. The cars aren't moving anyway. She gets out of the car and shifts her seat forward so I can climb out. We run to the other side of the road, to the other people who are standing at the foot of the gravelly slope that the animals are coming down from. Some people are feeding pieces of dry bread to the animals. After a while, I stretch out my arm. One of the animals approaches cautiously and touches my hand with its soft nose. But since I don't have anything in my hand, it quickly moves away. Did you see that! Mom is delighted.

When the line of vehicles starts moving, we go back to our car. We're driving slowly and I don't feel sick anymore. At one of the next curves we see a big black skeleton with its arms reaching to the sky. What's that, I ask. There was a labor camp here during the war, Dad says. The prisoners were digging a tunnel through the mountain. A lot of them died doing this work, and many of them were killed too. We'll be driving through that tunnel today.

Dad goes on with the story. He tells us about the camp doctor, a man named Sigbert Ramsauer, who decided whether people would live or die. He was responsible for hundreds of deaths. He was sentenced to life imprisonment after the war, but then he was pardoned a few years later. And the worst of it is—Dad's voice is getting louder—this man later worked at the hospital in Klagenfurt, and eventually he had his own private practice. But what about having a conscience? And what about all those people who knew what he had done during the war? What happened to their conscience?

I don't know what Dad is talking about; I don't understand and I'm not really interested so I stop listening. Instead, I imagine being in stores with shelves full of toys. On one shelf there are characters from *Star Wars*. On another, there are superheroes. On a third shelf, there are soldiers, and on a fourth, cowboys and Indians. And on and on. I don't know when I start drifting off to sleep. When I open my eyes, I see my mother's smiling face above me. We're here, Bean. Come on.

That evening there are two new shiny boxes in my room. I take Superman off my desk and slowly open the first box. I open it carefully so I don't tear the cardboard and so the tape doesn't damage the picture of Luke Skywalker on the back of the box. When Luke is out, I place him next to Superman and start on the second box. I can barely believe it: Darth Vader. None of my friends has any characters from *Star Wars*. In the store Mom said I should pick the nicest one, one that I know. But when I saw these two *Star Wars* figures, I knew it wouldn't be possible. But you haven't even seen the movie, she said. You don't know who they are or what it's all about. Yes, I do, I protested. I know everything! Martin saw the movie and so did Ali. They both told me about it. Many times. I know everything! They're the ones I want. Skywalker and Vader or nothing! Dad said to Mom that she also chose the things she wanted. That's different, Mom said. I'm not sure it is, Dad said; then he kissed her. It's a guy thing. In the end, Mom gave in. As we left the store, Dad said he and I would see the movie as soon as it came to the theater or television.

In one of the stores we went to we bought two bunches of bananas, a bucket of oranges, lemons, chocolate, and coffee. I ate a banana before we left. It didn't seem particularly special. I don't know why it's such a big deal that there aren't any bananas in our stores.

Although the light in my room is off, I'm still staring in the direction of my desk, where Superman, Luke Skywalker, and Darth Vader are standing. Superman is almost half the size of my two new figures, but that doesn't bother me. Right now I'm the happiest boy in the city, maybe in the whole world.

14

ON SUNDAY AFTERNOON we go to Elvis's. Uncle Fikret phoned Dad on Wednesday to invite us. We'll have coffee, he said, and the kids can play together.

I have Luke Skywalker and Darth Vader with me in a big bag. I can't wait to show them to Elvis and Ali. When we get there, I go straight to Elvis's room. Mom says something to me but I don't hear her. Well, I do hear her but I don't listen to what she says. It's not important what she said. What's important is what I have in my bag. Look, I cry, pulling out first one figure then the other. What do you think? You've got Darth Vader and Luke Skywalker, Elvis exclaims in amazement. Where did you get them? I tell him we went to Austria. At first Dad said I could have only one, but in the end he let me have them both. Of course, Elvis says excitedly. There's no point in just having one! He picks up Luke and starts carefully moving his arms, legs, and head; then he sets him down in front of him and says he's terrific. He pulls out a big box of toys from beneath his bed and turns it over, so everything comes tumbling out on the floor. Now we can really play!

This is Captain America, he says, pushing a blue-and-red action figure over to me. Do you know him? No, I say. My uncle gave him to me. That time when, you know. Right, I say as I look at the figure; then I look at Elvis. Does it still hurt? Are you kidding? I forgot all about it. He waves his arm. So what does it look like now? What does what look like, Elvis says. You know, your thing. What does it look like now that it's circumcised? Is it different? Of course it is. Elvis stands up, unzips his fly, and pulls it out. I'm surprised when I look at it, but I'm even more surprised when I look at the door, which has just swung open. Ali steps into the room.

What are you doing, little brother? Are you crazy, he laughs. Best put that worm back in your pants. For fuck's sake, you're not homos. He comes over to me and pats my head. My face has turned red because he caught us, and I can't bring myself to look at him. Ali says, I'm not going to tell anyone. I heard you got some new action figures. If you want, I can tell you how it all began. How what began? I look up. The story of *Star Wars*, of course. Ali turns serious now. It's not some children's fairy tale. It's not some sort of nonsense. And if you ask me, there is more to come. They won't stop at just one part. Someday they'll make a second and third part too. Because there's a lot more to tell.

By now Elvis has zipped up his pants and sits down with us. Then we both listen as Ali tells us the story.

A while later Defne joins us. She sits on the bed and listens to Ali. When I glance up at her, our eyes meet. I feel embarrassed and quickly look away. I look at Ali for a while, then Elvis, then

SEBASTIJAN PREGELJ

Defne again. Again our eyes meet. Just like before, I look away, but from the corner of my eye I can see that she's smiling. I feel hot all over. I try to calm myself, to follow what Ali is saying, but my thoughts keep returning to Defne. I try not to look at her. If Ali or Elvis sees us looking at each other, it's over. They'd start teasing us and asking us when we're getting married. I look at Ali, at his lips, so I can more easily follow the words he is saying, but the words fall past me, as if they weren't connected at all, as if they had no meaning.

I'm eventually rescued from this misery by Aunt Farhana, who sticks her head into the room. Dessert's on. Come and get it. Yes! Elvis jumps up and immediately runs into the kitchen. Ali finishes what he's saying and looks at me. Well? What do you think? I think it's good, I say and follow him out of the room.

While we're eating dessert, Uncle Fikret tells us he's glad that we've come. Happiness is something everybody searches for and chases after, but friendship is something we have. Or don't have. Friendship is like a bird. It's not good if you keep her locked in a cage, because then she becomes sad. She needs to be free and come to your window on her own. If you set out food for her on the ledge, she'll make it a habit. She will keep coming to see you and will sing you a sweet song. But if you're not good with birds, she will come once and then leave and won't come back. Then he sits up a little straighter and extends his hand to my father across the table. I remember our first visit here and how our fathers were always shaking hands. I thought it was funny, or maybe not funny, but at least a little strange. I had never seen anyone shake hands as much as our fathers did that day. Later, they didn't shake hands as often. They only offered each other their hands at the beginning, when they arrived, and then at the end, when they were saying goodbye. But now they are doing it again.

I almost forgot, Uncle Fikret says, jumping up from the table. He goes over to the low chest where the television is and opens a drawer. He brings back two photographs. From last time, he says with a smile. I had copies made for you. The photos pass from hand to hand. Aunt Farhana tells her children to hold them by the edges so the pictures don't get covered in finger marks. The grown-ups look at the photos more carefully and hold on to them longer. We kids look at them faster. Finally, Mom puts the two photos in her purse. But first she wraps them in a piece of newspaper.

When our plates are empty, Dad looks at his watch and says it's time for us to go. Next time, you'll have to come to our place, Mom says. In the front hall, Uncle Fikret goes up to Dad, takes his arm, and says in a half whisper that if he ever needs marks or schillings again he should come to him.

15

LIFE IS REALLY unfair sometimes. Bad things happen to good people.

On Tuesday morning the plane on which Ana and her family were flying for a short vacation crashed into the side of Mont San-Pietro on Corsica. All the passengers and crew members died—180 altogether. Mom and Dad told me what happened that afternoon, but I didn't understand. I couldn't believe it; I didn't want to believe it. Of course, I know what death is, but it's grandparents who die, great-uncles and -aunts I don't remember, elderly neighbors I haven't seen in years; even Tito died. But not my friends.

On Wednesday morning we are sitting in class. Everybody knows what happened. When Miss Nada comes in, she doesn't say anything for a few moments. But then she wipes her eyes and tells us about the accident. She tells us that our classmate and her family were on the plane, and that this is truly a great tragedy, a great loss. We will all miss her very much.

Ana's chair is empty. Alenka, who sat with Ana, can't stop crying. I look at the empty chair and think maybe Ana will be here tomorrow anyway. Maybe all of them are wrong. But what do I know. I'm only eleven and I don't understand anything yet. I don't know anything. But it could happen, I think. If she's here tomorrow, then her mother will be here on Friday to pick her up early, just like she picks her up early every Friday because on Fridays they drive to Koper to visit her grandmother. And then her brother will still be singing at school events and all the girls will still be in love with him, with the boy in the blue sweater with the big yellow sun on it.

But it doesn't happen.

The next few days I spend a lot of time staring at the empty chair. I'm still waiting for the morning when I walk into the classroom and see Ana there.

But Ana is still never there. The only thing that really reminds me of her is the chocolate commercial on TV. Each time it's on, my parents say they can't understand it. How can they keep showing this commercial? Even if most of the people who see it don't know, it still isn't right. As for me, I'm glad the commercial for Ana's chocolate is still being shown. Whenever I watch it I feel like Ana is still with us, that she's still here, and that everything is all right. She just didn't come to school. That's all.

A few weeks later, the commercial for Ana's chocolate disappears. It's replaced by a new one. The chocolate is the same but the child in the commercial is different. For a few evenings I wait for the commercial with Ana to appear again, but it doesn't.

So, like other people, I still think of Ana only now and then. Next year, when we move up a grade, Ana's chair won't be there.

There won't be anything to remind me of her and then, for many years, I won't think about her.

Only later, when Mom and I, or maybe only me, are going through the family photo album and I see the girl with dark hair in one of our class pictures, I'll remember her again. I'll be happy that she is still there, in that grainy photograph. I'll be happy that she is still there with all of us, captured at a moment when everything in life was fine and good.

And when I grow up, I will believe that the children in that photograph are living their lives, which have nothing to do with our lives. It doesn't matter what we grew up to become, what we do for a living, or who we are living with and where. In the photograph we are exactly the same as we were back then, all of us, even Ana, and everything is happening that was happening then. Time flows for a good four years, and then, on the last day of November, it rewinds. Everything that happened at school up to that point, we instantly forget, and so do our parents. Again it is the first day of school. Our mothers are fiddling with our hair and straightening our clothes as our fathers tirelessly take pictures of us. Again everything starts over. And again and again.

16

RIGHT AFTER WINTER vacation, our homeroom goes with the B homeroom to the School Activities Center in the mountain village of Zgornje Gorje. Our teacher has been telling us for weeks about all the things we'll be doing and learning over the course of our stay. The parents all attended a special meeting, where they were told what our daily routine would be and what we would need to bring with us. Mom and I went around to different stores to buy anything on the list I didn't already have. On Sunday afternoon she laid out my clothes on the sofa, and Dad brought up the big brown duffel bag from the basement storage unit. Mom put everything inside it, telling me what each thing was and where it was, as if I wasn't standing right next to her watching what she was doing. Dad stood to the side and laughed. I'm sure none of you will wash yourselves or change your clothes there. Well, maybe you'll change your clothes, but you're certainly not going to wash. Mom kept telling him not to talk nonsense.

Now I'm standing in the dormitory next to my bunk. Rok is above me and Elvis is two beds over. Peter's not here because he got sick. Soon the gym teacher walks into the room. Boys, are we all ready, he asks in a loud voice. He takes a quick look at us and leads us to the cloakroom, where we change into our ski boots, and then outside into the snow. With our ski boots on our feet and our skis in our arms we set off for the hill behind the Center. The teacher says that we first need to do a test. I have to see how well you all ski, and then I'll divide you into groups. Starting tomorrow, you'll be skiing in groups based on your skill level. So show me how good you are. Do your best.

I want to be in the same group with Rok, but in the end I'm not with either Rok or Elvis. Rok skis a lot better than I do, and Elvis doesn't even know how to stand on skis. That sucks, I say as we go back to the Center, where all we do is change out of our ski boots; then we go on a hike with our teacher Mr. Miran. We trudge through the deep snow for about half an hour. Everybody is soaked to the bone and exhausted. We've had enough of this; we want to go back to the Center, but instead we keep walking. Until Matic makes a snowball and throws it at the teacher's back. Mr. Miran, a lanky, bearded man, turns around slowly and frowns. I think, This is not good. He's angry and he's going to punish us, just like in gym class when he makes us do frog jumps for every foul, which he calls anything that in his opinion we're not supposed to do. But amazingly, he leans down, makes a snowball, and throws it at one of us. All at once we start running around, shouting, making snowballs and throwing them at each other. Then we form groups. Some of us gather around Matic. The girls move away and we start attacking the B homeroom, who have gathered around the teacher.

Half an hour later, back in the dormitory, we quickly change and hang our wet clothes on the warm radiators. Soon, another teacher, Miss Mojca, arrives and says that it's six thirty, time for supper. We get in line and follow her to the dining hall, which will also be our classroom for the next few days and, on Tuesday and Thursday evening, a disco. After supper, we sit on the rug in the dormitory. Some of us are playing cards; others are reading books or comics.

The next day right after breakfast we go to the ski slope. My group goes straight to the chair lift and then to the top of the mountain, while the other groups stay below. Our ski instructor, Mr. Matej, tells us to hurry. We're going to have the best snow!

We ski in a line until lunchtime. Sometimes someone falls and we wait for them to get to their feet, and sometimes someone wanders off somewhere on their own and again we wait. Unlike Mr. Miran, Mr. Matej doesn't get upset. He keeps repeating that there's time. But it would be best if we used the time for skiing. It's such a fine day today, he exclaims.

After lunch we have an hour free. Matic puts on his ski jacket and says he's going to the store. We all stare at him. The day we arrived they said we're not allowed to leave the Center on our own. What are you going to buy, Rok asks. Snacks and stuff, Matic replies. They don't give us anything here. It's unbelievable! Anybody coming with me? We look at him, and then, for some unknown reason, I stand up and say, I'll come. Anybody else? Matic looks around the room. Nobody? Okay, but don't ask me later, Can I have some of your chocolate? Can I have some of your chips? He laughs. Then he turns around, opens the door, and slips into the hallway. I hurry after him.

In the hallway I look to make sure we don't run into any teachers. Downstairs, we change into our boots and go outside. At the corner of the building we see Miss Mojca, who is smoking and talking with somebody, but the other person is behind the corner and we don't see them. We think maybe it's Mr. Miran, but it could also be Miss Alenka. Matic slaps my chest and starts running through the snow in a different direction. Without hesitating, I run after him. When we get to the road, we're wet to our knees. We look left and right, then run across. On the other side, we run to the entrance of the store. When we're inside, Matic rubs his hands and, still catching his breath, grins as he shouts, Did you see? Did you see? They didn't even notice! Of course they didn't. They don't have a clue. We can come here every day.

We walk up and down the aisles and find the shelves with the cookies and snacks. Matic takes a big bar of chocolate, some Neapolitan wafers, and two bags of potato chips. I stand there looking at all the delicious things and can't make up my mind. Actually, there isn't that much to choose from, but the choice is still too big for the amount of money I have with me. Or is it with me? I freeze in horror. I feel my pockets with my hands, then reach inside them. I realize I left my wallet in my duffel bag. And now here I am in the store with no money. I can't go back, but I can't pay either. I think about asking Matic to lend me some money but decide against it because I don't want to owe him any favors.

I lean around the edge of the shelves and look at the check-out lady, who is sitting at the counter reading a magazine and waiting for us to bring our selections to the cash register. I consider exactly what I could take. I choose the mini chocolate bars. They're small enough to slip easily into my pockets. Slowly, I walk to where Matic is and then back again. Matic asks me if I have everything I want. I tell him I'm not going to buy anything today and that I just came to have a look. For tomorrow. Matic shrugs and goes to the counter. Now's the time, I think, as I hear the lady talking to Matic. She's asking him where we're from and if we're here for the whole week.

I reach over to the second shelf with my right hand and grab a fistful of mini chocolate bars. I turn toward the checkout counter as if I'm intending to take them there, but instead I shove my hand into my pocket and let them drop. My heart is racing, my lips are dry, and my arms and legs are shaking. Even so, I grab a few more mini chocolate bars and slip them into my other pocket. Then I go to the counter where Matic is paying. The checkout lady looks at me. I stop.

I can't move. I'm sure she saw me, or maybe she sees my bulging pockets. I tell myself there's still time. I can still put everything in my pockets on the counter and say I forgot to take a basket. I can still say I forgot my wallet and will come back later or maybe tomorrow. I can still do that. But when Matic is holding a full bag of snacks in his arms, I simply follow him out and, at the door, say goodbye. You boys come again sometime, the checkout lady says as we leave.

Outside, my heart is still racing. I'm scared the checkout lady really did see me and that at any moment she will run after us, grab me by the sleeve of my coat, pull me back inside, and empty out my pockets. I'm scared she will yell, You little thief. What should I do with you? No matter what I tell her, no matter how much I beg, in the end she'll call the police. The police will call the teachers. And suddenly the store will be full of people. The checkout lady, the police officers, Miss Mojca, Mr. Miran—all of them will be looking at me and asking, Why were you stealing? What's wrong with you? What should we do now? If some random person from the village should at that moment happen to walk into the store and see us, he will ask the checkout lady in a low voice what happened and she'll whisper to him, The boy's a thief. What else could I do? I had to call the police. It's best that they take him away. But what happens next will be a hundred times worse than the police taking me away. The checkout lady, Miss Mojca, and Mr. Miran will decide that they have no choice but to call my parents. I imagine my mother and father staring at me in silence, in front of all these people. I'm sorry. I am so, so sorry. I don't have the words to say how very sorry I am. But now it's too late. You did what you did, I hear my father reproaching me. You can't go back and make it right. What's done is done. I can feel my eyes filling with tears, my nose dripping. I didn't mean to. I'll never do it again. Never ever again. I'm sniffling. I wipe my eyes with my right hand and see Matic running across the road.

I take off after him and at the same moment I hear loud honking. I run as fast as I can. I see a car out of the corner of my eye and the angry face of the driver, who is shaking his fist at me.

Everything's okay. Everything's good, I tell myself once I'm across. You are really something! Matic looks at me wide-eyed.

You jumped right in front of that car. It came that close to hitting you. Didn't you see it? But despite my fear of the car, which almost killed me, right now I mainly just want to take a deep breath and shout for joy at the top of my lungs. The fear of being hit by a car has completely obliterated my fear of the checkout lady. And the fear of being hit by a car is a lot less than my fear of having to stand in front of my parents in a store full of people and stare at the ground while everyone is whispering that I'm a thief.

No shit! I look at Matic and laugh.

The checkout lady didn't notice anything. She didn't realize what I had done. She didn't come after us. Everything is okay. Everything is good. I'm saved! My heart is beating happily as if I just learned that Mom and Dad are letting me get a dog. Not a goldfish or a hamster, but a dog! The only thing is—I can't go back to that store. But I don't want to go back to the store. I don't give a damn about the store! The best thing in the world would be if they closed the store tonight and didn't open it again until next week and the checkout lady never returned to work. That would be the best thing in the world.

Matic and I run through the snow and stop by the wall of the Center. We walk carefully past the pile of snow beneath the windows; then we run to the entrance and slip inside. We quickly take off our coats and boots in the cloakroom and then tiptoe up the stairs. The others are still playing cards, or racing toy cars around, or lying on their beds reading.

Matic drops onto his bed, opens a bag of chips, and starts munching them loudly. I crawl onto mine and furtively empty my pockets, so nobody can see. I push the mini chocolate bars under the blanket. I would love to give them all away at once because I can't bear to look at them, but Matic would know that something isn't right. He would soon figure out that I had stolen them. So I carefully push them one by one under the blanket. Later, when my classmates are asleep, I will open them slowly and eat them. I won't like the way they taste and in fact will want to throw up. When I took them, I didn't notice that they were *rum bars*. Is there anything more disgusting than rum bars? I will barely be able to keep them down. But I have to get rid of the rum bars at any cost. They are evidence and the evidence must be destroyed. I will keep eating them until nothing is left under the blanket but the empty wrappers, which I will stuff beneath my pajamas, go to the lavatory, and throw into the trash. Even if somebody finds them in the trash can, they won't know who put them there. I will be sick to my stomach, but somehow I will keep them down and not throw up. Then I will try to forget all about those mini rum bars. And for a while I will succeed. But later, every time I see them in a store, I will remember how that winter, when I was eleven or twelve, I stole some rum bars from a little store beneath the snowy mountains. I will remember the fear gnawing at my bones and the disgusting smell and even more disgusting taste of those rum bars. Only many years later, when the chocolate factory has stopped making rum-flavored mini chocolate bars, will I truly be able to forget them. But it will be a long time until then.

I am eleven years old. I am lying on the bed and slowly pushing mini chocolate bars under the blanket. I make sure that none of my classmates see me.

17

EVERYTHING IS BACK to normal on Monday and by Tuesday I have the feeling that we were skiing last year, not a few days ago. But then there is terrible news. On Wednesday, when I return from school, I find my mother weeping on the sofa in the living room. My father is over by the balcony door rotating a cigarette lighter between his fingers. At first I think they're getting a divorce. I have been afraid of that ever since it happened to my classmate Tina. I don't dare ask what's wrong. I just stand there and look at them, until Dad comes over, strokes my head, and says, Grandma has died.

I look at him and don't understand. On the one hand, I feel glad that he and Mom aren't getting a divorce, but on the other, he has just told me something terrible. It can't be true. After all, it wasn't that long ago we were sitting at the table eating salty soup, three kinds of meat, and five kinds of dessert; my cousin Janez was talking about the Opel Kadett, Matija was playing the accordion, and Petra was dreaming about some boy she'd let kiss her. And now this. No, I say, shaking my head. Grandma is at home. Maybe she didn't hear the phone ring and didn't answer. Or maybe she and Grandpa were outside. Maybe their phone's not working. You know, sometimes it doesn't work. I look at Dad and hope that he slaps his forehead and says, You know, you're right. I didn't think of that. It's a good thing we have you. Of course, I don't believe this. Still, if anything could be different, then that is exactly what would happen now. But he says, Aunt Katja phoned and told us. Dad wraps his arms around me and hugs me tight. I swallow hard and look at him. Did it hurt? No, it didn't. One minute she was still alive and everything was fine, and the next minute she fell asleep and passed away. She didn't feel a thing. She fell asleep and left. Where did she fall asleep, I ask. Was she in her bed? It was at the kitchen table, Dad says. She fell asleep at the table. It was as if she just dozed off after lunch.

She dozed off after lunch? Really? I run into my room and throw myself on the bed. I know Grandma died because of me. What else could it be? Because she was always telling me that Jesus suffers for our sins; she was continually repeating that we are all sinners. But at the time I could never think of what sin I had committed that would cause Jesus to be so brutally beaten up. But now I know. Grandma was warning me in advance. She wanted to keep it from happening; she wanted to keep me from doing anything for which Jesus or anybody else would have to suffer in my place. Every chance she got she told me, Do not steal. Do not lie. Honor your father and your mother. But it was no good. Her words went in one ear and out the other. They did not reach my heart. So I lied and stole! That's why my grandmother died. The next time I'm in the choir loft and glance at Jesus, he's going to look me straight in the eye and whisper, It's all your fault. If you hadn't stolen, your grandmother would be sitting below right now praying in a pew. She prayed a lot for you. And now, boy, what will become of you?

I close my eyes tight. Who says I have to sit in that choir loft ever again? If Grandpa finds out it's my fault Grandma died, he'll never look at me again. If Mom finds out that Grandma died because of me, she won't love me anymore. Maybe she'll send me to an orphanage or reform school. I don't know. For a few moments my entire body is aching with fear. I clench my fists as if I'm gripping at branches while I dangle above a bottomless pit. My strength is giving out. I know I won't last much longer. Then, all of a sudden, I feel tremendous relief, which immediately covers up any feeling of guilt and drives away my fear and pain. Nobody knows about it! Except for me, nobody knows that I stole anything! And if nobody ever finds out, then everything will be okay. Everything will be just the way it was before. What's a few candy bars, anyway? Could Grandma really have died because of a few mini rum bars, which I didn't even like and which made me so sick that I nearly threw up? Of course not, I think as I wipe away my tears.

A little bit later we leave the apartment. My parents are going to see Grandpa but first they drop me off at Martin's. Superman, Luke Skywalker, and Darth Vader are going with me. Dad and Uncle Gorazd have a brief conversation. Was she sick? Did you see it coming, my uncle asks at the apartment door. No, Dad says, there were no signs that anything was wrong. Quite the opposite. She appeared healthy and was looking forward to her next sixty years. And then this happens. But you know how old people are. Even if she had been to the doctor's, even if he had told her something, she would have kept it to herself. She didn't want to be a burden; she didn't want to put anyone out. But I don't know. He lightly punches Uncle Gorazd's shoulder. I'm off. I want to get back as soon as possible.

The moment we're in his room, Martin starts telling me about the Scouts. He was at their winter camp, where they learned all about surviving in nature. Under winter conditions, he emphasizes. Do you know what that's like? You have no idea. He shakes his head. In winter all sorts of plants don't grow. So you don't have any fruit or berries to eat. There aren't even grasshoppers or snails, which you could stuff into dough with your thumb and cook up a meat roll in the embers. It's excruciating, I tell you! I don't know what "excruciating" means, and I don't ask. Martin said it with such conviction that everyone but me must know the word.

Soon I take my action figures out of my bag. Martin looks at them, but he's not as excited as I thought he would be. He picks up Vader, moves his legs a little as if he's running, but then puts him down again and asks, So are you going to the funeral? Yes, I say. You know you'll see your dead grandma in a coffin. Aren't you afraid? He tilts his head. No, I say. Why? Do you think you'll have the courage to touch her, Martin continues. What? I don't understand the question. Do you think you'll have the courage to touch a dead person? How do you know she's not a zombie? You reach out your hand to touch her and when it's above the corpse, your grandma opens her eyes, grabs your hand, and bites it off, Martin whispers. My grandmother is not a zombie,

I say. She didn't used to be when she was alive, Martin says, wrinkling his forehead. But now that she's dead, are you sure? She isn't, I insist. Stop it!

Okay, okay. Take it easy. Martin leans back; he doesn't want his folks to hear me shouting. He knows they would be in the room at once. They would ask him what he'd done to me. And if I squealed and told them what he said, he would be in trouble and maybe earn himself a box around the ears.

Want to see a Scout knife? Martin switches topics. Sure, why not, I say, because I really don't care. Martin hops over to the wardrobe, opens it, and brings out a big hunting knife. He places it in my lap and says I can take it out of the sheath. Only be careful you don't cut yourself. It's sharp as shit. I grip the leather sheath with my left hand and the handle with my right and slowly extract the knife. The blade shines under the light. What do you do with it, I ask curiously. I cut rope, branches, anything. If I was attacked by zombies, I could defend myself with it. I nod and slip the knife back into the sheath. I don't say anything. The Scouts seem interesting and I'd like to hear more about what they do, but ever since I got there, all Martin talks about are zombies. I think that's stupid and it's making me a little scared. Martin knows how to talk so it chills your blood. Plus, he's a couple of years older than me and knows things that I don't, which is why I mostly believe what he says.

Have you ever actually seen a zombie, I ask a bit later. Don't ask—they're horrible! They're corpses and their bodies are decaying, but still they walk around like living people. And they're really evil. As soon as they see that something's alive, they want to kill it. Animals, people, they don't care. He waves his arm.

And they walk really slow, but you can't escape them. All of a sudden they're all around you. It's epic! That's another word I don't know, but I repeat it after my cousin. Epic.

Then I hear Aunt Taja calling from the kitchen that supper's ready. Pancakes. Pancakes, Martin shouts. I love pancakes! He races into the kitchen, but before he sits down my aunt sends him to the bathroom. First we wash our hands, right?

Would you like milk too, she asks when I'm seated at the table. Yes, please. Cold or warm? Cold. I'm repeating what Martin said. Actually, it doesn't matter to me. Mom never gives me cold milk. She's afraid it'll make my throat hurt and I'll get sick. Aunt Taja doesn't worry about such things, so she pours cold milk for both of us.

My uncle doesn't eat as many pancakes as the rest of us. After only two, he says they're delicious but he's full. He pats his stomach, gets up from the table, and goes into the living room, and the next moment we hear the television. When Martin and I finish later and go into the living room, I freeze. The television is in color! I just stare at it, even though it's only the news. The people on television are all wearing clothes of different colors. Then some cars appear. They're also in different colors, just like in the parking lot outside. I look at Martin and ask how long they've had a color TV. Not too long, he replies. But I'll tell you, you quickly forget how it used to be. I can't even imagine what it was like watching TV without color, he says. Black-and-white is the pits. It's not even real TV. It's only half TV. Martin! I hear my uncle's voice from behind the upholstered sofa. Don't be pompous. I'm not! I'm just saying. Right, you're just saying, my uncle snorts. Then there's the click of a lighter, followed by smoke rising from behind the sofa, and my nostrils fill with an odor that I sometimes like and think is pleasant but other times smells awful to me and makes me nauseous.

Martin goes to wash his face and hands and change into his pajamas; then we sit in front of the TV and watch a movie. I fall asleep waiting for my parents to arrive.

In the morning I wake up in my bed. At first I'm surprised because I'm not wearing pajamas, but then I remember everything that happened the day before: Grandma died, so I went to Martin's. We had pancakes; then we watched television. I guess I fell asleep. Mom and Dad must have gotten there late so they carried me to the car. Then when we got home, they didn't even wake me up; they simply undressed me and put me to bed.

I get up and go to the kitchen. Mom is drinking coffee at the table. When she sees me, she smiles, stands up, and comes over and gives me a big hug. How are you, Bean? Did you sleep well? Did you have a nice time yesterday? Yeah, I say, wriggling out of her arms. It was good. And you know what? I'm almost shouting. They have a color TV! It was like in the movies. Really? Mom smiles. That's nice. She strokes my head and says she's going to make breakfast. When are we going to get a color TV? Mom shrugs. I don't know if she even heard me. I don't know if she even understood. I'm talking about a color TV! Maybe I should talk to Dad about it. He'll understand.

On Thursday, I take a note from my parents to school, and on Friday morning we go to the funeral.

On the way there I feel sick, but I don't say anything. The fact that we're going to a funeral is so much worse. And the fact that Grandma is dead is the worst thing of all. Mom keeps wiping away tears. Dad is doing his best to distract her and so is constantly talking. Mostly she doesn't answer him. Mostly she is silent and keeps moving her handkerchief from her right to her left hand and back again. When we get to the cemetery, there are already lots of people there. Mostly it's my aunts, uncles, and cousins, but there are also some of my grandparents' neighbors. Before we go over to the others, Mom tells me to be on my best behavior. Please, she says as she takes my hand, squeezes it gently, and lets go.

The coffin is in the cemetery chapel; it's surrounded by wreaths and floral arrangements. There are candles standing on the floor in groups of four and six; they are decorated with black bows. In front of the coffin there is a photograph of Grandma sitting in front of their house. The right side of the picture has been cut off. Later I hear Uncle Tone say that Grandpa was on the right. They cut him out, of course. Otherwise it would look as though they had both died. To me it makes no difference. If Grandpa was in the photo next to Grandma, I would know everything was fine. At the moment when the picture was taken, everything was fine. Everything was good. They were both smiling; they looked happy, enough for a hundred years back and a hundred years ahead. Now Grandma still smiles in the picture, but Grandpa isn't there.

Grandpa is sitting in the back, behind the coffin, on a wooden chair. Although he is somber, he still looks like he's smiling. Ever since he got his dentures he appears to be smiling all the time, and when he opens his mouth, you can see the gleam of his new white teeth. While Mom and Dad are still next to the coffin, I run over to Grandpa and hug him as hard as I can. Grandpa looks at me and strokes my head. You're a good boy, he says. Of all my grandchildren you're the one I love most.

My parents soon come over and I circle the coffin. I look at the wreaths and read the writing on the ribbons. Some ribbons are black, others green, and still others are red. Some are the colors of our flag. They all have writing on them, mostly in gold, but on two of the wreaths it's in silver. On all the ribbons the letters are big and well-rounded, so the writing is easy to read. The wreaths are mostly from my uncles and aunts and their families, and a few are from neighbors. I recognize the names on the wreaths. There is only one wreath with names I don't recognize. I'm curious about who brought it, but I don't ask anybody. I would probably keep wondering who brought this wreath with the black ribbons with the names I don't recognize if one of Grandma's neighbors, an old lady named Vida, had not at that moment climbed onto the metal frame supporting the coffin, which she leaned across as if she was trying to crawl inside it.

I glance over at my cousins, who are directly across from me. They're smirking and pointing at the neighbor lady. Then one of them whispers something and they all chuckle and laugh until Aunt Katya scolds them and sends them away. The old lady, meanwhile, is no longer leaning into the coffin. Now she is standing in front of Grandpa, pressing his hand and telling him something.

I would like to see Grandma, I think, and go to where a few minutes earlier Vida had been standing. I grab the edge of the coffin with my fingers, step onto the metal frame and pull myself up as high as I can. Suddenly Grandma comes into view. She looks like she's asleep, only her skin is white, as if it's covered in the wax

SEBASTIJAN PREGELJ

that drips from the white candles in church. Her hair has been carefully combed and her arms are crossed over her chest. Her face is peaceful, like she's asleep and dreaming beautiful dreams. It doesn't look like she was in pain when she died. If she had been in pain, she'd be all twisted. But Grandma isn't all twisted; she is calm, just like I remember her. She is wearing a white blouse, the same one she got for her birthday, which she said was too beautiful for just anytime. Today isn't just anytime, I think to myself. I stand on tiptoes so I'm a little bit taller; then I reach over and touch Grandma. First her hand, then her face. I love you, I whisper. And I'm sorry. Then I hop down and go back to the wreath with the black ribbons and the names I don't recognize.

When it's all over, we are sitting in a restaurant—the grown-ups at a long table, the children at a shorter one. Grandpa is sitting in the middle of the long table; next to him, on either side, are Aunt Katja and Aunt Marija. They are telling him it was a beautiful mass, that the priest gave a beautiful homily, and that Mama could not have asked for a more beautiful funeral. If she could have seen it, she would be happy. And there were so many people! And they brought her so many wreaths and flowers! They talk without pause, as if they are trying to distract him so he doesn't notice. But how can he not notice that Grandma isn't sitting next to him and that he is alone and from now on he always will be alone? At first, of course, my aunts and uncles will come to see him every day, since they all live very close, but for the most part Grandpa will sit alone on the bench in front of his house.

At our table, my male cousins talk about motorcycles and cars, and my female cousins whisper about boys. I hope it will be over soon so we can go home.

When it's already quite loud in the room, the priest enters. They don't talk about him the way they talk about other people, but always with the greatest reverence. Even Janez, who still acts like he's smarter than everybody else, never says anything bad about the priest. I heard that on Wednesdays and Saturdays Bertica goes to tidy up the church, and that Matija has played the organ at morning mass a few times. I don't care what either of them does. No matter how conscientiously Bertica removes the dry flowers, brings in fresh ones, sweeps, and dusts, it won't bring Grandma back. No matter how beautifully Matija plays the organ, Grandma will never again be sitting in a pew with her hands folded together, her eyes gazing out in front of her, not at the altar, not at the stained glass window, but somewhere farther away, as if she was looking at the other side and could see what was there. Which is why she could always speak with such confidence about angels and heaven.

The tall priest, all in black, greets us in a loud voice and everyone immediately falls silent. Let us begin with a prayer, he says with no regard for the conversations he has interrupted; then he crosses himself and starts to pray. When the prayer is over, he smiles and says he is sure our mother is already looking down on us from heaven. She is with the angels singing on our behalf. She is happy to see you all gathered together like this. He rubs his hands. We too should rejoice with her. And follow her example. Then he sits down at the table.

On the way home I think about whether heaven actually exists or if it's imaginary, the way Santa Claus is imaginary, the way the deer that pull his sleigh are imaginary, and the elves that make the toys and wrap the gifts. To the best of my knowledge, no one who anyone might know has ever died, gone to heaven, taken a stroll there, and come back to tell people what it's like. The one person I know who came closest to this was Uncle Valentin, when his heart stopped, but fortunately, as soon as he started mumbling that he couldn't breathe and his chest hurt, Aunt Meta ran to the neighbors, who had a telephone, and called the ambulance. Just as the ambulance was pulling up to the house, my uncle's heart stopped. The paramedics did not delay. They managed to revive him with cardiac massage and electric shocks. They themselves were surprised. Uncle Valentin spent a few days in the hospital and then came home. Now he tells everybody that he's not afraid to die because it's beautiful on the other side. When you ask him what he saw, he doesn't know how to tell you about it. He just keeps saying that it was beautiful. So that much we know.

For Grandma's sake, I want heaven to exist. For Grandma's sake, I want her not to be wrong and for there to be fat little cherubs and slender-waisted angels up there, and I want Grandma to be among them and happy, to be singing with them in the angelic choir and looking down on us from above. If there is a heaven up there, then I am sure it smells of fresh cakes and pies, the kind Grandma liked to bake for us down here. More than with words, she tried to convince us that heaven existed with her baking. That was my Grandma. And we believed her. Her cakes and pies were tangible proof.

18

OUR SCHOOL DANCE is today, the last Wednesday in May. We've been getting ready for it for about two weeks. Mr. Boris, the physics teacher, is in charge of organizing things. Borči, as we like to call him, is younger than all the other teachers, and he understands us. He doesn't pester us about stupid things. He even lets us chew gum in his class. So long as we pay attention to what he writes on the chalkboard, other things don't bother him.

While we're carrying tables and chairs out of the dining hall, which is where the dance will be, Matic says to me that Alenka is already a real chick. Just look at her, he says, as if we are two grown men. Look at what juicy peaches she has! And below, too, he says, I bet she's hairy down there. Right? He pokes me with his elbow. What do you think? I don't know, I say and start laughing. Basically, I don't really care if Alenka's hairy down there and to me her peaches seem more like apricots. Besides, I think she's annoying and she doesn't interest me. But I don't tell Matic that. I just laugh and look down at the floor.

I remember the medical exam we had at the start of the school year. After measuring and weighing us, the doctor told us to sit on the benches. The boys sat on a long bench on one side of the locker room, the girls on a bench on the other side. The doctor walked up and down between us, talking about how girls' bodies are different from boys' bodies, and women's bodies from men's bodies, and what eggs are and what sperm is, and how a child is made, and so on. We boys thought the whole thing was funny and kept smirking and making faces and laughing until the doctor told us to stop. Then I got red in the face, looked down at the floor, bit my tongue, and could barely hold in my laughter, while some of the other boys kept on laughing until the doctor threatened to call the teacher.

Now I'm looking down at the floor again. I think it's funny. I think Matic is funny. Not long ago, all he wanted to talk about was *Rambo* and *Rocky*. When he talked about the bloody scenes from either one of these movies, we were all riveted, even though he was saying the same thing over and over. Matic's father is the director of a big company. For New Year's he bought the family a video player. Later, when he was in West Germany, he brought back all three movies about Rocky the boxer as well as the brand-new war movie *Rambo*, which had not even come to our movie theaters yet. We've asked Matic several times if we could watch the movies at his place, but he says his father won't allow it.

When *Rambo* finally came to a movie theater here, it took me two weeks to get up the courage to ask Dad to take me. He said it's not for children. So instead of *Rambo*, we went to *E.T.* What can I say? I liked it, but it wasn't something I could boast about seeing to my classmates, and certainly not to Matic. He'd say it was for babies.

Now not even Matic talks anymore about *Rambo* and *Rocky*; he suddenly stopped telling everyone all the time that Sylvester Stallone is the greatest actor there ever was. Now all he wants to talk about is girls. Actually, he doesn't talk so much about girls in general, just about Alenka. Matic is in love with her. This is obvious to everybody, although he doesn't say it himself. He's constantly talking about how Alenka is the hottest chick in class. He says he likes her peaches and that she's hairy down there. And since he's the tallest and strongest boy in our class, nobody contradicts him.

Matic has big plans for the dance. We'll start dancing, and then during a slow song we'll hold each other a little. He nudges me with his elbow again. Then I'll ask her if I have a chance. I am nodding even though I don't really know what that means, let alone what it means if a girl says yes. If she says no, I know it means she's not interested in the boy. But I don't know what happens if a girl tells a boy yes. Does that make them boyfriend and girlfriend? Matic obviously knows what it means. He says he's going to make out with Alenka.

At a few minutes before five, Matic's father arrives. He's got a full stereo system with him in the trunk of his big BMW. A few of us boys help carry the components into the dining hall. Andrej carries one of the speakers; Rok carries the other. I carry the box with all the cables. Matic and his father bring in the amplifier, the cassette player, and the turntable, and then the records. We boys stand around the stereo system inspecting it and admiring it. It's a real monster, Matic says. You'll see.

We're gonna have a great time. Just be careful, Matic's father says. Who's in charge here? Borči comes over and says he's responsible for the dance and for us. Matic's father nods; then he asks what time the dance will end. At nine o'clock, the teacher says. Okay, I'll be here at nine thirty, Matic's father says. Then he sticks his right hand into his pocket and leaves.

We continue to admire the stereo system for a few minutes, until Borči reminds us that we haven't finished taking out the tables and chairs and that there's more work after that too. We run to the other side of the dining hall, leaving only Matic next to the stereo system.

Half an hour later the dining hall is ready, and the song "Hello, Hello," Yugoslavia's Eurovision entry, is coming from the speakers. The boys from our class are again gathered around the stereo system, and now kids from other classes are starting to arrive.

I don't exactly know what to expect from the dance. My parents told me to have a good time, behave nicely, and watch what I do. No silly stuff! And dance with a cute girl, Dad said with a wink as I left. I'm not sure if I want to. There are some girls I like in our class, but it's nothing more than that. I'd rather hang out with the other boys and talk about guy stuff. With girls I don't know what to talk about. Matic has no problem with girls. He tells them stupid things and they laugh. Tadej is also good with girls. So is Andrej. But for some reason me and the other boys aren't. Andrej likes Sanja from 5C. Tadej likes them all. And he says he could have them all. Only I don't know what he would do with them if he actually had them.

Borči turns off half of the lights, and suddenly the dining hall is transformed into something entirely different, something unknown.

Boys and girls are mixing together in groups, but the boys are still mostly talking about the stereo system Matic's father brought, which doesn't seem to interest the girls much. For a while Matic was in the same group as Alenka, but then he left. It's not time yet, he shouts in my ear when he comes back to us. There are too many in a bunch. When there are that many all together, you don't have a chance. Remember that!

Later, Peter, Elvis, and I head to the lavatories. The music remains behind us. We're talking about other things. And we would have kept on talking if Sršen hadn't appeared in front of us. When he sees us, he blocks our way. Well, what's up? You like it? The dance, I mean. Or did you boys want to be by yourselves a little, because you're not all that interested in girls? He laughs. You know what we call freaks who aren't all that interested in girls? He pulls out a crumpled pack of cigarettes and lights one up. The three of us just stand there looking at him. We wait to see what happens next.

Sršen is in the eighth grade. Everybody is a little afraid of him, even the teachers. But Elvis, Peter, and I haven't had any problems with him for a while. He leaves us alone because, as he himself says, he has better things to do. Smarter things, none of that childish shit. Nevertheless, whenever we see him, we try to avoid him. When he surprises us, we start walking slower, ready to break into a run at any moment, although it's been a long time since he's chased us. So in that sense things have changed, especially between Sršen and me. A few times he has even stopped to speak to me one-on-one. It was mainly him who talked; all I could do was listen, nod, and say nothing.

We heard that he likes to hang out with some guys from the vocational school. Actually, it's not so much that he hangs out with them as he's their leader. They call themselves a gang and skip school a lot. Mostly they walk around the neighborhood. People say they control a certain territory. People say it was Sršen and his gang who broke into the newsstand at the bus stop. Jovo, the salesman, was frantic in the morning. He kept walking around the plastic kiosk, holding his head in his hands and asking loudly who's going to pay for all the damage. But it could have been worse. The thieves took a few cartons of cigarettes and some booze. But they could have set the kiosk on fire. That would have been much worse. People say that Sršen and his gang broke into a few garages in the area and stole some car radios and snow tires. People say that they break into storage units and that they were the ones who broke into the janitor's apartment because they knew he was going to be away for a few days. People say that from time to time somebody gets beaten up for no real reason, just because they happened to be walking by at the wrong time. People say that the police leave Sršen and his gang alone because his father is a member of the State Security Service. These are all things that people say, which is why everybody is a little afraid of Sršen and his gang. Whether any of it is true, nobody knows.

While we're waiting to see what happens next, Sršen smiles and says, Have a good time, boys. Then he blows a thick puff of smoke in our faces and disappears down the hallway.

We keep standing there for a few moments as if we're waiting for the smoke to clear—and with it the danger of Sršen beating us to a pulp—but then we shrug and go to the end of the hallway, where we sit down on the windowsill. Like we always do when the danger has passed, we laugh and tell each other, in whispers, that Sršen has the face of a pig: a big, fat, bristly head, tiny eyes, even tinier teeth, and a teensy-tiny brain. He's a pig and a half!

When we start to feel calmer, Peter says his dad is going to buy him a computer. He says it's the way of the future. He says it would be good to learn as soon as possible how to work with computers because of the endless possibilities they offer. Some things we can already imagine, but the vast majority of things that will happen in the future are completely unimaginable today, Peter says. He's talking the way he heard his father talk. One day computers will do all the work for us. One day they will be smarter than us. He takes off his glasses and wipes them on his shirt.

I don't know if it's possible for a computer to be smarter than the person who makes it, but I don't say this because I don't know. I've heard about computers mostly from Uncle Gorazd, who is excited because where he works they have a supercomputer. He likes to talk about all the things their supercomputer can do, but I only half listen to him because I'm not so interested. If I had paid closer attention, I could say something now, but as it is I'd rather not say anything. I tell myself I should ask him about this the next time I see him. If I remember.

Elvis and Peter and I talk a while longer, but then we return to the dining hall, where ABBA is playing. Next to the stereo system, where earlier it had been mainly boys from our class hanging out, now only Matic is there, with Alenka beside him. All the others are dancing or standing by the edge of the dance floor in small groups. In one of these groups I see some of my classmates, including Barbara and Tina. Let's go over there, I say and walk toward them. Elvis and Peter follow. For a few moments we stand off to the side, as if we're waiting for someone to notice and invite us to join them, but then we mix in with them.

I am standing right next to Tina, who is swaying to the music and now and then grazes my shoulder. I like it. I, too, start moving my feet to the rhythm. I take half a step closer to Tina and now she's touching me even more. I think this means something; otherwise, she wouldn't be constantly touching me. If she wanted, she could dance in a way so she doesn't touch me, but she doesn't do that. I think she's telling me something although she isn't looking at me. I am waiting for it to happen, although I'm not sure what's supposed to happen.

When our eyes meet much later, my heart skips a beat and I feel hot all over. Just a few minutes earlier I was prepared to ask her, as soon as she looked at me, if she was having fun, but now my mind is suddenly a blank. There's not a word anywhere. I just smile and nod; then I act like I'm totally into my dancing. Our shoulders touch a few more times. At every touch, it's as if there's a big anthill beneath my belly button and a column of ants is marching out of it. The tiny insects divide up. Some continue their subcutaneous journey down my arms, others go down my legs, and yet others are between my chest and my belly, while some go even lower. I've never felt anything like this. It tingles and it's sweet, but mainly I like it.

At home, I lie for a long time in my bed and stare at the ceiling. The last song is still echoing in my ears. I think about Tina. I like her. I like the way she laughs and the way she talks, although we haven't really talked very much, and when we have, it was always about school—about homework, papers, quizzes, stuff like that. I would like to talk to her about other things too.

At home in my bed everything seems simple. It seems like we could easily strike up a conversation; the words would just come on their own, with no awkward silences where I wonder what I should talk about now and what after that. At home in my bed everything is clear and simple. In my mind, Tina and I are talking and laughing and every so often we touch each other with our arms or legs. And each time we touch, we flinch a little and quickly move our arm or leg away, but then not long afterward we touch again. And then one time when we happen to touch each other again like this, Tina doesn't move her arm away and I don't move mine either. Cautiously, I start stroking her arm and then she strokes mine. Then I take her hand and hold it for a long time.

There are more and more ants. Now they're not just under my skin; they are crawling out. My whole body is tingling. If I pulled off the covers and turned on the light, I imagine I'd see my body crawling with tiny insects. As if I'd been captured by Indians, stripped naked, tied up, and smeared with honey, and then tossed on a giant anthill.

19

A FEW DAYS ago, as I was leaving Elvis's, Ali caught up with me on the stairs. I have something for you, he said as we walked down the stairs together. Oh yeah? I looked at him. What? Here, have a look. He pulled a magazine out from under his sweater and pressed it into my hands. When I looked down at what I was holding, I froze and my heart beat faster. On the glossy cover there was a naked woman and, above her, in red and yellow, the word *Start*. Ali smiled. What do you think? There are more like her inside. Put it in your bag so nobody sees. He waited as I removed my backpack, set it on a step, and slipped the magazine in with my notebooks. Let's go! Ali jumped the last steps and ran out. I was directly behind him. We went together as far as the traffic light; then we split up. Ali hurried on to the gas station, and I crossed the street to go home. It was only when I was in the middle of the street that I remembered I hadn't thanked him, or asked if he wanted me to give the magazine back to him. I probably should, I thought, and when I do, I'll thank him. As

I walked home, I was thinking about where I could hide the magazine so my parents wouldn't find it. In the end, I decided I would put it with last year's notebooks. I could hardly wait to be alone so I could look at all the women in the magazine without being disturbed.

Not too long ago, these things didn't interest me. I remember how it was whenever we collected scrap paper at school. The entire week we'd bring in bundles of old newspapers and magazines, either neatly tied up with a cord or yarn or stuffed into plastic bags, depending on the person. We brought the paper to a long room next to the janitor's apartment. There was a door at either end. At one end it was an ordinary door, like the ones in our classrooms, but at the other end it was a garage door. The room was wide enough for a van or a car with a trailer to enter. When this long room was full of scrap paper, boys from the seventh and eighth grades would sneak in and dig through the paper. They were looking for bundles of magazines and, inside them, magazines with naked women. Whenever they found one, the boys would set it to the side and then later smuggle them all out. They carried the magazines under their sweaters and jackets or in their backpacks. Any way they could. The janitor would be angry because now the scrap paper was everywhere and no longer in neat bundles. How am I supposed to load this on the trailer, he'd shout after them. One page at a time? Stupid brats! I'll show you! The boys would laugh at him from a safe distance, but they didn't want to provoke him too much. He could follow them back to their homeroom. And then what would happen? One time he came to a homeroom when he caught two boys smashing light switches after school.

Another time, he dragged a kid from 8B into the homeroom by his ear; someone had jammed a wooden match into the lock on the math classroom not long before an exam, so it was impossible for anyone to unlock the door. The teacher tried in vain a few times to stick her key into the lock. When she saw it was no good, she called the janitor. But the janitor couldn't do anything either. He said he would have to take the lock apart. The exam was canceled for that day. Then, a few days later the janitor, completely by chance, caught a boy jamming a wooden match into the lock on the faculty conference room. He sneaked up behind him and grabbed the boy's left ear with his right hand. The boy started screaming, but it didn't help him. The janitor did not let go until the principal rushed into the hallway to see what the screaming was about. Not for a second did the janitor doubt that this was the same boy as before, although he denied it. And so on. But the janitor had never yet come to a homeroom because of dirty magazines. And the boys knew that. So they just laughed and said there wasn't anything he could tell the teacher. Because he couldn't say he was there because of dirty magazines! That's why it's never happened and it never will happen, they kept saying. But what did happen was that some seventh graders surrounded me in the lavatory and showed me the centerfold from one of those magazines and screamed in my face, You like naked ladies? Wanna fuck her? I didn't know what they wanted from me. I ran out, and the boys laughed and shouted after me that I didn't even know what my thing was for. I didn't care so long as I got away from them.

Sometime later, I saw Sršen a few times in the locker room handing out magazines and receiving them from the boys who were returning them. He carefully inspected every one of the returned magazines—first the front and the back, then the centerfold, and then all the other pages. As he did this, he would nod his bristly head and mutter, Good, fine. To the boys he was lending to, he would yell, Bring it back on Friday. In exactly the same condition. No funny business! If it's wrinkled or torn or a page is missing, you're paying for it. Understand? The boys would nod and put the magazine into their backpacks with greater care than they ever showed toward any schoolbook. Sršen, meanwhile, like a librarian, would watch them with a serious face and jot down everything on a sheet of paper. Whenever a new boy showed up, he had to pay the membership fee. Two hundred dinars for three months, Sršen would tell him. That's the lowest I can go. It's not much more than a single magazine, and you can borrow a different one every week, right? That was his response to anyone who was surprised that he wanted money. Sršen's Naked Boobies Club has only first-class material. You remember that!

One time he saw me watching him. He winked and gestured me over. I went. Sršen took me by the shoulder, pulled me closer, and put his arm around me, as if we were best friends. So kid, if you want, I'll lend you one. Look, he said, taking a magazine from his pile and holding up the cover to me. She's the one for you, don't you think? Her boobs are just the right size so they don't scare you too much. Do you want her? Thanks but no, I said, shaking my head. You don't have to join the club, he grinned. I'll lend it to you for free. So how about it? No, thank you, I said and pulled away. Have it your way, he said with a shrug.

These things still didn't interest me then; nudity didn't excite me. That was right before summer vacation. But a few weeks later, when we were at the seaside, it started. Swaying breasts quickly caused me a certain *embarrassment*. First I would cross my legs to keep it from happening, or at least so no one would see. Then I covered myself with a towel. That didn't help at all and it was obvious I had a boner. I'm sure everyone must have noticed, but luckily nobody said anything. If Mom or Aunt Taja had even mentioned my *embarrassment*, I would have sunk into the ground. Martin maybe could have helped me. He could have told me how he deals with these situations. Does he jerk off before we go to the beach or something? But, of course, I didn't have the guts to ask him. I don't know what he would have thought, but I am sure this would have given him a new opportunity to tease me. I figured it was best if I worked things out on my own.

And I did—as soon as we got back from the seaside. I usually did it at night in my bed, but sometimes during the day I would lock myself in the bathroom. I didn't want anyone to hear me so I kept flushing the toilet. But then Mom started asking, Is everything all right? And when I came out of the bathroom she had a worried expression. But I would just look at her and try to get to my room as quickly as possible. What could I say? Should I have told her? Should I have said, I'm great, Mommy, now that I'm done. I imagine she would keep pestering me, as if I was a little kid who still needed help going to the bathroom. Done what, Bean? And then? What should I say then? That it had been great jerking off?

As if that wasn't enough, the dreams started. The first time it happened I was totally confused. The next time it happened, at least I knew what was going on. I would have a beautiful dream, and then I'd wake up with my pajamas wet between my legs. Now it happens almost every night. I'm no longer Superman in my dreams, and I'm not flying, but instead I'm making out with a grown woman. Usually, it's the woman from the cover of the magazine Ali gave me, but sometimes it's one of the women inside. And occasionally I dream about the new music teacher at school. It doesn't make any difference. It's just as nice with all of them. At first she caresses me; then she holds me so tight I can feel her soft curves. It's wonderful. Until I wake up. For a few moments everything is still okay, but then I feel how my pajama pants are wet and sticky between the legs.

I'd like to know if Ali has more magazines like this and what the women in those are like. I think he probably does. And probably the women in them are all very different. Based on what I've seen so far, there are some big differences. Not just in the size and shape of their breasts, but also in whether they are hairy or smooth down there. I'm curious why some of them are hairy and others are smooth and which is better. I would be happy with any of them, even the ones on the black-and-white pages. Although I'm not exactly sure how it's supposed to work. But I'm sure the woman would show me.

I'd like to know if Elvis knows about Ali's magazines. I think he must, but I'm not sure if Ali lets him look at them. If he doesn't, then Elvis probably takes them himself when Ali's not at home. I expect there is no corner of their apartment that Elvis doesn't know about. So he must also know where his brother keeps his magazines, in what order they are, and which way they're turned. That's very important. Otherwise, he wouldn't be able to return them to the same place and exactly the way they were. Otherwise, Ali would soon realize that Elvis was going through his stuff. Maybe he would pretend not to notice, or maybe he'd box his ears. He'd tell him to never ever go through his things again or else. Of course, he wouldn't believe that Elvis would keep his hands off his magazines. But what could he do about it? Squeal on him to their mother?

I, too, know every corner of our apartment, but that doesn't help me at all. I've never found such a magazine among my parents' things. Although the drawers in their nightstand are full of things, and there are even some magazines there, there are no naked women in them. The closest thing is Mom's thick Neckermann's fall/winter catalog. It contains everything, from hunting rifles and electric drills to women's lingerie. Those pages are almost as good as *Start*. Some of the women are wearing lingerie you can see through. You can see their nipples. On some of them, the nipples are small and pale; on others, they're big and dark.

I would like to get my hands on that sort of magazine. Only how? I have money, but I can't imagine going to a newsstand and telling the man behind the counter that I'd like to buy *Start*, especially if someone was standing behind me. But even if there wasn't anyone behind me, I doubt if the man at the newsstand would sell me a magazine for adults. He'd probably tell me to scram. Or he'd say *Mickey Mouse* was more my style. If I told him it wasn't for me but for my father, he'd say in that case my father should come and buy it himself.

20

ON SATURDAY AFTERNOON, Martin, Aunt Taja, and Uncle Gorazd come for a visit. Uncle Gorazd tells Dad he's recently been
assigned to a new work group that's researching electromagnetic
waves and developing antennas for military needs. It's confi-
dential information, he says, raising his right index finger. Dad
laughs and says he must be doing all right financially. When you
work for the military, there's money! Uncle Gorazd wags his
head. Well, yes, there is a little more, that's true. But not like
you might think! Oh, come on! Dad keeps at it. No wonder you
bought a color TV! I bought the color TV for the Olympics, Uncle
Gorazd says. Now that will be something to watch! A spectacle
like we've never seen before and won't see again! Next year, from
February eighth to the nineteenth, Sarajevo, and Yugoslavia too,
will be the center of the world. You'll see! Yeah, I'll see, Dad says,
still laughing. He's laughing because he's not really into sports,
whereas my uncle is the opposite; his world revolves around
sports and competitions. Dad doesn't go to competitions. He

likes downhill skiing and ski jumping, but he watches the competitions at home, from his armchair. Mom and I do the same. Sarajevo, my uncle exclaims. Now that will be a show. I know what we are capable of in this country. I know all the great things we can achieve. History will be written in Sarajevo. That's why I think you need to buy a color television. Let your family enjoy those historic moments in color. I know how you love skiing, how you love ski jumping! Cut it out, Dad says with a wave of his hand. Meanwhile, I'm watching to see if he's going to give in. There's a chance he'll give in to my uncle's persuasions. Uncle Gorazd doesn't usually stop until he gets what he wants. If that happens, then Dad will say, Okay, fine, Gorazd. Take me to that Rozman fellow of yours. Then on Monday he will go to the bank and withdraw some foreign currency, and on Tuesday afternoon go with Uncle Gorazd to *that Rozman fellow*, and they'll come back with a big cardboard box printed with the logo of ITT, Philips, Sharp, or Sony. Mom will probably say we can't afford it, but, nevertheless, that evening we will all be sitting in front of the new set, staring at the screen and exclaiming that this really is something else. It's like being at the movies, if not better. But Dad doesn't give in. Unfortunately.

Mom and Aunt Taja watch for a while as their husbands argue. Mom is probably hoping that Dad won't give in, but at the same time I'm convinced she'd be glad to watch movies and shows in color. When Uncle Gorazd eventually gives up, Mom and Aunt Taja start talking about other things. I hear Mom say there's only one thing she's afraid of: growing old. I look at her. My mother is young. And beautiful. I don't know what she's talking about. And I don't understand when she goes on to say, I just can't imagine it. Imagine what, my aunt says. You can't imagine having wrinkles? You can't imagine having liver spots on your hands? Not that. Mom shakes her head. I can't imagine having only a few years left, and even then not knowing how many. Oh, come on now! My aunt hugs her gently. We're still young, you know. Why should you be worrying about growing old? Where is all this coming from? Can you imagine what you'll look like in ten years? Aunt Taja doesn't wait for an answer. I'll tell you. You'll look the same as you do now. And in twenty years? You'll still be beautiful, only maybe with a couple of crow's feet and maybe you'll have to dye your hair. And in thirty years? Even then you'll be beautiful, only with more wrinkles, and you definitely will dye your hair. But that's a long way off! You're just a few years past thirty, and here you are talking about growing old! As for me, it's not growing old I'm afraid of. Aunt Taja shakes her head and, for just a second, presses her lips together. I'm afraid of not growing old. I'm afraid I won't ever get gray hair or wrinkles or put on weight. I'm afraid I won't live to see any of that because something might happen first. You know how many diseases there are out there. You know how many accidents happen every day. My neighbor Manca, who works at the hospital, tells me horrible things. Breast cancer, ovarian cancer, skin cancer. That's what I'm afraid of, my aunt says. But I try not to think about it. Ever.

Martin and I look at each other, shrug, and go to my room. Martin talks for a while about what it's like in the Scouts; then he says he has something to tell me but I have to promise not to let anybody know. Okay, I say. You swear? I swear. Good. He wets his lips. I'll tell you. I have a girlfriend, he blurts out. She's a Scout too, like me. Oh! I look at him in surprise. I had thought it would be some really big secret. Now I'm a little disappointed, but I don't show it. What's her name? Eva, Martin says. But don't you start teasing me. You know I won't. I smile and glance at the shelf where Superman, Darth Vader, and Luke Skywalker are standing. It would be stupid to ask my cousin who has a girlfriend if he wants to play with plastic action figures. So instead I ask him to tell me more about the Scouts, and Martin starts talking.

We have our Scout meeting every Friday at five. Mainly we learn things, like how to tell directions in the wild without a compass. You can tell directions by the sun, my cousin explains. Or you can use your watch to tell directions, or a stick and shadows, or the moss that grows on trees or the rings on a tree stump, or even plants, based on the way they grow on rocks, and at night you can use the stars. Of course, that's just a few ways you can do it, he says. We're also learning how to tie different knots, how to make a poncho out of a tent fly, how to make a tent out of a few tent flies, and stuff like that. Every two weeks we go on a camping trip, no matter what it's like outside. A few raindrops or snowflakes won't stop a Scout! Last Friday we went to Mount Grmada, and before that to Mount Krim. In two weeks we're going to Mount Slivnica. What do you do on these trips, I ask. We try out the things we've been learning. Last Saturday we made ponchos and tents. Then we made a fire and cooked hot dogs. It was great. Lynx, our troop leader, promised us that one day we'll make an actual raft and take it down the river. Imagine that!

Usually, each troop goes on its own camping trip, but for Mount Slivnica, Lynx said he was going to ask Owl if our troops can go together. Who is Owl, I ask. Owl is the leader of the Foxes. And who are the Foxes? Eva's a Fox! Martin winks at me. Get it? Each troop has its own name. We're called the Deer. I remember Martin's hunting knife and his green shirt with the badges. Do the girls haves knives too, I ask. Of course, Martin says. How else could they survive in the wild? Are they supposed to wait for the boys to show up? Sure, the girls have knives too, and they also have to know how to make a poncho and a tent from a tent fly, and how to tell directions without a compass.

But listen to this, Martin says a little while later. In the summer we're going to go for ten days to the jamboree. It's on Lake Bohinj. I'm definitely going, and so is Eva. Are you going to be in the same tent, I ask with a smile. Are you crazy? Martin jumps up. There are only two people in a tent and both of them have to be from the same troop. Boys together, girls together. But we'll have plenty of opportunities. You know, like when we're helping in the kitchen and washing the dishes in the stream during the day, and then around the campfire at night. I'm going to take my guitar with me. Girls like that. You play guitar? I'm surprised. A little. There's still enough time before summer for me to learn the chords for all the Scout songs and for some other songs too. You can imagine what's going to happen, right? First we'll sing a few Scout songs, then a few other songs. Everyone will be around the fire, then later there'll be fewer and fewer of us. But the guy with the guitar stays to the end, right?

I'd like to know what he thinks he and Eva are going to do when they're alone together, but I don't ask. Martin would say I was being stupid. I can just hear him, You know what boys and girls do. Or don't you?

I think I'd like to be a Scout too. Only they have to come to our homeroom first. They'll probably come at the start of the new school year. They'll arrange it with the teacher and then make a presentation about what they do. Anyone who's interested can join. I am definitely going to raise my hand. Mom and Dad won't have any objections either. Why should they? They're always saying I should spend more time in the fresh air. They're always saying I should be out walking in nature more. And who spends more time in nature and the fresh air than the Scouts?

21

MEDAL! WE'VE GOT a medal, Dad shouts. Bronze, if not better. Way to go, Jure! Way to go! Mom and I are partly watching Dad and partly watching the television screen, where the decisive minutes of the giant slalom competition at the XIV Olympic Winter Games in Sarajevo are unfolding. I have never seen my father so excited. His face is totally red, as if all his blood has rushed to his head. He's shouting and jumping up and down in our living room, totally indifferent to the neighbors. I wouldn't even be thinking about the neighbors if Dad wasn't always reminding me whenever I played my music too loud that we're not the only ones in the building. And now here he is jumping and shouting like a crazy person, even though, as he himself says, he doesn't really care about sports. But I have to admit I'm also feeling a kind of indescribable joy now that it looks like Yugoslavia is about to capture a medal.

We watched the first run of the competition at school. The teachers now set up the biggest possible television they could find on the tallest possible stand in the same auditorium where, on that first day, they showed us the movie about the red balloon. As many of us as could fit in the auditorium watched the slalom competition, which our teachers said would be historic. Bojan Križaj has a very good chance of winning a medal, they told us. Anybody who couldn't fit in the auditorium watched it in the big gymnasium.

Before the competition started, the teachers told us that we had to be quiet and calm. No misbehaving! If you misbehave, we will turn off the television and go back to our lessons. At first we were all talking excitedly, partly because one or maybe even two classes had been unexpectedly canceled, and partly because we were going to be watching a competition in which a Yugoslav skier might very well win a medal. But as soon as the principal stepped into the auditorium, we fell silent. We sat there quietly, with our eyes on the screen, even during the commercials.

Everyone was waiting for Bojan Križaj to ski. We imagined that it would be like in the movies. That even years later we would remember these magic moments and relive them over and over. We would talk about the smallest details with each other, each one of us an expert, and we'd compete to see who could describe Križaj's run most precisely and vividly.

But ultimately, what stayed with us was not Bojan Križaj's run, but Jure Franko's. When the first run ended, Jure was in fourth place, which looked very promising. Bojan, however, was in twelfth place, which didn't look so good, although the teacher said that everything could still change.

We went back to our classrooms at the end of the first run, but actually classes were over for the day. By lunchtime nearly everybody had rushed home. It was a Tuesday, and most of us were supposed to remain at school until our parents got off work, but this was no ordinary Tuesday. After only four hours at school, we all rushed home to watch with our parents as Yugoslavia won its Olympic medal.

Now I am sitting next to Mom in the living room and watching partly Dad and partly the TV screen. When Jure Franko was on the slalom course, the commentator had been more or less silent. Only during the interval did he note how Jure had been significantly faster than Boris Strel. You could hear the fans in the background. Even when Jure reached the finish line, the commentator said little more than that taken all together Jure had been significantly faster than Boris. What this might ultimately mean, he said dryly, will be determined by the performances of Franz Gruber, Andreas Wenzel, and so on.

Now Dad is jumping up and down and shouting. We've got a medal! A medal! When Max Julen, the top-ranking skier from the first run, takes off down the course, Dad stops shouting. Mom holds her breath and clenches her fists, while I stare silently at the screen. I'm watching the seconds and the tenths of seconds. I hope he won't make it. The Swiss have enough gold medals already and we don't have any. But in the end, the Swiss skier comes in first, and our Jure second. We've got a medal, Dad keeps shouting. Now I'm shouting it too. We've got a medal!

SEBASTIJAN PREGELJ

22

ON FRIDAY AFTERNOON we go to Elvis's. Uncle Fikret has invited us for cake to celebrate the end of the school year. Ali isn't there. Uncle Fikret says he's almost never home these days. He almost never goes anywhere with us anymore, except when we go to Bosnia to visit our relatives. He has his own friends. Dad says, Birds have to leave the nest, and Uncle Fikret agrees. Ali's a good boy, Mom says. At least you don't have to worry about where he is or what he's up to. It's hard for young people these days. It's hard to always know everything and be so smart, she says, glancing in my direction as if she wants to tell me something. Things were different in our day. She looks at Aunt Farhana. Our parents didn't have as many worries with us. But Ali is a good boy, she repeats. Uncle Fikret nods; then he looks at Aunt Farhana and asks if she'll bring the cake to the table.

While we're eating, Mom says she is happy and proud of us both. You boys have finished seventh grade, she says, reaching out and stroking my head as if I'm five years old. Eighth grade is next, and then secondary school. She smiles and looks at Elvis. Do you know what school you're going to? Elvis shrugs and doesn't say anything. I'm always saying he should go into electrical engineering, Uncle Fikret says. Whoever does that will always have a job. That's the way it was in my day, that's the way it is now, and that's the way it'll be in the future too. That's why I tell him what a person likes is one thing, but what puts food on the table is another. Also, he adds with a grin, I don't want him to end up driving a cab like his old man. The boy's too bright for that. Well, there's still time to decide, Mom says and looks at me. Jan doesn't know either yet. Electrical engineering, Uncle Fikret repeats.

When the plates are empty, Elvis says we're going to his room. Take Defne with you, Aunt Farhana says. All right, Elvis says before running off down the hall. When we're in his room, he flings himself on the bed and asks me what I feel like doing. I don't know, I say, sitting on the chair by his desk. Elvis and I don't usually hang out together at school and we don't usually walk home together anymore either. We each have our own friends. But Uncle Fikret still thinks we're best pals and Elvis doesn't want him to think otherwise. Sometimes he tells his parents he and I are going out somewhere together, and sometimes he tells them he was at my place. If he tells them he's going to be with me, Uncle Fikret stops asking questions. And if he's late getting back, even then his father doesn't usually ask anything. That's fine by me.

It's too bad Ali's not around. Elvis told me not long ago that his brother hangs out with some boys who get together in Lenin Park. Mainly they just talk, but sometimes the oldest one,

Musa, gives them an assignment. Usually to read something. Musa brings them photocopies of texts, which he hands out and says they should read carefully before their next meeting. Musa is teaching them the *abjad*—that's the Arabic alphabet, Elvis explains. He's teaching them some Arabic words. He's going to teach them the language. Elvis talks more about Musa than he does about Ali. But what Ali and his friends are doing doesn't sound like much fun to me. It sounds more like school.

Defne asks me if I have a girlfriend. I look at her in surprise and shake my head. Who told you that? I glance at Elvis. I didn't say anything, he says, raising his arms. Maybe you did and forgot. No, I didn't, Elvis insists. Okay, so you didn't, I say. For a minute or two, the three of us are silent; then we all burst out laughing. And suddenly the conversation starts to flow. We're talking the way we used to. Elvis is telling us about the most recent Bundesliga football matches. He lists all the scorers and the number of goals, predicts the results of upcoming matches, and at several points brings up the goalkeeper Toni Schumacher. Toni's unbeatable. Even if the defense isn't doing its job, Toni saves the day!

I'm not really into football, but I enjoy listening to Elvis. Also, I learn just enough from him so that when the other boys in class talk about the game, it's not all news to me.

Elvis says he's going to get his hair cut like Toni. Shorter on top, longer in back. He pulls a crumpled football card out of his pocket and hands it to me. There's a picture of the goalkeeper. See? Like that. Dad's gonna kill you, Defne says. Oh please, Elvis exclaims. You come home with a haircut like that, and you'll see what happens, Defne says. He'll grab you and drag you to his own barber. Uncle Mihajlo will give you a bowl cut or shave your head, then you'll be happy. Defne smirks. Anyway, your hair's straight. Toni's is curly. So what makes you think the barber can even cut your hair like that? So are you gonna get a perm? Boy, are you stupid! You don't have a clue! Elvis waves his hand. Not about football, not about haircuts! Oh yeah? Defne stands in front of him. Well, I'd like to see you with that haircut of yours. Go right now and I'll give you the money for the barber. You're on! Elvis extends his hand to his sister so they can shake on it, but at the last moment, Defne pulls hers away. You're an idiot! She frowns and takes a step back. Well, you're a bigger one!

So what do *you* think? Defne turns to me. About what? I look at her. About that stupid haircut, she says. It's not stupid, Elvis cries, but Defne doesn't respond. She is looking at me and waiting for my answer. I don't think anything, I say. Some of the older guys have that kind of haircut. Even grown men have that haircut, Elvis adds. Fine! Defne lifts her arms. Do whatever you want with your head. And as for you, you could at least be smart enough to say something to him. She gives me a nasty look. But . . . I stammer out. But nothing, Defne says angrily. He might listen to you.

I look at her in silence. Defne has a beautiful face. I remember how we used to exchange secret glances across the table. Whenever our eyes would meet, I'd turn red. I still like Defne.

SEBASTIJAN PREGELJ

23

I AM LYING in my bed reading a book and listening to Iron Maiden. A few days ago, I bought the record without the cover from Matic. He had cut up the cover and hung it in his room; then he sold the record to me for half price. If he hadn't been talking about Iron Maiden and nothing but Iron Maiden for the past two weeks, the way the eighth-grade boys had been talking about the band, I wouldn't have been interested in them. The problem is that everybody talks about them, but other than Matic nobody actually has their album. His father still won't let us come to their place. So our only chance to hear them fell through. But after everything I've learned, I didn't have to *hear* the record anymore; I had to *have* it. Eventually, Matic said he'd sell it to me. But just the record, without the cover. I cut up the cover and hung it in my room, he told me. I didn't care about the cover. I brought the money to school and Matic brought the record. When I got home from school, my parents were out. So I ran into the living room and put the record on the turntable. A minute later the drums started pounding; a minute later the guitars started playing. This music is completely different from what comes out of the speakers when my parents play one of their records. Don't get me wrong; I like the Beatles and the Rolling Stones. Jean-Michel Jarre is even better. But Iron Maiden is the best. They are exactly what has so many times been swarming in my head, only I couldn't describe it, because it's hard to describe music in words. My heart went wild the first time I heard them. That very day I copied the record onto an old cassette, and I've been listening to it constantly ever since. When I'm at home alone, I listen to the record in the living room. We have big speakers and the music is rocking so loud it's like Iron Maiden is playing in our apartment. But when Mom and Dad are home, I listen to the cassette in my room.

Rok doesn't like Iron Maiden. He has a few cassettes by the Slovenian punk group Pankrti and one by Videosex. He says the lyrics are good. When we're at his place, that's what we listen to, but I still prefer Iron Maiden. It doesn't really matter. Rok and I have other things both of us are interested in. For a while now we've been in the Scouts together, and we're also both in the journalism club and work on the school newspaper. Most of the time we don't write anything; we just help distribute it when a new issue comes out.

Last summer Rok and his family moved to a place not far from us. Since then we spend all of our free time together. Mostly we hang out at home, sometimes at my place, other times at his, but occasionally we go into town and every so often to a movie. Rok's father laughs and asks if we're going out to look at girls. The questions he asks remind me a lot of Uncle Gorazd.

They're both the same. Rok and I say we're not going out to look at girls, but in fact we don't care what he thinks. We're old enough to check out the girls if we want to, we say, laughing as we roam the streets.

I still like my classmate Tina. But I also like Defne. I don't know how I'm supposed to decide. I don't know how other boys decide, and I don't know how adults decide. I think Tina knows I like her, but I don't know what to do next. Do I do anything? Do I wait for her to make the first move, or at least give me a sign? But what kind of sign? What if I don't understand it? What if I miss my chance? Will she start going out with somebody else, the way the girls in eighth grade go out with secondary school boys? Those boys have mopeds, and some of them even have Vespas, and they know where to go to make out with girls without being disturbed. We don't have any of that. Besides, I don't think my parents would ever let me get a moped. They say mopeds and motorcycles are dangerous. Whenever I ask them, they start naming everyone they knew who died in a road accident. I have no idea if all these people ever really lived and then died on mopeds and motorcycles, or if my parents are just making up names to frighten me. Rok too. I don't think his parents would ever let him get a moped. Matic, on the other hand—I have no doubt that he'll get one in the eighth grade. That's what he told us. Once when we were talking about motorcycles and girls, he started bragging, My dad's going to buy me a Vespa for my birthday. And if I handle it responsibly, he's going to buy me something bigger when I'm older. As for me, I can only dream about having a moped. Just like I dream about girls.

My classmate Tina knows that I like her but she doesn't do anything. As for Defne, she's in love with me and would do anything for me. I see the way she looks at me when I'm at their place or they come over to ours. But I don't know what's supposed to happen. I think it would be awkward if Defne was my girlfriend. For one thing, our families are friends, and even more than friends. I call her father "uncle" and her mother "aunt." Her little brother is my classmate and her older brother is my friend. I have no idea how they would look at us. I have no idea if they would approve. I think they probably wouldn't. Besides, everyone would be worried that something might happen. And what if we broke up? So maybe it's best if we don't even start and Defne isn't my girlfriend.

Maybe we could just make out a little. That would be easier. We would keep it between ourselves and nobody would give us any disapproving looks. But I don't know if girls are okay with that. I don't know what Defne would think if I said I just wanted to make out a little with her. Girls want more than that. Girls want to hold hands; they want you to go out with them—to the park, the movies, the disco. Only later do you get to make out a little with them. Denis, one of the older boys, was telling us in the hallway at school that he had to work really hard before he got to make out with a girl, and then all she let him do was touch her a little; all she let him do was put his hand under her top a little.

Things usually happen on their own. You have to wait; you have to be patient. But that's exactly what's tormenting me. I don't want to wait anymore—I want something more than the women in *Start* magazine.

SEBASTIJAN PREGELJ

24

THAT WAS FIKRET, Dad says in a serious voice as soon as he hangs up the phone. Ali's in the hospital. What happened, Mom asks, worried. He says he doesn't know exactly, Dad tells her. There was a fight. Ali was hit a number of times on the head with a blunt object and now he's in intensive care, but he's out of danger, fortunately, Dad explains as I stand in the doorway of my room and listen. A fight? My mother can't believe it. He was hit on the head with a blunt object? But they're children! That's what Fikret told me, Dad says.

Sršen, I mutter through my teeth. What did you say? Dad looks at me. Nothing, I answer. No, you said something. You said Sršen. I nod. It could've been Sršen. Because that's the way it's always been. Sršen calls Ali a gypsy. And every time he and his gang run into Ali and his friends, they attack them. It's nothing new. Nothing new, Dad shouts. I flinch. What do you mean nothing new? The boy was nearly killed! Do you understand? Fighting is one thing, a couple of punches and kicks; but hitting someone enough to send them to the hospital, that's another thing altogether! Yeah, I know, I say, looking at the floor. Don't you dare look down! Dad takes a step toward me. Talk to me, boy! Tell me everything you know! Samo, Mom cries, jumping between us. What's wrong with you? Leave him alone! And as for you, young man, she says, turning to me. Tell your father what you know. But I don't know anything. Oh, you don't know anything, do you, Dad shouts. I'll show you what you know! He reaches out to grab me but I slip away. Samo, Mom screams. Calm down! I am calm, Dad says. Just wait till you see me angry! Stop it! Mom lightly pushes him away. Ali's in the hospital, but it's not life-threatening, right? So it's not as bad as it could be. And it won't help anyone if you're shouting and threatening. Dad takes a step back, leans on the low sideboard, and gives me a baffled look. I won't ask you again. Tell me everything you know!

I told you everything I know, I say. So that's it, is it? So if the police come, you'll tell them only as much as you told me and won't remember anything else? And then when they put some pressure on you, you won't sing like a bird? Look, I say. I take a breath and slowly exhale through my nose. Everyone knows what Sršen's like. Everyone's afraid of him. But not me, not so much. I don't know why, but he leaves me alone. So what's your business with him, Dad asks suspiciously. Nothing! He just doesn't hassle me. Dad nods. He just doesn't hassle you. When he says this, he screws up his face and mimics my voice. But Ali? What's his business with Ali? You'll have to ask *him* that, I say. I'm warning you, boy! He starts coming toward me again, but Mom steps in front of him. Stop! Enough! I'm not stopping until the boy tells me everything he knows. And until he does— Well, what until he

SEBASTIJAN PREGELJ

does? Mom looks him in the eye. Maja, stop coddling him, Dad snaps at her. You know what will happen if there's an investigation. You know what will happen if the police get involved. Don't you think we should know everything first, or would you rather hear it later and be surprised? Be surprised? Mom is alarmed. What does our son have to do with any of this? Dad shrugs. I don't know. Apparently nothing. But also, apparently, he knows something. That's the point, Dad shouts. When there's a police detective standing in our apartment, or the boy's down at the police station, there won't be any of this nonsense then! Then . . . then it'll get damn serious. You're exaggerating, Mom says. No police detective is coming here. And in any case they're not going to take Jan down to the police station just like that. He's a minor! We'll be with him. And he didn't do anything! Oh, Maja! Dad waves his right arm at her and goes into the kitchen. You just don't get it, do you, he mutters.

What don't I get? Mom goes after him. Tell me what I don't get! What's there to understand here? Apparently, now you're the one who knows something! Well, I know what happened to Gorazd, Dad says. He had some dealings with the police. He messed up once, but it wasn't his fault. And now? He's still under a cloud. If he was under a cloud, he wouldn't be doing work for the military, Mom counters. You think they don't check everyone who works for the army? I'm sure they do. And not in some casual way either. I'm sure they're very thorough. But enough about that! She turns to me. If you know anything at all, you tell your father! Right now, young man!

They call themselves the Hornets. But you already know that! I shrug my shoulders. One time they robbed a newsstand.

They set a few crates on fire. They jammed matches in the locks in the storage units and set fire to the mailboxes in a few of the buildings. They hang around outside the school. They once keyed the principal's car and let the air out of her tires. They beat up the janitor. But you know all this already! I go into my room and shut the door.

I throw myself on the bed and think about Ali. Of course I'm concerned that he's in the hospital. But on the other hand, who can stop Sršen? Who can do anything to him? The moment he appears, everybody is afraid of him. And when he's with his gang, we all get out of their way. I glance at the shelf where there is a trophy and a few medals. I went to karate because of that pig head, I say. Then I jump out of bed and start doing push-ups. At fifty, I stop. I'm still in good shape, I say to myself. Then I go to the window and look out. It's getting dark outside. Most of the cars have their lights on.

I imagine Ali lying in the hospital bed looking out the window. He doesn't see the street or the car lights; he doesn't see any cars or traffic lights; he only sees the sky, which is slowly getting darker.

Then I imagine Sršen and his gang of pigs. They're probably in some basement sprawled out on sofas and armchairs, smoking. They're belching and laughing their heads off, until Sršen says, Okay, that's enough rest. Time for work! And our work is having fun! So let's go! He stands up and runs outside with the other guys right behind him.

I think about how I, too, was attacked a few times. I remember the first time they surrounded us at the garages. And the second time. And how we were afraid of them and how we are still afraid of them. I remember how I was attacked on various occasions, but it was usually just slaps, some flicks, a kick or two, all because I didn't want to go. I was attacked because I didn't want to leave my friends on their own. My friends got it worse than I did. But even then it wasn't so bad. A little blood, a tooth knocked out, a broken pair of glasses, some torn pants. No one had to go to the hospital. And there were no police.

And now? What if the police really do come here? The thought of those grim men in gray uniforms with the white belts makes me break out in a sweat. Everybody knows what Sršen and his gang get up to. It's no secret. But nobody says anything. And if I tell them what I know, are they even going to believe me? Would it even help? I doubt it. They'd want proof. Words aren't enough. But there isn't any proof. I saw Sršen stealing the nameplates off cars, but that's probably not enough for the police and, anyway, that was years ago. I could tell them he slapped and flicked me a few times. But that won't be enough either. We had a fight in school. The principal dealt with it. And everything else? Everything else I merely heard about. The janitor should tell them that they beat him up. But if he hasn't told them by now, then he probably doesn't intend to because he's scared. The principal doesn't have any proof that they were the ones who keyed her car. The people in the apartment buildings don't have any proof that it was Sršen and his gang who set fire to their mailboxes; they don't have proof that they broke into their garages. If they had proof, something would have happened by now. And so I'm back to the beginning. If the police come here, what am I going to say to them?

Whatever I say, there's still Sršen's father to think about. We all know about him. If not for him, something would have happened by now.

Old Sršen really is old and looks more like Sršen's grandfather than his father. He walks with a slight limp and wears a raincoat in both summer and winter and wears tinted glasses both day and night. He dons a regular hat in winter and a straw hat in summer. Whenever he walks past someone, he says good afternoon or good evening, but I've never seen him actually stop and talk to anyone.

When we were smaller we were afraid of him. If we were kicking a ball against a wall, he didn't have to say a word when he walked by. He just stopped and looked at us. Then we'd grab the ball and run away. If we were playing near the entrance to his building, it was the same. We'd leave the moment we saw him coming. And if we were sitting by the garages, it was the same. As soon as we caught sight of him, we'd get up and move to the other side.

I once heard my father say that old Sršen works for State Security. At the time I didn't know what State Security was, but from the way Dad said the name, I figured it wasn't anything good. When I asked him what it meant, he waved his arm at me and muttered that it wasn't important. He didn't want to tell me anything. He said I was too little for such things and wouldn't understand. From then on I knew that working for State Security was a bad thing—such a bad thing that nobody ever talked about it. Just like nobody ever talks about the diseases their friends and relatives have; just like nobody ever talks about the bad things that happened to someone.

I understand more now, but when it comes to certain things, Mom and Dad still act like I'm a child, like I was still in the first grade. I don't know when this will end. It drives me nuts.

I remember that Ali is in the hospital. I expect we'll go visit him. I wonder if he'll at least tell *me* what happened. He can trust me. I won't tell anyone, least of all the adults. Because I don't trust them. Mom and Dad would first ask me if that's what Ali actually said. Then they'd ask me if that's exactly what he said or did I add anything, since I have such a wild imagination and they often don't know what's true and what I'm making up. They'd ask me if those were his exact words in that exact order because a different order could change the meaning. Who else could I tell? Uncle Gorazd? Aunt Taja? Definitely not them, because they would tell my parents and then it would be the same thing, only worse. Besides, I never talk to them about these sorts of things. How would I even start? And then later, Mom and Dad would ask me why I told my aunt and uncle but not them. They would think it wasn't right. They'd say I should always tell them first. Always! So who else could I tell? Uncle Fikret? Never! Because that's the same as if Ali told him. But Ali didn't tell him because he doesn't want him to know.

Ali has no reason to worry about me. I won't tell a soul.

25

ROK AND I roam the city streets almost every day. We get good grades, so our parents basically leave us alone.

Every so often, if I get home at night later than we agreed, Mom and Dad ask me where I've been, what I was doing, and why I'm so late. They ask me why I smell like cigarettes and if I was smoking. They ask me if I've been drinking alcohol. My answer is always the same. I tell them that Rok and I went out. Out where? They want me to be specific. Just out. I keep it short. I say I smell like cigarettes because people were smoking all around me. And I haven't drunk any alcohol. But, in fact, Rok and I do light up now and then and occasionally we have a beer. But we only really smoke and drink when we run into the girls we hang out with: Hana, Lea, and Meri—whose name is actually Marija but everyone calls her Meri because she says it sounds better, and also she looks like a young Meryl Streep. They're students at the Secondary School of Health Studies. They call us their kids. But they don't think we're children or childish, and whenever we run into them, we stay together until Rok and I have to go. If we happen to meet someone they know, they introduce us, and they never go off with somebody and leave Rok and me behind.

We'll teach you kids everything, they said with a laugh the first time we were all sitting together on the back of a wooden bench in the park. Lea lit up a cigarette and after a few puffs handed it to me. It was exciting to take the cigarette from her hand, to touch her slightly and then put it, still moist, in my mouth. It was exciting to realize that just a moment before this very cigarette had been in the mouth of a woman. But then after my first puff I started coughing, my eyes teared up, and I was embarrassed because we had told them earlier that we smoked.

We'll teach you kids good things and dirty things. But cigarettes and alcohol are essentials. Here, have a sip, Hana said, pushing a wine bottle into my hands as soon as I stopped coughing. It'll get better, you'll see. I took a sip and passed the bottle on. It quickly circled back and I took another sip. Before long my head was spinning and I felt nauseous. The girls laughed. Rok, meanwhile, was drinking and smoking as if he'd been doing this every night since first grade. You'll get used to it, Meri told me. And then you'll like it. You'll see, she said as she stroked my head.

Every time we say we have to go home, Meri, Lea, and Hana invite us to go somewhere, to the Palma disco or the K4 club or Student, but we can't. You don't know what you're missing, they say, laughing as they go on their way, while we get on the ten o'clock bus.

I'm no longer interested in my classmate Tina. Nothing ever happened between us; we never even really talked, since I couldn't find the right words, and Tina couldn't either. It's different with Hana, Lea, and Meri. I don't have to think; the words come on their own. Nothing is difficult. Same with them, too—they're always talking about stuff that Rok and I are interested in.

Then there's Defne. Nothing's going on with her either, although something did happen. And what happened was more than I dared to hope. But it happened only once, and completely out of the blue. Later, we cleared the air and that's how we left it. A few months have passed since then and nothing has changed between us. It happened one Saturday morning when, for the first time in a long time, I went over to Elvis's so we could go out for a while, but he wasn't there. Defne said he'd gone to the store. He'll be back soon. Ali was out too, and Uncle Fikret was working. Only her mother was at home. Mom's in the kitchen making lunch, Defne said. She won't bother us. Come on. She took me by the hand, led me into her room, and carefully shut the door. Then she stood in front of me. Want to see it? Excuse me, I said, not sure what she was asking. I asked you if you wanted to see it, she repeated and stuck her thumb under the top of her sweatpants and slowly pulled them down. Then with her index finger she grabbed her white panties and pulled them down too, in just the same way. At first I saw a few tiny hairs; then there were swirls of hair like I'd only seen in magazines and at the sea but never so close up and on a girl I was interested in. My heart was pounding, the veins were throbbing in my neck, and my mouth suddenly went dry. Defne pulled her panties down a little more and looked at me. Would you like to touch it? I stared at her in amazement; I could hardly believe this was actually happening. Don't be afraid. She took my hand

and pressed it between her legs. Do you like it, she said, looking into my eyes. Don't move your fingers, she told me, but you can pet it a little. Just a little, not too much. I don't want anything to happen, understand? From the surprise of it all, I was already hard. Defne smiled and drew my hand a little bit forward, then a little bit back. That feels good, she sighed. Okay, that's enough. And all at once she pulled my hand away, drew up her panties, and then, a moment later, her sweatpants. Right then the door to the apartment opened and Elvis came in. Defne was not the least bit flustered. She dashed out of her room and said, Jan's here. He's waiting for you. Left alone in her room, I first sniffed my hand, which had a very particular smell. I liked it. Then I grabbed at my pants, because I still had a hard-on, which I tried to make less obvious. When Elvis entered the room a second later, he didn't notice anything. So are we going, he asked. Yes, I said; then I looked at Defne and said, Bye. The next time I saw her she told me, in just a few words, to forget it. Nothing happened. It wasn't anything. I looked at her silently and nodded. But in fact, I could hardly say it wasn't anything, since after it happened I kept dreaming night after night about being in her room with my hand between her legs.

Hana, Lea, and Meri are different. Of course, I sometimes imagine being with them—first with Hana, then with Lea, and after that with Meri. But they act almost as if they were boys. They're not afraid of anything and nothing seems too dangerous to them or out-of-bounds. When we sit with them on the back of the bench in the park, they tell us what happened the previous time, after Rok and I went home. They tell us how they walked across Cobbler's Bridge on the balustrade, which is wide enough so it's not too hard. You know, Hana says, like in the movie *Hang On, Doggy!* where Matic jumps in the water after the balloon. And then Jakob the dog jumps in after him. Only you can't look down! Lea laughs. And when you get to the columns on the bridge you can rest a little. Meri was flapping her arms like mad but in the end she made it across. Oh, stop! Meri shoves her in the shoulder. You know I'm scared of heights. Then we went to the train tracks and lay down right next to them. It was insane, Lea exclaims. When the train was coming, I thought we were gonna die. The rumbling got louder and louder and the ground was shaking. And then the train came. We almost went deaf from all the noise and the whistle! I don't know about Rok, but I could easily imagine what it would have been like to be there.

I often think about what I need to say to Mom and Dad so they'll let me stay out longer. Dad I would somehow bring around—if nothing else, I could tell him it had to do with girls and he'd understand and give me permission. I don't know what I need to say to Mom so she'll give in. Is there even anything I could say?

Eventually, Rok comes up with an idea. You'll sleep over at my place, and I'll sleep over at yours. Problem solved. What? I look at him in confusion. Then he explains. You'll sleep over at my place, and I'll sleep over at yours. But actually you won't be sleeping over at my place and I won't be sleeping over at yours, because we'll be going out. Get it? I nod. But what if my parents call yours? Or yours call mine? That won't happen, Rok says with certainty. Why would they? Have they ever? No, I answer, but then I've never slept over at your place and you've never slept at mine. It'll be fine, Rok says, brushing the matter away with a wave of his hand. Don't make extra worries for yourself.

The next time we're in the park with the girls, Rok officially announces that on Friday we'll be going with them. Great. Hana smiles. But where? What do you mean where, Rok says with a frown. We'll go wherever you go. It could be K4, it could be Palma, it could be the Tourist Club. Yuck! Meri grimaces. The Tourist Club? Rok blushes; he knows he said something wrong. We don't go to the Tourist, Meri informs us. We don't wear pink tops and parade around for guys with Vespas. Okay? Right, Rok says. He's embarrassed and so am I. How do we know where they go and don't go? It's true they've never mentioned the Tourist Club, but the girls in our class talk about it all the time. So we assumed it was a place people go. Palma and K4 are fine, Lea says. Maybe we can check them both out. Maybe we can, Meri says enthusiastically. You kids have got to see them.

At school the week drags on and on. Tuesday we have a math test, Wednesday a Slovenian test, and Thursday I have an oral exam in English. On Thursday we get the math test back. C's OK, I say and push the paper to the edge of the desk. Rok got a B. No worries. Everything is as usual, no complications, no surprises. At gym class we sit on the bench and chat. Soon Elvis joins us. The three of us are sitting there and laughing until the teacher comes out of the office. You three, he yells. On the court right now! Each of you take a ball. A healthy boy should enjoy chasing balls! Right, I say. I thought that's what dogs like to do. We all burst out laughing, but then we start throwing balls at the basket anyway. We don't want the old fart to freak out on us; we don't want any needless problems.

When gym is over we go to the locker room. While we're changing, Matic takes off his underpants and starts jumping around. Who's got the longest? Well? Come on, cowards, let's see what you got! We're all laughing and trying to get out of the way of his dick, which he's shaking at us. It's only when he hears the teacher shouting from the gym that somebody needs to put all these balls away that Matic calms down. When we're dressed, we dash down the hall and up the stairs to our chemistry class.

Chemistry is my toughest subject. No matter how hard I study, I don't seem to understand. Rok is better at it. He basically understands everything, but he can't explain to me why a certain chemical reaction falls into one group and not another or how chemical reactions are categorized by their reaction mechanism.

After I got two bad grades on chemistry tests, first Dad, for a while, and then Mom have tried to help me, but with no success. But it turns out that chemistry is Hana's favorite subject. If you need any help, just ask. I'll do my best to take care of our kid, she says as she lights a cigarette, takes two puffs, and hands it to me. I have a puff, blow the smoke out, and hand it back to her. Will you really help me? Of course I will, she says. Right here, I ask. Don't be silly. We don't study in the park. In the park we have fun. You can come over to my place, or I can come to yours. Whatever you want. I think about it for a few seconds. I don't know what Mom and Dad would say if I brought Hana to our place. They'd see right away that she's older than me. They'd want to know how we know each other and so forth. I don't want to have to explain this to them, so I tell Hana I'd rather go to her place. Fine, she says, patting my leg. Just say when. Maybe Tuesday? It's a deal. She gives me her address and tells me which bus to take and what name is on the doorbell.

On Friday morning I can hardly wait for Rok to arrive at school. When he shows up just before our class starts, I see that something's not right. It's canceled, he tells me. What's canceled? I look at him. English? He shakes his head. I don't give a damn about school. Our night on the town is canceled. I can't go because we're all going to my aunt and uncle's for the weekend. And you are *not* going to go without me. Promise! I promise, I say. I'll call Hana and let her know. You have her telephone number? Rok is surprised. No, but I know what street she lives on and I know her last name. That should be enough. I guess so, Rok says. Then the teacher comes in and we stop talking.

That afternoon I find the number in the phone directory and call Hana. A woman's voice answers; she tells me Hana isn't home right now and I should try again later. I thank her and say goodbye. In my room I put on Iron Maiden and open *The Master and Margarita*. Meri said this is the best book ever, so I borrowed it from her. At first I have a little trouble following it, but the story soon pulls me in and I don't hear either the music or my mother when she gets home.

You're here? She looks at me from the doorway. How was school? I glance at her over the top of the book and say, I'm reading. Really? She comes over to me. What are you reading? I show her the cover. Isn't that a book for grown-ups? I am grown up, I tell her as seriously as I can. Of course you are. She smiles and casually strokes my head. Will you help me with lunch? Sure, Mom, I say, just so she'll leave and let me finish the chapter. Then I go to the kitchen and set the table.

Dad, as usual, gets home a little before three. He's in a good mood because it's Friday. But then he's normally in a good mood. He gets upset sometimes when he watches the news and sometimes when he's reading the paper. Then Mom tells him to stop watching or reading and he'll feel better. But Dad doesn't stop. He tells her that turning off the television isn't the solution for bad news. The TV isn't the problem. The newspaper isn't the problem. Mom leaves it at that because she knows it won't end. She nods and says in a low voice that it's whatever you decide it is.

At lunch I tell them that Rok and I were talking about me sleeping over at his place. What? Dad looks at me. Why? Mom turns to face me. We'd like to go out for a while and then maybe watch some movies. I don't understand. Mom puts down her fork. Why would you sleep at his place? You could come home. Of course I could come home, but that's not the point, you know? No, I don't know. She is not giving up. If Rok lived farther away, then I'd understand. Well, at least *you* get it, don't you, Dad? I look at him. Well, I guess so, he says with a shrug. He doesn't want to take my side but he also doesn't want to say that Mom is right. Just forget it, I say. I'm not doing it anyway. Not doing what? Again Mom doesn't understand. I'm not sleeping over at Rok's tonight because he's going to visit his uncle. Oh, I see, Dad says with a soft growl. So the matter's settled, right? He smiles. Actually, it's not, I say. I'll sleep over at Rok's some other time, okay? Mom and Dad look at each other. I still don't understand why, Mom says. Leave it, Dad says. We'll talk about it when the time comes. Let's talk about it now, I say. But why? Mom stands her ground. Because it's what everybody does! I

SEBASTIJAN PREGELJ

raise my voice a little. On Fridays and Saturdays it's normal! Girls sleep over at girls' places and guys at guys'. Oh, right! Dad laughs. At first I thought you meant girls sleep over at guys' places. Stop it, Samo! Mom shoots him a look. That's not funny. She turns to me. We'll work something out. I'll call Rok's mom if that's what you want. All right? All right, I say and go back to eating. I'm halfway there. The ground is prepared.

26

ON TUESDAY I go to Hana's. They have a big apartment with high ceilings. Hana has a piano in her room. Do you play, I ask. No, she says. So why do you have a piano? It's a long story, Hana says. It's an old piano. My great-grandfather was a musician and he had it delivered from Graz. At the time it was something special. When he died, the piano was at my grandfather's, and then at my aunt's. When my aunt died, it came to us. Our relatives said our apartment was big enough; plus, it was the closest to my aunt's. They sold my aunt's place, but they wanted to keep the piano in the family. Something like that. She shrugs. I see, I say, and go over to the piano. I carefully lift the keyboard cover and run my fingers across the keys, pressing hard enough so they go down a little, but lightly enough so there's no sound. It's nice, I say. Oh yeah? Hana smiles. So tell me, did you bring your notebook and textbook? Of course. I slip the canvas bag off my shoulder. Come over here. Hana sits at her desk, where there's a chair for me too. Let's see what's giving you trouble.

As I sit at the desk with Hana while she looks through my notebook, I think, what a nice room she has. The piano makes it special. I've never seen anything like it. But even without the piano, this is the room of an adult woman. There is nothing childish about it. My room is the complete opposite. Superman, Luke Skywalker, and Darth Vader are still on my shelf. Sure, on the wall over my bed I have a few pictures torn from magazines of Iron Maiden, Kreator, and Motörhead, but there are two big boxes of Lego blocks under my bed and, on my dresser, a globe with a light bulb inside that makes the world glow in bright colors when you switch it on. I still have children's books on my bookshelves, mixed in with a few slender volumes from an encyclopedia, an English–Slovenian/Slovenian–English dictionary, and books from the two series *Slovenian Classics* and *One Hundred Novels*, and on my wardrobe door there are animal stickers, like a ladybug and beetle, which I used to get from the bank every time I deposited money. I think to myself, I have to redo my room. The way it is now, I don't ever want Hana or any other girl to see it.

Then I look at Hana as she pages through my textbook. Here, in this room with a piano, she seems completely different from how I've known her up to now. Without her makeup and black work boots she doesn't look that much older than me. I like her. When she turns to me, our eyes meet. Well, she says with a smile, are we going to study or not? Show me where we should start. I lean over the open textbook and turn a few pages back. This is where we are, I say. Hana laughs. If you want to understand this, you have to understand what came before. She turns a few more pages back. Then she starts asking me questions.

At first, for a while, I answer them quickly, then there are longer pauses and painful silences in my responses. During one such pause there's a knock on the door. What is it, Hana asks curtly. The door opens a crack and a woman peeks into the room. Are you going to offer your friend anything to drink? Maybe a glass of juice? We're studying, Hana says sternly. Then she looks at me. You thirsty? Want some juice? No, thanks, I'm fine, I say. I'll bring some anyway, the woman at the door says. When she brings the juice, she introduces herself. I'm Vida, Hana's mom. I'm Jan, I say, and offer my hand. Before she leaves she asks me if I'll be staying for supper. No, thanks, I say. But maybe you will, Hana says. You can if you like, Hana's mom says. I'll make a little extra. When she shuts the door behind her, Hana rolls her eyes and shrugs. Okay, now where were we? She turns a page and puts a new question to me for which I have no answer, so she pushes the textbook to the edge of the desk. She pulls a blank sheet of paper over to her and starts drawing on it with a pencil as she talks. As Hana is drawing and writing and talking, everything becomes clear to me. I understand. And when she tells me to repeat back to her what she said, I do it perfectly. Then Hana pulls the textbook over and asks the same question as before, when we stopped. Now I answer it correctly. And the next time that I can't answer something, Hana again takes an empty sheet of paper and starts drawing and writing.

That's enough for today, she says when we reach the page in the textbook where we stopped in class. Outside, it's already getting dark. Maybe you should come another time too. You're not so great with some of the basics. Some things you understand

SEBASTIJAN PREGELJ

and can do, but others you have trouble with, she tells me. But if you don't understand one thing, then you're not going to understand the next thing, right? She ruffles my hair. But you'll see. In the end you'll know everything. Don't worry. Chemistry isn't something you can just memorize. You have to understand how it works. I'll help you.

Are you and Rok coming to the park on Friday? She quickly changes the topic. Sure, we'll be there, I say. So we'll see each other soon. She stands up, takes a couple of steps, and throws herself onto the bed. Come here. It's more comfortable. She pats the pastel bedcover. Or are you afraid I'll bite? She frowns when she sees me hesitate. No, I'm not afraid, I say and lie down on the bed next to Hana.

I took ballet in primary school, she says. My mother is always saying that we're a musical family. But other than my great-grandfather there's not a single musician among us. She lifts her legs high above her head. Great-granddad was Russian. Aleksandr Aleksandrovich Kaganov. When they had a war over there, he fled here. He was planning to sail to America, but he didn't make it. He got as far as Trieste, and then decided to go to Ljubljana. He thought he would be a concert pianist, but nothing came of it. But he did find the love of his life here. Hana glances at me. He found Valentina, my great-grandmother, and fell in love with her. Her parents didn't want to hear a word about her marrying some Russian. But in the end love triumphed. Again, Hana glances at me. Well, that's the way my mother tells it. Hana slowly lowers her legs and laughs. But who gives a shit! She hops off the bed and crosses to the other side of the room where there's a record player.

What do you want to hear? Motörhead? AC/DC? I don't care, I say. So, Motörhead. Hana picks up the black album cover, pulls the record out, and sets it on the turntable. Soon the room is throbbing with wild music. Any second now, she says, turning to me, my mother will be here. You'll see. She'll knock on the door and yell at me to turn it down. And before I can say anything in response, there's a knock on the door. A moment later I hear Hana's mother, Turn that noise down! You can't be studying to that racket! We're not studying anymore, Hana shouts back. Then she comes back and jumps on the bed. So what d'ya think? Do you like it? She looks at me. I nod. And what about me. Do you like me, she asks, bending her head a little so her soft hair falls over my face. I'm instantly hot all over. I look at her and can't utter a sound while all my blood is rushing to my head and I'm sure I must be red as a beet. Forget it, Hana says and rolls to the other side of the bed. I thought maybe you did. But it's no big deal. She crosses her legs in the air. But I do, I half whisper. Don't apologize, Hana says. After all, we're friends, right? She reaches over and touches my arm.

Later at night, as I lie in bed, I can't get Hana out of my mind. We're on her bed, on the pastel blanket, and her soft hair is tickling me. Hana has a very special smell. She leans over me and asks if I like her, and I say I do. Then her lips touch mine and my heart becomes a grenade that's just about to explode.

27

ON SATURDAY WE go to a wedding. My parents are in a good mood. They're constantly laughing. Then my mother turns to me and says, We'll be going to your wedding before long. I roll my eyes. You'll see, Mom continues. It can happen just like that. It sure can, Dad pipes up. Now, what's the name of your chemistry tutor? Oh yes, Mom says. Hana, isn't it? When am I going to meet her? Never, I say, shaking my head because I know they're just teasing me. They're getting on my nerves. They're acting like children. And I'm not wild about going to Janez's wedding either. I'd much rather go into town tonight, meet up in the park with the girls, and see Hana. Ever since she's been tutoring me, I think only about her. It's not that Lea and Meri aren't great, but Hana is the one I really like. I want her to be my girlfriend, but that probably won't happen. When I look at her I see an adult woman, and when I look at myself I see a child. Hana sees it differently. Once she told me that I'm more mature than any of the guys in her class.

When we finally reach Aunt Mimi's house, from where, in an hour or so, we're all going to drive in a long row to St. Stephen's Church and then on from there, people immediately start decorating our car. They tie a big bow to the side mirror, stretch a red ribbon across the hood, and tie a white one to the antenna. My aunt says a few words to me, but she doesn't have time to chat today. There's too much going on. My cousin Petra, who since we last saw each other has become a real woman, is going from groomsman to groomsman with a basket of tiny bouquets, which she carefully pins on our lapels. When she comes to me, she tugs my ear and says, Be careful you're not next. You've got to be kidding, I say. I'm just saying, be careful that you don't end up like Janez. She runs her right hand down her front and then at her belly she makes a wide arc. She winks at me and whispers, Understand? Uh-huh, I say, but Petra apparently doesn't believe me. She's pregnant, she whispers. That's why there's a wedding. She walks slowly away. I watch her. She looks exactly like her mother, only younger. She's wearing makeup, like she always does, and is in high heels. The heels sink into the ground, but Petra knows how to walk in them. She has wide hips and big breasts, which she makes no effort to hide, unlike the girls at school.

A little later I see Bertica. I remember our school lessons. I still feel a little embarrassed, but that was a long time ago. I wave to her and she comes over to me right away. I haven't seen you in ages, she says. And now you're taller than I am! She gives me the once-over. So how are you doing? Fine, I say. And you? I'm finishing school. I'm going to be a teacher, she says, her eyes beaming. Of course you are, I say. Only now you won't be teaching teddy bears, but actual children. You can't imagine how I'm looking forward to that! Bertica claps. I love it when we guest teach in real classes. Don't get me wrong—the older kids give us trouble sometimes and like to tease us, but the younger ones are real sweethearts.

Right then my uncle comes up to us holding a silver tray filled with small glasses of schnapps. You're old enough now to have a drink, he tells me. If you say so, I say and pick up the closest glass. I drink it in a single gulp. While I'm trying not to grimace from the burning in my throat and the disgusting taste in my mouth, which together feel like I've swallowed a ball of fire, I look at my uncle. He's old. I remember how not so long ago he was still in the prime of his life, fit and muscular, but now his body looks like it collapsed; he has rings under his eyes, heavy jowls, and a wrinkly neck, as if he's become a turkey above his shoulders. You certainly know how to drink, he says enthusiastically. Have another! No, thanks, I say, and put the empty glass back on the silver tray.

Bertica, still next to me, is staring at me. So, do you have a girlfriend? No, I say. No you don't have one or no you don't want to say? I shuffle my feet and look down. That's what I thought. My cousin smiles. You don't want to say. What's her name? I'm not telling you. I feel like laughing. Come on, you can tell me. Who am I going to tell? And even if I do tell somebody, what's the big deal? It's Hana, I say. Hana, Bertica repeats and just looks at me. A moment or two later it occurs to me that I should have asked her if she has anyone. That could be the only reason she asked me, but I didn't think about it and just blurted out the answer. What an idiot. So how about you? I look at Bertica. Do you have a boyfriend? Don't be silly! My cousin waves her arm at me. So you do! No, I don't. Yes, you do! Fine, Bertica says. There's someone I'm seeing. We've been to the movies a couple of times. And had a drink together. What's his name? It's not important, Bertica says, shaking her head. Come on, I told you! I keep at her. Well, all right. Bertica looks at me from under a lock of hair. It's Brane. His name is Brane. And? Do you know him from school? No, Bertica says. He works. He goes to a job. And he has a car, she adds. And his own place. So I guess there'll be a wedding soon. I don't think so. Bertica shakes her head. Why not? Well, I just don't think so, she says. At this moment we're interrupted by loud honking. A gleaming Opel Kadett drives up to the house, and Janez steps out.

I learn later from Petra that Brane is twenty years older than Bertica. She can't bring him home because her parents are against her having anything to do with such an older man. In the end, it'll turn out that he's married, Petra says with a wry smile. In the end, there'll be lots of tears. I just hope he doesn't knock her up first, she whispers. Know what I mean? I hope it won't be like what happened with Janez. From Petra I learn that Janez had his eye on a different girl. But he wasn't the only one hovering around her. Petra places her warm hand on my leg. Lots of boys were hovering around Beti the hairdresser. He started seeing Alenka so he wouldn't be alone. It didn't seem to be serious. More of a weekend thing. More about making out in the vineyard hut. And then this happened. But maybe Alenka is what Janez actually needs. Maybe with her he'll calm down. Beti the hairdresser will be driving men crazy for years to come. Even if he had won her, who says she'd have stayed with him? But even if she did, he would be jealous. He would have been miserable. He would probably always be hanging around the beauty salon. He would probably always be asking her why she had to wear such short skirts and tight tops. As if that's not why he noticed her in the first place! Alenka is different, Petra says. Still waters. Know what I mean?

From Petra I also learn that for the past few years my aunt and uncle have been sleeping in different rooms. My aunt in the bedroom, my uncle in the living room, if he even comes home. Mostly he sleeps in the cottage, which is what they call their vineyard hut. Mostly he doesn't come home. I don't want to be like my parents, she tells me. I want to be happy. My folks aren't. Maybe they were once. But if they were, it didn't last very long. Just look at them now! It'll take three or four glasses for them to relax. And in the morning, when we get home, the bed in their bedroom will start creaking again after a very long dry spell. In the morning they'll be together. But after a few days it'll all go back to what it was before. I don't get it. I don't think Papa has another woman. I don't know what the problem is, Petra says. Do you feel like dancing? She hops up. I don't know how, I say. What do you mean you don't know how? She's surprised. People don't dance where you live? You don't go out? I go out, I say. But we don't go dancing. Although we do have a lot more discos and clubs than you do here. That's what I want, Petra says. To go to the city. But only if you and me go out. You know all the clubs. You'd know where to go. I guess so, I say. But I don't know if you would like it. Why wouldn't I? My cousin frowns. Because it's different, I say. Yes, I know it's different. I hope you don't think I've never been to a disco before! I hope you don't think all I know are farmers' bars and village festivals! I didn't think that, I say apologetically. If you come for a visit, I'll take you out. Of course I will.

Janez and I exchange a few words; then I sit down next to Grandpa. He looks content. Mostly he's quiet and is watching the others. When I sit down next to him, he puts his arm around me and says, There's my boy. Tell me how you are. What are you doing these days? Why don't come visit more often? I hardly recognize you. Your parents have nothing but good things to say about you, you know? Are you really being that good? I suppose, I say with a smile. Yes and no. You know how it is. I glance at him and all at once I feel my grandfather's warmth. I'm finishing eighth grade. And then I move on. What do you want to be, Grandpa asks. I'm not sure. Mom and Dad say I should plan to study law or economics. Lawyers and economists have good jobs, and a good job is the foundation of everything. That's what they tell me. But what about you? He looks at me. What do you want? I'm not sure, I say. I'm interested in a lot of things. But I don't know if there's any one thing that I'd want to do my whole life. Well, don't worry about it. Grandpa smiles. You'll do what you want to do. You're smart enough. Just keep studying. It's important that you get a good education. Right? Life gives and life takes away. Grandpa reaches for his glass and takes a sip. But if you have a good education, it's a little easier sometimes, a little more bearable. I wanted to keep studying. I was the best student in my class. But in the end they sent my older brother Karel to the city to study. There was only enough money for one of us. My parents said the eldest had priority. At first Karel did do some studying, but later he basically got lazy. He never finished school and he never returned home either. He was smart enough to find his way in the city. And in fact nothing truly bad ever happened to him. Well, it's not important, Grandpa says and reaches for his glass again.

I could sit with him until morning. Even if he didn't say another word. I'd like to visit him more often. The last time my parents came for a visit, I told them I had to study. And the time before that it was Rok's birthday. There was always something. And that something always seemed more important to me. Now, sitting next to Grandpa, I feel that when I'm with him everything is always fine, always good. No problem is too big and no annoyance too terrible. Grandpa always finds the right words. I look at him and smile. I want to tell him that I love him but the words won't come. That's okay. I'm sure he knows it, even if I don't say it.

Sometime later, my uncle brings in the accordion and Matija straps it over his shoulders. Soon he is playing. I get up and go outside for air. It's cool outside. The stars are out. I look at the sky. I don't remember when I last saw a sky so full of stars. The stars are constantly flickering. There's not a patch of empty sky. Even if it seems so at first. You just have to look long enough.

From somewhere Petra appears. She asks me if I smoke. I shake my head, but when she takes a pack of cigarettes out of her purse, I ask her for one. I thought you didn't smoke. She smiles and lights it for me. I think about how I much like it when Hana lights me a cigarette. She presses it between her lips, takes two puffs, and hands it to me. The rim of the filter is moist, and that simply thrills me.

28

HANA AND I meet up right after school. She laughs and says there's something she wants to talk to me about. My heart is pounding. I think, The moment has come. Hana isn't like other girls. We're not going to the movies so that somewhere in the middle of the film we can shyly hold hands and then, right before it ends, kiss. Hana will tell it like it is and I can hardly wait. Shall we go to the Skyscraper, she asks. Sure, I say, because I don't care where we go. We can go to Lenin Park; we can go to the Skyscraper. So long as we're together, it's not important where we go or where we are.

While we're waiting for the elevator, I tell her that my grandfather helped build the Skyscraper. Really? Hana looks at me and smiles. Was he an architect? No, I say, a construction worker. I'm not exactly sure what he did. We're in luck, she says and pulls open the door when the elevator stops on the ground floor. It usually takes forever to get here. Wait, she cries and puts her hand across my chest just as I'm about to step in. Always look to make sure it's really there. Never step in without checking. Never assume. The door could open and there's no elevator. It's happened before—someone's fallen into the elevator shaft and died. Here? I look at her in surprise. Not here, Hana says, somewhere else. Oh, I say. But the car *is* here. Yes, it is, Hana confirms. But you must always look first. I wouldn't want anything to happen to you. I wouldn't want you to fall into the elevator shaft and die. Understand? I understand, I tell her. Then I step into the elevator, wait for Hana to enter, and press the button for the rooftop terrace.

Do you feel it? Hana puts her hand on her stomach. It's moving so fast that my stomach can't catch up with the rest of my body. I'm not sure, I say with a shrug. In America the elevators are a lot faster, she says. Which is understandable, because people have to go to the fiftieth or eightieth or hundredth floor! If the elevators all went as slow as this one, it would take half a day before you got to the top. That's why they have super-fast elevators there. I would probably throw up the first time I rode one. Do you feel sick, I ask. She shakes her head and says, But in a super-fast elevator I probably would.

When we arrive at the top, we do a circle around the terrace. Hana chooses a corner table with a view of the castle. Is this okay? I nod and can hardly wait for her to get to why we've come so high above the city. I look at her and think how lucky I am. I have liked Hana since the day I met her. At first, I saw her as a girl who is nothing at all like the girls I know at school. She and Lea and Meri don't constantly huddle together, whispering things that are not for the ears of boys; they don't giggle at every word Rok and I say, even though we say some really stupid things sometimes. When we're in town, Hana isn't self-conscious and does what she feels like doing, and if anybody says anything, she lets them know exactly what she thinks. Over time, at our chemistry lessons, I got to know a different Hana, one who is friendly, tender, and caring, like a caring mother—except that with my mother this all makes me angry and I tell her I'm not a child anymore, but I like it when Hana is caring. But Hana is only like that when it's the two of us, and even then not always.

I like Hana in very particular way. I like everything about her. I often, secretly, look at her breasts. I can't help myself. The girls at school are always careful to avoid any unnecessary touching, but Hana doesn't mind it when I touch her. Whenever we all get together, she gives me a big hug, both when I arrive and when I'm leaving, and it feels so nice I get goose pimples. The girls at school always bashfully cover up their breasts, even if they don't have much to show, but with Hana I sometimes feel like she's parading them in front of me on purpose. As if she wanted me to take a good, long look at them. I can't stop thinking about her, especially recently. In the morning when I wake up, my first thought is about Hana, and at night before I fall asleep I think about her. I think about her on the way to school, during class, during the breaks between classes, and on the way home. Every day I can hardly wait to see her. Also, no one in my class has a girlfriend like this. When they see us holding hands and kissing, they won't be able to say we're just friends. And there's something else too. If we do become boyfriend and girlfriend, Hana will start opening worlds to me that have so far been hidden between the covers of *Start* and similar magazines. I'm sure there are all kinds of things she knows about and can do.

Hana waits until the waiter sets her coffee and my Coke on the table and leaves; then she looks at me and repeats what she told me in front of the school. There's something we have to talk about.

How long have we known each other? She purses her lips and answers her own question. About two years, I think. You were still in seventh or eighth grade, right? And now you're a freshman in secondary school. Something like that, I agree. I could easily calculate the number of months, which I think is more like a year and a half, but Hana has already moved on. A lot has happened since we met. You've grown up. And, she smiles, so have I. It shows, doesn't it? She pushes back some hair that was hanging in front of her eyes. I really care for you. She looks at me. You're the best friend I have. I wanted to tell you that. Then she takes a deep breath, pauses a moment, and says all at once, I have a boyfriend.

What? I look at her and feel all my blood rush to my head and then, like a torrential stream, drain into my limbs, which are getting heavier and heavier by the second, like sandbags filling with water. My head is humming and I don't understand what Hana has said. Or I do understand but don't want to. I probably didn't hear it right, I think. But, of course, I heard it right; I just don't want to understand it. Hana has a boyfriend!

Hana reaches across the table and takes my hand. Hey, why are you so quiet? Did I surprise you? Aren't you happy for me? Did you think . . . oh, you little idiot! She puts her hand over her mouth for a moment. You thought I was going to say something else, didn't you? You thought it was you. She wrinkles her forehead. You thought that you and I . . . Is that what you thought? No. I withdraw my hand. I didn't think that. But you did. Hana stands up, comes over to my side of the table, and puts her arms around me. I'm sorry. I didn't realize. Didn't realize what? I glance at her and quickly look away; I feel my eyes filling with tears. It never occurred to me that you and I . . . well, you know, that we would be a couple. It never occurred to me that you might feel that way about me. I don't, I say. Don't be like this. Hana hugs me harder. I thought . . . Leave me alone, I say, extracting myself from her arms. I'll survive, okay? Of course you will, but it's not about that, Hana says and goes back to her side of the table. For a few moments she doesn't know what to do; then she takes a sip of coffee. She says she hasn't drunk anything so bitter in a long time. It needs sugar. She takes a packet of sugar, opens it, and sprinkles it into the cup. Then she stirs the coffee with the tiny spoon and takes another sip. It's still bitter, she says.

Her words hang in the air. I don't hear them. My eyes rest on a man sitting a little farther on. The man is wearing a black hat. I think to myself, Men don't wear hats anymore. I suppose some still do, but so few it's hardly worth talking about, so this man seems special. I look at him and can't take my eyes off him. I feel like this has happened before. The man is reading a newspaper and smoking. The gray smoke from the tip of his cigarette rises in a thin column until a slight breeze pulls it to the side and tears it apart. The man lays the newspaper across his cup and glass, as if he's thinking about what he has just read. He slowly lifts the hand with the cigarette, takes another puff, and turns toward me. Before our eyes meet, I glance at Hana. Suddenly I can hear what she's saying again. She is saying I'm cute and a

SEBASTIJAN PREGELJ

sweet boy but a woman needs a man and Boris is a man. Boris lives in the student village. He's a student at the faculty of civil engineering. He needs a few more classes to get his degree. Once he graduates, he'll have no trouble getting a job. Civil engineers are almost guaranteed work, if not here then abroad. There are lots of them in Libya and Iraq.

I don't care about goddamn Boris or what he fucking studies and I don't care about what kind of fucking job he can expect. I don't want to know anything about him. I don't want to hear a word about him from Hana's lips.

I'm going home, I say and stand up. Hana looks at me. She stops talking, looks at me awhile, and then asks, Will we see you on Friday? Are you and Rok coming to the park? I don't know. I expect you'll be with Boris. No, I won't, Hana says. I'll be in the park with Lea and Meri. Boris is going home for the weekend. It's been a few weeks since he's seen his parents. . . . So we can see each other. She stands up and walks over to the glass doors, behind which the counter with the cash register is located. I'm just a step behind her. But then I feel a hand on my shoulder, stopping me. Don't you remember me, the man in the hat asks. Did you forget? I gave you a coin. It had your lucky number on it. Go look for it. He lets go of me and I hurry after Hana, who is paying. I'll pay, I say when I come up behind her. Don't even think about it, she replies. I invited you here and I'm paying.

Neither of us says a word in the elevator. I stare at the door and wait for the elevator to reach the ground floor. Hana is looking at me. I can feel her eyes on me but I don't look at her. Before the elevator stops, Hana grabs me, leans into me, and gives me a big kiss. Our lips are together for what seems like an endlessly long time. I'm so surprised I can't breathe and my eyes are shut. When she lets go of me, she whispers, I do care for you. I really do. I want you to remain my friend. Tears are running down her cheeks. I look at her and don't know what to say. I know what I would like to hear her say, but I am certain that won't happen. I also know what Hana would like to hear from me right now, but since I don't believe we'll stay friends, I say nothing. When the elevator stops with a jolt, I turn around, push the door open, and run out. Say something, Hana cries after me. I stop and turn around. What am I supposed to say? I don't know, Hana says. Say what you feel. If you love me, say that you love me. How will that help me, I ask. You'll say it. It will be from you, Hana says. And what about you? I rub my eyes, which are full of tears. But I already told you, Hana says. Yes, you told me. I turn around and go outside. I start running across the street, past the policeman, and across Lenin Park toward the bus stop. As I run, I feel the tears. I pull a handkerchief from my pocket, wipe my eyes and nose, and continue to the bus stop. I stand at a distance from the other people there.

On Friday evening I don't go into town. I tell Rok that we have a family dinner at my aunt and uncle's. For the first time in quite a while I watch television with my parents. When the movie is over, I go to bed. I lie there for a long time on my back, staring at the ceiling and thinking about Hana. Tears are running down my cheeks. They won't stop. Everywhere hurts.

In the days that follow, I make sure always to avoid Lenin Park and I don't go down any streets where I think I might run into Hana. I don't want to see her. Not ever again. I want to forget the whole thing as soon as possible. On Wednesday, Rok asks if we're going out on Friday. He asks if we're all meeting up. I have no choice but to tell him that we're not. I'm not going out with them ever again. But you do what you want, I say. What happened, Rok asks. I'll tell you another time.

29

ANOTHER TIME MIGHT be too late, Mom says. Grandpa is seriously ill. We're not going to wait for him to be released from
the hospital. Maybe they won't even release him. Maybe he'll
stay there until the end. I don't know. She wipes her tears. And
Meta . . . I don't understand why she waited until today to call
me. He's my father too! I'm sure he'll be home in a few days,
Dad says, trying to calm her. Some people live for years with
cancer. Three, five, even ten years! Some people—quite a few,
in fact—fully recover. I know, Mom says, sobbing, but others
die very quickly. Three months, six months, a year at most after
the diagnosis. And this is my father we're talking about, not
some statistic. Do you understand? Like I told you—Dad puts
his arms around her—we'll go to the hospital and talk to the
doctor. Then we'll know where we stand.

A little while later we're all in the car. Mom is quiet. Dad is
talking because he wants to dispel her dark thoughts, but she
doesn't answer him, so when he runs out of things to say he

turns on the radio. Ever since this morning, when Aunt Meta called to tell us that Grandpa was taken to the hospital two days ago, there's been a knot in my stomach. It's like the feeling I get before a test, only worse. And my legs are shaking a little. The last time they shook like this was when the Hornets were standing in front of me and my friends, but that was a long time ago. I look out the window. I'm not thinking about anything. I watch the countryside slipping past. But I'm not interested in meadows and forests, hills, white roads, trees, birds, and deer.

An hour and a half later, in the hospital room, the knots in my stomach and chest are gone and my legs have stopped shaking. Grandpa looks good. He's laughing and telling us he's all right. What did you think, he says, holding my mother's hand. You thought I'd be staying here for good? They've examined me and in nine days I'm going to Ljubljana for an operation. That's all.

That's all, Mom says, while Dad, in the corridor, is keeping his eye out for nurses and doctors. He's already asked three or four nurses where he might find Dr. Turk, but nobody knows. They tell him Dr. Turk has many patients. He'll be here when he's completed his rounds. Then he'll have time to talk to you. Don't worry.

Come here, Grandpa calls me over a few minutes later. When I sit down on the edge of the bed, he takes my hand. So tell me, are you okay? I nod and mutter, Uh-huh. Well, so am I, he says, smiling. When I see all of you, I'm okay. I wouldn't want to have to stay here. He shakes his head. It's always noisy. At night I hear moans from the rooms on either side, and during the day, it's my roommates' visitors. And the food is terrible. He grimaces. I can't wait to go home. Just another day or two.

That much a person can put up with. He smacks his lips. But I've been through worse. When your mother was your age, I was in the hospital for two weeks. My appendix burst. They barely saved me. They told me that if I had gotten there any later I would have died. But that's the way I am. I'm a fighter. Well, that almost did me in back then. I woke up one morning with a pain in my belly. Later I started throwing up. We all thought it was the flu. But I kept on throwing up and the pain got worse. It was late November and the fields were already covered in snow. Lojz took me on his moped to a nearby village, where the medical center was. No one had a car back then, Grandpa explains with a smile. The doctor examined me and said it was my appendix. You have to go to the hospital, he said. Right away! But I had no way to get there. If I called an ambulance it could be too late. My only option was for Lojz to take me on his moped to the city. I felt each and every pebble. I held on to him with both hands so I wouldn't fall off. I was clenching my teeth and every once in a while I had to lean over to the right or left to vomit. I was very careful not to vomit on his back. Grandpa laughs. When we got to the hospital, my teeth were chattering from the pain and the cold. The people at the hospital were amazed: first, because of how I got there; second, because of the state I was in; and third, because I was still alive. I went straight under the knife. The appendix had already burst, so it wasn't a simple operation. But somehow they managed to patch me up. And look at me now! Is there anything wrong with me? Not a thing! He smiles and squeezes my hand. When I'm home again, you'll come for a visit, okay? Yes, I promise. Of course I will. I'll come during vacation. I'll stay with you a whole week. You don't have to promise that, Grandpa says. I'll be happy if you come for a day.

I look into Grandpa's eyes. They fill me with calm. I know he's going to pull through. Everything will be fine.

Two hours later, on the way home, we're all feeling much better. Mom and Dad are talking quite a bit. Dad says, Grandpa looks good, certainly too good to be in the hospital. Mom is happy too. She says, Maybe it wasn't as bad as we thought. It wasn't, Dad confirms; he talked to the doctor. Dr. Turk says they caught it early enough. They'll remove the cancerous tissue when they do the operation. Grandpa will need some follow-up tests over the next few months, but that's a good thing. If they didn't get all the cancer and it starts growing again, they'll catch it right away. Also, it's important to remember that in elderly people the disease advances more slowly. For the most part Mom and Dad leave me in peace.

We're home in time for the evening news. Dad turns on the television and starts staring at the screen. A reporter is saying that radioactive particles were discovered on workers' clothes in Sweden, in the vicinity of the Forsmark Nuclear Power Plant. This evening we don't worry too much about the radioactive particles that were found on the clothes of some Swedish workers. We're all in a good mood because Grandpa is feeling better. In any case, the news about the radioactive particles is just one of many different news stories and it doesn't seem like anything serious. Only later will reports reach us that there had been an accident in Ukraine the day before. And only much later will we learn the full extent of the accident at the Chernobyl Nuclear Power Plant, where an explosion occurred during regular maintenance work. This produced a radioactive cloud, which air currents carried across the Ukrainian steppes and over a large part of Europe, eventually reaching America. Immediately after the explosion, firefighters started attacking the flames on the ground, while the army helped them from the air, and by morning the fire had more or less been subdued. Many years later, we will learn that an even bigger accident had been averted by two workers, who were sent to open the valves for releasing the radioactive water. They saved millions of lives, but like numerous firefighters and plant workers, they died at the scene of the accident. On that first day, 203 people were taken to a nearby hospital, of whom 31 died in the days that followed. The authorities evacuated 150,000 people. The city of Pripyat was evacuated entirely, and its former residents will never return. On anniversaries of the event, news teams will prepare segments about the worst nuclear accident of all time. The first few years they will report mainly about the victims; they will present all the details of the night when the explosion occurred. We will learn that most of the team that initially tried to limit the effects of the accident died within a few weeks. In the years that follow, there will be reports about the disabled and deformed children born in Ukraine and Belarus. We will see terrible images and hear all kinds of statistics. I will never be able to forget the image of a hydrocephalic child who looks like he could be a visitor from another planet, or the calf with two heads and the sheep with three pairs of legs. Later still, news teams will start visiting the abandoned city. We will watch clips of deserted homes. After fifteen or even twenty years, everything will still be just as it was left by the former residents, who were allowed to take only the most necessary essentials, their documents, and a little food, since they were supposed to be coming back in a few days. They departed the city in a convoy of two hundred thousand buses. After fifteen years, the plastic doll will still be in the crib waiting for a child's hand to pick her up and hug her; the teakettle will still be on the stove and the plates will still be on the table. A wedding picture will still be hanging in a corner above the table—a young man and woman, a few groomsmen and bridesmaids, and in the background a concrete monument with the date 1970. Everyone is smiling and, to judge from the photograph, beautiful times await them. But the view through the window will be different. The streets and courtyards will be overgrown with vegetation, and wild animals will have migrated into the city. We will see clips of the deserted amusement park with its gigantic Ferris wheel, which had been scheduled to open on May Day, and of wolves running in the streets. We will see monuments to the heroes of a forgotten era and, on buildings, giant red stars, golden ears of wheat, and silver hammers and sickles. Scientists will estimate that the city will not be safe for human habitation for the next one hundred thousand years. But this evening, when we get back from the hospital, we do not yet know any of this. And even if we were to know some small part of it, this would in no way cloud our joy. We are all happy that Grandpa is feeling better. It looks like it's not as bad as we feared.

In bed, I spend a long time thinking that I must not go back on my word. I will spend part of my vacation at Grandpa's.

Before I fall asleep, the outlines of the house and then the road appear before my eyes. Beside the road there are flowers on which honeybees and bumblebees are grazing. Beyond the flowers lie meadows and fields, and in the background there is a forest. I hear the buzzing of the insects and the sound of the wind, which blows now from one direction, now from another. The sun is warm but not scorching. I am walking. My step is light. The air is sweet in a very particular way. I fill my lungs with it. I don't have a care in the world.

30

ROK AND I are sitting in a corner of the pub Under the Linden. We are still best friends, but because we go to different schools now, we don't often see each other during the week. Sometimes we run into each other at the bus stop and sometimes by our buildings. We do, however, get together basically every Friday and almost every Saturday. When there's nothing better to do and we don't know where else to go, we go to Under the Linden. So far no one there has asked us how old we are. We can drink beer and smoke cigarettes in peace. In the summer, the terrace is packed, but we don't care; we don't mind being inside. We don't go there for the fresh air.

While we're waiting for our drinks to arrive, I ask Rok if he still gets together with Lea, Meri, and Hana. He's surprised. Rok and I last saw each other a few days ago and not much has happened in the meantime. He shakes his head and tells me he's seen them a few times since then. By *then* he means when I said I wasn't going back to the park where we used to meet up, and in fact I never did go back. He shrugs and says, It was a little . . . well, I don't know what it was really. It wasn't like it used to be. Hana didn't come at all, and with just Lea and Meri there, it was like we didn't know what to do. Before we went to Palma, we'd sit in the park, passing a bottle around and saying whatever popped into our heads. The girls are in their final year at school, so they have to study a lot. But I tell you, it's not the same. They were asking about you. How you are and what you're doing. They wanted to know if you're ever coming back to the park. They don't hang out with Hana anymore. I told them what happened between the two of you. They said she's a bitch. Ever since she took up with Boris, they don't see her anymore except at school. And even at school she's often absent. She'd rather be making out with her lover man, they said. Boris recently found a job and . . . Okay, enough, I interrupt Rok. I'm not interested. I'm really not interested why Hana doesn't have time for school. And I really don't care who she is with and what she is doing. I get it, Rok says. She screwed with your head. No she didn't, I say. I screwed with my own head.

I look out the window and give Rok a nudge so he'll look too. The waiter, Antonio, has put a couple of pizzas down on an empty table and is now handing out the napkins and silverware to some patrons. We both know what's going to happen. Soon some sparrows dart over from the bushes nearby. Brazenly, they alight on the pizzas' doughy edges and start pecking at them like mad, pulling at them with their tiny beaks and trying to tear off pieces, while the pigeons on the ground wait patiently for their share. Rok and I wait to see who will notice first. It's not long before a man with a mustache shouts, Hey!

What the hell! Those sparrows are hopping all over our pizzas! The waiter waves his arm and hurries to the pizzas. Birds have to eat too, he mutters as he chases away the sparrows. They retreat to the closest bush, from which they carefully observe the situation on the pub terrace.

Rok and I, too, would have probably gone on observing the situation on the terrace if we hadn't heard a scream coming from behind the doors that lead down to the restrooms. Startled, I look for the source of the piercing sound. Rok turns too. While we're still wondering what to do, a young woman appears at the swinging doors shouting that there's a dead body downstairs.

Now a few men get up and run over to the swinging doors and down the stairs. Soon even more people are headed to the swinging doors and finally Rok and I go too. Someone needs to call an ambulance, says one of the men who are now hurrying back up the stairs. When the waiter Antonio runs in, everyone stands back as if he was a police officer. They make room for him to go downstairs and see for himself what has happened. He soon returns, somewhat pale but also determined. He hurries to the bar and, on his way, asks loudly if anybody has called an ambulance yet. They're on their way, a skinny waiter replies; he's new there. Good, good, Antonio says, and stops hurrying. Give me something strong, he tells the new waiter, and then a moment later gulps down the drink the boy has poured for him. After that, he returns to the swinging doors and starts shooing people away. Move, please. Step away. Go back to your tables. Excuse me, please, he says as he goes down the steps to the restrooms. Is anyone here a doctor, he asks. Or maybe a medical student? Anyone? No? If not, then please move away.

The paramedics are on their way. The police are on their way. Make room!

Everyone is trying to guess what happened. Do you think she was killed, a girl asks her boyfriend, who doesn't reply but cranes his neck as if he is trying to see or hear something else. It was murder, miss, says the older man standing behind her. Maybe it was something else? What else could it have been? Rok and I glance at each other. The man looks like he knows. We see him here on occasion drinking espresso standing up—he says he doesn't have time to sit down; then he runs across the street, where he has a photocopying place.

Now we manage to push our way to the front of the crowd, but even then there is nothing to see and not much to be heard either. Muffled sounds are coming from below; we catch a word or two now and then but mostly it's just mumbling. We know there's a dead woman down there, but we've known this for a while now and so has everyone else. At the sound of sirens, people start glancing at the front door.

Make room, a voice says firmly. Out of the way, please. Step aside. Two police officers in gray uniforms enter. Now people are moving apart so the policemen can get to the stairs. One of them goes immediately down the steps, but the other turns toward the crowd and says, What is it, people? What are you waiting for? What are you staring at? Maybe somebody here knows something? Would anyone like to give a statement? The portly man who had earlier said it was murder speaks up. Comrade officer, I believe a murder has taken place downstairs. A woman has been killed. Is that so? The policeman looks at him. How do you know this? Were you downstairs? Did you see something?

He takes a notebook from his pocket and asks the man his name, address, and year of birth. That's enough for most of the onlookers to begin retreating. Rok and I stand there watching as the policeman returns his notebook to his pocket and runs down the stairs. Meanwhile, everyone who was still downstairs comes back up.

We go back to our table. Rok pulls out a packet of cigarettes. We light up. Well, this is a fucking mess, he says. I wonder what happened. I don't think anyone was murdered, do you? I don't know, I say. Well, we'll see. It's like the beginning of a movie. A dead woman is lying on white tiles. A good starting point. Then cut to everything that led up to it. Then cut to the hunt for the killer. So what do you think? He puffs out some smoke. I suppose you're right, I say. Soon we are talking as if nothing has happened.

A while later, the paramedics emerge from below. The body on the stretcher they're carrying is completely covered. The two policemen are behind them, and the waiter Antonio is behind the policemen. He goes behind the bar, while the policemen walk among the patrons and look us over. They stop next to each person and ask where they were at the time of the murder. Then they take down their information. They eventually stop at our table. Rok and I freeze. We were sure the policemen would walk past us and now here they are standing in front of us. Aren't you two a little young to be hanging out in pubs, the first one asks, raising his left eyebrow. How old are you anyway, the second one asks. Fifteen, I mumble. Sixteen. How old are you *now*, the mustached man says with a frown. Fifteen or sixteen? One of us is fifteen, the other sixteen, I say. The policeman nods. And your parents—do they know you're here? I don't know, I say. Maybe not. I see, the policeman says. Well, in that case it's best you go home. So they don't worry. And so I don't worry. All right, we say. We grab our coats and are about to leave when he stops us. Ah-ah-ah, just one more thing. I need to take down your information, he says. He licks the tip of his index finger, turns a page in his notebook, and looks at us. Just in case.

What a fucking mess, I say when we're outside. What if our parents find out the police took down our names? They won't, Rok says as if he knows all about it or has had some experience with this before. Those cops were just acting smart. Nothing will happen, you'll see. If the police took down the names of every witness for each and every event, and then went around to every person on the list, how many cases would they ever solve? There were so many people there today, those two cops would be doing nothing for the rest of the year except going around and taking down statements about who saw what when. But in fact nobody saw anything. Nobody knows anything. At least none of us who were upstairs, right? So there's nothing to worry about! He spits on the ground and waves his arm. You really think so, I ask, still doubtful. I know so, Rok says firmly.

On the bus we don't talk. I'm scared. I'm scared the police will come to my home. I'm scared they'll tell my parents everything. Mom and Dad will find out where we were and that we were drinking and smoking. And that somebody was killed. Mom will go crazy. I can imagine her shaking her head and trying to choose her words carefully but then finally exploding, Do you have any idea what a mess you've made? Don't you realize it could have been you who died there? What are you even doing at such a place? Dad would be standing to the side and, eventually, he would add, The police took your name down. Now you're in their files. Guilty or not, you're in their files. And that isn't good. Look at your Uncle Gorazd. This happened to him and he's had no peace of mind ever since.

On Monday there is a small item in the newspaper saying that M. K., a woman, was found dead at a popular Ljubljana tavern. The case is still under investigation, but according to current information there are no signs of a violent death. On Tuesday, Rok and I run into each other at the bus stop. By now we know everything. The woman who died by the restrooms at Under the Linden was Mara the cleaning lady. She had a table and chair in the hallway. She had a metal box on the table where she kept the money customers left her when they used the restrooms. Since payment was not mandatory, most people left nothing, but some would toss in a coin or two. There were rolls of toilet paper stacked on the edge of the table and various cleaning agents on the floor.

What a shame, Rok says. Just imagine. You spend your whole life cleaning bathrooms and in the end you die in one. Fuck. Really, I agree. Fuck. The funeral's tomorrow, Rok says. Do you think anyone'll go? Do you think this woman, who had so many people walking past her every day, will have anyone at her funeral?

We could go, I say. Are you crazy? Rok is surprised. But then he cocks his head and says, You know what? You're right. Let's go! We'll tell our teachers we're going to a funeral. If you say you're going to a funeral, they don't usually ask too many questions. And if anyone does ask whose funeral it is, we'll tell them it's our Aunt Mara's. We go to different schools so they're not going to find out, right? And no one's going to ask anything else. After all, she's our aunt. It wouldn't be appropriate. Just don't forget to wear black tomorrow.

The next day, an hour and a half before the funeral, Rok and I meet at the Bavaria Court bus stop. From there buses go in every direction and twenty minutes later, when we get off at the stop for the cemetery, we go straight to the display case with the funeral notices. Rok appears to have done this before. Everything is clear to him. He runs his finger down the front of the display case until he comes to the name Marija. That's her. Wasn't her name Marica, I ask. Do you see any Marica on the list, he says, looking at me. That's just what people called her. But her real name was Marija. Hundred percent. Anyway, there are five funerals today and three are for men. So the women we have to choose from are Marija and Danica. Which would you choose? Good, I say. Let's go.

Rok takes us to the right funeral chapel, where a few people are standing. Among them we see Antonio, who is staring into space. Since we don't know any of her relatives or who is who, we keep to the side. We think, however, that the oldest man there is probably her husband and that the two younger women are her daughters. The older woman could be a sister, cousin, or friend. Then there's Antonio, who we guess isn't part of the family because he's a coworker. There are two older couples on the other side of the chapel. Maybe they're more distant relatives, or friends, acquaintances, or neighbors. There are no other people there. We stand where Antonio can't see us and try not to be conspicuous.

SEBASTIJAN PREGELJ

Forty-five minutes later, when the service is over and we're about to leave, Antonio runs over and stops us. Hi, guys. I saw you earlier but I couldn't—well, you know. It's nice of you to come. Our Mara was a woman and a half. I said the same thing to her husband too. A woman and a half. Do you want to get a drink? Thanks, I say, shaking my head no, but because Rok doesn't answer, we end up going to a pub nearby. What're you having, Antonio asks us when the waiter comes to our table. A small beer, Rok says. Apple juice, I tell the waiter. I'll have a pear brandy and some mineral water, Antonio says. He tells us again how glad he is to see us and asks if we knew Mara personally or were in some way close to her. Not really, we say. Then it's even nicer that you came. He is pleased. When the waiter brings us our drinks, Antonio lifts his glass of brandy. To Mara, he says. To Mara, we repeat.

Antonio wipes his mouth with the back of his hand and says that Mara was a gem of a woman. Very meticulous, and so devoted to her work. Everything shined, didn't it? It sure did, we agree, everything shined. Where will I find another woman like that? Antonio rotates his glass. Women like her don't exist anymore. Today women are so fussy. They all want to work in an office. None of them wants to get their hands dirty. They all have polished nails. But not Mara. No, Mara wasn't like that. In the morning, she liked to arrive fifteen minutes early, and at night, she liked to leave half an hour late. She cared about what our customers thought of her work. She cleaned everything before the first ones arrived, even though it was already clean from the night before, because Mara was always the last to leave. And at night, she cleaned everything so there would be less work for her in the morning. And as honest as the day is long! Mara was the kind of woman you don't often meet. I could give her the keys to the pub and sleep soundly at night. Hell, I could give her the keys to my own home and sleep soundly. Antonio is nodding to his own words. At the end of the day she would count up all the money people put into that metal box of hers and bring it to me at the cash register. Before the holidays, I would tell her to keep it. Yes, sometimes I'd let her keep the money she collected. As a kind of bonus. But she would put up such a fight! As if she had drawers full of cash at home. But in the end I managed to convince her. I'd tell her she had earned it, and that as her boss I could give it to her. I did the right thing, didn't I? Rok and I nod.

Our glasses have been empty for a while, but Antonio is still talking. Eventually, he notices the empty glasses and calls the waiter over; he orders three pear brandies. We toast each other's health. Antonio and Rok empty their glasses in a single swallow, but I'm not fond of hard liquor, so after taking a sip I push my glass over to Rok and say, Drink mine too.

Once we're outside again, Antonio asks us how we got there. The bus, Rok says. I can give you a lift, Antonio offers. No need. The bus stops right in front of our building, I say, although that's not really true. All right, guys. Antonio raises his arm to say goodbye and hurries to the parking lot.

On the bus, we're mostly quiet. Rok says a few times that Antonio is like a character from the movies. I don't say anything.

SEBASTIJAN PREGELJ

31

IT'S BEEN A long time since my aunt and uncle have come for a visit. Now I'm disappointed that Martin didn't come with them, although I wasn't actually expecting him. They usually come by themselves, and when we go to their place, Martin's either not at home or has just left. Uncle Gorazd says he's out chasing girls. Aunt Taja shoots him a look and tells him not to talk nonsense. Then Dad asks how the military work is coming along. You wouldn't believe it, Uncle Gorazd says enthusiastically. We're making all kinds of things and money's no object. We've hired two new engineers. One in computer science, the other in telecommunications. These things are changing at the speed of light. All at once, the future is now! He laughs. Don't be ridiculous, Aunt Taja says, trying to stop him, but my uncle won't be put off. Evgen—that's the second guy's name—says it's only a matter of time before the two fields merge. He says he doesn't know how it's going to happen, but it will happen soon. He says wireless telephones are coming. The Japanese, the Scandinavians, and the Americans are all competing to see who'll be first. The prototypes have been around for a while, and the Americans have even put the first of these devices on the market, but ordinary use is still a while off. But keep an eye out, he says excitedly. Things are moving lightning fast. Things we can barely imagine today are the reality of tomorrow. That's how it will be with telephones. Before long you can expect to see a phone that doesn't need any wires. And this will change everything. You'll be able to carry it with you—and I'm not talking about the cordless phones we have today. What people call cordless phones still need a unit with a cord, and their range is still very limited. You can't go across the street and make a call with it, let alone take it to the other side of town with you. Why would I want to use my phone on the other side of town, Dad wonders. There are phone booths everywhere. Uncle Gorazd says, Imagine something like a walkie-talkie, only without restricted frequencies—it's a telephone! It's part of a telephone network. You see? Phone booths? Forget about them! Wireless phones are ideal for mountain cabins and isolated farms, and I won't even mention the army! But in other ways too. Understand? I do understand, Dad says, but I genuinely cannot imagine why it might be a good idea for me to carry around a phone. Oh, but just you wait, my uncle says. You'll see! It's like compact discs for music.

I look at him and think his head is going to explode if he can't get everything out. Uncle Gorazd's head is full of wires and circuits and chips! It's full of things we can barely understand. It's like he's trying to explain a rocket to a monkey. But in the end, a chimp did go to space before a person did, and I want to laugh when I imagine Uncle Gorazd trying to explain to a chimp why it's a good thing to have a telephone you can carry around that doesn't need a wire.

Dad looks at him and says nothing. Haven't you read about them? You don't know what's going on in the music industry? Uncle Gorazd is a little surprised. You, who always turned up the music so loud the neighbors would start banging on the walls and ceiling with broom handles? Then he shakes his head. No more reel-to-reel tapes, no more vinyl records, no more cassettes! From now on, just compact discs. Music on a compact disc is completely static free. No scratches, no jumping. The disc itself is practically indestructible. You can throw it on the ground, pour water on it, even drive a car over it. And it's fine! And you can put more music on it than you can on vinyl. A whole lot more. And it's much smaller too. Can you imagine? I guess, Dad says because he doesn't know what else to say. We were in Frankfurt this fall at the trade fair, my uncle tells him. And companies were presenting these compact discs. They were presenting them as something that is already here. Because it is! The music stores there have special shelves for compact discs, and people are buying them. I tell you, it's the future of music. Throw away your records! He laughs and looks at my mother, who is simply listening to him. Then he looks at me. He's waiting for somebody to ask him something, but he's told us so much in just a few minutes that it's hard to ask anything.

You're badgering him, Gorazd, my aunt says. You're always badgering people with your telecommunications and those music discs. I'm not badgering! It's the future. The future is knocking on the door! Like color television. Not too long ago we thought we'd never have it here. After all, a few years ago no station was broadcasting in color! And then what happened? Everything changed overnight. And today? Today even the Gorenje company makes color TVs. There's a color TV in almost every home. This is called progress. Even Samo here bought one, he says with a grin. You're badgering him, my aunt says again and turns to my mother. You see? This is what they've done to him at work. I think it's the radiation. He's losing his hair and all he thinks about are wires and chips. He can't talk about anything else. The older he gets, the crazier he gets. He should be thinking of buying a little house by the sea, where we can get away for the weekend. Come with me, Mom says. She gets up and goes to the kitchen. My aunt follows her.

My father and uncle go out on the balcony. Why don't you join us, my uncle calls to me. I'm not going to let you have a cigarette, but some male conversation won't do you any harm. The more you know the better. You're in secondary school now, same as Martin, but you'll have to decide soon enough what comes next. Isn't that so? He looks at Dad. That's true, my father agrees. Martin's going into computer science, my uncle says. Computers are the future. He'll get a job right away. And a job with computers will open every door. Even abroad. Where do you think you can get the best education? Here? In Zagreb? Belgrade? No! Everyone's going to America. Even Martin. But of course, first there's the army. Yeah, Dad says, the army. But you know the right people and can probably arrange something so Martin won't be sent too far away. Probably, my uncle says with a shrug. I have to speak to the colonel the next time he comes. I need to get him alone. The colonel acts tough, but in fact he's a softie. I'm sure of it. So I'm not too worried. We'll arrange something for Jan too, he says. Now where were we? Right! He does a little hop. Computers. Computer science.

I'm not interested in computers, but I don't tell my uncle that. I am, however, interested in anything connected with music. Do you have any of those compact discs, I ask Uncle Gorazd. I have the two discs I got in Germany, he says, but I don't have a player for them. Right now they cost an arm and a leg. Two arms and a leg, Dad adds and they both burst into laughter. It's one of their old jokes.

What do you think you'll study, Uncle Gorazd asks as he lights a cigarette, takes a deep drag, and holds the smoke in his lungs. We're both telling him he should go into law or economics, Dad says. I see, my uncle says, slowly exhaling the smoke through his nostrils. Law or economics. Good. They're good too. But if you ask me, computers are the way to go. Information technology. The Americans call it IT. Not many people know anything about it today, but tomorrow—you'll see—tomorrow everyone will realize it's where the future lies. You're just starting out. He touches me lightly with his index finger. And information technology is also just starting out. I mean it's not new; it's been around for a while, but right now there are some major advances starting to happen. If you're one of the first in the field—and you can be—you'll have the advantage. Do you understand what I'm trying to tell you? I nod.

So how are things otherwise? Uncle Gorazd flicks some ash off the tip of his cigarette. Any girls, he asks. Things are fine, I say. Now I regret coming out on the balcony. I know what my uncle is like. Now that he's started drilling me, he won't let up.

The more I avoid answering, the harder he will press. But at the same time I'm glad. Uncle Gorazd is special. I've often thought it would be fun having a father like him. I used to envy Martin, although I wasn't exactly sure why. It was just a feeling. Uncle Gorazd finds his way. He doesn't wait; he connects the dots. Dad is different, I think; he's more reserved. He wants to think things through first; he wants to be sure before he does anything. That's why Uncle Gorazd bought a color TV before we did. That's why he bought a German car, while we're still driving one from Czechoslovakia. They go shopping in Trieste almost every month, while we've gone twice to Klagenfurt. But what do I know.

32

I HAVEN'T SEEN much of Rok recently. He has a girlfriend now and spends most of his time with her. So I'm at home more. Whenever my aunt and uncle come over—and recently they've been coming over more often because Martin is in the army—I mostly listen to them talk about my cousin. Uncle Gorazd, through his connections, arranged for Martin to train as a reserve officer in Zadar. He got Colonel Nikolovski alone one day, told him his son was doing his military service in the autumn, and asked if there was any way to arrange something. The colonel first congratulated him and then said that something can always be arranged. So while other boys were receiving draft notices with the names of cities they had never heard of or couldn't find on a map of Yugoslavia, Martin's draft notice said: *Zadar*. Uncle Gorazd says it's not too bad. He says the base is like a second-rate hotel and that life at the reserve officers' school is a lot different from life on an ordinary army base. Even so, Aunt Taja's eyes are always filled with tears and she keeps repeating that it's horrible for the boy. My father tries to reassure her by saying that every boy has to go into the army and that every boy also comes back. But the boy who goes in comes back as a man. Aunt Taja just shrugs, and then she and Mom usually go into the kitchen and close the door. They cry a little and laugh a little. Meanwhile, Dad and Uncle Gorazd go out on the balcony and smoke. As for me, I prefer to stay in my room. All four of them get on my nerves.

Right before Martin left for the army, there was a massacre at the army base in Paraćin. For months afterward, Aunt Taja was beside herself with worry. Uncle Gorazd kept telling her that Paraćin was in Serbia, while Zadar was in Croatia. But my aunt wouldn't hear any of it: an army base is an army base; the military is the military. If some boy named Aziz killed the soldiers in Paraćin, then another Aziz could do the same in Zadar. And she is probably right. The Aziz who shot the soldiers in Paraćin was not someone who caused problems, but all the same, just before his service was ending, he went nuts and shot his sleeping comrades in the dormitory. He killed four and wounded five. Then he fled. The military police soon tracked him down and surrounded him, but then, according to official information, Aziz committed suicide.

Mom has been urging me to write to Martin for a while now. She says he's bored and must be awfully homesick and that letters from family can help, because when he reads them he feels like he's with us, if only for a short time. I think it's a stupid idea. We've hardly seen each other these past couple of years. Besides, I don't know what I'd write him about. Do I tell him what's going on with me? Nothing is going on with me. Nothing

SEBASTIJAN PREGELJ

I could write about. Ever since Rok and I have been spending less time together, less has been happening to me. I could tell him I'm hanging out more with Matej now, but why would he care about that? Dad sometimes tells me that when I'm in the army I'll want to get letters too. And if everyone says they can't write me because they have nothing to say, then I won't get any. It's as simple as that.

Then one day I make up my mind, sit down at my desk, tear a page out of my notebook, and start writing. After a few opening sentences, I get to the point. I write that there's something I often wanted to ask him but never found the right moment. Maybe it's now. Maybe it's now when you're not standing in front of me and we're not looking at each other. By now you're wondering what I'm going to ask you. I know. It's a strange way to begin a letter. Well, this is what I'm curious about. I hold the fountain pen in the air a few seconds, then continue. The year I got a bike for my birthday, we all went to the Skyscraper Building. There wasn't anything particularly unusual about it. We played on the rooftop terrace, running and chasing each other. I remember how we tried to look through the binoculars. There were four of them, one on each corner, and maybe they're still there. But we couldn't reach the eyepieces and eventually gave up. Well, to make a long story short, after we left the terrace and were already on the street, a man came flying down from the Skyscraper. One moment he was alive and falling. The next moment he hit the ground and was dead. We were the closest to him, but we didn't run to help him; we ran away. When I looked up at the sky, I saw a black hat falling a little behind him. One of our parents turned my head away. After that I didn't see anything else. I remember running as if we were fleeing the scene, as if we were guilty of something, as if we somehow had something to do with the man jumping off the building and killing himself. But I don't think we had anything to do with it. How could we have? None of our parents knew him. If they had, they would have at least said hello to him, right? But this is what I want to tell you. When we were still up on the terrace, this man grabbed me by the arm and held me. Don't ask me if I'm sure it was the same man. Of course I am sure. Otherwise I wouldn't be telling you this. Anyway, you ran on and didn't look back, so you didn't see anything, but I stayed behind at his table. The man smiled at me and gave me a silver coin. He told me to take good care of it and that my lucky number was on it. I have the coin right in front of me. It's an American quarter dollar. It has the year it was minted on it: 1952. I'm writing to you because I want to know if you remember this event or know anything more about it. I know a man jumped off the Skyscraper and I have the coin he gave me just before he did. But that's all I know. And you? Did you ever overhear anything at home that your dad might have said to your mom when he thought nobody was listening? Well, that's basically it. Otherwise, I hope you're well. Your dad says your base is like a second-class hotel. I hope that's true. When you're here on leave, let's get together!

I lie on my bed and examine the American coin. I hadn't thought about it in a long time. I found it when I was cleaning my room. I put it in the wooden box where I keep coins. I've been keeping them in that box ever since Grandpa gave me a few coins from old Yugoslavia, from when we still had a king, and a few from the occupation, when we had Hitler marks and Mussolini lire. After that, I started telling people I collect coins. Uncle Gorazd would bring me coins from his business trips abroad. There was a time when he was traveling a lot to Eastern European countries. After each trip he'd give me a coin or two from the country where he had been. Mom would always tell him not to give me money, but he said that rubles, or florints, or zloty, or levs aren't worth much and it's more a souvenir than anything else. He told me they aren't old coins, but they will be one day. My uncle still travels a lot, but the past few years it's been mainly to Western countries. He doesn't bring me coins anymore. He still thinks of me, though, and brings me something small. Recently he brought me a six-pack of Coca-Cola. That first day, during the snack break at school, all my classmates noticed when I pulled a can of Coke from my bag. Tjaša asked if I would give her the empty can. I'll make it into a holder for my colored pencils, she said. I smiled and gave it to her.

I lie on my bed and think about all sorts of things. At one point I remember Hana. I'd really like to know how she's doing. Is she happy with that Boris of hers? Did she ever finish school? Does she have a job? Do they have a child? When I think about it, Boris has everything: a job, a car, an apartment. What have I got? None of that. I have a bicycle I ride around on and I have some pocket money. That's hardly enough for me to promise Hana anything. But what could I even promise her? I'm still in school. How am I supposed to get a car and an apartment? How am I supposed to get anything? How am I supposed to make plans for the future? It drives me fucking crazy. I really don't know why she was in such a hurry. I don't understand. She lived in a big apartment in an old house. She had a big room and a nice mother. She had a piano.

Then I think of Elvis, Ali, and Defne. I heard a long time ago that Ali was hanging out with guys who were reading and discussing religious texts. They all grew beards. Then he was in the army. I heard he had problems there, but I don't know what kind. That's the way this country is, Uncle Fikret said once when we were at their place. They don't like people who read and think for themselves. They don't like people who pray. But people who pray don't mean any harm. Well, it doesn't matter, he said. My son returned alive and healthy and everything is fine. Later I ran into Ali in front of the central post office. He had a beard and was wearing dress pants. He was even thinner than usual, or maybe the dress pants and white shirt made him look that way. When he saw me, his eyes lit up, as if the black embers in his eye sockets had caught fire. He opened his arms and embraced me like a brother. We didn't talk much because my bus pulled up only seconds later. I hopped on. Ali raised his arm to say goodbye and then went on his way.

Elvis is the same as always. He seems fine to me, but Uncle Fikret sighed a few times and said it would be easier if he was more like his brother. Elvis goes to the Secondary School of Economics. As far as I know, he doesn't have any problems there. Whenever we run into each other—which happens so rarely it's like we live in different cities and not in the same neighborhood—we mostly talk about the old days. We talk about the stupid things we all did together. Whenever we run into each other, I think we should get together again sometime. It could be fun. But then I never call him and he doesn't call me.

I lie on my bed with the quarter-dollar coin between my fingers and think about how strange it was the last time my parents and I were at Elvis's. On the one hand, I still felt that Uncle Fikret and Aunt Farhana loved me just the way they did when I used to bring my school bag there so Elvis could copy out what he missed when he was absent. But on the other hand, this was the first time I noticed how different we were. With every word that was said and the silences that followed, I felt like we were drifting farther and farther apart from each other.

Then Uncle Fikret told us that Defne was getting married. Why, that's wonderful news! My mother clapped her hands in delight. When's the wedding? In the spring. In Sarajevo, Uncle Fikret added. In Sarajevo? Dad was surprised. Yes, that's what we agreed and it will be better that way. Muslims in Sarajevo live differently than we do here. Don't get me wrong, he said. Everything is fine here. Jobs and salaries are better than in Bosnia, or for that matter anywhere else in Yugoslavia, but for a true Muslim there isn't even a prayer hall here, let alone a mosque. Where are we supposed to pray? We get together at the homes of friends and acquaintances, he said, patting down his mustache, but it's not the same thing. My brother, Nadir, who lives in Sarajevo, has been telling me for a long time that things are different there. Things are changing. We spent two weeks with them this summer. We got to know a lot of people and had a lot of conversations. My brother has been urging me to move to Sarajevo. He said I could just as easily drive a cab in Sarajevo as in Ljubljana. He would find us a nice apartment or a house. But that's not for me, Uncle Fikret said with a wave of his arm. But Defne is going to move to Sarajevo. It'll be best for her. Her future husband earns good money. He has his own business and a big house. Oh, I see, Mom said, glancing at Defne, who was sitting next to Aunt Farhana. Neither of them said a word all this time. Defne was smiling and looking at us as if the conversation was about somebody else. On the way home, no one said anything for a long time. Then, when we were in front of our building, Dad said he didn't get it. Sarajevo! Who is this future husband anyway? Does she even know him? You don't think she knows him, I asked. I don't know, Dad said. I have no idea what's going on.

I am lying on my bed. I don't know what happened to Uncle Fikret, Aunt Farhana, and Ali. I don't know if it also happened to Defne. It happened least of all to Elvis. Back at home, Dad sighed and said that we were drifting apart. Did you notice? Farhana had a scarf on her head. Maybe she didn't have time to wash her hair, Mom said. Oh, please, Dad continued. You're not going to say that in all these years this was the first time Farhana didn't have time to wash her hair? And what about Ali? Did you see that photo? Are you going to say he has a beard because he didn't have time to shave? And Defne! That tops everything. To me it sounds like they sold her off. For goodness' sake, Samo! Now you're going too far, Mom objected. They spent the summer in Sarajevo and the girl fell in love. And maybe, well, you know, she got pregnant. I suppose, Dad said and marched into the kitchen, where he poured himself a glass of schnapps. This was the first time I'd seen my father take the bottle he kept for guests, pour himself a glass, and down it in a single gulp. Then he switched on the TV and didn't say anything else.

I am trying to figure out when everything changed. Was it when Rok and I were talking about the movies we'd seen? Or when we were sitting in the park with Hana and Lea and Meri and passing around a bottle of white wine? Or when Hana was tutoring me in chemistry? Or when Aunt Marija was admiring her new automatic washing machine? Or when my cousin Janez was polishing his Opel Kadett? Or when Uncle Gorazd was installing his chips and circuits? Or when we thought Grandpa would die but in the end he pulled through and now he looks like he could live to be a hundred? Or when we were waiting for wireless phones and compact discs to arrive? Or when people started coming to Uncle Boštjan with questions and asking him to show them the unmarked graves in the forest? Or when I learned that Sršen's father was not just an ordinary State Security agent but that he had a particular assignment, and twenty years ago, he was given the apartment where he lives because the man in the apartment above him had to be kept under surveillance since, although he was old, he was dangerous? Or when I couldn't imagine how the old man on the fifth floor could be a danger to the country? Or when Aunt Taja was shuddering to think that some other Aziz might go nuts, pick up a rifle, and shoot her son? Or when I was still waiting to have my first real girlfriend?

33

A FEW DAYS ago, when I was in town, I ran into Sršen. My first thought was that the man taking care of the grocery carts in the basement of Maximarket looks a lot like Sršen. His big bristly head and protruding ears caught my eye. He also walked like him. I said to myself, That man is the spitting image of Sršen, and the thought of him gave me chills. Then a second later when I got closer, I saw that it actually was Sršen. I quickly said hi as I walked past. I didn't want to stop and I hoped he wouldn't even notice, but no, Sršen ran after me, placed a heavy hand on my shoulder, and said, It's nice to see you, kid! Don't get the wrong idea. He squeezed out some spit from between his teeth. This is just a cover. I didn't ask what kind of cover it was or what he was really doing. How are you, he asked, as he walked alongside me. I'm fine. I wagged my head and stopped. Suddenly Sršen didn't seem as big as he used to be. He was still taller than me, but I had the feeling he had spread out. Before it was only his head that was big, but now his rear was too. He

SEBASTIJAN PREGELJ

was in loose jeans and work boots, with the store's white smock over a plaid shirt.

This is the best spot in the city, he said. You learn everything here. Information is gold if you know what to do with it. He brought his finger to the tip of his nose and smiled. That's all I'm telling you. Nothing else. You're still going to school like a good kid, right? Yes, I said. That's good, he said and gave me a poke. Because you're smart. Of all those little faggots we used to pick on, you were the only smart one. You can go far, he said protectively. You just have to learn. Learn what? Well, you have to learn what pays and what doesn't pay. Do some calculations. Know what I'm saying? Think back a little. He wrinkled his forehead. How many times did you get a beating from me for no good reason? Well, you got it because you're stubborn. Because you didn't want to listen. If you had listened to me, you wouldn't have gotten it. But since you didn't, I had no choice. I had to give you the same beating the others got. Because of them, not because of you. And I felt bad about it, too, because I liked you. He grabbed the back of my neck and gave it a squeeze. Come by some afternoon at three, when I get off. Or some evening at nine. We can go for a beer and I'll tell you more. If you're interested. I nodded and told him I was running late. Of course, Sršen said. He let me go and, almost simultaneously, pulled out a pack of cigarettes, lit one, took a drag, and said softly, See you, kid.

On my way to school I thought how, after all these years, it was still unpleasant running into Sršen. I knew it would be a long time before I again took the passageway under Maximarket, where it always smelled of white, fluffy loaves of bread as light as clouds, which people were prepared to wait hours and hours for.

Now I am lying in my bed thinking about Sršen and his father, that grim old man in a raincoat with a hat on his head and tinted glasses on his nose. The body under the raincoat has shrunk; that's easy to see. Not very long ago he still seemed powerful and dangerous. Now, suddenly, he's a little old man. I've noticed the same thing with lots of other people. It happens fast, overnight almost. One day a person is the same as ever, and the next they're someone else entirely, at best a shadow of themselves. That's exactly what happened to old Sršen. He changed overnight into a little old man. But a nasty and spiteful old man. At least that's the way he seems. So even now, when I see him on the street, I still try to avoid him.

His name has come up several times recently in conversations between my father and uncle. Whenever they get together, they talk about how some things are changing fast, like technology, for example, which we can barely keep up with. Other things, meanwhile, remain the same, like the State Security Service. You don't want to have anything to do with those guys, not even today, Uncle Gorazd says. Military intelligence too—they're constantly sniffing around our offices and labs. I don't know if they understand anything, but that only make matters worse.

Dad and Uncle Gorazd say that there's no shortage of people like old Sršen. And it's not just old men. They have younger colleagues in their ranks too.

Whenever they talk about old Sršen and his comrades, Uncle Gorazd will flick his lighter for no good reason and say they're still holding all the reins. Maybe recently we've gotten the

SEBASTIJAN PREGELJ

feeling they're easing up, but it's not true. The moment they start to feel threatened, they'll tighten their grip again. They're not going to allow any changes, at least not the kind that would put them in a worse position.

Uncle Gorazd says State Security agents listen in on a huge number of telephone calls. How do you know that, Dad asks, although he knows where this is going because they always talk about the same thing. How do I know? My uncle's voice goes up a notch. We make the bugs. There are two types of microphones. One goes in telephone receivers, and the other, which is a little bigger, can go anywhere else. That second type is most often installed in a corner behind a wardrobe or cabinet. Somewhere no one will find it. I tell you, we don't make these microphones for the hell of it. And if you ask me, they're not just tapping truly suspicious people. Anyone can end up on their list. They install these listening devices in homes and offices, vacation cottages, hotel rooms. Everywhere.

Dad and Uncle Gorazd say old Sršen is one of them. At home he has headphones and a tape recorder. He listens and records what happens in the apartment above him. There's at least one such Sršen in every apartment building. Someone who's always listening. Recording. Taking notes. Making copies. Reporting. So, no, I wouldn't say they're easing up, my uncle says, shaking his head. They're just giving us the feeling that they are. For the most part, people are happy with the little they have. It's enough that they can cross the border to buy things. They're happy that nowadays they're not hassled so much by customs officials. Some things you smuggle in, other things you pay duty on. Most people think that's fair. Everybody complains about the economy and politics, but nobody does anything. It's like we're waiting for things to happen on their own. But Samo, nothing happens on its own! You know that. You're a historian. Besides, we're not young anymore. We can wait another ten or twenty years, only by then we'll be well past fifty—almost sixty in fact. It'll be easier for Martin and Jan, Dad says. Changes need time. Or a revolution. But you don't want another revolution.

You don't want another revolution, Dad repeats. The émigrés in the Americas and the dissidents in Germany are getting louder and louder. People who fled in the nick of time and others who survived the postwar massacres are starting to raise their heads. Do you really want them to come back? Do you really want them to make the changes? I don't, Dad says firmly. If they make changes, it'll be like it was before the war. That's all they know. And besides, I have no doubt they'll take revenge. They think it's their right. The Home Guard, the Ustaše, the Četniks—they'll all return to Yugoslavia. And, you see, we don't need them. If they return, we won't be going forward; we'll go backward. It'll be 1941 again, and again everything will start over. And I don't want that for myself or for my son, Dad says, frowning. But does that mean I have to support the party, the army, and the State Security Service? You see, it's not that simple. Dad gives Uncle Gorazd a light punch on the shoulder, a sign that it's time to go on the balcony for a smoke. They don't talk about these things on the balcony. Somebody could overhear them. You never know. So when they're outside, they talk about entirely different things.

Whenever my uncle and father are talking about changes, I always listen. They talk in a way where you can't tell if the people they're talking about are good or bad. The good people are also bad in a way, and the bad people are also good in a way. So how do you decide? At school we're learning about external and internal enemies. We're learning about separatists and irredentists. We're learning that they are bad. The difference is that we know our external enemies—we know who they are and can prepare ourselves against them—whereas the enemies who live among us we mostly don't know. That's why internal enemies are more dangerous. This is what our socialism teacher tells us. This is what our national defense teacher tells us. So I eat up everything I hear at home. My father and uncle always tell me I must never breathe a word of anything I hear them say, not at school or anywhere else. But I'm old enough that they don't have to tell me that. I know what to say and what not to say. Still, my father and uncle are careful. They tell me you can never be too careful.

When I listen in on their conversations, my ideas about old Sršen only get wilder. In my mind I see him cautiously opening his door, slipping into the hallway, and hurrying up the stairs. He stops for a moment in front of the door to the apartment above his and quickly rings the bell. Convinced his neighbor is not at home, he then uses a special tool to unlock the door and, like an old cat, slips into the apartment. I see him putting on gloves. Then, with well-practiced movements, he takes the telephone receiver apart, removes the old microphone, and replaces it with a new one. He frequently checks his watch. He wouldn't want his neighbor to surprise him. When the receiver is again in one piece, he places it on the cradle. He glances at the bookcase in the living room. He runs his eyes across the titles of the books. The only thing that looks suspicious is a book with its spine turned toward the wall. Old Sršen is an experienced old cat; he knows it's a trap. Nevertheless, he takes the book from the shelf, looks at the title, and smiles; then he returns it to where it was and carefully nudges it in a little so it's not quite even with the other books. He installs another new microphone in the hanging lamp above the kitchen table, another behind the chest in the living room, and a third one in the lamp on the nightstand in the bedroom. The last bug he installs in the air duct in the bathroom and cautiously leaves the apartment. Back at home, he puts on his headphones and makes sure that all five microphones are working properly. He nods with satisfaction and switches on the tape recorder. He stores the old microphones in a desk drawer.

I sometimes talk about such things with my classmate Matej. What do State Security agents actually do? Are they like James Bond, with numbers instead of names? Do they carry special weapons? Do they drive fast cars equipped with all kinds of gadgets? Do they often shoot people? And if they do, then why don't we hear anything about it? Obviously, the television stations and newspapers don't report such incidents. But if they do occur, then people would surely hear something about them and there would be rumors. Like the way people know something about the postwar massacres, or the apparitions in Medjugorje and the messages from Mary, or the books that are smuggled into the country and then get passed from person to person, hand to hand. I still remember the title of one of these books: *Tito—Angel or Devil?* Someone had driven down from Austria with a whole trunk of them. When they were being loaded into his car, he didn't know what he would be transporting. That's *our* business, he was told. And this was enough for him. He was lucky. When he got to the border, neither the police nor the customs officers ordered him to open the trunk. It was probably late at night and the man in the car was alone and didn't seem at all suspicious. It wasn't until he got home that he realized what he had driven across the border. People usually succeed if they aren't aware of the danger, Matej said, as if he was an expert on the subject. If the man had known what he was carrying, he would have been nervous. And his nerves would have given him away. Police and customs officers smell fear like dogs. In any case, half an hour later, three or four cars pulled up to his apartment building. The books were loaded into the cars, which then disappeared into the night. Later, one by one, the books started circulating through the population.

Matej says communism will die like a starved dog. Then we'll have capitalism and democracy. He says only then will we see any real possibilities open up for us. He also says Slovenia will split from Yugoslavia and become an independent state. My father and uncle also talk about this from time to time. Only when they do it sounds more like wishful thinking, but when Matej talks about this, it sounds like everything is ready and it could happen at any moment.

Matej lives across town. His parents have a house in Ljubljana and an apartment on the coast, in Piran, which they call their weekend getaway. When Matej's parents are at their weekend getaway and Matej is home alone, we all get together at his place. He invites some of his classmates to come over, both guys and girls. And his old friends from primary school also come.

Matej does his best to get us to mingle, and he partly succeeds. Among the guys, I've chatted a few times with Gregor, who's a guitarist with his own band. They used to play punk, but now they're into heavy metal. The next time they have a concert, I'll be there. Among the girls, Natalija caught my eye; she has long hair and goes to the Secondary School of Natural Sciences. Natalija always comes alone. I'm sure that if she had a boyfriend, she would bring him. Other girls bring their boyfriends and occasionally some of the guys bring their girlfriends. Whenever we get together, we first go to a grocery store nearby, where we get what we'll need for the party. The guys stick to beer and Stock brandy, the girls to screwdrivers. Personally, I don't care. I try not to get drunk, or if I do, at least not right away. That's why I drink Stock and Cokes. I pour the Coke almost to the top, with just a splash of brandy, no more. When the glass is full, you can't tell how much is soda and how much is Stock. The guys leave me alone. The ones who drink beer always have a full bottle in their hand. You can see how much beer is in the bottle. You know how many bottles everyone's drunk. Even before one bottle is empty, they're already holding the next. That's why the beer drinkers are the first to pass out. From time to time someone throws up. If he gets to the toilet on time, all's well.

Most of the girls at Matej's parties smoke, even the ones who normally wouldn't. And we all smoke when Robert brings weed. The joint is passed from person to person. To me the weed always seems the same, but some people like to stare at the glowing mix of cannabis and tobacco and state with authority that it's even better than last time. Some people get stoned very quickly. Then they wander around with their arms stretched out, grinning and laughing until they drop onto the sofa or knock something off a shelf or run into a wall and lie still. But I don't know. Maybe I don't know how to smoke it properly or maybe it doesn't affect me so much. All I get is a disgusting aftertaste in my mouth.

It's Friday and I'm sitting with Matej on his terrace. While the other guys are in the living room looking at the new records Gregor has brought and the girls are in the kitchen preparing snacks, Matej and I, like always, are talking about Secret Security agents. Matej keeps saying they're toothless dogs. No need to be afraid of them. I don't know, I say. We've got one living on our street and I always hate running into him. Really? Matej looks at me from under his brow. I tell him about old Sršen and the man who lives above him. Now that's interesting. Matej scratches his head. I'd really like to get into his apartment. He's an old man, I say. You might find a book or maybe a letter or something— I don't mean the old man above him, Matej breaks in. I mean the agent. *His* apartment? I'm surprised. Why? What do you think you'd see? I don't know what I'd see, Matej says, grinning. I have no idea what to expect. But I'd like to get into his apartment. I'm sure I'd discover something. Forget it! I shake my head. Oh yeah? Matej smiles. Let me tell you: you can get into any apartment. And you don't have to wait for the guy to leave. No need to break in. Listen. He leans over to me. I can ring his doorbell and say I'm there to read the gas meter, or the electric meter or something. But it doesn't take very long to read a meter, he says, more to himself than to me. I have an even better idea! I can say I'm writing an article for the school newspaper. Get it? I can ask him for an interview. Do you think he'd agree? What would you tell him? I frown. That you're investigating how State Security agents live? Well, not that! Matej smiles. But I could say I'm writing an article about the last days of the war or something similar. Don't you think he was a Partisan? Don't you think he was around then? Well, he's not *that* old. I shrug and do a quick calculation of how old old Sršen would have been at the end of the war. Sixteen, I say. Sixteen what? Matej doesn't follow me. Well, off the top of my head, I'd guess he would have been sixteen or seventeen when the war ended, I tell him. Well, there you go. Matej is satisfied. Back then everyone was a Partisan. It didn't matter if you were sixteen, fifteen, or sixty-five, you could still be a Partisan. Why not? If he wasn't a Partisan, he was at least a message boy.

I would have told Matej more about old Sršen if some girls didn't just then come out onto the terrace. One of them is Natalija, who glances at me and smiles. I sit there for another minute; then I get up and go over to her. It looks like she is intentionally standing a little apart from the other girls. She says that it's finally Friday and Friday is the best day of the week. Saturday is still good, but Sunday already gives me a bad taste, because the next day is Monday. So Friday is definitely the best day. And now here we are again! She smiles. And I get to see you again, I blurt out and a moment later regret it. Natalija smiles and tells me not to overdo it.

Meanwhile, the guys are passing around the cover of *Fatal Portrait*. Gregor is saying it's an indisputable classic, even if it is a new release. With some albums you just know right away they're a classic. Others need time to acquire that status. But most are ordinary shit that gets played for a year or two, or not even that long, and then everyone forgets about it. But *Fatal Portrait* is a classic. The music is blasting from the speakers, but everyone is mostly listening to and assessing King Diamond's screeching voice, which some of the guys like but most don't, although nobody says this because Gregor is insisting it's a classic and they think they just need to get used to it. The girls, meanwhile, are in the kitchen having their own sort of fun.

Natalija takes my hand and leads me to the front hall. She leans against the wall, pulls me over to her, and kisses me. Her kisses are moist; she is soon out of breath, as if she just ran the 100-meter dash. Then she grabs my hands and moves them to her breasts. I can feel her stiff nipples. I can feel myself getting hard. She bites me lightly on my lower lip, and I try to reach under her top, but she stops me. Not so fast, big guy, she whispers and bites my neck. Come with me. She gently pushes me off her and hurries up the stairs. Suddenly we're in the bathroom. Natalija switches on the light above the sink and turns on the water in the tub, which starts to fill. She kisses me like it's the last day on earth. What you do today, you do, and what you don't do, you miss out on. I'm scared I'm going to come before anything even happens.

Natalija takes off her top, grabs my shirt, and yanks it over my head. She presses herself against me. She's still in her bra, but even so it feels like she's naked. So, she smiles, aren't you going to take it off me? I kiss her shoulder and reach behind her back. I don't know a thing about undoing a bra. I struggle with it a bit. I hope she won't notice. But she notices. Not much experience, huh, she whispers and unfastens it herself. Now I feel her breasts against my chest. I feel her tongue playing with mine. My head is spinning a little. As Natalija is licking my lips and my chest, I try to think of anything else. I close my eyes.

My mind is a complete blank. I can't think what to think about. Even with my eyes shut, I can still see Natalija's breasts, still feel her tongue and her breath, and I think I'm going to explode. But then from somewhere, the image of old Sršen steals into view. That old bastard is the answer, I think with relief. Never have I been so glad to see him.

As if I'm watching it in a movie, old Sršen drives up in a dark-colored car and parks a couple of doors down from Matej's parents' house. It's Friday afternoon and the State Security agent knows that on Fridays Matej's parents go to Piran. Sometimes their son accompanies them, but sometimes he doesn't, so the agent is cautious. About an hour later, when the family car drives away from the house, the old man steps out of his vehicle, leans against the hood, and lights a cigarette. He takes a few puffs, then strolls over to the metal gate in front of the house. He rings the bell twice and waits. When no one answers, he tosses the cigarette to the ground, steps on it, opens the gate, and enters the front yard. At the door, he again rings the bell. As expected, nothing happens. The house is empty. He pulls a leather case out of his pocket where he keeps a small tool, which he uses to unlock the door.

Soon old Sršen is in the front hall. He quickly looks around; then he goes into the living room, where the telephone is. Now the game begins. Although he has plenty of time, since the house will be empty until Sunday afternoon, he works quickly and carefully. First, he installs some bugs on the ground floor; then he goes upstairs. Just as he thought, there's a second phone in

Matej's parents' bedroom. He installs another listening device there and, while he's at it, looks through the contents of the nightstand on Matej's father's side; then he moves on—to the study and Matej's room. He puts a bug in every room. When he finally comes to the bathroom, he's surprised there's a fan in the air duct. But the old bastard has installed bugs in all kinds of places. The fan is nothing but a small hiccup in an otherwise routine procedure. He quickly looks around and decides on the bottom edge of the cabinet where they keep towels and cosmetics. He gets down on his knees and carefully positions the microphone. Then he lifts himself up, runs his hands over his knees, and straightens his back. Nodding with satisfaction, his eyes fall on the bathtub. It is wider and longer than an ordinary bathtub. He thinks to himself, They sure like their luxuries in this house. That old couple had this sort of tub put in because they like playing their little games in the bathroom. He knows what pigs like them get up to. And as for the son—oh yes, without a doubt the boy brings girls here. And he sometimes lets a friend use it too, to mess around with some young tart. A friend like Jan. The old man lifts his head. Our eyes meet.

34

I'M SPENDING THE first week of February at my grandfather's. We all drove up together Saturday morning; then, in the evening, Mom and Dad went home and I stayed. Grandpa and I watched the news, had a quick supper, and went to bed. Grandpa goes to bed early and gets up early. He usually gets up at dawn. He says it's the most beautiful time of day. I don't get up that early.

I read for a while in bed; then I turn off the light and sink into the darkness. I listen to the soft ticking of the old wall clock, which Grandpa's grandfather brought back from Vienna more than a hundred years ago. People say he was smart enough for two. First, he finished the four-year primary school in the village, where the parish priest noticed how intelligent he was. The priest talked to the parents about the boy; then he sent him to school in Ljubljana. After a few years, the boy was sent from Ljubljana to Vienna. Nobody remembers exactly what he studied or even if he got his degree. He probably didn't, because if he had, there would be a framed diploma hanging somewhere in the house or, what's more likely, he never would have returned to the village and not only would there be no framed diploma, there would be no wall clock either. Whatever happened, ten years later Grandpa's grandfather came home. With him he brought one suitcase full of fancy clothes and another full of books, and, in a big knapsack, a pendulum clock, which he simply called his *pendulum*, which is what Grandpa still calls it. In those days a clock cost a small fortune, so people came from far and wide to the house to see the *pendulum*. Grandpa's grandfather was not the only person who owned a clock, but his clock was the only one of its kind anywhere around. And to me it still is.

Painted on the clock there is a picture of a woman in light-blue clothes; she is wearing a hat and has a pink face, pink hands, and red lips. There is a landscape in the background, and everything is framed by a lacy border, which looks like it could be pure gold, more for a church than for a picture on a clock. Just as the clock's thin metal pendulum moves back and forth, so too do the dark eyes of the woman in the hat. Left, right, left, right. To the end of time, for as long as somebody keeps winding the clock.

The clock chimes once every half hour, and on the hour it chimes the time. Two metal weights keep the clock from stopping. Grandpa pulls them up every morning, always making sure they don't knock against the casing. When I was little, I often asked him if I could pull the thin chains that move the weights, but he never let me. It wasn't until he decided I was old enough, and had the proper feeling in my hands, that he softened. After that, whenever I was here during summer vacation, it was my job to wind the pendulum.

Many years from now, the old wall clock will resurface in my memory. I will remember its soft ticking, its metallic chiming, and the moving eyes of the woman in the hat. And after Grandpa's death, when the house is empty, I will tell my mother I would like to have the old clock. At first she'll be reluctant; she'll say she doesn't know if she can take it, but eventually my father will support me. He'll say that if anybody wanted it they would have taken it by now, but they probably all think it's junk. So it's better if Jan has it than if one of the uncles tosses it into the attic or the trash because it's not as precise as a Japanese digital clock. And so, many years later, Grandpa's clock will come to me.

Now I am lying in bed sinking into the darkness. Even now, when Grandma is no longer here, the bed linen in Grandpa's house has a very particular smell. The cloth is not as soft as at home, but it smells much nicer. Mom says this is because Grandpa dries the laundry outside, near the meadows and forest. It's the same with Grandpa's bread. It's not as soft as the bread we buy at home, but it smells much better. Grandpa has a small electric mill in the basement, which he uses to grind grain into coarse flour; he makes the dough and bakes the loaves in a bread oven, just as he and Grandma used to do. Grandpa's bread is black on the bottom and has a hard crust. When I was little, Grandma used to cut the crust off for me because I couldn't bite into it. But the inside of the bread smells better than any cake. It's the same with Grandpa's hands. They're big and covered in deep wrinkles and cracks, never pink but always brown, and darker in the cracks, but they are warm and soft when he hugs me or strokes my head.

In the morning, I dress quickly and run across the snowy yard. Grandpa is in a small workshop behind the barn. In the past, he would only be in the workshop in the winter and then only when the weather was bad, when it was impossible to work outside. But these days he often stays inside even when it's warm and sunny. When I was little, I used to spend whole days with him in this workshop. While Grandpa made trellis posts for vineyards, I would play with the leftover pieces of wood. Grandpa would tie the posts into bundles of ten. Each time he had a bundle, he'd smile and say, A hundred dinars. That's how much he got for ten wooden posts.

What are you making, I ask as I enter the workshop. Grandpa looks at me and says, I made a wheel bolt. He tells me the back wheel on the cart has been wobbling for a while. So now I made a new bolt for it and I think it'll be okay.

On Tuesday morning Uncle Boštjan stops by. He's delighted to see me. He asks me when I arrived, how long I'm staying, and how school is going. Then he asks Grandpa what we've been doing. While we're telling him, he nods and says, Uh-huh, uh-huh . . . uh-huh, uh-huh. When we don't have anything more to tell him, Uncle Boštjan scratches his neck and says to Grandpa that *those people* were here again this morning. Same folks as last time, two men and a woman. Again they were asking me questions. They said I didn't have to answer, but not saying anything wouldn't help anyone, not them and not me. At most, it would only help the people who committed the crimes. All they wanted from me was to tell them where their relatives were.

Same folks as last time, you say? Grandpa stares at Uncle Boštjan. And what did you tell them? I said I didn't have time now and, besides, there's snow and ice and it's not safe. They said I shouldn't be afraid because times are changing. A lot of things are going to change. Then they said goodbye, got into their car, and drove to the forest. They turned onto the path and went from there on foot. So what do you think? Uncle Boštjan looks at Grandpa. Should I tell them what I know? I think it's time, Grandpa says with a nod. I think we'll have to start talking about this too. Then he stops, as if Grandma had just walked in. Grandma never put up with any talk about *those things*. What *those things* exactly are I've been trying to piece together from the bits and pieces I hear now and then. Whenever they talk about *those things*, they lower their voices. They're talking about things that happened during the war and right after it. They're talking about the Partisans and Home Guard, the Italians and the Germans; they're whispering about the people the Partisans killed during the war and right after it.

I know you lost a brother, my uncle says. No need to mention Lojze, Grandpa says, shaking his head. The war took people from all of us. We were also lucky. We lost Lojze, but the rest of us survived. Our family came out of it all right, even though we had people on both sides, and either side could have killed us. Or maybe that's why they left us alone. I don't know. You didn't really have a choice, Grandpa says. You went with whoever found you at home. That's how Lojze went off with the White Guard, and me with the Reds. It could've been the reverse. They knew about the two of us. They had everyone counted and listed. Also, there were people in the village who passed on information to one side or the other or both. Like a lot of other boys, Lojze and I tried to hide. But we both ended up going off with an army. Lojze was sixteen; I was fifteen. I came back; Lojze didn't. Mama would go around to people who knew something, but they didn't want to tell her anything. At first, they were silent, but later they told her to stop asking, stop digging. You lost one son, but you still have one left. Many people lost all their sons and all their daughters. You still have one. In the end, we all had a pretty clear idea where Lojze was. If he had been able to save himself, he would have let us know he was alive. If he had gone to Austria, he would have written to us. If he had gone to America, he would have written to us. But Lojze didn't write to us. That's just the way it was.

What happened, I ask. My uncle looks at me and says, The people who surrendered and the people who were captured— they were killed. With no mercy. They were shot and thrown like dead cats into ravines and caves. Brother killing brother. People could hear the shooting. The shooting went on in the forest for a few weeks after the war ended. It was mostly at night. During the day it was like nothing was happening. Of course, people knew very well what was happening, but they were frightened and didn't dare go into the forest. They refused to even think about it, let alone talk about it. They stayed home, said nothing, and were happy to be left alone. Four years of war had been enough. And when it was all over and there were no more gunshots coming from the forest, and the Partisan army had left, they still didn't go into the forest. They never went there again.

Later, every so often, a Partisan veteran might say something in a bar. One might start boasting, another might start crying and ask the relatives to forgive him. Uncle Boštjan frowns. But people just turned away. They didn't want to hear. They knew this was a moment of weakness and the next day everything would be the same as before.

They were all victims, Grandpa says. Even the ones who did the shooting. For them it was maybe worse than for the ones who ended up in the ravines. I knew a few of them, and one or two are still alive. Do you think they shot them because they wanted to? Let me tell you, they never had a moment's peace afterward. They were afraid to shut their eyes. And the older they got, the worse it got. The dead, they said, are coming back. They said they were climbing out of the ravines, coming to the village, and knocking on their doors and windows. Many of them put a bullet in their own heads because they couldn't take it anymore. A few are still alive. Grandpa nods at his own words. But don't ask me to tell you who! Just like I didn't tell our side after the war which of our neighbors were with the Whites, I have no intention of saying now who did any shooting. But let's leave it. Grandpa waves his arm. And not talk about this in front of the boy.

Soon it won't be a secret anymore, Uncle Boštjan says. People have started coming here and asking me if I know anything, and if I don't then who does, and who would be willing to say something. If I don't say anything, somebody else will. I know, Grandpa says. The time has come. We'll let the ghosts come out of the forest. But what I'm afraid of is that then there will be no more peace. Up to now one side has always been in the right, and now the other side will try to prove *they* were in the right. I'm afraid it'll be brother against brother again. I'm afraid it's all repeating itself. But you can tell them what you know. You weren't there. You're not guilty of anything, not what one side did or what the other side did. You're too young. But you know what you heard from us old folks. And you know where the places are that no one ever goes.

After he says this, Grandpa walks over to the stove and puts the water on for coffee.

Uncle Boštjan leaves at around eleven, but Grandpa remains in a serious mood. There is worry in his eyes. It's best if I don't ask him anything. It's best if I keep quiet.

35

MARTIN WAS HERE not long ago on a ten-day leave. He said it's a fucking mess, especially in Kosovo, which is where they sent him after Zadar. There are war conditions there although nobody ever talks about it. Somehow he'll survive. Some guys don't. When we asked him what he meant, he told us it was like he said. Some don't survive. They're sent home in sealed caskets. Nobody talks about it. You only find out if you know someone.

Until recently, the army was said to be the living tissue that held together the nations and nationalities of Yugoslavia. Now all at once you hear how officers are coming down hard on Albanian and Slovenian recruits in particular. More and more draftees are thinking about how to avoid the army, but it's not so easy. You either need good and reliable connections or, once you're in the army, you have to fake a nervous breakdown. You can also pretend to have mental problems, and then you don't have to go into the army at all, but it'll be on your record for the rest of your life. Most guys don't want that because later it's awkward to have to always explain you only did it to get out of serving in the army. Martin said that, personally, he hasn't had any special problem with the officers, and there aren't any Albanians in his unit so he can't say what it's like for them. Albanian recruits don't stay in Kosovo; they're mostly sent to Montenegro, Serbia, and Bosnia.

Sršen's military service, I heard, was postponed a few times. His father must have contacted one of his old friends and arranged things. In the end, however, Sršen had to go into the army just like other guys, but then he came back after only a few weeks. I don't know what happened and, frankly, I don't care.

We haven't seen my aunt and uncle since Martin went back. Dad calls Uncle Gorazd now and then to ask how he is, how Taja is, if he's spoken to Martin at all, and whether we'll see each other anytime soon. Uncle Gorazd says he and Taja are fine, and that Martin's also fine, all things considered, but that things have become tense at work. They have him on a new project. Dad asks what sort of project it is. Uncle Gorazd says he's not allowed to say. You're not making atomic bombs, are you, Dad asks to get a rise out of him. Or are you? Don't talk nonsense! My uncle is angry. Especially not on the phone! You know what telephones are like! For fuck's sake!

In March there is a surprise. Mikhail Gorbachev, the leader of the Soviet Union, visits Yugoslavia. People talk about him like he's a movie star. Ljubljana is his first stop. At school, in our first class, the socialism teacher talks to us about it; beaming with excitement, he says more than once that this is a historic moment. Up to now only two Soviet leaders have ever visited Yugoslavia: Nikita Khrushchev and Leonid Brezhnev.

Brezhnev visited our country no less than three times, our teacher exclaims. He and Tito were very close. At Tito's funeral, which was attended by all the major world leaders, Brezhnev was accorded a special honor. He sat in Tito's six-door Mercedes limousine. That tells you everything. And now Gorbachev is here!

The teacher says a few words about this man who began his career working in a factory and then studied law. I'm not really interested so I only half listen, and then by the end of class I've forgotten everything I heard. I wouldn't have given Gorbachev a second thought if my father, when he was watching the evening news, hadn't started screaming and shouting for Mom and me to come quick. We both run into the living room, terrified that something horrible has happened. Like a heart attack. Or a stroke. Or the start of World War III. Or I don't know what else. But it's nothing of the sort. Dad is sitting there in the armchair, leaning forward and pointing at the screen, where we see Mikhail Gorbachev's bald head with that purplish blotch in the middle. Look, Dad is shouting. Do you see? Then it happens. The camera rotates a little and, for a split second, right next to Gorbachev, we get a glimpse of Uncle Gorazd. It's my brother, he cries. Do you see?

The last time Dad was shouting in front of the television like this was when Jure Franko skied his second run at the Sarajevo Olympics. But then I was shouting with him. Now Mom and I just stare in silence at the television screen. Seeing Uncle Gorazd on the evening news really is a surprise, but it's not enough of one to make me start shouting and jumping up and down. But it's different with Dad. Even when the camera shifts back to the general secretary of the Soviet Communist Party, he's still shrieking, Gorazd and Gorbachev! Do you see? Do you see?

There will be more talk about Gorbachev's visit. In the years and decades to follow, it will grow into a legend, one that goes something like this: Iskra Delta was a high-tech company that organized the automation of numerous Yugoslav factories; it was also one of the first companies to manufacture a personal computer. That is one side of the story. The other side is more interesting. Under the careful monitoring of agents from the State Security Service and military counterintelligence, Slovenian computer scientists developed the basis for the information network used by the Chinese to connect the police stations in China's biggest cities. A large number of Chinese then started appearing in Ljubljana, but no one was really interested or upset by this. At the same time as the Chinese, American and Russian spies also began arriving. The Chinese lived in a student dormitory, while the Russians and Americans lived in hotels. If it had been purely a matter of economic interests, the company would have continued to develop and grow, but the geopolitical and intelligence interests were more powerful. The Americans feared that knowledge could be leaked to the Russians through the company, while the Russians were calculating that if the company failed, they would be able to snap up some highly trained specialists. Gorbachev's visit represented the beginning of the end. The State Security Service faced a dilemma of conflicting interests. The decision was made overnight. The agency prevented the company director from meeting with Gorbachev and withdrew its support and assistance from the company. Instead of the director, the general secretary met with my uncle. The Soviet leader's visit remained in the news a couple more weeks, but when the excitement died down, the company, far from the eyes of the public, waded into financial difficulties and quietly collapsed. The Chinese immediately disappeared from the city, followed by the Americans and, last of all, the Russians.

My father telephones my uncle as soon as the news is over. Congratulations, he shouts into the receiver. Mom, from the kitchen door, gestures to him to keep his voice down because the entire building can hear him. Now I see why you don't have any time, Dad says at the end of their conversation.

Personally, I don't care that much. I am lying on my bed paging through *Mladina*. Matej buys this magazine every week and then talks on and on about everything he's read in it. So a few days ago I bought a copy. Most of the articles I don't find particularly interesting and I can barely understand them. I quickly reach the end. I stash the magazine under my bed and stare at my dresser, where, from a different time altogether, I still have Superman, Luke Skywalker, and Darth Vader. If Mom had her way, they would have long ago been put away in a cardboard box somewhere in our storage unit, or, even worse, she would have given them to some kid who has no idea who they are. He wouldn't have given a second thought to breaking their arms and legs and finally pulling off their heads. They don't bother me, and they don't bother the friends who come to see me. And none of the girls from my class who have been in my room has ever said anything about them either. So Superman, Luke Skywalker, and Darth Vader will remain on my dresser for a long time to come.

36

A FEW DAYS ago, the State Security Service made several arrests in the city, working in conjunction with the military. Two journalists from *Mladina* and a junior officer are now sitting in a military prison. They have been accused of publishing military secrets. People have been out protesting ever since. Matej and I have been to a few of these protests. While to me it doesn't seem like there are many protesters and I don't think a handful of people will change anything, Matej is excited. He says there are more and more people each time. Just look around! If it keeps up like this, next week there'll be a hundred of us. And a hundred is not a small number!

We see more of my aunt and uncle these days. Uncle Gorazd complains about the conditions at work. He says he's constantly under the eyes of officers from military counterintelligence. Colonel Nikolovski is no longer around and Knežević has been replaced by someone named Nikolić. My uncle says Nikolić is like a vicious dog. He digs his teeth in and doesn't know how to let go. Dad asks him what's going on, but my uncle says he's not allowed to say because under the new rules everything that happens at the company is a military secret. And, well, you see how things are today; those fellows got their hands on some minor document that had been designated a military secret and now look where they are. In prison. If I tell you more, I'll be considered guilty and so will you, he says, shaking his head. Then he and my father go outside, have a smoke, and talk about other things.

I can hardly wait for the weekend, when we'll be at Matej's. Each time I hope Natalija will be there too. She basically acts like nothing happened, but what we did in Matej's parents' bathroom has happened twice since. Once on the steps to the basement and another time in the garage on the hood of the family car. Natalija says she likes the danger. Sex in bed is for old people, she told me a couple of weeks ago as she bit my ear, grabbed me by the hand, and pulled me after her. It's boring. If you yield to passion somewhere people can catch you, that is something else entirely. The very thought of fucking on the stairs behind the door makes me completely wet. I feel like Matej knows what's going on and so does everybody else. Natalija is loud. When she's about to climax, the veins in her neck stand out, she gets red blotches on her breasts, her nails dig into my back, and she starts shouting.

Other than at Matej's, Natalija and I don't see each other. I would like to see her more often, but she says she doesn't want any sort of relationship. She says life should be enjoyed in the here and now. Nobody knows what tomorrow will bring. As for me, I would be happy knowing that I would see her tomorrow. But I won't. That's why I can hardly wait for the weekends when we get together at Matej's.

Matej isn't so much interested in women as he is in the demonstrations organized by the Committee for Human Rights. He says something has to give soon. Things can't stay the way they are. You'll see.

My parents are worried. They know Matej and I go to the military court building on Roška Street, which is where the protests are held in support of the political prisoners. They say it's going to cause me problems in the army and with getting into university. They love sending boys like you and Matej to Kosovo, my father tells me. You can be sure that there have been undercover cops taking pictures of everyone right from the start. Martin told you what it's like in Kosovo, in case you forgot. And remember this too. Matej's parents may have connections somewhere, but we don't. So you'll have to go wherever they send you.

I'm not worried about the army. There's plenty of time for things to change before I have to do my service. Maybe they'll even end mandatory service. Some people are saying Yugoslavia should replace the draft system with a professional army. If that happens, I'm not going anywhere.

Today at school, at the start of our last class, the history teacher said that history is happening on the streets. Here and now. Anyone who wants to go to Roška Street can go. He left the classroom door open behind him. Naturally, we all left. Most students went home or into town, but some of us went to the military court building.

Now it's not just fifty or a hundred protesters in front of the yellow building. Matej says there are at least a thousand of us. A thousand, he cries, tugging excitedly at my sleeve.

A tall man with a beard reads out the demands of the Committee for Human Rights. This is followed by a few short speeches by others. The sound system isn't very good and I can't make out much. Despite this, I clap loudly when the others clap and boo when the others boo. Somebody unfurls the flag of the Socialist Republic of Slovenia on the stage, but with the red star cut out of it. We're all waiting to see what will happen. We expect the police to move in and remove both the flag and the man who is waving it, but they don't. Maybe it's because there are so many of us. The small groups of policemen are merely observing the situation from the side.

When the demonstration is over, everybody goes their separate ways. Matej is beside himself. He keeps on repeating that there were a thousand of us there. Man, can you believe it? A thousand!

The moment I get home I tell my parents that our last class was canceled because the history teacher said we could go to the demonstration. I say there were at least a thousand people there and tell them about the flag without the star. Dad listens to me. Then he says he'll go tomorrow to see for himself what's happening. Mom is silent. On the one hand, her silence upsets me, but on the other, I know exactly what she would say. She would say, yet again, that I have to be careful. She would remind me, yet again, about the undercover police, the police files, the photographs, and all the problems I could be making for myself. If she said anything to Dad, she would ask him over and over if he's sure that's wise. For the sake of his job, for the sake of his family. But Mom is silent. Dad, however, surprises me. All at once I am happier than I have been in a very long time. Do you promise? I promise, Dad says. He says that at work they've been talking quite a lot about what's happening in the country. Some believe that it's bad; others, that it's very bad and will end badly too. They've been talking about Dobrica Ćosić and Slobodan Milošević. In their opinion, these two men are inflaming hatred and tearing Yugoslavia apart, even if they claim otherwise. But then he concludes, If you don't see something with your own eyes and hear it with your own ears, how can you know what it's about? How can you even have an opinion? And since it's happening right here and right now, there's nothing for me to think over. After he says this, he goes to the window and looks out.

Every age brings something of itself, he says, drumming his fingers on the window frame. We're quick to think that what we've had up to now was bad and that what is being promised us will be much better. But that's not always the case. Still, humans aren't designed to stand in place. We have to move forward. Otherwise we would still be living in the trees. We would still have tails, Dad says with a smile as he continues to gaze out the window. We stumble our way through history. Sometimes with our heads held high, but mostly hunched over. History teaches us nothing. See? He looks at me. That sounds strange coming from a historian. But it's true. If there was anything we could learn, things wouldn't keep repeating themselves. That scares me sometimes. What we have isn't even so bad. We have homes and jobs. It's true we can't get everything in the stores and we have to stand in line for cooking oil and sugar, and if we want chocolate, bananas, or lemons, we have to drive to Austria or Italy, but we're not hungry. And most of all, we have peace. That's what I want to tell you. Maybe not everything is the way we want it to be. Maybe it's not like what we see in Austria and Italy. But we have peace. And peace is the most we can have. You probably think what I'm saying is stupid. Again, he looks at me. But I'm telling you, peace is like fine porcelain. It can easily break. And when it breaks, well, who's going to find all the little pieces and put them back together into one whole? No one. He shakes his head. What's happening now . . . It's not just happening here; it's not just about a few young men. In previous times, these kinds of demonstrations would have been broken up by the police. If the police couldn't do it on their own, the army would come to their aid. There would be nothing about it on the radio or television. Or if the protests were too massive to cover up, they would accuse foreign countries and Yugoslav émigrés of being involved. But now? Yugoslavia might seem big and strong, but in fact it's more like a porcelain cup on the edge of a table. If anyone accidentally, or even deliberately, gives it a nudge, it will fall and break into pieces. And if it breaks into pieces, then I'm afraid we might all end up cutting ourselves on the shards.

37

I AM ON my way to the draft board with the letter that arrived two weeks ago. I am the first of my classmates.

Yesterday, we had lunch at my aunt and uncle's. Martin was there too, for the first time in a long time, and I was genuinely glad to see him. While Mom, Dad, my aunt, and my uncle were all in the kitchen talking about whatever they talk about, I was with Martin in his room. My cousin was telling me about the architecture program he's enrolled in at the university. He said there were a number of cute girls in his year, but it was one of the older students who had caught his eye. Her name is Mojca. I expect I'm not the only one who's noticed her, however, because she's a real babe. Oh yeah? I was surprised. What about Eva, from Scouts? Eva? My cousin burst out laughing. You've gotta be kidding! That's ancient history. I nodded and didn't ask him anything more. That's the way it is with Martin: if he wants to tell you something, he'll tell you on his own. If he doesn't want to tell you something, no one can drag it out of him. He said his father was still pressuring him to switch from architecture to computer science. He says I'll lose a year, but that's nothing in comparison with all the years I'll waste studying the wrong subject. The old man's insane. Martin gave my shoulder a punch. Sorry, dear old Dad, but chips and circuits simply do not interest me. Besides, there are no women in computer science, or if there are, well, you know . . . Martin makes a face like he's about to vomit. And how about you? What's new? He looks at me and stops talking. There is nothing new with me, or what there is, I didn't tell him. Natalija, for instance. My cousin would think it's terrific that I'm getting laid with no strings attached, but I want something different. Then there are the protests and demonstrations. My cousin would think it's crazy that I go to them because he himself is not allowed to. His father has driven it into his head that he must not even dream of such a thing because he—Uncle Gorazd—could lose his job over it, or something worse could happen, and Martin respects this because he understands the seriousness of the situation, as Uncle Gorazd told us in praise of his son. In the end, I tell him that I received the letter from the draft board a few days earlier and have my interview tomorrow.

Don't worry, my cousin said. It's just to gather information. They don't make any decisions there. You'll have these old farts sitting and smoking at a long table and asking you what you think about the Yugoslav People's Army and which branch you'd like to serve in. They tell you you'd make a good paratrooper, and you end up in a submarine. It's stupid. Just don't philosophize too much. And always keep looking at them. If you look down at the floor, they'll ask you what's wrong. Just say you have no problem with the army and you'll go anywhere they send you. That way they will do all the talking, not you.

But a little later, without me asking, Martin started telling me about his own experience in the army. I looked at him with something like admiration. In this respect at least, he has become a man. When men don't know what to talk about, they start talking about their experiences in the war or army. They soon become animated. Up to now I've seen Grandpa do this—he's the only one who was in the war—as well as my various uncles, who have all been in the army. Although Dad and Uncle Gorazd were also in the army, they never talk about it. And now Martin is doing this too. I listened with interest to what Martin had to say. It was like it was happening to me. He told me that for forty-five days he had been on guard duty with shoot-on-sight orders. That's guard duty under extremely dangerous circumstances, where guards have to shoot without any warning, he explained. Did you ever shoot anybody, I asked. No, Martin said. I didn't, but Siniša, a buddy of mine from Vukovar, did. He killed three Albanian terrorists and was given a week's leave for it.

Later he told me his worst experience was always the walk from the guardhouse to the town. The Albanians would be watching for us from the side of the road. I had to talk in a loud voice so they could hear me from a distance. They left us alone because I'm a Slovenian. The year before, three of our guys got stabbed on the same road. What about in the town, I asked. They were nice in the town. When they heard my Slovenian accent, I got free desserts, Martin said.

I have the folded envelope in my hands. I check the address and cross a dusty gravel courtyard. The sign on the door tells me

I'm at the right place. As I'm going up the front steps, the door opens. A boy comes out, glances at me, and hurries off. When I'm in the building, there's nothing to look for. The corridor leads directly to an office with the door wide open. Inside I see a long table behind which three men are chatting. Two are in civilian clothes, and the third is wearing a Yugoslav Army uniform. I stop in front of the door and am about to knock when one of the men notices me. Come on in, kid, he says, gesturing to me with a cigarette in his hand. Hand me the letter and take a seat. There is only one chair on my side of the table, so there's nothing for me to think about. I give the man the letter inviting me to the interview and sit down. I look at them and wait. Cigarette smoke is rising in three columns from the table. The other two men stop talking. I look at the man I gave the letter to. He reads out my full name and asks me how I am. I'm fine, thank you, I say. The man asks me if I know why I'm here. I nod. Good. The man passes the letter to the man sitting next to him and looks at me. You're a bit on the short side. Now let me think. After a short pause, he exclaims, You could be a courier. Yes, the man next to him nods. A courier. Good idea. The man at the far end is in a green uniform with gold stars and gold trim on the shoulder boards. Only where should we send you? What do you think, the man asks me. I don't know, I say with a shrug. You see, there are boys who care about preserving Yugoslavia, and other boys who would like to destroy her. When he says this, I begin feeling hot. I look at him and wonder if knows that I go to the demonstrations. Is that why he mentioned boys who would like to destroy Yugoslavia? I can feel my heart racing. But you seem like a fine young man to me, the man with the gold stars says with a smile. You don't want to destroy our country. No, you'll defend her. Isn't that right? Yes, sir, I assure him. If that's the case, then you should be careful whom you associate with. Right? Right, I say and feel my arms and legs turning into chewing gum.

A courier, the first man says again. I look at him. As he's stubbing out his cigarette, he tells me that couriers played a vital role in the People's Liberation Struggle. There weren't any telecommunications back then. And if war breaks out again, you see, the big question is how the telecommunications would work. People like your uncle are doing their very best to develop instruments that flawlessly connect the front lines with the rear and the infantry with aviation. But the enemy is also developing all sorts of instruments that could disrupt electromagnetic waves. When he mentions my uncle, my stomach tightens into a knot. Who else are they going to mention?

Now I am sure they know everything. They know who I associate with, where I go, what I say, and probably even what I think. They know about me and Matej and they know about me and Natalija. I look at the first man. Martin's words are engraved in my memory. If I look down at the floor, they will start asking me what's wrong. So I mentally count to ten. I look at the second man and mentally count to ten. I look at the third man. Then I look back at the first man.

His forehead is full of wrinkles. How old is he? Fifty? Fifty-five? Not too long before retirement. His hair is totally gray. I notice the gold pin on his suit in the shape of Tito's signature. His hands are large and hairy. He is wearing a gold wedding ring on his left hand and, on his right, a ring with a heavy black stone. He doesn't look like a bastard, but looks can be deceiving. It's the same with teachers. Some look like they're nice and friendly, but they're actually real bitches, while one or two have the reputation of being bitches but at some crucial moment they turn a blind eye to a mistake you made and give you a higher grade. The second man is younger. He is thin and pale. I think he could be anemic or even have some disease that keeps him from being a soldier. It's not clear if he ever was a soldier. He has thin hair, a hooked nose, and a mustache. He is agreeing with everything the first man says. He doesn't ask me anything. Now and then he glances at me, but mostly he's watching his cigarette burn slowly down on the rim of the ashtray. It's as if he's only smoking to keep the others company, when in fact cigarettes make him queasy. It's the same with the girls at school. They all smoke at Matej's, but if you watch them for a while, you see that only three or four are actually inhaling; the others are just blowing the smoke out. The third man seems the most dangerous of the three. Not only because of the uniform; his accent is dangerous too. He's speaking Slovenian, but you can hear he's not used to the language. As he watches me, he taps the tip of his pencil on a sheet of paper. I am sure that he is the one who ultimately decides who goes where.

That will be all, the first man says. I give a start. Unless you have any questions? No, I say. So you can go, the second man says and stands up. Let's get some air in here. It's really smoky. He goes over to the window and opens it all the way. I hear the birds singing outside. I quickly stand up, say goodbye, and leave.

As I'm walking, I think that it wasn't entirely like Martin told me. But he did get some things right. It was good that I kept looking at them. If I had looked down at the floor, they would have started drilling me and I'd probably still be in there. Those three men know everything. They would have tested me like in the movies, to see if I was telling the truth. And then later they would analyze my answers. They would try to find the common denominator of the lies and the common denominator of the truths I was telling. And from that they would draw their conclusions. It's fucking insane.

I'm walking faster and faster. I want to get to school as soon as possible. Whenever we had a general physical or a medical exam for some educational camp, we were never in a hurry to get back to school. We'd take as much time as we could. Whenever I had a dentist's appointment, I'd ask Mom to write me a note excusing me for at least half the day. But now I'm almost running to school. I can hardly wait to tell Matej everything that happened this morning.

Half an hour later I don't believe it: Matej is almost indifferent to what I tell him. I told you they're all assholes, is his only response. Yeah, I know, I say, not giving up. But you should have seen it. They knew everything about me. Did they mention any names, my classmate wants to know. No, no names. I shake my head. Well, yes, they did mention my uncle. And they told me to be careful who I associate with. That's hardly specific, Matej says. They were bluffing. They don't know shit. They were waiting for you to blurt out something. Did you? No names, I say. No information. I only answered *yes* or *I understand*. You did good, Matej says. Rage is growing inside me. Matej's patronizing attitude is really getting on my nerves. I'm not saying he doesn't know more about these things than I do. But it was me sitting in front of the draft board, not him. I'd like to see how smart he would be in my place.

During the next break I more or less ignore Matej. And during the main break, I go outside. I sit at the end of the bench where the girls who smoke hang out. Saša offers me a cigarette; then she asks what's going on between me and that Natalija chick. The other three girls start giggling. How should I know? I shrug. Don't be embarrassed, Saša says, ruffling my hair. But if you're interested, maybe *we* could get together sometime. I can't tell if she's pulling my leg or means it seriously. I don't want to play the fool, so I tell her to just say when. The others start laughing again, and Teja says she's being a skank. Why? Saša defends herself. He doesn't have a girlfriend. When the bell rings for the next class, we run inside. When school is over, I sling my bag over my shoulder and quickly leave the classroom. On my way out, I wait to see if Matej's going to run after me and say something. It doesn't happen, although we usually go part of the way together. I try to figure out what happened. Did I do something wrong? Did I say anything I shouldn't have?

It's stuffy on the bus and there's a bad odor, so I get off a stop early and continue on foot. I go past the garages and, at the end of them, just like in the old days, head toward the park with the swings. I see Rok there. Hey, Rok, I call to him and raise my right arm. Hey, man! Am I glad to see you! Rok runs over to me and gives me a punch on the shoulder. It's been like a thousand years. So what have you been up to? Not much, I say. I'm just on my way home from school. I didn't mean that! Rok laughs. I meant in life. Well, I met with the draft board today, I say. No fucking way! Rok becomes serious. What'd they say to you? Nothing in particular. They asked a bit, listened a bit. So where are they sending you, he wonders. They didn't say. One

SEBASTIJAN PREGELJ

of them said I could be a courier. The second one agreed. And the third one didn't express an opinion on the subject. So maybe I'll be a courier. Oh, come on, Rok says. If you ask me, they're still playing Partisans and Germans. Can you believe it? And what about you, I ask. How are you doing? Now let me think. Rok frowns, pauses a few seconds, then gives me a big grin. I'm doing good. Real good. From his pocket he extracts a pouch of tobacco mixed with pot and a pack of some rolling papers and sits down on a swing. As he pushes himself backward and forward with his legs, he rolls the joint, finds his lighter, lights it, takes a drag, and holds the smoke in his lungs a long time. No fucking joke, that really hits the spot, he says, exhaling, and holds the cigarette out to me. I sit on the swing next to him, take the cigarette and inhale. After a few drags, I begin to feel dizzy. Strong stuff, I say. The best. I've got a friend who gets me the very best. If you're interested. I don't answer.

A little later we're swinging on the swings and laughing so much we've got tears in our eyes. First we laugh about those three guys on the draft board, then about the people walking by, and finally about the birds flying above us. Wait, wait! Rok hops off the swing, falls down, and, laughing hard, picks himself up. Come on! He stretches an arm out to me. We're gonna do something. I hop off the swing and only barely land on my feet. I wipe my teary eyes with my sleeve, sniffle, and run after my friend. Soon we're in a grocery store. Rok goes first to the bread section and takes a loaf of white. I watch him and wonder why he's buying a whole loaf. Maybe to take home. If he was hungry, he'd most likely just take a roll. I don't have a clue. This way! Rok hurries between the shelves, stops at the wine, and stares for a long time at the bottles. Tell me, he says, grabbing my shoulder, which one's the cheapest? What are you gonna do with it? Which one's the cheapest, he repeats. This one, I think. I point to the row of bottles on the bottom shelf. The label shows a man in a hat carrying a white goose. Rok bends down, picks up the bottle, and starts laughing. Just look at that picture! Fuck! Just look at it! That guy! I tell you—that guy's a fucking sodomite, Rok says in a loud voice. Okay, cool it. I'm trying to calm him because people are looking at us. Rok is clearly a lot more stoned than I am. He's acting like a mentally impaired child. Come on, Rok, let's go. I tug at his sleeve. Okay, let's go, Rok says as he stumbles toward the cash register with the loaf of bread and bottle of wine.

Once we're in line, he quiets down for a while, but then he starts asking me if the lady in front of us is wearing a wig or if that's her real hair. Cut it out, I tell him. But I really want to know, Rok insists. It's so pretty. He holds his hand out as if he's about to touch it, but at the last moment I grab his wrist. Pull yourself together, I say sharply. But I'm fine, Rok says. I ran into my old schoolmate and I'm happy, he tells the woman standing behind us. Uh-huh, the woman says with a nod. She is probably hoping that's the end of it and he'll turn around again and leave her alone. But Rok is already staring at her shopping basket, which is filled to the brim. Ma'am, he says to her, you sure have a lot of stuff. You're having a party, right? Come on, stop it! I tug his arm. I'm scared that someone in the store might know me, or know my parents. They could tell them how Rok and I were acting. What would I say at home? That Rok went crazy? That he was like this before too, only the signs of mental illness weren't so blatant? The lady's gonna have a party, Rok tells me. Wanna go? She didn't invite us, I say. I grab the bottle he's been holding and set it on the counter in front of the cashier. Then the bread too. Pay, I tell him. Rok pulls out his wallet, counts out the money, and puts it on the counter in front of the cashier; then he grabs the bread and wine and shouts, Bye-bye! He stumbles out of the store, and I follow him.

Rok starts running toward the garages. I want to tell him to stop and calm down a little, but I can't get the words out. Maybe I should leave him by himself. He wouldn't mind if I left because he probably wouldn't even remember I was there. But he's so stoned, I'm afraid something could happen to him.

At the garages, he sits on the low concrete wall and starts breaking the bread into pieces and throwing it onto the grass. Then he opens the bottle and pours the wine over the bread. Now I understand what he's doing. Rok, don't do this, I say. It'll be funny. He looks at me as he tears the wine-drenched bread. You'll see. It'll be funny. His hands are sticky with wine and covered in crumbs. Here, birdie birdie! Here, birdie birdie, he calls to the pigeons. Here, birdie birdic birdie!

Before long, the first pigeon flies down near the bread. Soon there are more and more of them. The pigeons greedily pull at the soggy bread and gobble it down while also pushing away the sparrows who would like to join the feast. Watch what happens now. Rok nudges me with his elbow. The fun's about to start. There are about to be some aviating problems.

When nothing happens, Rok hops off the wall. Go! Go! Go! He's waving his arms to frighten the pigeons, who start jumping all over each other and flapping their wings. A few of them lift off the ground right away and then start circling, rising and falling, until one bird slams into the window of the closest building. Did you see, Rok shouts with delight. Did you see that? It's fucking crazy what's happening to them! Even birds gotta have fun, right? Rok turns to me and says he's going home. I'm tired. And he wanders off across the grass.

I sit for a few more minutes on the concrete wall and watch the pigeons. New birds have arrived and some of the old ones have come back. All of them, without exception, are pulling at the wet bread and gulping it down. After a while, some can't even take off and are twirling on the grass, others somehow do take off but soon fall back down, while still others don't fall down but circle weirdly in the sky. Rok is already far away when I grab the bottle and what's left of the bread and throw everything into a trash can. I'm glad there's nobody around. I go past the garages and take the shortest way home. As I'm about to enter our building, I realize I don't have my bag with me. I must have left it by the swings. I run back. It's still there. That's something at least.

38

I OPEN MY eyes. Outside I hear the sound of a bugle and, everywhere around me, shouting and the clinking of metal. I lift my head and see a few boys in green underpants and white undershirts and a few soldiers in uniform. For a moment, I'm still half-asleep and confused, but then like a bolt of lightning it hits me: the army. Strumica, Macedonia. Fuck. I arrived in the city yesterday on the last bus. It was already night. We were met at the bus station by soldiers who drove us to the base. First we reported to the officer on duty; then we were taken to a yellow building that a raucous noise was coming from—the kind of welcome party you don't want, I thought, but have no choice but to go to. It doesn't matter. That's what I decided before I left: I am going away and this one year will be whatever it will be. I will switch off half my brain. I will do whatever is required of me and whatever everyone else does. Even the biggest idiots get through this. So I will too.

In the dormitory, it was explained to us that we'd be getting our uniforms the next day. For now you'll stay in your civvies.

And as long as you're in your civvies, army rules only half apply. So make good use of this last night, a pimply-faced guy with an eagle's beak of a nose told us with a laugh. Maybe some lucky fellow will get to stay two nights with us. That's a good thing. Even if you don't have a uniform, the time still counts toward your military service. But don't expect more than that.

Then he turned on the record player. The speakers started crackling, and the accordions and trumpets sounded like there was a band of rowdy Mamelukes in the room. That's Bosnian heavy metal, pimple-face shouted and started singing along with the music as best he could. The guys who were already in bed covered their heads, while the others were sitting around and laughing. We all looked like imbeciles on their last day out. I shrugged and threw myself on an empty bed. I was one of them now. I had become them. Good night.

I jump out of bed and do what I can to put the covers in order. I stand for a while beside my bunk, but then, like the others, I sit down and wait for whatever's going to happen. Pimple-face looks like he's been up the entire night. He's walking up and down the room. First he tells us we don't know how to make a bed but that's okay because they're going to teach us. Just like they're going to teach you how to sew on buttons and fold your shirts and pants, your underpants and undershirts, all to the width of your cap. Then he says we're lucky. This base has a good reputation. It won't be too bad here for the most part.

At some point I go to the bathroom. I see concrete sinks, urinals, and stalls with squat toilets. There are no doors on the stalls. They are tiled floor to ceiling. There are brown finger marks on the tiles. I discover that if somebody is squatting opposite you, you're looking at each other. I go back to the dorm and throw myself on my bed.

At six thirty we go to breakfast, and after breakfast to the raising of the flag. The sound of a bugle comes from the loudspeakers; the soldiers stand at attention. We are somewhere behind them. Probably so we're not too visible. The duty officer reads out the orders of the day. After the orders of the day we go back to the yellow building and wait. Pimple-face tells us mail is delivered between nine and ten and that's when our documents will arrive. Until then you can enjoy yourselves; then they'll come and get you. When you have your uniform, fun's over. When you have your uniform, you're soldiers.

At eleven, the first soldier arrives with a few sheets of paper. The guys whose names he reads leave with him. Pimple-face says they're lucky. Artillery. Then a few more soldiers arrive with papers, until only two of us are left in the dorm. When the last one comes and reads out our names, pimple-face says, Infantry, recoilless rocket launcher. You two are fucked. Good luck.

The soldier takes us to the storage rooms where we each get a tent fly; then they toss into it everything I'm supposed to get: socks, undershirts, underpants, long underpants, thermal underpants, pajamas, four shirts, two pairs of pants, sweater, overcoat, gloves, two caps, undercap, shoes, boots, belt, water canteen, a smaller bag the kind certain kids carried to school, a big duffel bag, and a red star. When the tent fly is full, we return to the building by the square where the flag is flying.

We climb the steps to the topmost floor. The last sixteen steps are made of wood and creak beneath our feet. When we're at the top, we find ourselves in a classroom. At one end of the room there are wooden stands with rifles and other equipment; at the other end there is a chalkboard with a picture of Tito above it. In between there are two doors. Here we are, says the soldier who brought us here. I look at the bunks in the dormitory. On each bed there is a sticker with a name. The names are written in the Cyrillic alphabet. If there had been more than just two empty beds, it would have taken me forever to find my name. There are three mattresses on the bed and a metal locker next to it. I put the tent fly and everything that's in it on the floor; then I lay the mattresses, one after the other, on top of the spring mesh frame. I sit down, open the metal locker, and have no idea where to begin.

After a while an officer comes in. I stand up and salute. He asks me where I'm from. I say Ljubljana. I like boys from Slovenia, he says. They're fast learners and shoot straight. I hope you're the same. Have they shown you how to make your bed and put your things in the locker? No, sir, I say. Okay, wait. Private Eskija! Kenan Eskija, the officer calls from the door. Here, sir! A soldier runs up to the door. Help out the new kid, the officer orders. Yes, sir, the soldier replies and comes over to my bed. In the next ten minutes he explains everything to me: how to put my clothes away, and that everything in the locker has to be folded to the same length as the cap; how to make the bed, how to fold the pajamas, and that most guys don't sleep in pajamas because that way you don't need to fold them in the morning; it's only a problem if there's a night check. Then we have to put our pajamas on and in the morning fold them. He tells me he's from Ilidža, in Bosnia, has two brothers and a sister, and an uncle who lives in Slovenia, in Kranj. He got here two weeks ago. If you need anything, just ask.

When I am done folding everything, I put on the uniform, stuff my civilian clothes in a bag, and put the bag in the locker behind the overcoat; then I go to the classroom. The soldier on duty shouts that we need to get ready for lunch. When everyone is assembled, we hurry single file down the stairs, out the door, and across the park to the mess hall. We stand in a line that weaves from the building all the way to the first trees. Some guys move into the shade—the September sun is very hot, as if it was late July or early August. More than anything, the line reminds me of being in primary school. We wait to get our trays, which we then take to get our food: stew and bread. Some guys take two pieces of bread, some three, and some even more. I take one piece, follow the others, and sit at the same table as everyone in front of me. As we eat, I look at the guys from our dormitory. I had the same feeling the first time I stepped through the door of my secondary school. When I got to the classroom, I took a quick look at the kids who were already there and determined that I knew by sight two girls who had been at my old school, but in a different section, and no one else. Since everybody was looking at me, I quickly asked the closest boy if the seat next to him was free and sat down. He asked me if I was taking any sports and I asked him what primary school he'd gone to, and we soon found ourselves in a conversation. It's not so different here. You ask a guy where he's from, he asks you the same, and somehow you soon find yourselves in a conversation.

We have some free time after lunch. The officer tells us we should chat. Get acquainted. You need to know each other like you were brothers. Because for at least half a year you will be brothers. You'll be dependent on each other—a lot more than you might imagine today.

Those of us who have only recently arrived sit in a circle. We all introduce ourselves in a few sentences. Dušan from Nikšić, in Montenegro; Robert from Zagreb, in Croatia; Radovan, or Rade, from Užice, in Serbia; Siniša from Belgrade, although it turns out later that he's actually from Kočetin, a village of five hundred people about a hundred kilometers from Belgrade; Blaže from Skopje, in Macedonia.

The guys who have been in the army since the spring do their own thing and pay no attention to us. Later, I learn that they're waiting to find out if they'll be redeployed somewhere else or will stay here. Everybody wants to stay here. There's only one place people get redeployed to: Kosovo. And nobody wants to go to Kosovo. It's no secret that the bases there have been taken over by the police and special forces, while the regular army is always in the field. In Kosovo, there's an emergency situation. But in six months things will be different. When it's time for my class of recruits to be redeployed, many of the Serbs will want to go to Kosovo. They will go to headquarters, present themselves, and request to be sent there.

Two soldiers in our dormitory are preparing to go home. Marko has three days left; Haris, nine. Marko and Haris are proof that it will one day be over, although I am not thinking about the end. It's too far away. There's no point. If I let myself start thinking about the end, it will all seem even farther away.

At night I have a hard time falling asleep. Everything feels like it's happening in a movie. It feels like I'm in it by mistake. I should be in the audience, but instead I somehow ended up on the screen.

39

I AM SITTING on the left wheel of the recoilless rocket launcher, smoking. A sharp wind is blowing across the snowy landscape. Soldiers are sleeping in trench shelters behind me. Or most likely not sleeping. I haven't slept a single night since we've been in the field; it's too cold in the trench shelter. I merely closed my eyes and tried to get warm enough so I wouldn't shiver all night. For a while it helped if I flexed my muscles, but you can't do that forever. And when I stopped, I started shivering again. Both nights felt like they would never end.

I'm on watch until midnight. You might think that freezing in the open air is worse than freezing in a trench shelter, but it isn't. When we're on watch, we have a fire, and that is a luxury. While the others are freezing eighty centimeters below the surface, their whole bodies aching from lying on frozen ground, and trying in one way or another to warm themselves on shared bedding under shared blankets, when I'm on watch I can stand right next to the flames.

The moment I went on watch, I went over to the fire, tossed a thick log on it, and let the flames lick my legs. When it became too hot for me, I took a step back. My pant legs quickly cooled down and the cold returned. So I moved closer to the fire again. Now I'm trying to thaw out my boots. They were completely white from snow during the day and completely frozen. Even if I had wanted to, I couldn't have untied them and taken them off. When I stuck the tips of my boots into the flames, they started smoking. I thought to myself, I won't just thaw them out, I'll dry them too. And sure enough, before long I could feel my toes again. I could even move them! The laces were soft again and, if I wanted, I could have untied them. But why would I do that? It's the same with my hands. During the day, my fingers were hard and rigid, with no strength at all in them. I couldn't even open a can of food, or rather, I had to struggle; it was like using the can opener on a tank. So as soon as my fingers got good and warm, I opened all the cans I still had from the previous days. First, I treated myself to canned ham, then to a blend of goat and mutton with big white chunks of fat, and, last of all, fish. With my eyes half-closed, I took the sardines out of the oil and relished every bite.

Now, as I sit on the left wheel of the recoilless rocket launcher and smoke, I tell myself it could be worse. Blaže, for example, is coughing up blood, but the officers say he's faking it because he wants to go to the army hospital. The army hospital is in Skopje and Blaže is from Skopje. He just wants to go home, the officers say with unwavering conviction, so they're ignoring him. Kenan has blisters from his boots. In the ambulance they opened the blisters with a scalpel and bandaged his feet. Since then the soles of his feet have hurt him so much he can barely walk, but he's not giving in. He says he'll survive. That's how things are with those two. Their situations are definitely worse than mine, although that's not much comfort. The bad stuff that happens to other people doesn't make the cold any less terrible for me.

I'll get through it somehow, I keep saying to myself. Somehow we'll all get through it. I haven't yet heard of any unit returning from the field without a soldier because he froze to death. Although other kinds of accidents do happen, both in the field and on base. A few years back, an officer told a group of privates that they shouldn't be afraid of antitank mines. They're designed to be activated by the weight of a tank. But a man is not a tank, he said. Then he placed a mine on the ground and jumped on it. The seven soldiers who had been standing in a semicircle around him trying to overcome their fear all died with him. Another officer had his right arm torn off when he was firing a recoilless rocket launcher. And last winter a truck skidded off the road. The two soldiers sitting next to the driver were crushed. On base, a few years ago, there was an explosion in the boiler building. When it happened, the soldiers were all standing in formation and about to raise the flag. Pieces of tiles came flying off the roof of the low building, along with glass, bricks, and human flesh. The five soldiers next to the boilers all died. And ever since, the radiators in the dormitories have been cold. They remain there as confirmation of the truth of the story, but the dormitories are again being heated by small cast-iron stoves. And so on and so forth. Accidents happen and the stories about them spread from person to person. How many are really true nobody knows. But so far nobody has frozen to death.

I check the time. Half past ten. More than half of my watch is behind me. A little before midnight I will wake up Siniša and lie down in his place. He's fat, so I hope it will be warm there.

I remember very well how, on the sixteenth of November, I was lying on a bench soaking up the rays of the sun. I was glad they had sent me to Macedonia. It was as warm as late summer in Ljubljana. Then, on the nineteenth of November, I was woken up by the sound of metal scraping asphalt. Before I could get out of bed, Rade was shouting that it had started snowing overnight. Fucking hell, look at all that snow! In a second we were all at the windows. The square was cleared before reveille, but it was soon covered again by fresh snow, which was whirling in the gusts of wind. As soon as the raising of the flag was done, the soldiers on duty started shoveling again. They shoveled snow all day and late into the night. They shoveled it again the next morning before the flag raising, and then, again, all day. On the third day the snow began to let up, and on the fourth it stopped altogether. Then the freezing cold set in.

Today is the twenty-fifth of November, our third day in the field. We have another four days in the mountains above the town. On the twenty-ninth of November—Republic Day—we will march back through town in a column, singing. This will be a show for the people, Second Lieutenant Cvetkovski told us a few days before we left for the field. They'll see their finest sons—despite snow, ice, and cold—singing at the top of their lungs. Our singing will pay honor to the great holiday.

A single week doesn't sound like a long time, but these are the conditions: the entire landscape is covered in snow, the temperature stays at fifteen below during the day, and at night

SEBASTIJAN PREGELJ

it drops at least another ten degrees. This might be tolerable if the wind wasn't constantly blowing.

I have my collar raised and my undercap pulled down around my neck. I'm wearing everything I was given: thermal underpants, regular long underpants, winter work pants, short T-shirt, regular shirt, sweater, and overcoat. I have two pairs of socks on my feet. Despite all this, the cold is chilling me to the bone.

I stand up from the wheel of the rocket launcher and go to the fire. As I wait for my thighs to start roasting, I look out over the landscape. Under different circumstances I would like it. The rounded hills have been blown smooth by the wind. They gleam in the pale moonlight like scoops of vanilla ice cream, with a dark-chocolate sky above them and an occasional flickering star like a tiny bit of orange peel. There are clouds in the sky but you can barely see them. If a caravan of camels were at this moment to appear out of nowhere, I wouldn't be surprised, not even if the camels were cautiously stepping from star to star. Here, absolutely anything seems possible.

My cigarette is almost down to the butt and I use it to light a new one. For a few moments I gaze at the flames. The fire seems alive. The fire is my friend.

Before we left for the field, there was a fight in our platoon. Dušan punched Siniša in the mouth, splitting his lip and knocking out a tooth. The lieutenant said we were lucky. Since it was a Montenegrin who punched a Serb, there wouldn't be serious consequences. If it had been the other way around, and a Serb had punched a Montenegrin, that, too, would have been okay. But if by chance an Albanian had punched a Serb, or a Serb had punched a Slovenian, well, then there would be hell to pay. Motherfucking hell! If that had happened, we'd have to report it on up. A commission would be sent here from Skopje and the soldiers involved would have to go before a military tribunal. That's how it is these days, Cvetkovski said, shaking his head. When we get back from the field, both Dušan and Siniša are going to have to spend a week in detention. And time spent in detention doesn't count toward your military service. But there won't be any worse consequences for either of them.

It had been an ordinary evening. Siniša was sitting by the iron stove reading aloud the personal ads in *Hot Stuff*, one of Yugoslavia's first porn magazines. Mostly they were from men boasting about the size of their dicks and looking for women for a good time. There was the occasional ad from a woman, but I never believed they were written by actual female readers. I'm sure somebody at the magazine must write them. For someone who's naive, these ads are proof that *Hot Stuff* is read not just by men but by women too. They're proof that Yugoslavia is full of open-minded women looking for a good fuck. And the best way to reach these women is through an ad in *Hot Stuff*.

If an ad was signed by a guy from Slovenia, then, during the evening reading of the personals, that guy had to be me; if the author was from Bosnia, it was Kenan; if he was from Serbia, then it was sometimes Siniša, other times Rade. And so on. It was the same every time we got a new issue. Siniša would sit by the stove and read the ads out loud. The rest of us would laugh and shout and throw pillows at one another. Eventually, the person who had brought the magazine would disappear. Everyone knew he was jerking off. The rest of us would wait our turn.

Maybe we wouldn't get the magazine until the next day, or the day after that, but it was still better than nothing.

That evening there was an ad in which a Montenegrin man from Budva wanted to meet a man who was interested in something more than just hanging out together. Wasn't it you who wrote that, Siniša said, looking at Dušan over the top of the magazine. I didn't know you Montenegrins were faggots, he said, laughing. Dušan then jumped out of his bed, walked over to Siniša, and dared him to repeat what he had just said, if he had the guts. We were all howling with laughter. Even Siniša was laughing and, still laughing, repeated what he had said a minute earlier, adding that now he wasn't sure if, in the field, he would have the guts to sleep next to Dušan in a trench shelter. Dušan took a swing and, in one blow, knocked Siniša off the chair. It was like he was Mate Parlov or Damir Škaro. Blood was dripping on the floorboards, and a tooth flew beneath a bed. What the fuck! We were all instantly on our feet, grabbing hold of Dušan, whose face was bright red with the veins bulging on his forehead and neck. Calm down, man, we cried as we dragged him back to his bed. And don't you do anything to make things worse, said the two guys who picked up Siniša off the floor, after which he ran straight out of the room. It would have all ended all right if, on his way to the bathroom, Siniša had not run into the duty officer.

Robert, who was the private on duty that day, was ordered to get Lieutenant Cvetkovski. About half an hour later, the second lieutenant was in the office of the duty officer. First, the two men discussed the situation; then, they called Dušan and Siniša to the office. The rest of us waited in the dorm to see what would happen.

The duty officer said they could both expect detention when they got back from the field. He confiscated the porn magazine and ordered them to return to the unit. The officers exchanged a few more words, after which Cvetkovski went home and the duty officer leafed through the magazine in peace.

I return to the rocket launcher and sit back down on the wheel. I smoke and look out at the landscape. In another forty-five minutes my watch will be over.

I still have two hundred and ninety-five days until the end of my military service. It seems like it will never end. I have been here for an eternity, but if I count the crossed-off days on my calendar, then at the moment when I take Siniša's place in the trench shelter, there will be only seventy such days. Fucking hell.

How many more times will I have to rush, as I soap up under cold water and rinse the soap off under scalding water, so that in the end, when they shut off the water without warning a minute later, I'm not still covered in soap? How many more times will I have to sew buttons onto the shirts I get from the laundry? This baffles me. The shirts I give to the laundry all have buttons, but the shirts I get back are buttonless. It's like some button-eating animal lives in the laundry room. How many more times will I have to stand an hour or two in line to make a phone call, so I can talk to my father, my mother, or Saša for five minutes while the guys behind me are tugging and pushing and trying in every possible way to get me to hang up? How many more times will I have to squat in a cubicle without doors while I stare at the guy who's shitting across from me?

My parents ask me how things are going. Fine, I say. What am I supposed to tell them? I myself don't know what's more

SEBASTIJAN PREGELJ

terrible: communal shitting or listening to Lieutenant Stojanović explain to us, during our political instruction, that the
situation in the country is complicated but that our job is not
complicated. Our assignment is to preserve the constitutional
order and territorial integrity of Yugoslavia—even with force
if need be. Lieutenant Stojanović says that separatism is growing stronger in Slovenia and Croatia, that the influence of those
people who would like to destroy the country is growing stronger, those people who shit all over Comrade Tito, the People's
Liberation Struggle, and the benefits of the Revolution. Week
after week he tells us there are people who want to see Slovenia
and Croatia become part of Germany. He warns us about the
real and present danger of infiltration by Ustaše terrorists. It
would not be the first time, he says. In the period since World
War II, hostile émigrés have, within Yugoslavia, carried out forty terrorist actions, in which at least thirty people have been
killed and twice that number wounded. In this same period,
outside of Yugoslavia, they have carried out over six hundred
anti-Yugoslav attacks! And more than a few diplomats were
among the dead. But we are ready, Lieutenant Stojanović says,
raising his voice and shaking his fist. Every so often he looks at
me. Every so often he looks at Robert. As if we represented all
those Slovenians and Croatians who want their countries to
join Germany, as if we were the two people responsible for the
Yugoslav Army being in a state of permanent readiness, as if we
were the ones keeping Lieutenant Stojanović awake at night.
But what do I know?

In the days before we left for the field, we watched on the
seven-thirty news as people gathered at the Berlin Wall and

stayed there until the border was opened between East and West Germany. We saw the demonstrations in Prague and heard about the unrest in Romania. Just before we left the base, Lieutenant Stojanović hammered a nail into the wall of his office and next to the picture of Tito hung a second picture—of Slobodan Milošević.

Everything that was happening on the base and on television is far away from this snowy landscape and the icy wind that is blowing across it.

I light another cigarette. When it's finished, I'll wake Siniša.

Sometimes I think about whether there really will be a war in the end. I wonder if Lieutenant Stojanović could be right. Does he know more than we do? And if there is a war, who will fight against whom? That is not clear to me. Who will we be pointing our guns at? Who will we be shooting at? Whose war will it be?

Right before I flick the butt into the flames, I think, It will eventually be over. Anyway, I'm full now. Before my watch I was hungry as a wolf, but during my watch I ate my fill. Now I stink of canned fish. But it's a good stink.

40

ROBERT IS SPINNING in the middle of the office with his arms spread out. The Tiger Glue has done its work. He squeezed half a tube into the polyvinyl bag that now lies on the floor while Robert, as he spins, tells me again and again that I should try it too. Come on, he insists. It's good. I won't do it, I say. Then don't be a pussy and put on GBH or PTTB, he shouts. As you wish. I reach my arm out, change the cassette, and push play.

A little while later, Robert is sprawled out in the armchair. We don't have it so bad here, he says. Before I can answer, his head slumps to his chest. I look at him and say in a low voice that we really don't.

When the six months of training were completed, most of the soldiers were sent to Kosovo. About a thousand of us, maybe even less, remained on the base. People are saying Yugoslavia signed an agreement under which its larger military bases have to be at least one hundred kilometers from the border. I have no idea if this is true, just as I have no idea how big a base has to be to be considered larger. But all indications are that our base is emptying out: more soldiers are leaving every week and there are no new arrivals.

We have been lucky. Most of our platoon was assigned to headquarters. My responsibilities are writing the orders of the day—based on Major Stanković's instructions—and cleaning the offices of some of the senior officers. An office is clean when the ashtray is empty and there are no ashes on the desk. I empty the ashtrays every day, I wipe the desks every day, I vacuum the offices once a week, or maybe I don't. I have no other jobs. Robert handles the coffee. In the morning, it's crazy here—all the officers want coffee the moment they arrive. During the day almost nothing happens. Still, Robert always needs to be available. Rade is the base commander's driver. Kenan works in the post office. Kenan is friends with the guys from the fire squad. They have a plot of weed growing behind the pigsty. The weed can't be bought for money, but you can get it in exchange for alcohol, which Kenan provides. Kenan has more alcohol than any bar in town. It's very simple: in the morning he sorts the new mail and package notices by unit; then, in the early afternoon, he distributes the packages to the soldiers. But first he has to open and inspect each one to make sure it doesn't contain any alcohol or drugs. If a package contains no more than one bottle of alcohol, he confiscates it; if there are two or more, he takes one bottle, but it's like he doesn't see the other bottles. He's supposed to hand the alcohol over to an officer the next morning, but Kenan's no fool. The good stuff we drink; the bad stuff he hands over. Some of what he keeps back he trades for weed. Kenan shares what he has with us, which is why we love him. If

SEBASTIJAN PREGELJ

the base ever selected a soldier of the month, it would be Kenan, at least as far as those of us at headquarters are concerned.

There is a loft above the pigsty with straw and pig feed, and there you can have a gypsy girl. One of the firemen makes the arrangements, but we don't go there. We're happy enough with magazines like *Hot Stuff*.

At headquarters, besides us, there are also the guards. On every floor, there's a guard at the head of the corridor and another by the stairs. Some of the senior officers have additional guards. There is one in front of the door to the base commander's office, another in front of the door to the office of the colonel in charge of military counterintelligence, and two a floor higher, who guard the office of the lieutenant colonel in charge of the signalmen, whose coded teleprinters are kept behind two bulletproof doors. The guards change every week. We get along well with them. They warn us with a kick at the door that the officers are coming. In exchange, I lend them magazines. Some of them wait until their shift is over, but others jerk off while on duty. It makes no difference to me. What's important is that they return the magazines. I keep my library under the carpet. The magazines are arranged side by side, so you don't notice when you're walking on them. I started with a few magazines I inherited, but in just a few weeks the collection had grown. I'm not as strict about them as Sršen was in our school locker room. I store them and lend them, but I never make any threats. The lending fee can be anything but money. Payment can be made right away, as with the guards, or I can wait. Nobody ever forgets to pay. Not the barber when I need a haircut, or the cooks when they dish out the food. The guys in the platoon get the magazines for a longer time. If a copy gets ruined, I replace it with a new one. Everything's been much easier since they opened the duty-free shops. And I can bring anything I want onto base in my duffel bag.

Even the officers know this. Not a day goes by that one of them doesn't call me into his office. Behind closed doors, he presses a banknote into my hand and places an order for brandy or vodka. I slip out in the afternoon, when the only people left on base are the duty officers. There's a store not far from the base where the beautiful Vangelija works. I'd heard about her even earlier, before I was assigned to headquarters, when I could only leave the base twice a month. The other soldiers flocked in droves to the beautiful Vangelija, but I never went there. Since I've been at headquarters, however, I see her a lot. Not only is the store where she works nearby, it also has everything I need, which is basically brandy and vodka. Only I don't find the beautiful Vangelija to be especially good-looking—her charms are of a different sort.

The shelves at the beautiful Vangelija's store are organized in a very particular way. Items are arranged not by groups but by price. The cheapest items are on the lowest shelves. The higher the price, the higher the shelf. But the beautiful Vangelija can't reach the highest shelves. She needs a ladder. And when she climbs the ladder, she gives you something to look at. The beautiful Vangelija does not wear panties.

The guys say I'm lucky. Brandy and vodka are not on the topmost shelf, but they're high enough for the beautiful Vangelija to need a ladder. So I get a show every time.

I go to the store on days when rank-and-file soldiers aren't allowed to go into town. I arrive at the store with my duffel bag, in which I bring the empty bottles and leave with the full ones. From time to time I take something small for myself. Mostly things from the lower shelves. When I pass through the main gate of the base, the soldiers on duty never inspect me. I suspect they know I'm carrying something but they don't know who it's for. The alcohol could be for the base commander or one of the senior officers, and then they would be in deep shit. At least that's what they think. But, in fact, no officer would want to expose himself like that. If I was ever caught with alcohol at the gate, those bottles of brandy and vodka would be my problem. But the soldiers on duty don't know that.

Every time I return from the beautiful Vangelija's store, I have to describe in detail what happened. At first I would tell the other guys what actually happened, but they refused to accept this and thought I was holding something back. They wanted more, so I started adding things and making stuff up. Now when I tell them my story, the guys laugh and punch me in the arm and say I've got it better than winning the lottery. And maybe I do. Once, however, I told them the beautiful Vangelija was in fact not as beautiful as everyone says. They went nuts. So you'd be happier if Goce served you? Fat, hairy Goce, with no pants on? Come on, cut the crap and admit it: she's a real fox! Admit that you're lucky. Any one of us would trade places with you in a heartbeat. Unless you're a faggot. Since then, I try to come up with the best possible story with the most details I can think of. And pretty much I do.

Afternoons I most often spend in Robert's semibasement kitchen or in the classroom with the TV. After supper we're all usually in the dorm. There we clown around awhile, drinking and smoking, and then fall asleep. Nobody comes to wake us in the morning; nobody makes us do morning exercises; nobody checks on us. We just have to be ready by the flag raising.

On Friday and Saturday nights, Rade and I go outside on the balcony, each with our own bottle. There we drink from taps to reveille. It's a kind of ritual. At the end Rade hugs me. He tells me I'm a good friend, a true comrade. He tells me he's a communist with a heart, even if he's not a member of the party. He says you don't have to be a member of the party to be a good communist. Just look at the Federal Assembly. Everyone in it is a party member, but tell me, he asks, are they good people? Fuck them, I reply.

Every time we're on the balcony, Rade tells me about the kind of women they have in Užice. They're so good you can lick all ten of your fingers, he claims. But nobody ever gets the best ones because they're too good for any local boy. But if you came to visit me, they would all be ours. He grabs the back of my neck with his sausage-like fingers. They love Slovenians. You could have the very best one, and I'd get all the others because I'm your friend. So will you come to see me when we're on the outside again? I will, I tell him although I doubt it. Events in the world and in Yugoslavia have recently been happening so fast, one after the other, that you almost don't notice them, but they're piling up. I feel like it won't be long before something cracks beneath the weight of all these changes.

And where will I be when it does?

In late December, because of the events in Romania, we were in a state of permanent battle readiness. Every evening we watched the news, and every morning, standing in formation, we listened to the lieutenant's explanation of what was happening in the country next door, where mass demonstrations had erupted. On December seventeenth, protesters in Timişoara clashed with the army, the police, and members of the secret police. The next morning Lieutenant Stojanović said that we had probably heard about the disturbances in Romania but nobody knew exactly what was happening there. It seems very likely that British and American agents are involved, that they're stirring up the populace. But the Romanian army will soon get the situation under control. Even if there are foreign agents in the country, we need to remember that usually the only people who join them are drunks, drug addicts, faggots, and other scum who can be bought for a few filthy dollars. Honest citizens know their place! Honest citizens cannot be fooled!

Three days later the protesters occupied Timişoara and set off for Bucharest. On December twenty-first, there were clashes in the capital, with a significant number of dead and wounded, and by the next day the clashes had spread to every city in Romania. For the final time, President Nicolae Ceauşescu addressed the Romanian people from the balcony of the palace; they booed him. Soon afterward, the protesters stormed the palace, but Nicolae and his wife, Elena, at the last possible moment, lifted off from the roof in a helicopter and escaped.

At some point, when it became clear that Ceauşescu was a lost cause, the army joined the protesters; the secret police alone remained loyal to the president. Lieutenant Stojanović told us the next morning that the situation was serious but the Romanian army was on the side of the people.

The army forced the helicopter carrying the Ceaușescus to land. On December twenty-fifth, in the city of Târgoviște, a quick trial was held, which was followed by the execution of the presidential couple. Three days later, when all the world's television stations were running clips of the shooting and the dead couple, Lieutenant Stojanović said the overthrow of the dictator had been justified. He did not comment on the trial or the execution. He added only that, as a result, the instability in the region had probably ended and Romania's internal problems were no concern of ours. Our concern was our own country. Our task was to preserve the constitutional order and territorial integrity of Yugoslavia.

We rang in the new year with a few smuggled bottles of brandy. Not enough to get us really drunk, but it cheered us up a little.

A conference was announced for January ninth at the Cankar Centre in Ljubljana on the topic of Slovenia's secession from Yugoslavia. The next morning, after the raising of the flag, Lieutenant Stojanović called me into his office and asked what my relatives at home had told me about this in our phone conversations and what the other soldiers from Slovenia were saying about it. I said I wasn't interested in politics and didn't know what other people thought because it wasn't something we talked about. Well, ask around a little, he suggested. Maybe someone will say something. If you hear anything, come to me, he ended.

In late January, the Slovenian and Croatian delegations walked out of the 14th Congress of the League of Communists of Yugoslavia. The next morning, Lieutenant Stojanović was again enraged. He shouted that maybe we really did want to join the Krauts! But the army had clear orders and would never allow that.

Two days later we went into the field. No more watching the evening news or listening to morning lectures about the state of the country. On the first day, we reached the small town of Valandovo; on the second, the village of Josifovo. In between, we performed a few tactical exercises—we dug foxholes for artillery, staged attacks and retreats, and, on both days, in the evening and late into the night, dug trench shelters, where we slept. The late January cold was easing up, but there was a sharp wind blowing off the Vardar River.

In the town of Demir Kapija, the patients at the local psychiatric hospital were excited by the long column of soldiers; they ran back and forth along the fence, some of them barking at us but most of them saluting us fist to temple, the way they had seen it done in Partisan movies. Two days later, we reached Kavadarci and then, finally, Krivolak.

The next day we had a munitions drill. In the morning, Second Lieutenant Cvetkovski talked at length about how in previous years his soldiers had always been the best. I want this year to be the same!

As we were all getting our rocket launchers ready, Lieutenant Stojanović came over to Robert and me. Maybe it would be best for the army if the two of you didn't shoot, he said. I don't understand, sir, I replied. All sorts of things are happening these days, the lieutenant said through his teeth. You're being trained for six months by the finest officers of the Yugoslav Army. And I have to ask myself, What are we going to get out of this? It's possible that in a few months we'll be looking at each other from opposing sides. I don't understand, sir, I said again, although I knew very well what he meant. That's when Stojanović went crazy. Like fuck you don't understand, he shouted. Comrade Soldier, you will not take me for a fool! You will not fuck with me! I remained silent. Fortunately, Second Lieutenant Cvetkovski came over. Stojanović left and Cvetkovski didn't ask any questions.

After the drill we cleaned our launcher and waited to hear the scores. When the soldiers from the Prilep base finally finished shooting, it was clear that we had come out on top. We had been told that the best squad would be rewarded with a week's leave. Siniša hugged me like a little kid. He was jumping up and down and shouting that we were the best. Second Lieutenant Cvetkovski treated us to two rounds in the canteen; then Lieutenant Stojanović came over and said that was enough. Without another word we left for the trench shelters.

During our days in the field, the Soviet Union ended its one-party system, while in South Africa, Nelson Mandela was released from prison after twenty-seven years. Most of us had no idea who this smiling Black man with the raised fist was, but we knew the Russians were our friends. What happened there made a difference.

When we were in the field I had a conversation with the driver Darko. He had come to Macedonia from Croatia. He said we had it good here. It's a fucking mess in Croatia. He said the army was moving from base to base. We had no field training, he whispered. A little way past the town of Slunj I stopped to take a crap. The officer yelled for me to hurry. When I looked up, the surrounding hills were full of people. At first I thought it was the army. But it wasn't the army. They were Četniks. Fucking Serbian nationalists. When I asked the officer what was going on, he told me to look straight ahead. Not left or right, not up, only straight ahead. Just follow the trucks, he said. Don't fall behind and everything will be fine. I couldn't get Darko's words out of my head. Lieutenant Stojanović had been going on about the Croatian Ustaše and the Slovenian Home Guard, and now Darko had added Serbian Četniks to the mix.

When we returned from the field, there was no reward of a week's leave. The lieutenant said nothing. The second lieutenant even asked him about it once, but he didn't get an answer. Our six-month training period was approaching its end. We waited to see what would happen.

In his own way, Lieutenant Stojanović was right: it was the army that was holding Yugoslavia together. But he was also convinced that a few Home Guardists and Ustaše, pickpockets, and faggots never stood a chance against the third most powerful army in Europe. There's still plenty of room in the prison camp on Goli Otok, he thundered. If need be, the army will step in to help the police keep order on the streets. Then there will be peace. Then nobody will dare let out a fart. Yugoslavia will survive!

About this he was wrong. In the months that followed everything went to hell, including the third most powerful army in Europe.

If I had known then what was coming, on my last day I would have given every soldier I had spent that year with a big hug and kissed them on both their cheeks. If I had known what was coming, I would have told them that I hoped they survived. I would have told them that I hoped they never had to kill anyone. But instead we just laughed like crazy, had one last beer at the station in Skopje, told each other to go fuck yourself, and boarded the train that took us to the future.

41

I AM LYING in bed and thinking, It's finally over. Everything is finally over. Good.

It is good that I'm home. It is good that war didn't break out when I was in the army, although even now I cannot imagine who we would be fighting against. We heard all kinds of things, but we didn't believe them. The officers talked about Slovenian and Croatian separatists, about Home Guardists and Ustaše returning to Yugoslavia from Austria, Germany, America, Canada, and Australia. You'll see! But the more they talked about them, the more there were pictures of Milošević hanging in their offices and the more there were Serbian recruits requesting to be sent to Kosovo. Little by little, fear got under our skins, as if we sensed that the time was coming when everything would be different, a time we were not prepared for. We often got drunk. When we were drunk, the anxiety went away. When we were drunk, things were a lot simpler, easier to solve, clearer. At least for us. In the end, not a day went by that, after emptying a few bottles in one office or another, we didn't hug each other and say that everything would be okay. Look: Siniša's a Serb, I'm a Slovenian, Kenan's a Bosnian, Robert's a Croatian, Rade's a Serb. And do we have any problems? None at all! So can Croatians, Bosnians, Serbs, and Slovenians all drink together? Yes, we can! Can we all eat off the same spoon? No, we can't. Yes, we fucking can. Of course we can! Fine, that was the wrong question. Fuck it. But the point is that we all get along. We hugged each other and laughed. As if we really believed that, when the time came, anyone would ever ask us anything.

I've been home for three weeks now and I'm still not entirely sure it's real. I'm still not entirely used to the bathroom having a door and the hot water not running out in the shower. I can barely believe there are no more bugle calls, no more sewing buttons on or cleaning rifles. No general, no lieutenant, no corporal. No more *I understand, sir!* No more *Like fuck you understand!* Sometimes I'm afraid it's all a dream, although in the army I never dreamed about being home. Even so. Soon the bugle will start playing, followed by the morning run and exercise, washing, making the bed, rushing to breakfast, rushing to the flag raising, and finally Lieutenant Stojanović and all his threats about Germans and Americans, Greeks and Bulgarians, Romanians and Albanians, Slovenians and Croatians, separatists and irredentists, smugglers and pickpockets, artists and faggots. He'll be shouting and spraying us with his venomous spit, which doesn't wash off because it's like tar, like a fungus you don't see at first but that quickly spreads and spreads until in the end all you see is mold, deadly mold.

SEBASTIJAN PREGELJ

The first few days I was constantly in town. I wanted to walk down streets I knew, to touch buildings and walls, benches, bushes, and trees. If I touched them, it meant they were there. If I didn't, then maybe they weren't there at all. I spent hours sitting in the bustling city, drinking coffee and listening to the people around me. I watched them and thought, everything is normal. There was no Home Guard in the city, no Ustaše or Četniks, no German or American agents. Nothing but entirely ordinary people. Doing entirely ordinary things. Rushing here and there. Some of them weren't doing anything in particular. Like me, they were sitting and watching the world around them. When it started to rain, I didn't seek cover like everyone else. I let the drops fall on me. They seemed soft and warm. They seemed friendly.

I remembered how once, long ago, I was standing with Peter and Elvis on the hill behind our apartment buildings. We were in the second or third grade. We weren't in school because it was a holiday. We were waiting for the airplane to come. Every year on this day an army plane would fly over the city and drop leaflets that said: *Long live the Liberation Front!* It was a cloudy day and the wind was blowing. Then raindrops started to fall. We just stood there waiting, staring into the sky. Every so often a ray of sun would penetrate the gray veil of clouds, but despite this the raindrops were coming down faster and faster. Peter's mother shouted a few times from their window that we needed to get out of the rain, but we pretended not to hear her. A little later there was thunder and then it started to pour. The few people who had been walking their dogs retreated to the garages to wait out the rain, but we didn't budge from that hill. And then it happened. First, we heard the rumble of the engine, then the silver plane appeared against the gray sky. It was flying low, right above the apartment buildings, and heading straight for us. At that very moment, the sun shone through the clouds. It was raining buckets and the sun was shining. Just before the plane was directly overhead, leaflets started dropping out of its sleek belly. We took off down the hill, running across the wet grass as fast as we could. Quickly, we began picking up the wet sheets of paper and soon our arms were full of them. Not until we had as many as we could possibly carry did we go to the garages, carefully deposit our little stacks of paper on the curb, and thoroughly examine them. We compared the piles to see who had more. Elvis had the most leaflets, Peter the fewest. I was somewhere in between. Elvis took a few from his pile and gave them to Peter. Then he gave a few to me as well. At that moment we were the happiest boys in the city. I could feel the happiness tingling in my chest. We split up and each of us distributed the leaflets in the mailboxes in our own buildings. Any leftovers we took home with us. I remember how soft, warm, and friendly the raindrops felt to me when we were standing on the hill that day. But that was a long time ago. Strange I should remember it.

With Mom and Dad I talk as if nothing had happened: Do we need anything from the store? What's for lunch? What's the movie on TV tonight and are we going to watch it together? They never ask me about the army. They probably think I would tell them if there was anything to tell. But there probably wasn't. I guess not.

Saša and I got together the day after my return. When I stepped through the door, we looked at each other for a few seconds, then I hugged and kissed her. A moment later Saša bit me; then her teeth were grabbing at my lip and she started pushing me lightly toward her room. From the front hall we went down the long corridor, discarding clothes along the way, and ended up in her bed. How I missed you, Saša kept saying, until her words were lost in ever-louder gasps and sighs. When, out of breath and drenched in sweat, we finally took a break, she asked me what was going on with us. What do you mean *going on*, I asked. Are we a couple or aren't we? I don't know, I said. Were we a couple before I left? Or were we just getting together now and then? Did you wait for me or were you with somebody else? Well, you know, she said softly, I was with someone else. Then she quickly added, But just a couple of times. He didn't mean anything to me. Do you understand? I do, I said. Are you angry? No. What about you? She looked at me. Were you with anyone? Just the beautiful Vangelija, I smiled. Then I told her about the beautiful Vangelija and her store. Saša laughed.

In the evenings I meet up with friends. The first was Peter. I happened to run into him one morning. Later that afternoon we went into town. We sat outside the Golden Ship pub and laughed like hell. When it got dark, we went to the nearest phone booth and called Elvis. Elvis wasn't at home, but Uncle Fikret, who was thrilled to hear from me, said he was all right. Elvis got back five days ago, he said. Come and see us sometime. I will, I promised, although I didn't really mean it. Elvis came by the next day. We all went out together.

A few days later Rok phoned me. We met up right after lunch. We sat on top of the garages and talked. Stupid shit mainly. I told him about the plot of weed, the beautiful Vangelija, and the whorehouse above the pigsty. I told him about the alcohol from the packages, and about Rade and the women of Užice. Rok told me about the Romanian women who crossed the border because they could earn as much money in one night in Yugoslavia as they did an entire week at home. They'll jerk you off for 100 dinars, he said. He told me how one winter night they drove them from Zrenjanin to the border. On the other side of the border, people are outraged and the army is trying to capture the president. And meanwhile, we were patrolling our side. But one night our patrol got lost. And in the morning the corporal, who's as dumb as shit, sees a road sign and realizes we're a good ten kilometers from the border—inside Romania. So we hid until dark and then cautiously started making our way back to Yugoslavia. If we heard even the slightest noise, we'd lie low and wait. We didn't want to run into any Romanian border guards or the rebels or the police, but, more than that, we were scared shitless because we'd heard there were landmines all along the border. Luckily, everything worked out in the end and we made it back. The base was going crazy. They thought we'd been captured or even shot, but when it turned out that we were alive and well, people started suspecting that we had defected to the Romanians. Can you believe it? Rok laughed. The colonel accused us of treason. What did you take to Romania, he shouted. What the fuck did you tell them? He interrogated each of us separately for hours, but in the end he decided it was basically what we said it was. Then the next day a commission headed by some general arrived from Belgrade. They, too, questioned us in detail. In the end, the corporal was rewarded with a week's leave for getting us back safely to Yugoslavia. What bullshit!

Who was it who took us into Romania in the first place? Then Rok said he was going to the coast that weekend and asked if I wanted to join him. Thanks, but no, I said. I'd rather stay here. I just want to be here for a while.

I thought a few times about calling Matej, but I always changed my mind. He can call me if he feels like it. I don't even know if he's back yet. Mom told me about Peter and Elvis, and Rok himself called me. But I have no idea where Matej is. And I'm not really sure I want to see him anyway. We hadn't been hanging out together as much as before. I expect he's thrilled by everything that's happening. I'm sure he's joined one of the new political parties and could even be part of its leadership. I imagine he talks about nothing else. But right now what I want most are for things to be normal and ordinary. My ears are still ringing with slogans: *Protect Brotherhood and Unity Like the Apple of Your Eye! The Revolution Endures! Tito After Tito!* etc. At first, when everything was still new to us, I felt like I had fallen into some parallel universe where time stood still, where Comrade Tito was still alive and still leading the nations and nationalities of Yugoslavia, who all lived together in brotherly harmony. Tito was still the supreme commander of the armed forces, only he was no longer driving around the country in his Mercedes, which is why we never saw him. By winter, however, it was clear nobody believed a word of it. Still, day after day, the officers kept repeating the same old crap. It was like they took us for morons. Only later did I realize that in fact they didn't give a shit what we thought. They knew we were powerless. So right now, what I want more than anything else is peace. No big slogans. What I like talking about most is what's for lunch, what's on TV tonight, and what movie we should go to: *The Godfather Part III*, *Misery*, *The Hunt for Red October*, or *Night of the Living Dead*. My friends and I talk mostly about stupid shit. Nothing about plans, nothing about the future. Until October, when classes at the university start, my time is my own. Until then I'll do only what I like and what truly makes me happy. Everything else can wait. That's why Saša and I saw each other again the very next morning and the day after that.

We get together a little after eight every weekday morning. Since I still wake up at five o'clock, waiting until eight seems like an eternity. But so what? When I remember that I'm lying in my own bed and don't have to get up, the world seems incredibly beautiful and simple to me. Saša likes to sleep a little longer, so I wait until eight. Also, I prefer to wait until both her parents and mine have left for work. I don't want either hers or mine to know about us. At least not that we see each other every day. So a little after eight, but never later than eight thirty, I ring her doorbell. We don't waste words, we don't play games—we go straight to bed. We fuck like the world is about to end. Sometimes we don't even make it to the bed. Sometimes it happens right in the front hall. Once it happened on the kitchen table and twice in the bathroom. One more time, then everything will be gone. But we soon realize that the world didn't end and we still have time for a little more cuddling. Then we hug and caress and kiss each other until eventually Saša climbs on top of me or I pull her beneath me. In the end, we take a shower and go our separate ways.

Ever since I got back, Dad keeps saying now everything will change. When he says Slovenia is going to secede from

SEBASTIJAN PREGELJ

Yugoslavia and then everything will be different, he seems to be sure of what he's saying. It can't be stopped now, he says, shaking his head. They can try to stop it with the army, but America won't allow that, and the Russia that once would have supported Belgrade doesn't exist anymore. It's possible that the army could try to seize power. I'm not saying it will, but it's possible. And it's possible that we'll have to fight back. I'm not saying we will, but maybe we won't have a choice.

A few days ago, Uncle Gorazd told us that one morning some army trucks pulled into the courtyard at his company. The soldiers, led by Nikolić and accompanied by military police, cleared everything out of the offices. They took all the computers and all the files. We managed to hide a few things, but not much—it was a surprise to everyone when the army showed up. Now the offices are empty. We still go in to work but mostly we just stare at each other. The director has promised us new computers, but they won't do us much good without our files. That's a year's worth of work down the drain.

And you, he asked me on the balcony, pulling out a pack of cigarettes. All three of us lit up. How was it? I tell him it wasn't anything special. It could've been worse. They could've sent me to Kosovo. Something could've happened, but it didn't. See? Uncle Gorazd tapped my shoulder with his right index finger. That's good. You were lucky. And what about our guys? Have they called you yet? What do you mean *our guys*? I didn't understand. Territorial Defense, he explained. That's our army now. No, they haven't. He just got back, Dad said. That's exactly why I asked, my uncle said. They've mostly been calling up boys who just got back. Martin spent fourteen days last month doing military exercises. Some guys try to avoid it. They go into hiding. But I don't think that's right. Who's going to stand up to the Yugoslav Army if there's a . . . well, if things keep intensifying? We have to show them we're not afraid.

I am lying in bed and thinking that a lot of changes occurred when I was away. I'm hearing new things. What a year ago was only whispered is now being said aloud. Some things sound good, others less good. I feel like nobody really knows what comes next.

42

THE MOMENT I come in, I can tell something's wrong. Mom and Dad both have that kind of face. I stand at the door and wait for them to tell me.

It's Aunt Taja, Dad says at last. She's sick. She has cancer. What, I say. She has cancer. She hasn't felt good for a while now. She would throw up sometimes. She told herself it was nothing, that it couldn't be anything. Not at her age. She didn't tell your uncle. When she started to feel worse, she went to the doctor. He immediately sent her to be tested. She got the results yesterday. She told Gorazd and Gorazd told me. Are they going to operate, I ask. Of course they are, Dad says. The doctor said it would be soon, since cancer patients are given priority in the waiting lines. He also said they found it in time. It would have been better if she had come sooner, but what's important is that she didn't come too late. Some people come too late. They come when there's nothing that can be done. Sometimes the surgeon just opens them and closes them up again. Sometimes not even that. But fortunately, Aunt Taja came at the right time. I nod and sit down at the table. Mom tells me there are leftovers from lunch in the refrigerator. Have something. I'm not hungry, I say. When I was coming up the stairs, I was hungry. I was hoping there would be something left over from lunch in the refrigerator. I was imagining cold chicken, bread, and mayonnaise, or maybe French salad. Now I don't feel like eating. I'm thinking about Aunt Taja. They're going to operate on her soon. I hope everything will be okay then.

Eat something, Mom tells me as I go into my room. Let him be, I hear Dad say. I shut the door and throw myself on the bed. I saw my aunt and uncle not too long ago. It was like always. How can things go wrong so fast? One day everything is fine and good, and the next day everything is bad and wrong. I turn onto my side and shut my eyes. I'd like to fall asleep. I'd like to sink into a deep sleep and wake up yesterday, when everything was still okay with my aunt, although it wasn't really okay, only we didn't know that it wasn't. And if you don't know something, it doesn't scare you, it doesn't gnaw at you, it doesn't exist.

Not everything is okay with my aunt, but I hope she'll be one of the lucky ones. I hope the operation will be successful and she will quickly recover and the disease will not return. After all, Grandpa is still alive and they discovered his cancer a long time ago. Grandpa is one of the lucky ones.

But maybe Aunt Taja won't be lucky. Maybe the operation won't be a success. Maybe she won't be around very much longer, I think. Maybe when they open her up they will see there is nothing they can do. They'll sew her up and send her back home. Uncle Gorazd and Martin will watch as she fades. At first she will do everything she usually does at home as if nothing had happened. Then she will gradually stop cleaning and straightening up. She'll start apologizing to Uncle Gorazd, who will wave his hand each time and say it doesn't matter. Leave it, he'll say. I'll do it. Then one day she won't make dinner because she spent the entire day sitting in her armchair. She will say she's worn out and can't even get up. Uncle Gorazd will wave his hand and order pizza. Soon she won't be able to take a shower on her own, and later she'll even need help getting out of bed. The home-care nurse will come twice a week but that won't hardly be enough. Uncle Gorazd and Martin will have to take care of her. They will have to feed her, help her to the bathroom, wash her, dress her, and turn her in the bed. No matter how much she eats or doesn't eat, she will get thinner and thinner until in the end she is nothing but skin and bones. She will look at them with black-circled, sunken eyes and try to smile. She will have cracked lips and weirdly big teeth. Uncle Gorazd and Martin, each of them privately, will wait for the end, because every day Aunt Taja is getting worse and worse and suffering more and more. She is suffering from the pain and suffering even more when she sees what she has become and what their life has become. But not today, not yet, they will think. They will hope it's tomorrow.

Nobody knows what will happen.

43

LECTURES BEGAN IN late October. For now, I'm going to all of them. For the most part they're interesting, but that feeling in the big lecture halls, especially, is something completely different from what I felt in the overcrowded classrooms at my secondary school. I never did like secondary school.

Saša and I still get together, but a lot less often than before. I see Peter now and then, mainly when we run into each other at the bus stop, but it's been a while since I last saw Elvis. Matej and I got together once. It was strange, and I haven't entirely shaken that feeling of awkwardness. I was thinking the whole time that it was a big mistake. I shouldn't have phoned him and we shouldn't have met up. Matej says the time is coming when Slovenia's thousand-year dream will be a reality. It will be the end of humiliation and slavery. He speaks in elevated tones, as if he was talking about religion, revelation, the parting of the sea, or I don't know what else. In just over an hour, I drank three bottles of beer, smoked eight cigarettes, and said about twenty words. When we parted, I sighed with relief.

Elvis has gotten strange. I don't know what's up with him. He answers my questions in short sentences, as if he doesn't want to tell me everything, although I don't ask him anything unusual. His eyes dart this way and that as if there is something he's hiding. He told me his parents now have a cage on their balcony where they keep quails. What do I care about some fucking quails? Defne is living in Sarajevo with two kids and a third on the way. She is happy. As for Ali, Elvis says he doesn't know where his brother is. I don't have a clue what's going on in that family. In my opinion, Elvis knows where Ali is but he doesn't want to tell me. Instead he talks about quails. It's enough to drive you fucking insane.

It's good I have Rok. With him, everything is like it used to be. We go out and goof around. Most of the time we're at Under the Linden. Rok still smokes weed, but only now and then. Sometimes I join him. When we're stoned, we talk about the old times. About school and Batty, about Tito's portraits, and about the guy who was jerking off by the train tracks. We can talk about those things again and again. Sometimes we remember other things too: how I fought with Sršen and ended up in the principal's office, and how we stuck a match in the lock to the physics classroom and thought we could get out of the test that way, but then the teacher took the class to an empty room next door, handed out the test, and said we would only have whatever time remained and that if it was less time than we would have had otherwise, well, we could only blame ourselves for that. Some of the girls were angry at us for this. We talk about how at the end of the school year, in the art room, we squeezed out tubes of tempera paint through the window onto the people below, until finally a man came storming into our homeroom with a yellow stripe down his black suit. The homeroom teacher summoned our parents to the school and we all had to collect money for a new suit. At home, of course, there was hell to pay. But everyone in the class blamed someone else and nobody really knew whose idea it was in the first place, so no one squealed and no one got punished.

It's the same as always at Under the Linden. Antonio still works there. Ever since Mara's funeral, he treats Rok and me as old friends. Sometimes he gives us a round on the house. Then he says, To Mara. You guys know what a gem Mara was. When this happens, we can't refuse. We know what a gem Mara was, we say, and drink to her memory.

The days pass slowly, one after the other. It rains almost every day, and it's getting noticeably colder out.

Aunt Taja was operated on early this week and the prognosis is good. The doctor is optimistic, and so is Uncle Gorazd. He and Dad went out and got drunk. Mom didn't get angry; just the opposite. She laughed and said he came lumbering home like a badger and then snored like a bear.

Six weeks after the operation my aunt went on a pilgrimage to Medjugorje. The place is known for its apparitions of Mary. The first one happened ten years ago. Mary appeared to six children and ever since she has been sending messages through them to the world. The authorities are not happy about the apparitions, and not even the Vatican wants to recognize them, but nevertheless people flock in droves to this small Herzegovinian village.

It can't be real, Uncle Gorazd said, when my aunt told him she was going on the trip. But in the end I agreed, he said when he stopped by my father's office on his way home from work on Thursday. Go if you think it will help you, I told her. Taja said she wasn't sure it would help. But it certainly couldn't hurt me. And she went.

Ever since she returned from that pilgrimage, she's been going to church and brings us Mary's messages. She says there's going to be a big punishment for all our sins. The only way we can soften it is through prayer. The leaflets she leaves with us linger on the kitchen table or on the counter for a while, but eventually Mom or Dad tosses them in the receptacle for old paper. From time to time I pick one up and read it. Dad says it's nonsense. It can't help. Mom doesn't agree. She says it couldn't hurt. It can only help her. And if it helps her even a little, that's a lot. It's more than anything else has. Am I right? Yes, you're right, Dad says and backs down.

Aunt Taja has invited Mom to go with her to mass sometime. You'll see, Father Lovro is different. Every month he takes a group to Medjugorje. You don't have to be a believer to go. It's enough that you're willing to open your heart. And anyone who's been there once knows how . . . well, it opens your eyes. Father Lovro gives us hope and strength. Mom is reluctant. She says she went enough times to mass as a child. You can't do it because of others, my aunt says, not wanting to give up. You have to do it for yourself. For your family. You'll see what a positive effect it has. Maybe some other time, Mom says. And that's where she left it.

A few days before New Year's, Saša tells me she can't go on like this. Maybe we could be a couple. But if there had been anything of that there, we would be one already. But that's not how you feel, is it? No, I say. Well, then that's too bad, she says. Tears are trickling down her face. I have never seen her cry before. I hug her, although at that moment I wish I could vanish from the room, like a magician at the end of his performance when he wraps himself in his cloak, which a few seconds later falls to the ground and the magician is nowhere to be seen. People are astonished. They look and look and can't believe their eyes. They don't know whether to clap after such a finale. Who are they are clapping for if there's nobody on the stage? In the end, they rise in silence from the upholstered seats and leave the auditorium. They whisper, How did he do that? How is that possible? Saša hugs me, then she pushes me away. Go! Just go!

The things they are saying on the seven-thirty news are not at all promising.

44

EARLY THIS MORNING tanks rolled onto the streets of Maribor. When the telephone rang a little after nine, I knew it was for me. As the situation in Maribor and other parts of Slovenia was being shown on television, I was expecting this call. Right after we declared independence, we removed the Yugoslav signs and flags on the border crossings and replaced them with Slovenian ones. The army received its command during the night and left the bases. They were ordered to occupy the border crossings. I got my backpack out of the basement; I have had it since I was called up for military exercises in late April. Mom unstitched the red star from my army cap and Dad told me to be careful, a few times. Maybe nothing will happen in Ljubljana, he said. But it doesn't look that way. I expect this is just the beginning. Don't try to be a hero.

Not long after that, I put on my backpack. I'm going now. I hug my mother. I hug my father. I step into the hallway and run down the stairs. My mind is blank, but the strange feeling in my stomach is like when the teacher calls you to the chalkboard. You don't know what's going to happen. I hurry down the street, cross the parking lot, and don't know what to expect. Everything is unknown. Everything is new and alien. It's not entirely clear if there's even a war. In my mental images from movies and books, wars start differently. During World War II, on the first day of its invasion of Yugoslavia, Germany bombed Belgrade. Japan attacked Pearl Harbor. In my mind I see explosions, ruins, smoke. But in our case, it's tanks and armored vehicles rolling onto the streets. The tanks crushed a few buses and trucks, which the Slovenian police and Territorial Defense forces had put there to stop the army's advance. That's basically it—otherwise the day looks entirely ordinary. The hedges by the apartment buildings are growing wildly into the air; the leaves on the trees are getting a deeper shade of green; the rose bushes on the well-tended lawns are coming into bloom. There is a puddle by the curb left over from yesterday's downpour. There are pigeons around it. They appear to have quenched their thirst a while ago and now are trying to keep the sparrows away from the puddle. Still, every so often, one gets past. It wets its beak, ruffles its feathers, flaps its wings, and leaves. But the road is emptier than usual. Although an empty road doesn't mean there's a war.

Early this morning, when I was watching the tanks break through the barricades and crush the buses and trucks, I felt angry. Everything inside me was shaking. If I had been there with a rifle in my hands, I would not have just stood and watched. But no one in Maribor used any weapons. As if this was just the last in a series of provocations where you needed to stay calm and keep your head. These past few months the Yugoslav Army has often tried to provoke us, but until today nothing like this has happened. The tanks stayed inside the army bases. Now several columns of tanks are making their way toward the western and northern borders. So it's obviously serious. Lieutenant Stojanović was right, I say to myself. They trained me, but today we stand on opposing sides.

It doesn't take me long to reach the district administration building. There are two lines of young men in the basement. They are here because they have been called up like me. When I present my military documents, I'm sent past the lines. I stand for a second in front of the last door; then I knock and enter.

Inside I see Vane, the captain I met at the military exercises in April. He looks at me and says he was right. I remember how at the end of our training, which we had with a unit from the special police forces, we all stared at him when he told us we shouldn't be surprised if we get the call soon. He said we would see each other again sooner than we imagined. We'll probably have to attack an army base or blow up some other military facility. You can't be serious, I thought. Now here we are.

We'll be getting new uniforms in a day or two, Vane says. Until then we'll wear the old ones. He hands out red armbands with the words *Territorial Defense* written on them. Wear them on your arms—so we can tell who's who.

Mint and Andrej haven't arrived, but the rest of us are here. Let's wait a little, Vane says; then he pulls out a pack of cigarettes and lights one. The smoke and the smell of the uniforms instantly take me back to the classroom on the army base in

Macedonia. I half close my eyes. It's the same smell, the same sounds, and it is just as unreal. It's all fucking insane.

I flinch at the clank of metal. Okay, this is what they have for us. Vane lays the guns on the green school desks. MP 40s, which you know as the Schmeisser, he says. I recognize the machine gun from Partisan films. It's what German officers, SS agents, and Partisan heroes all carried. Now I'm getting one too. I also get magazines, cardboard boxes with cartridges, and a leather bag. I load the ammo into the magazines and what's left over I put in my backpack. In the meantime, Vane prepares the pistols. Zastava M57s. Yugoslav. The Schmeissers are old. We got them from the police warehouse. It's possible they don't work perfectly. The pistols, however, are in pretty good shape. At least it's something. He stubs out his cigarette. The guys you saw outside aren't getting weapons for now. They'll have to wait for us to empty a warehouse. Which won't be easy. He shakes his head. But if it was easy, we wouldn't have called you, right?

In the afternoon we climb into a small yellow van, the kind postmen use for distributing big packages, and drive to the other end of Ljubljana. We learn that for the time being our base will be a secondary school dormitory. There's a Yugoslav Army base across from it. With about 200 meters of open space between them. Maybe less. Guys who arrived earlier than us are milling around outside the dorm. Since I don't know any of them, I stick with my platoon.

We toss ourselves on the beds in the dorm rooms. Duran Duran, Bryan Adams, and the Bosnian pop band Blue Orchestra are staring at us from the wall posters and a class schedule

SEBASTIJAN PREGELJ

is taped to a wardrobe. A girls' room. Smells like women, Frenk says with a laugh. Too bad they left.

There is something going on all the time outside the building, so a little later we go out again. We sit on a low wall by the steps and watch. When it starts to get dark, a white van drives up. Sandwiches and smokes, the driver calls out. There are a lot more sandwiches and smokes than men, so everyone gets two sandwiches and a few packs of cigarettes.

Before night falls, Vane organizes guard duty. I think it's good we're in Vane's unit. He obviously knows more than the others do; he's obviously more respected than the others. He'll know how to take care of the six of us, I think to myself.

Together we watch the evening news. None of it's good. Over the course of the day the Yugoslav Army occupied several border crossings. In some places there were clashes with Territorial Defense forces. Most extraordinary to me is that everything has been happening under the eyes of numerous civilians and armed police officers. People have been standing in front of tanks, throwing stones at them, and hitting them with sticks. They have been shouting and booing, and some were crying because they couldn't believe such a thing was taking place, but the tanks kept rolling on. When shots rang out, the people moved away; some would lie on the ground. When the shooting stopped, they got up and again approached the tanks. As if it wasn't serious.

We sleep in our uniforms with our boots on. Before I fall asleep, I think that anything could happen in the night.

Early in the morning we drive to the foot of Golovec Hill. Vane says we're going up. We need to see if anyone's there. By *anyone* he means Yugoslav soldiers. They could be at the observatory; they could be in some clearing. We need to be cautious and alert. He spits and lights a cigarette. We quickly arrange ourselves and start climbing the wooded hill. The slope is steep and covered in undergrowth, so we make slow progress. About halfway there, we hear voices in the distance and stop. My heart skips a beat. Like the others, I press myself behind the nearest tree and wait. I have my finger on the trigger. I feel beads of sweat collecting on my forehead. Soon we see a couple with a dog. The man and woman are talking in loud voices as they walk, with the smallish dog a few meters ahead of them, running and sniffing at trees and plants. Vane gestures to us to wait. I don't understand. Haven't these two heard what's happening? They could have run into the army, or we could have shot them. What the fuck, I think and take my finger off the trigger.

Once they're out of sight, we continue. Twenty minutes later we reach the observatory. There's an orange compact parked by the entrance. Vane walks up to the door while the rest of us wait in the woods. He knocks and goes in. A short while later he comes out. One of the astronomers is here. He says there hasn't been anyone else. We're the first.

When we return to the dormitory, a special forces unit is there. They're in camouflage and carry Korean SAR 80 rifles. They keep to themselves. So do we. Around noon the white van drives up. Lunch and smokes, the driver shouts. Everybody gets two schnitzel sandwiches with pickles and a few packs of cigarettes. While we're eating lunch, Mint joins us. We greet him like an old friend we haven't seen in a long time. He says he was at the seaside and couldn't make it back yesterday to Ljubljana.

Vane says clashes are happening all over Slovenia. He says we need to go to the Ljubljana Marsh. We ask him what we'll be doing there. Same thing, the captain tells us. We'll check to see if anyone's there. People have been calling to say that something is happening. We get ready and wait by the yellow van, which we're taking out of the city. We go through the villages of Črna Vas, Lipe, and Jezero. Then we drive to the foot of St. Anne's Hill. Vane turns onto a lane through the forest, drives a hundred meters or so, then parks the van behind some bushes and switches off the engine. We continue on foot. When the forest ends, we stop walking in a pack. We split up so the enemy can't shoot us all down with a single round of bullets.

Before the terrain levels out we come to the remains of a house that had been destroyed by the Italians in World War II. Vane tells us the Italians drove a blacksmith's family out of the house, but then the Partisans used it as a shelter where they could shoot at the Italians, who had turned St. Anne's Church into a military outpost with a stable. In the very spot where, before the war, people had prayed, now, during the war, there were horses shitting on the floor. We crouch for a while behind its low walls; then Vane, Frenk, and Mint move cautiously toward the church. First they walk around it; then they try to open the heavy wooden doors, but they're locked. Vane waves for us to come up.

While we are standing by the wall of the church, with Vane looking with his binoculars over the near and distant surrounding areas, we hear airplanes, shooting, and, a moment later, an explosion. The summit of Mount Krim, where the radio and television transmitters are, is engulfed in thick, black smoke.

When the smoke thins out a little, we see flames. My heart is pounding. My mind is a blank.

Vane says we need to get back. We go quickly down the hill. Once we're in the van, we have a smoke. There are wooden crates filled with munitions and explosives on the floor of the van. If we got hit, we'd be fireworks. Vane is driving cautiously and constantly looking up. The planes could come back. The yellow van is an easy target, he says.

Back in Ljubljana we learn that our side has stopped all the columns of tanks and that many soldiers from the Yugoslav Army have given themselves up. We watch TV. The reporters ask the soldiers what they were told before they left the base. They ask them what they think about everything that's going on. The soldiers are confused. They say they were dispatched to the border because Austria had attacked Yugoslavia. Some of them say nothing; others are wiping away tears. Now I know what I was afraid of in Macedonia, I think as I light a cigarette. I couldn't imagine what it would look like back then. Now my fears have acquired a form.

In the meantime, the Yugoslav Army carried out air strikes on the Brnik Airport, the Karavanke Tunnel, and the transmitters on Nanos, Boč, and Kum, as well as Krim.

We eat our schnitzel sandwiches and talk about what it was like on Krim. The guys in camouflage listen. One of them tells us they're anticipating the arrival of Yugoslav special forces from Niš. We're expecting them to attack Ljubljana. Somewhere in the background a raspy transistor radio is playing the song "It's Sunny Out and You've Mussed Up Your Hair."

In the evening we watch *Twin Peaks*. Every night we follow the story of Special Agent Cooper as he investigates the murder of the college student Laura Palmer. Frenk says Laura was a hot babe so he doesn't understand why anyone would want to kill her.

The war, it seems, has ended for today. Outside it is quiet. Our guards are in position around the dormitory, and our scouts are in position around the army base.

45

MOM AND DAD are at my aunt and uncle's, but I stayed home. I am sitting in front of the television watching the news. As clips of burning cities, charred corpses, and dead animals appear in succession on the screen, I wonder where my buddies are. Where's Rade? Where's Siniša? Where's Kenan? Where's Robert?

Did Rade do okay? Did he earn lots of money, bribe some army officials to lose his file, and escape being called up? Is he now in Užice, hanging out at the bars where the best women go? Or maybe he didn't earn so much money but still managed to leave the country. Was he lucky enough to have an uncle in Germany or Sweden who works in a car factory and could arrange a job for a relative? Did he leave for Stuttgart or Göteborg in time? Or maybe he didn't go at all but decided to stay? When times get tough it's only cowards who run; real men stay and fight for home and country. Maybe he had been attending meetings even earlier and knows the truth. I remember Rade's stories about his grandfather, Radovan, who he was named for. He told me about him on the balcony where we were emptying bottles. He talked about the column of Četniks on horseback; there were so many horses the ground was shaking. They would attack the Germans. But because they feared the enemy's revenge, all the soldiers they killed they buried. This way the Germans wouldn't find the bodies and retaliate by killing hostages. A few times in Bosnia they fought the Ustaše. They also attacked Partisans. In one of these attacks Radovan was wounded. A neighbor named Lazar recognized him. Lazar was a Partisan. He said he could save him, but he would have to join them. Then he shaved off Radovan's beard, removed all the Royal Army insignia, and carried him to the Partisan hospital. When the grandfather recovered, he rode horses with the Partisans. Then, for two years after the war, they rode around Kosovo burning villages and killing Albanians. What I fear is that Rade, like his grandfather, might have grown a beard and said to himself, To hell with everything, we Serbs have to defend ourselves against the Ustaše and the Turks! Then he might have gone to the nearest army base and joined the Četniks.

And Siniša? Is he hiding from the military police, who are searching the entire country for conscripts that didn't respond to the call-up? I find that hard to believe. In the village of Kočetin they would have found him right away. In a neighboring village, too, and I doubt he'd have gone anywhere else. Besides, Siniša is no coward. Siniša wouldn't go into hiding. In my mind I see him receiving his call-up papers. Feeling the weight of Serbia's glorious history, with rulers from Duke Dervan's son, who led the Serbs to the Balkans, all the way to King Peter II, who was stripped of his kingly rights after World War II and died in Denver, Colorado, Siniša says to himself, I will kill and roast just one more pig; then I will go. Before his departure, he would invite all his friends and relatives and, just as he said, roast a pig. He would pass out large pieces of the juicy meat, pour the slivovitz as if it were mineral water, and, when the feast was over, say, To hell with everything, the Serbs in Bosnia need our help!

And Kenan? Is Kenan a Muslim? A Croat? A Serb? In the past it didn't make any difference. Now everything makes a difference. The only thing that makes no difference is whether it's a Monday or a Friday. In the besieged city of Sarajevo, a sniper can kill you just as easily on a Monday as on a Friday. I remember when Kenan once got a package of sweets from home for Eid. So he's most likely a Muslim. Maybe he's in the city, or maybe he's somewhere in the Bosnian mountains in a muddy ditch shouting in the direction of the Serbian trenches, *Allahu akbar!*—along with volunteers from the Arab countries who have come to help their European brothers. The Serbs are not afraid of the Bosnians, but they are afraid of the Arab volunteers. There are horrible stories going around about their cruelty. Kenan is with them but he doesn't do much shooting, or even none at all, because it's important to preserve the ammo. He holds a curved Arab knife in his right hand. And he is determined to use it. He just has to get close enough. As he waits for the order to attack, he says to himself, To hell with everything, I'm going to slice one of their necks open.

And Robert, what about him? Is he still getting high on Tiger Glue under some bridge on the Sava River? When the war started, he would have had to stockpile it. If he checked the cardboard box it came in, he would have seen that the glue is made in Serbia. Once it ran out, it would no longer be available in Croatia. It's also possible that some time ago, before the war even started, he got totally high and fell into the river and drowned, so he doesn't have to worry about where to get his Serbian glue. A third possibility is that he got high at the wrong moment while watching the news. When they showed the fall of Vukovar and reported that Serbs had brutally massacred the wounded Croatian defenders in the hospital, he took one last hit from the bag, rolled his eyes and roared, To hell with everything, even that Serbian glue! He then put on his boots, headed to the office of the Croatian Defense Force, and signed up as a volunteer. They put him in uniform, hung a rosary around his neck, handed him a Kalashnikov, and sent him god knows where.

If it had been up to us, none of this would have happened. If we had our way, Rade would be strolling the streets checking out the women; Siniša would be slicing large pieces off his roasted pig and licking his thumb and index finger with every slice; Robert would be getting high on Tiger Glue in Tomislavac Park in Zagreb, where he's been going since he was a boy; and I would be on my way to visit Rade. But nobody asked us.

It looks like we'll all need Tiger Glue someday. We'll use it first to repair our broken souls and glue our lost limbs back on; then, we'll try to mend old ties and friendships. But that will be many years from now. Today it seems impossible. There are still too many bridges to destroy and too many houses to burn. Everyone has lost somebody and everyone wants revenge. If anything, people today need to forget their old friendships and break their old ties. Memories just make everything worse. They have to be blotted out. Otherwise, it's too hard to pour the gasoline and light the match; otherwise, it's too hard to pull back the bolt and fire on terrified, unarmed people.

At the moment, it seems, no glue is that strong. Not even Tiger Glue. But even so, many years from now we will try. And hope for the best.

Good luck, Rade. Good luck, Robert. Good luck, Siniša. Good luck, Kenan.

46

IT'S BEEN TWO years since Aunt Taja's operation. The cancer has not returned and for now things look good. My uncle has a new job. He says the work he did before gave him greater pleasure, but he's too old to kid himself and, anyway, the pay is good. Martin has abandoned his studies. My uncle says he should probably feel angry about this but he doesn't. The boy is smart; he'll get by. These are the times we live in. It's not important what degree you have, what's important is what you know and that you know how to get by. Maybe we'll start a company together, he says. We could import computer equipment. You're dreaming, my aunt usually tells him, and he quickly changes the subject. I quit smoking, he tells us. I haven't had a cigarette in eighty-seven days. My parents are happy for him. They congratulate him every time. I haven't seen Martin in ages.

In the meantime, Grandpa's cancer came back, so my parents visit him often. Sometimes I go with them. As soon as my uncles and aunts see our car in front of his house, they come by. They always say the same things. It sounds like they're worried about Grandpa but actually they're worried about themselves. They really get on my nerves. They talk right in front of him about what they're going to do if his condition gets worse. For now it's okay, they say. For now we can manage. But who knows what it will be like tomorrow, they sigh. Maybe we'll have no choice but to put him in a home. Grandpa puts up with it patiently, as if the conversation wasn't about him, as if it didn't have anything to do with him. Most of my cousins are married now, and some have kids. They're taking out loans and building houses. Bertica married a man who lives in Austria. Her husband has a big farm with state-of-the-art machinery. She doesn't have to work. They say she's a lady. She had a cesarean section when she gave birth, but there was a problem and now she can't have more children. It's such a pity, they say. Such a big farm and only one child. Petra got married too. But nobody calls her a lady. Whenever the conversation turns to Petra, they only say, Take too long to choose and you get leftovers. I don't see very much of my cousins. They don't visit Grandpa because they don't have time, or they only stop by for a minute or two. The same as I hear from Mom and Dad how my cousins are doing, so they hear from my aunts and uncles how I'm doing. The information goes in both directions. When I go there with my parents, I go to see Grandpa. It's him I love the most; it's him I most love being with. Grandpa is the same as he was, only he doesn't talk as much. His eyes, although cloudy, shine just as they used to. When I am with him, time seems to stop.

But usually I don't go with my parents. I prefer to stay home and hang out with Rok. We're more or less always together. If you were to ask me what a real friend is, I would say, A real friend is someone you can talk to endlessly about the same thing.

I ran into Matej a few days ago in town. His father has become a retailer. He owns three stores and is about to open a fourth. I sometimes go with Mom to the one nearest us so I can help her carry home what she buys, but Matej is never there, although we have seen his father a few times. There is a long counter in the store with two scales and the cash register. Behind the counter are sacks of flour, sugar, and salt, as well as metal containers with cooking oil. Other things are on the shelves: different kinds of pasta, several types of rice, salt, tomato paste, cookies. The sacks and containers bear the stamp *STATE RESERVES*. Matej's father doesn't work alone. You need connections, Matej explained. Then he told me that he ran into Natalija not long ago. Remember her? She asked about you. What did you say? I was curious. Whatever I felt like saying, Matej said, laughing, but then became serious. I'm joking. I haven't seen you in ages. What could I tell her? I said I had no idea how you are. So, you tell me. What should I say if I see her again? Whatever you feel like saying, I told him. Want to get a drink, Matej asked. Sorry, I'm in a rush. Maybe another time. We both knew what *another time* meant. As you wish, Matej said with a shrug. But if we hung out together, I could introduce you to the right people. And when I say the *right* people, I mean people you can profit from. Know what I mean? Successful people hang out with other successful people; losers hang out with losers. And in my opinion, you belong to the first group. I guess, I said. Then I lifted my hand to say goodbye and took off down the street. When I turned the corner, I wondered if I had made a mistake. Friends like Matej can be helpful. Whatever you need, they always know somebody who can either arrange it for you or knows someone who knows someone who can. I wondered if I had misjudged Matej. After all, he doesn't mean any harm. There was a time when we were inseparable, when we talked about State Security agents, about old Sršen, and stuff like that. I went to the parties he organized every weekend, and had sex with Natalija in his parents' house. But then he changed. We all changed. Everything changed. None of that is left now, and I don't miss any of it. Well, maybe Natalija now and then.

I sometimes run into Peter at the bus stop. Peter is the same as always. He's thin and tall, talks in a loud voice, and jumps from topic to topic. His way of presenting himself can attract attention, but when people realize they have no idea what he's talking about, they soon amuse themselves by watching somebody else. Peter's only interest is computers. He told me he's applied for some kind of American scholarship. We'll see.

Then there's Elvis. We run into each other on the street sometimes, and sometimes at the bus stop. Bit by bit, I've learned that Defne and her kids returned to Ljubljana on the first day of summer. They arrived by bus. They left Sarajevo in one of the last convoys organized by the Red Cross. The buses were stopped and searched a few times by the various armies. The soldiers took anything of value but, fortunately, let them keep their documents and, in the end, things worked out. In the end, they all arrived safely from the besieged city; in the end, they all arrived safely from Bosnia. Now they are living with her parents. Dad recently ran into Uncle Fikret. Uncle Fikret said they would manage somehow. There was a time when there were five of us living in the apartment. We lived comfortably. Now it's a bit crowded.

Defne is lucky she had somewhere to return to. I remember how much I liked her when I was in first and second grade. I liked her later too. With her big eyes, dark hair, and silky skin, she always seemed like a princess from some faraway island. I open the drawer in our living room where we keep family albums and photos from different occasions, such as my cousin's wedding, Aunt Taja's fiftieth birthday, and so on. Most of the photos aren't stored in albums but are still in the envelopes we got them in. You need to open each envelope if you want to see what's inside. I'm looking for two photos in particular, which were taken by Uncle Fikret. I remember how during our first visit he and Dad were constantly shaking hands. I remember how delighted Dad was at the time, and I remember how, on the way home, Mom couldn't stop talking about what good, kind people they were. At last I find the yellowed photos. One of them is of Elvis and me. I immediately look at the other one. I run my gaze across Dad and Mom, Uncle Fikret and Aunt Farhana, and then quickly across Ali, Elvis, and me, until my eyes are resting on Defne. I look at her and wonder what would have happened if, when I became interested in girls, I had summoned the courage to tell her how much I liked her. I have no idea. In the background of the photo there is a small television set with a lace cloth on top of it. Standing on the television is a picture of Tito that has a black ribbon across its upper right-hand corner.

I remember how, a few years later, Defne shut the door to her bedroom, where I was waiting for Elvis, while her mother was in the kitchen making lunch. She took my hand and pushed it inside her panties. Now she has come back. No longer a little girl, or even a girl at all, but the mother of three children. Defne is a grown woman. And I still feel like a little schoolboy with his bag on his shoulder, watchfully approaching the garages so the Hornets don't surprise him; I still feel like a little school-boy bringing notebooks to his friend so he can copy out what he missed when he was sick at home. It wasn't so long ago that I was sleeping in my boots, with a machine gun at my side and a pistol under my belt. It wasn't so long ago that life for a short time was a bizarre dream, as if I had been watching a war movie the evening before and then had such vivid dreams that in the morning I was convinced they were real. If I looked in a dream book, I would not find any interpretation for these dreams. But then, as soon as they ended, I saw my school bag in the corner behind the door. A little schoolboy.

I remember Elvis's room. I remember the two big boxes of toys he kept beneath his bed. I remember how, although it sounded horrible, I was ready to be circumcised for such toys. I told myself that for two big boxes of toys I would grin and bear it. Uncle Fikret had clearly explained to me what the doc-tor does, but I didn't know why it was necessary or why it was good. I still don't. I heard that guys who are circumcised can go longer in bed. But that's probably not the reason Muslims have their sons circumcised.

SEBASTIJAN PREGELJ

47

A FEW DAYS ago, old Sršen died. A black flag was hung out on the building where he lived. When there's a black flag hanging on an apartment building, everybody in the neighborhood starts asking who died. Before long everybody knows. News of the death spreads from mouth to mouth. It is accompanied by the possible causes of the death and numerous other details, some true, some imagined. Old Sršen was not just anybody. My mother learned of his death from an article in the newspaper; then my father read the article. The day after the funeral, the newspaper published an obituary in which it said the service had been private with only the family in attendance. I remember how we used to be afraid of him. Even later it was unpleasant running into him. People said all sorts of things about him.

Now old Sršen is gone. The article my parents read says he died after a short but difficult illness. I don't remember exactly when I saw him last, but I am sure he did not seem particularly ill. Over the years he had changed into a little old man with a stoop, but that's all. His broad-shouldered body had drooped, and his raincoat had become too big for him. And his limp was more obvious. But he did not seem mortally ill.

I ask myself what I will remember him for. What does he leave behind? Anything other than fear? I couldn't say. The old fucker I and everyone else had been so afraid of, who I spent my childhood trying to avoid, lived on in my wild imagination for years after I stopped kicking balls by the garages. An agent of the State Security Service. A character from the movies, dark and dangerous. When you least expect it, he emerges from a shadow and stands right in front of you. He hears even your softest whisper. It's impossible to keep secrets from him. Old Sršen knows everything; everything is clear to him. Even your thoughts. He only has to look at you. Or, in some cases, if a look is not enough, he uses his fists, his billy club, or the butt of his gun. Whatever is necessary. But I eventually forgot all about him. I had stopped hanging out with Matej, who would have given anything to get into Sršen's apartment—it was like he believed that all the secrets of the past decades would be revealed within those four walls—nor was I running into that shrunken man on the street anymore.

He died on Saturday. And on Tuesday he was buried.

Five years from now, Sršen will rise from the dead and, for a short time, come back into our lives.

But first, another old man will have to die in his ninety-ninth year, the same man that old Sršen had been keeping under surveillance, as part of his official duties, from 1972 right up to independence, and a few months afterward too, and then, on his own initiative, basically until he himself died, since he had never removed the listening devices from the apartment above him and continued to record everything while keeping meticulous notes. The old man's heirs will hurriedly empty the apartment. They will not discover the bugs in the telephone receiver, behind the wardrobe, or under the edge of the table. Any clothes that are still in good condition they will take to the Red Cross, and old newspapers and magazines they will toss into the paper receptacle, but the books they will pack in cardboard boxes and take to the used bookstore by the Ljubljanica River.

The owner of the used bookstore will put the books from the series *One Hundred Novels* and *Slovenian Classics* on the shelves. He will think to himself that those books will sell quickly since they're in good condition. The collected works of the Communist leader Edvard Kardelj, however, he will leave in a pile on the side. These books, he will think, won't sell. Maybe they will later. In some twenty or thirty years, when people look back nostalgically on the past. But even then, it doesn't seem likely that anyone will want to read this. Still, who knows how things will be in twenty or thirty years? He will ponder for a while what to do with these books; then he will pick up the one on top of the pile. *Volume 4. The Political System of Socialist Self-Management Democracy*. Now there's a surprise! The book is hollowed out, like in a movie. Only what's inside is not a gun, or rolls of hundred-dollar bills, or a diamond necklace, but rather an old, somewhat small photo album with black-and-white photographs and a hard cardboard cover on which the word *Youth* is written.

The man will be curious and open the photo album. Initially, he will think it must be about love, with old letters and photographs. Then he will see that it is something else. The first photograph shows a group of young men. In fact, they are not even men yet, but more like boys. One of them, to be sure, is sporting a mustache, but even so he does not look like a full-grown man. In the next photograph, the boys are in uniform and carry rifles. They are smiling and look like schoolboys headed to the woods to hunt rabbits. A few photos later, the young men are standing beside another man, who is tied up. In the next photo, they are standing beside a dead body. The boys are still smiling. Then there are more photographs of dead bodies. More dead faces. Men, women, children. Dead. Dead. Dead. Death. The end. The end of youth. On the last page there is a piece of paper filled with names.

For several nights the owner of the bookstore will have trouble sleeping. He will be wondering what he should do with the photo album. In the end, he will take it to the police station, where the officer on duty will escort him to Inspector Brecelj. The gray-haired inspector will turn the pages of the album and say to himself that there is no statute of limitations on crimes like these. He will take down the name and phone number of the bookstore owner, but later nobody will visit or telephone him.

The inspector will take a personal interest in the matter. Even after he retires he will continue to work on the case. He will drive from place to place; he will visit archives, museums, and parish offices. In the end, he will publish a book titled *Youth*. In it there will be photographs from the album. Somewhere toward the end of the book there will be a mention of old Sršen, which is when he will rise from the dead and receive eternal life.

Whenever anyone from our neighborhood appears in the newspaper, it soon becomes known in all the apartment buildings. The news travels from mouth to mouth. While some people may read the article for themselves, most people simply talk about what they heard. But old Sršen is not just anybody— he appeared in a book! That is completely different from being in the newspaper. The news will quickly spread throughout the neighborhood that a book has been published about old Sršen.

Because of those photographs from somebody's distant youth, I will never again know for sure if old Sršen was a good man or a bad man.

48

IT'S BEEN RAINING since the morning and is as dark outside as if it was evening and the day was slowly nearing its end. I don't feel like venturing out, but in the end I leave anyway to attend my classes. I get off the bus at Hotel Lev. As I walk across Ajdovščina Park, which not long ago was still called Lenin Park, I remember how many evenings I spent sitting on the back of a wooden bench with Hana, Lea, Meri, and Rok. We would smoke cigarettes and pass around a bottle of wine that seemed disgusting to me but I soon got used to it. It was marvelous. Skinheads would occasionally approach us, but since the girls always knew at least one of them, in the end they left us alone. I remember how I loved it whenever one or another of the girls would happen to touch me, and especially, eventually, every time Hana touched me. I remember how excited I would be at Hana's place. I thought it would happen any moment. Then she told me about Boris, her boyfriend. After that I stopped going to the park and we all went our separate ways.

The Skyscraper Building rises in front of me. A few minutes later, I enter the passageway that runs through it. On the left, there is a big window display of paintings. I stand there for a moment staring at a picture of a streetlamp with a pigeon beneath it. The lamp bathes the pigeon in a soft light. The darkness in the background is growing thicker. But the light is friendly and inviting. I go on. On the right, there is a shop window with hats. Again, I stop to look at the display. I ask myself if anybody still buys hats. I look at the plastic heads wearing all kinds of hats: classic hats, straw hats, berets; toward the back there's a top hat and, in front of it, a bowler. There is a hunter's hat in the corner and, next to it, an Alpine hat. A smaller section of the display is devoted to women's hats. In the corner, there is a small tilted hat with a veil. I think it must be part of a wedding outfit. But who knows?

Are you looking for anything in particular, the saleswoman asks when I enter. Something for my uncle, I quickly come up with. The saleswoman nods and asks me what sort of hats my uncle wears. The classic kind, I say. Like these. I go to a shelf on which there are gray, black, and brown cloth hats. Can I try one on? I look at her. Yes, of course, she says and waits as I pick a hat from the shelf, set it on my head, and look in the mirror. It makes you look serious, and older, she says as I inspect myself. Thank you. I return the hat to the shelf, say goodbye, and leave.

When I step out of the store, I make the quick decision to skip classes today. I turn left, and then right at the exit from the passageway, walk past the copy shop, make another right, and find myself in the building's imposing lobby. I call the elevator. From under the ceiling, the black stone heads are watching me.

In the café, I sit at a corner table. I order coffee with milk, open my backpack, take out a book, and start reading. When the waiter brings my coffee, I light a cigarette. I love the taste of that first puff and the sound of the crackling paper.

After a while, I open my wallet and take out the coin I was given right here, by a man I was sure was a magician, only it turned out he wasn't, or else he was a very, very sad magician, because soon afterward he threw himself off the building. If I didn't have the coin, I would think I had dreamed it. I would think somebody had told me about it or I'd seen it in a movie. But I am holding between my fingers a quarter dollar with the inscription *Liberty* and the year 1952. My lucky number, I whisper. I had initially kept the coin with my toys and then later in the wooden box where I had all my important things, but then I forgot about it. When I remembered it again, I found it and put it in my wallet. I have kept it with me ever since. I even had it with me in the army. I am slowly starting to believe that it actually does bring me luck, or at least keeps misfortune away.

There is a newspaper on the table next to me. Nobody's at the table, so I take it and skim the front page. NATO jets are enforcing a no-fly zone over Bosnia and Herzegovina. More and more people are fleeing to the enclave of Srebrenica, which in the spring was declared a safe area under the control of the United Nations. Armed clashes are escalating between Bosnian Croats and Bosnian Muslims. In Bosnia, it's now everyone against everyone. Despite the territory of the former Yugoslavia being under an arms embargo, tons and tons of weapons are being sold. Anyone who has them is selling them, and anyone who needs them is buying them. And everyone needs them. This summer,

SEBASTIJAN PREGELJ

at the airport in Maribor, they discovered 130 tons of Chinese armaments intended for Bosnia in crates marked as humanitarian aid. I think of the guys from the army. I wonder how they're doing. The war goes on and on, and seems like it will never end. Of course, it will end eventually, because every war ends eventually, even the Hundred Years' War ended, but all indications are that this war won't end anytime soon. All sides still have too many boys and men they need to send to the muddy trenches. Sometimes I think it won't end until all the cities are in ruins and all the villages are burned to the ground; until all the women have been raped, all the old men locked up in camps, and every child's childhood has been shattered. Where is all this hatred coming from? This will for destruction, torture, killing? I remember the old Partisan films. I remember the evil Germans, the bloodthirsty Četniks and Ustaše. Did they creep out of our television sets at night, when people were sleeping peacefully, truly peacefully, in their own warm beds, and now have resumed their bloody dance? Is that what happened? What magic will send them back into those wooden or plastic boxes and return them through the picture tubes to the film from which they emerged? I'm afraid nobody knows. So the slaughter goes on and on. And the world cares less and less. Even Boško and Admira, the Romeo and Juliet of Sarajevo, touched the heart of the world for only a few seconds. When the lovers—he a Serb, she a Muslim—were shot down on a bridge by sniper bullets, Admira crawled over to her dead Boško and died on top of him. For seven days their bodies remained on that bridge, which was in no-man's-land. And the world went fucking insane over them. It went fucking insane over love.

The Balkans are not the center of the world. Other things are happening too. America has a new president; the last Russian soldiers have left Lithuania and Poland; Czechoslovakia has peacefully split into two separate and independent countries, the Czech Republic and Slovakia; and Eritrea, too, has separated from Ethiopia and become a sovereign state. Intel has started producing Pentium processors; Jamaica's Lisa Hanna is the new Miss World; the movie *Jurassic Park* is filling cinemas; and every week *The X-Files* keeps us riveted to our television screens. We're all listening to Nirvana, Radiohead, and Depeche Mode. Meanwhile, my room is still rocking with Iron Maiden, Testament, Slayer, and King Diamond.

Rok and I go out to the clubs now and then. We look at the kids who want to have a good time, just as we did once. They act like the end of the world is near. Every Friday and Saturday night they get high; some of them have sex in the bathrooms, others do lines. Some of them will fuck up big time—they'll become addicts, pick up diseases, and wreck their lives or even die—but most of them, like us, will somehow survive. They will pull themselves together, get degrees, enroll in a graduate program or find a job, start families, take out a mortgage that's too big on an apartment that's too small, and dream about one day owning a house, a dog, and a minivan.

No one cares anymore about the war in Bosnia. The only ones still talking about it are those who have relatives there. I don't know what it's going to take for the world to wake up and stop the killing.

And the magician? Who was he anyway? My mother read or heard somewhere—I don't remember now—that he had come

SEBASTIJAN PREGELJ

here from America. That he was an American. How did he get here? And why did he choose Ljubljana? Why the Skyscraper? What destiny drove him to the café on the twelfth floor? Just before it happened had he been walking through the passageway, paused in front of the window with the hats, saw one he especially liked, went into the store, tried it on, and then paid and left? Was he determined even then to kill himself? Did he have second thoughts? Was he trying to decide between throwing himself under a train or throwing himself off a tall building? Or maybe he had no particular plans. Just as he happened to go into the hat shop, so had he walked into the Skyscraper lobby. He took the elevator up to the café, ordered a long black coffee, and lit a cigarette.

I will never know any of this. But I can imagine what I want. I can make up my own story. Maybe that's just what he wanted. Maybe he wanted me to remember him and think up a story in which he goes on living. Maybe that's why he gave me the silver coin. The American.

49

KID, YOU KNOW what's a gold mine? Sršen has a firm grip on my shoulders. A real El Dorado? I look at him in confusion because I don't understand the question. Well, just listen. I told you once, right here—but it was a long time ago; I don't know if you remember—that this was the best spot in the city. I told you that here you can learn everything. Remember? And that information is gold if you know what to do with it, right? Uh-huh, I say. Well, look at me. Take a good look. He lightly pushes me away. I take a step back and look at him. It's true; he looks completely different, and if I saw him from a distance, I wouldn't recognize him. He's wearing a silk shirt and a dark suit, with cowboy boots on his feet. Like a character from an American movie. On a body dressed like this, even that bristly head of his seems less bristly and therefore less conspicuous. No wonder I didn't notice him, and even if I had seen him, I would hardly have recognized him. I was walking through the Maximarket passageway when I suddenly felt a heavy hand on my shoulder.

A moment later I heard that familiar voice. Hey, kid! Boy, am I glad to see you!

I expect you're still at the university. Me, I'm a businessman, he says. So, do you know what's a gold mine? An El Dorado? He looks at me from under his brow. The refugee business. Shh! He raises a finger to his thick lips. I assist them on their way to a better tomorrow. To Austria and Italy. I help everyone— Croatians, Bosnians, Serbs, but also Albanians, Montenegrins, and Macedonians. I don't discriminate. I don't care where they come from, or where they're going or why. I pick them up at the southern border and get them across the northern or western border. There you have it. That's what I do, if you're interested. I nod, because I can't imagine why he's telling me this. I didn't ask him. Well, Sršen says, smacking his lips, if you maybe want to earn some money. Because you're smart. I can get you work. A bit on the side. Five hundred deutsche marks for a single trip. Two days' work. Piece of cake. Your old man has to work two weeks to make that kind of money. Interested? No, thanks, I say. That's cool. Sršen wags his bristly head. It's not for everyone. But you're a smart guy and there's money in this line of work. And the business won't last long. Once the war ends, there'll be no more refugees. It appeared overnight and it'll disappear overnight. Understand? I do. But I'm not interested. All right, fine. Sršen releases me. No pressure. I'm just saying.

You know I work with gypsy boy too. He licks his lips. Who? I look at him. Ali. Your friend, Sršen says. He's down in Bosnia now. Don't tell me you don't know that. He wrinkles his forehead. Sure I know, I say, although I don't know for sure, because nobody told me, but I've suspected this for a while since he couldn't be anywhere else. If he's not here, then he's there. There he's not just anybody, Sršen says. He has a position; he has power. In Bosnia, Ali joined the Wahhabis, and of all the motherfuckers down there, they're the worst motherfuckers. They don't spare even their own. What do I care what they get up to down there, right? But once in a while they need a favor. Once in a while there are people who need to be taken across the border, to the West. Well, in cases like that, I hear from Ali. I enjoy doing business with Ali. Sršen smiles. The Arab countries help them out with dollars, and Ali's never stingy. Well, enough about that, in case someone's listening. Want to get a Coke, he asks. A Coke? I look at him and smile. Yeah, a Coke, he repeats. Sure, I say.

Soon I am sitting with Sršen at a table next to a glass wall. On the other side are the remnants of a two-thousand-year-old Roman wall, and on this side is Sršen, who offers me a cigarette. Marlboro 100s. From Germany, he says. Best tobacco, best taste, longest pleasure. Have one. I take the cigarette, light up, and inhale. When I'm halfway through it, I say it's good. Of course it is, Sršen says. You think I smoke crap? I had my fill of crap in the old days. Now I can treat myself to something better. I deserve it. Know what I mean? I do, I say and take a sip of Coke.

As he's talking to me about one thing and another, Sršen's cinematic end appears before my eyes. In my mind I see a wild police chase. It goes something like this: It's night. Stars are flickering in the sky; crickets are chirping in the grass. As fast as he can, Sršen is driving a van filled with refugees down a winding road through a narrow valley. To the left and right are meadows, then cornfields. Sršen has the lights turned off, but

SEBASTIJAN PREGELJ

that does not fool the police, who have been expecting him for several nights. They received information that this is his regular route, and now they are following him at a safe distance. Sršen's not stupid. He soon notices that a vehicle is following him, but his van, with all the people it's carrying, is too heavy and too slow. He knows it cannot go any faster. He thinks for a while, although he has thought about such situations countless times on these long nocturnal trips. Each situation has its own solution, and this is one of the more expected ones. A few minutes later he suddenly stops the van, jumps out, opens the rear doors, and gets everyone out. Gesturing with his arms, he tells them to go into the cornfield, repeating again and again that he'll be back to pick them up the next day. Hide so they don't catch you. Hurry up! Run! Hurry, hurry! When the van is empty, he slams the rear doors shut, jumps behind the wheel, and steps on the gas. The police car is right behind him. Sršen knows they will have to decide whether to keep chasing him or go after the refugees, who are running through the corn like deer startled by a cracking branch. Checking the rearview mirror, he sees the police still behind him. Angrily he pounds the wheel with his right fist. He's going faster now that the van is empty, but it's not fast enough. The police car has caught up to him. When it tries to pass him on the left, Sršen pulls to the left. When it tries to pass him on the right, he veers to the right. When the road straightens out, he steps on the gas. He presses the pedal to the floor. Now he has a certain advantage, but it won't be for long. Sršen knows his chances are slim, basically nil. He makes the decision to give himself up. If he confesses everything and, in addition, throws in the name of some small fry, maybe he can save himself. Since he has no previous convictions, he can count on a light sentence, maybe even a suspended sentence. After the next sharp curve he steps on the brake and jumps out of the van. He stands in the middle of the road and waits. A moment later he's lit up by searchlights. He hears the screech of brakes and the sound of stones striking metal and scattering in all directions. The police car and the van are covered in the dust. Stop right there, the policemen shout. Don't make a move! Sršen has a cigarette in his mouth; with his right hand he reaches into a pocket for the lighter. There's a burst of gunfire. Sršen feels a sharp pain and is thrown to the ground. As he lies there, he sees figures approaching. Suddenly he feels very tired. He remembers he hasn't slept for three nights. He shuts his eyes. Just for a minute, a brief minute. Darkness. The end.

When our glasses are empty, he reaches his arm across the table and lightly punches my shoulder. If you change your mind and want to make some money, you know where to find me, right? Uh-huh, I mumble. Here, take them. Sršen pushes the pack of cigarettes over to me. Marlboro 100s. Best tobacco, best taste, longest pleasure. He grins. I should do ads for them.

On the evening news they show a clip of the Old Bridge collapsing into the Neretva River. The bridge, which had been built at the orders of Suleiman the Magnificent and for which the town that grew up on both sides of the river was named, had been there for 427 years. Legend has it that the architect, Mimar Hayruddin, fled Mostar just as the scaffolding was about to be removed. And that's not all. The architect, fearing that this slender construction of 456 stone blocks would not hold, had even made preparations for his own funeral. But the slender

SEBASTIJAN PREGELJ

construction did hold, and Herzegovina received a bridge with the longest arch in the world. They called it the New Bridge, and later, the Suleiman the Magnificent Bridge, but in the end it was the Old Bridge—*Stari Most*. Today, a little after ten in the morning, this very bridge, after days of systematic shelling, collapsed into the river.

But what is a bridge in comparison to all the people who have been killed on both sides, and to those who are yet to be killed? The bridge can be rebuilt. If people want to go from one side of the river to the other, if they ever again wish to sit at the same table, have a smoke together, drink brandy from the same bottle, and talk about the weather, they will build a new bridge. But the dead? Will anyone bring them back to life? Will anyone return the dead children to their mothers, the dead wives to their husbands, the dead husbands to their wives? Like hell they will.

Also on the news, they tell us that nine Sarajevo schoolchildren have been killed in crossfire; there is something about Rudy Giuliani, who a few days ago became New York City's first Republican mayor since 1965; and at the end, we learn that Roger Moore is feeling well after his prostate surgery.

My father is upset about the bridge; my mother feels sorry for the people.

50

GRANDPA DIED LAST night. It happened sometime between two and five in the morning. That's what my aunt was told by the doctor who came to confirm the death and establish its approximate time. He said that, given my grandfather's illness and age, there was no need for an autopsy.

Mom has been crying since morning. Dad tries to console her; he keeps saying that in a way this was to be expected. All things considered, Grandpa was with us a long time, long after he got the diagnosis. Mom is not consoled by this. I am grateful to have had my father for as long as I did, she says through her tears, but I'm still sad. Of course, of course, Dad keeps repeating; he doesn't know what else to say, so in the end he says nothing. He sits next to Mom and holds her hand.

I imagine that during the night, at a little before two, the rooster crowed so loudly it woke up the master. Grandpa got up, put his teeth in his mouth, stopped the pendulum in the living room, got dressed, stepped outside, locked the door, and shoved the key beneath the flowerpot on the window ledge. He went over to the chicken coop, grabbed the rooster, carried him to the barn, picking up the axe along the way, and chopped off the animal's head. Then he laid the dead rooster in the tall grass and left his home. He set off along a white path that rose slowly upward until, at sunrise, he arrived at the gates of heaven. Looking through the golden bars he saw a garden more beautiful than the one on the church ceiling. The gates opened and Grandpa went in. He walked for a while beneath some slender palm trees; then he saw a house, one that was just like the house he and Grandma had on earth. Grandma was waiting for him at the door, and a bright-colored rooster was strutting in the middle of the yard. Grandpa was surprised because Grandma was as young as the day he had married her. But from the moment he had stepped into the garden, he too was young and strong, only he had not noticed this yet. How glad I am to see you, Grandma said softly. How beautiful you are, Grandpa whispered.

I remember what it was like when Grandma died. I was in the fifth grade. Aunt Katja telephoned that time too. A few days later, we went to the funeral. It was horrible, because I knew death meant the end. Before then, the only person I knew who had died was my classmate Ana. But with her it was different. Of course, I missed her. She was my friend. But in the fall, when we changed homerooms, and later with other changes, my memory of Ana began to fade. I would still recall her from time to time, and smile to myself, but then she would again slip beyond the edge of my memory. That's not how it was with Grandma. It was only her who left; everything else remained as before. The woodstove was still there, with a pleasant-smelling fire crackling inside it; the glasses were still stacked on top of the low refrigerator and covered by a white cloth; the clock in the living room was still ticking, still loudly chiming the hour. So, for a long time afterward, whenever we went to Grandpa's, for at least a moment I was expecting Grandma to be there. If I didn't see her in front of the house as we drove up, I was sure she would be in the kitchen, or if she wasn't in the kitchen, then she would soon appear from the living room or the larder. A lot of time passed before I got used to her not being there and accepted the fact that she wouldn't be. But Grandpa was still there, and with him all the good feelings that filled their house.

Mom keeps crying. Dad keeps holding her hand.

I remember the last time we were at Grandpa's. It wasn't that long ago. He looked weak and pale to me. But, more than once, Grandpa said his test results were good and there was no reason to worry. If anybody's interested, the folder's right there on the refrigerator, he said, pointing at it with a crooked finger and smiling. But the years have caught up with me. I can't keep getting stronger and healthier every day, you know. The doctor tells me I'm in great shape. But then, he lies like a dog. He chuckled. I know that's not true. But I'm doing good for my age. I've got everything I need and more. I just tire out sooner than I used to. Last year I chopped the firewood myself, but I couldn't do it this year, he admitted. What I like best is sitting in front of the house in the sun. When I'm inside, I'm cold. My father was the same when he got old—he was always cold. Even in the middle of summer, he'd be in his cardigan and have his hat on. And look at me these days! Am I any different?

SEBASTIJAN PREGELJ

My father and mother, uncles and aunts—everyone was talking on top of each other, speaking loudly and saying anything, as if they were trying to distract him. It made me angry, because no one was listening to Grandpa. Maybe there was something he wanted to tell us that day, but he didn't get a chance. And now here we are. At a little before two in the morning, he left us and is not coming back.

My mind is swarming with all the stories he so enjoyed telling me. How many stories there were! Grandpa was not, in fact, a very good storyteller. He spoke slowly, and at times the story would grind to a halt because he couldn't find the right word or remember some detail. Then he would take so much time thinking about it that when he finally remembered and told me, I had forgotten what he had even been talking about. But Grandpa had a special fire about him. The kind of fire that allows even a singer without perfect pitch or a musician without a well-tuned instrument to captivate the listener.

Grandpa was never at a loss for a story, but I was the only one who enjoyed listening to them. I need to write them down, I think. I need to write down all the stories he told me and then ask Mom to tell me the stories he told her, if she remembers them. That's the only way Grandpa's memories will be preserved, and with them, our Grandpa. Otherwise, first his memories will disappear, and then, soon after, so will our memory of him. And this scares me.

As the day approaches its end, I gaze out the window. Darkness is settling on the city. In my mind I see Grandpa's house. I see the barn and the workshop, where he was spending more and more time each summer. At first, he would only be in the workshop if there was something he had to repair. Later, he spent whole days in that shed. I would often go to see him there and stay until day's end. Grandpa would do whatever he was doing and, at the same time, tell me a story. I would be both listening a little and not listening. I loved being around him. I loved the sound of his voice and the smell of wood in the shed, where the floor was covered in shavings and where knotty trellis posts stood in a corner. I liked it when the darkness was growing thicker outside and Grandpa would put a light on so we could stay a little longer. All around us was silence, interrupted only now and then by the barking of a neighbor's dog or a passing car on the gravel road. The silence that enveloped the workshop was thick and warm. I would look at the corpses of the horseflies and wasps that had found a way inside but not a way out. Most of them were on the windowsill. Although the windowpane was filthy, the insects thought this was where they could get out. To the very end they had hurled themselves at the glass, which was covered at the top in thin threads of old spiderweb, until eventually, depleted of strength, they lay motionless on the wide windowsill.

The insects on the windowsill appeared to be sleeping. They were lying on their backs with their little legs in the air. I sometimes thought about bringing a matchbox with me so I could take a few of these bodies home, but I always forgot. So they stayed there, along with my memories of those evenings with Grandpa. And maybe that's how it should be. There, those tiny bodies were beautiful in a very particular way. At home they would have been merely dead bugs, which my mother, if she had found them, would have tossed in the trash or flushed down the toilet, saying there really was no need for me to bring dead flies into the apartment. There would have been no point in correcting her that they weren't flies, but horseflies and wasps, let alone in saying that they were beautiful. And if she did happen to listen to me, she'd say in the end, I would understand if you were collecting butterflies. Butterflies are beautiful. But horseflies and wasps? For goodness' sake, Jan!

In my mind, those big, fat horseflies and their skinny, much smaller cousins, the elegantly pinched-waisted wasps, are even now, at this moment, lying on the windowsill. Even now they are holding their little legs in the air and dreaming. And in their dreams it is a long, hot summer.

51

HAVE YOU HEARD what happened? My mother surprises me with this when I come home. I have no idea, I say. Ali, Mom says. He's been shot. What? Where, I ask, although I think I know. Ever since there's been neither sight nor sound of him, he's been in Bosnia. I don't know when he left, but I know he's there. I had suspected this even earlier; then Sršen confirmed it for me. And I believe Sršen. Why would he lie to me? Not about Ali. Anyway, where else could Ali be? It had started long ago and could not have ended any differently. Ali used to hang out in the park with boys whose parents were mostly from Bosnia. One or two had parents from Montenegro, and one or two from Kosovo, but they weren't Albanians. At first they would just be goofing around, drinking and smoking. Then one of them started bringing photocopies of texts, which they would read and talk about. They started letting their beards grow, stopped drinking alcohol, and learned a few words of Arabic. Now and then I would run into him in town. Now and then I would see him from the bus. We never really talked because he was always in a hurry. There was only time for, Hey there! How are you? Fine, thanks. And you? Then war broke out and a few months later there was neither sight nor sound of him. Somewhere in Bosnia, Mom replies. Uncle Fikret phoned. He asked if we knew anyone at the foreign ministry. He's beside himself. The boy needs to be brought here as soon as possible, to the Medical Center in Ljubljana. He's severely wounded. Here they could maybe save him, but who knows what would happen if he stayed down there. Hmm. I nod and watch to see what she'll say next. I didn't know he was in Bosnia, she says after a pause. Did you? Not exactly. I thought he might be. I asked Elvis a couple of times but he wouldn't answer me. I mean, he did answer, but he didn't tell me anything. I figured he had to be in Bosnia. Where else would he be? After everything that happened with Defne. You liked Defne, didn't you, she asks with a curious smile. Oh, come on, Mom. I roll my eyes. But since you ask, yes. When I was bringing Elvis my notes from class, I liked Defne. She was a lovely little girl, Mom says. Well, at least *she* is safe. Yeah, I say, and go to my room.

I am lying on the bed and thinking about Ali. If he is as badly wounded as Mom says, then he, too, will be lying on a bed. And if he is conscious, then maybe at this very moment he is thinking about his childhood, or if he is unconscious, then maybe he is dreaming about it. It was beautiful and we had no worries, I think to myself. Sršen would show up occasionally and give someone a beating, but that was as bad as it got. And besides, he didn't dare go after Ali. He might threaten him, and they did fight. But since neither one was stronger than the other, and since they both had older and nastier friends, it never went further than that.

Then somebody gave Ali such a beating he ended up in the ICU. At the time I said it was Sršen, but looking back, I don't think it was. Sršen and his gang did other kinds of shit. I don't know why they would want to beat up Ali. By then, their paths never crossed. The first or second day after it happened, my parents visited him in the hospital, but they left me at home. They said it was because they were afraid of how Ali might look. They didn't want me to see anything horrible. They didn't want me to be scared. When they got back, they told me it wasn't so bad and Ali would be home soon. They also told me some of his friends had been there, older boys. A week or so later, Ali came home from the hospital, and two weeks after that I would see him again on the street or at the bus stop. But by then, we weren't hanging out anymore, so I soon forgot everything connected with the beating and the hospital. I don't think it was Sršen. But I never asked Ali and he never said anything about it.

If Ali is thinking about his childhood, I wonder if I am part of his memories. How does he remember me? I still love him. I don't love the adult, bearded man who is lying wounded on a hospital bed somewhere in Bosnia. I love Ali the way he was when, every so often, he would come into Elvis's room, sit on the floor, and tell us stories from *Star Wars*. I love the Ali who stopped me on the stairs and shoved *Start* magazine into my hands. I love the Ali who, in the hallway at school, knocked Sršen off me and kicked him and then all three of us had to go to the principal's office. Ali was a fantastic boy. Ali was the greatest boy, like the brother I always wanted. And now? After all this fucking shit that's been happening, what has he turned into? What has he become? There's a tear trickling down my face. *What the fuck, Ali?* It could have been different. It should have been different. If back then, when we were sitting in Elvis's room, we had imagined our future, we'd have imagined it differently. In our future, there would have been no war. In our future, we would have stayed here. Defne wouldn't have married so young and moved to Sarajevo, and Ali wouldn't have been learning Arabic words in the park. We would be living the most ordinary lives, and again everything would start over. We would collect stickers with pictures of footballers, basketball players, cowboys and Indians, fighter planes, and racing cars, which we would paste into albums printed in the Serbian town of Gornji Milanovac. Those stickers had a truly special, intoxicating smell. We would exchange our doubles and tap them in. We would dig a hole in the dirt and shoot marbles for hours, with the winner taking all. But Ali would always give Elvis and me our favorite marbles back. We would ride our bikes all over the neighborhood and beyond—in Šiška, Koseze, and Dravlje; in early summer we would ring the doorbell of a house with a cherry tree in the yard, and Ali would ask the owner if we could climb the tree a little, and he would let us but tell us not to break any branches; and in the fall after school, when the days were still long and warm, we would ride around the apartment buildings and Ali would point to where some cute girl lived—he'd tell us her name, what class she was in, and the name of her homeroom teacher. In winter, in Elvis's room, we would page through *Start* together and talk about women. Elvis and I would copy everything that Ali did; we would feel safe in his presence and try again and again to impress him with what we could do. Life would have been predictable. Primary school, secondary school, a job. Maybe at some point university. It doesn't matter. In the end, almost imperceptibly, we would turn into people like our parents, although that wasn't what we wanted because we were expecting something more, only we didn't know how to imagine what *something more* looked like.

What, back then, was *something more*? In our eyes, the aunts and uncles who worked in Italy and Germany had quite a bit more. They had bigger cars—Audis, Mercedes, and BMWs—and in their homes they had dishwashers, remote-controlled color televisions, and stereo systems with hundred-watt speakers; they lived in twenty- and thirty-story towers. Cousins who came here for a week or two during the summer had quite a bit more; they were different from us both in the clothes they wore and the toys they brought with them. We didn't care about the clothes—it was our mothers and neighbors who noticed them—but we envied them the toys. Still, we were satisfied with our plastic guns and toy cars with the wheels falling off, and we were sure there was nothing we lacked. Such was our world. If back then we had wanted something more, it would have been a metal cap gun and a toy car with doors you could open.

When we were sitting in Elvis's room, we never tried to imagine the future. We never talked about what it would be. We did sometimes talk about what *we* would be when we grew up. About that, yes. Ali said he was going to join the pirates, and I wanted to be a trash collector, the guy who stands at the back of the truck. All three of them laughed at me. Elvis said he was going to be an airplane pilot, and Defne, shrugging, said she couldn't decide if she wanted to be a doctor or a kindergarten teacher. We later changed our professions a few times and then stopped talking about the subject because we thought it was childish. Anyway, you can't know what you're going to be. So we didn't worry too much about the future.

In Elvis's room everything was fine and good.

Now bearded Ali lies wounded on a hospital bed somewhere in Bosnia. I imagine him in a T-shirt with dark holes and blood-stains on it. I imagine him with a needle in his arm that supplies him with nutrient solutions and medicine. I don't want it to be that way. I close my eyes.

In my mind, Ali is again sitting on the floor in Elvis's room. He is telling us about Sandokan and his men, who are fighting against the British occupiers. The story is very exciting, but then it is interrupted by the doorbell. Ali says it's for him, jumps up, and runs into the front hall.

When he opens the door, there is a muddy trench yawning in front of him. Shots and explosions can be heard in the distance. Ali runs through the door. When he is on the other side, he is no longer a boy. He is a young man with a beard and in a uniform. Several dead men are lying beside the wall of the trench. We will not give up so easily! Ali pulls back the bolt on his automatic rifle, looks out of the trench, aims, and starts firing on the attacking soldiers, who believe the hill has already been won. Some of them fall; others take shelter and start shooting back. There are at least ten of them. Ali is all by himself. Not for the first time. More than once it's been him against everyone else. Ali tosses the empty magazine and loads a new one. He's shooting left and right. From time to time a bullet whistles past one of his ears. Each time Ali thanks the Gracious and Merciful One that it missed him. When the magazine is empty, he crouches down to his dead comrades. He quickly checks their magazines. One of them is still full. He takes it, glances out of the trench, and waits. Silence. For a moment he thinks the attackers have pulled back. One of them probably said that since they don't know how many are still in the trench it's best if they wait for reinforcements, but what he was thinking was that he doesn't want to die. Not on a crappy day like this when the fog is coming in and his skin is as clammy as a frog's. Not for some fucking little hill that's only on the survey map; you can't find it on any normal map because it's so insignificant it doesn't have a name. Ali wipes the sweat from his forehead with a filthy arm and smiles. What pussies. Then a shot rings out. A powerful blast knocks him against the muddy wall of the trench. His legs give way and slowly his body sinks down. When he's on the ground, he feels a burning in his chest. It's like he swallowed a flaming bullet. Fuck. He grabs at where it hurts. He feels his hand becoming warm and wet. Blood. He turns toward where the trench begins. He is trying to drag himself there, back to where he came from. He remembers the door at the beginning of the trench. If he opens the door, he will be saved. On the other side of the door there is a large front hall with a lustrous parquet floor and white walls. He will drag himself inside and kick the door shut. We will hear him. We will run to him and carry him into Elvis's room. Elvis will double-lock the front door. I'll call the

ambulance. There's been an accident! Hurry! Please. Defne
will run to the bathroom and come back with a wet cloth. She
will wipe up the muddy, bloody floor. Mom and Dad can't find
out about this.

Ali shuts his eyes.

I shut my eyes.

About Sandorf Passage

SANDORF PASSAGE PUBLISHES work that creates a prismatic perspective on what it means to live in a globalized world. It is a home to writing inspired by both conflict zones and the dangers of complacency. All Sandorf Passage titles share in common how the biggest and most important ideas are best explored in the most personal and intimate of spaces.